FROM THE MIND
OF ARTHUR BYRON COVER, AN
AUTHENTICALLY NEW ADVENTURE
IN THE BESTSELLING WORLD OF

PLANETFALL

"Only three times in my life has a writer kicked my sense of reality around the block and made me like it. The first writer was Theodore Sturgeon, the second was Roger Zelazny. And now, Arthur Byron Cover. Each time the effect was similar—my universe expanded, as though I had just for the first time seen the night skies through a telescope."

Delap's F&SF Review

"Cover tends to use sf imagery and plots in a wryly arbitrary fashion, to achieve sometimes moving statements about the world."

The Science Fiction Encyclopedia

"An unusually talented author . . ."

Michael Moorcock

Other Avon Books in the
INFOCOM™ Series

WISHBRINGER® *by Craig Shaw Gardner*

PLANETFALL®

Arthur Byron Cover

A Byron Preiss Book

AN **INFOCOM**™ BOOK

AVON BOOKS  NEW YORK

PLANETFALL: THE NOVEL is an original publication of Avon Books. This work has never before appeared in book form. This work is a novel. Any similarity to actual persons or events is purely coincidental.

Special thanks to Joel Berez, Mike Dornbrook, Steve Meretsky, John Douglas, Patrick Nielsen Hayden, and Gwendolyn Smith.

AVON BOOKS
A division of
The Hearst Corporation
105 Madison Avenue
New York, New York 10016

Copyright © 1988 by Byron Preiss Visual Publications, Inc.
Cover painting copyright © 1984 by Infocom, Inc.
Published by arrangement with Byron Preiss Visual Publications, Inc.
PLANETFALL software copyright © 1984 by Infocom, Inc.
PLANETFALL and the INFOCOM logo are trademarks of Infocom, Inc.
Library of Congress Catalog Card Number: 88-91503
ISBN: 0-380-75384-7

Cover and book design by Alex Jay/Studio J
Edited by David M. Harris

First Avon Books Printing: August 1988

AVON TRADEMARK REG. U.S. PAT. OFF. AND IN OTHER COUNTRIES, MARCA REGISTRADA, HECHO EN U.S.A.

Printed in the U.S.A.

K-R   10   9   8   7   6   5   4   3   2   1

Chapter One
Song of the Flytrap

"AS YOU KNOW, sir, the upcoming Diplomatic Conference is shaping up to be one of the most important summits in the history of the Third Galactic Union so far. Perhaps more important, even, than the one that resulted in the creation of the Stellar Patrol."

Admiral Boink blinked. "I know that," he said.

"Then you also know that if our mission escorting various ambassadors to the conference is to be successful, we must travel over one hundred hyperparsecs through the ultradimensional void in exactly nineteen chrons. That's not much time."

Admiral Boink blinked again. "I know that too. Why are you telling me this? It's not my responsibility the drive conked out when we passed through the trails of that nova."

"Our superiors will little note nor care about the contingencies we've had to endure. They will care only that we showed up on time. The tremendous sacrifices we've endured in the name of truth, justice, and the bipedal way will be, in their minds, merely worth a tiny footnote in the multivolumed bibliography of the historical records of this sprawling, multifaceted galaxy of ours. Of course, in real life, which is where we're living right now, it's possible the more loathsome the sacrifices, the greater the eventual glory. Who knows? Provided we do show up on time, you and I—possibly even the entire crew—might receive a medal."

"Humph. I've got plenty of medals." Indeed, his scintillating dress jacket was covered with so many medals that some were pinned on his sleeves. Admiral Boink liked receiving medals. In fact, another ceremony was scheduled for seventy-five hundred, and his preoccupation with deciding which medal he should get this time was a niggling detail distracting him from the impending crisis. Too bad he had received all the commonplace ones so many times already. They weren't much fun by now. Perhaps he could convince one of the alien ambassadors that he deserved one of their native honors. Of course, he had better ask before the impending crisis became common knowledge. He pursed his lips. "Did I hear you say . . . 'loathsome sacrifices'?"

"Close. I was hoping that would get your attention, sir. Yes, loathsome sacrifices, including various degrees of ignominious humiliations, encompassing degrading debasements and despicable dishonors."

Boink's shoulders stiffened. As much as he liked medals, he disliked making sacrifices, especially in the line of duty. He was a white-haired man, with a white moustache and white sideburns, dark blue eyes and a ruddy complexion. His forehead was broad, his chin jutting, and his nose bulbous. Over eighty years old, he took considerable pride in not looking a day over fifty. Which is why he became distracted by his reflection in the plate glass over his desktop, leaning over for a closer examination. "What's that?" he asked, pointing at his cheekbone in the glass. "Some kind of rash?"

The reflection of the red-haired Lieutenant Colonel Second Class Coryban moved closer to his. He looked up at her and was immediately lost, as he usually was, in those creamy jade-green eyes—in those eyes of ice, as cold and distant as her personality. Her red hair was fixed beneath her kepi, lending her high cheekbones and prominent chin an austere air. The cut of her fatigues fitted so inexactly that it was difficult to make even a rough guess about the shape of her figure, though the discernible hints were sufficiently tantalizing for a red-blooded, virile biped to take a chance upon discovering the truth; if he could survive her initial reaction, that is. Boink had no doubt any risk would be worth it. The way her lips pressed tightly against her teeth when she smiled convinced him that when her hair was down about her shoulders, she was a veritable heart stopper.

But naturally she was currently staring sternly at him, causing something to deflate in his heart. Boink invariably felt many, many moons over a hundred and fifty whenever Coryban looked down her turned-up nose at him.

"No, it's not a rash," she replied with the faintest trace of sarcasm. "It's a smudge on the glass."

"Oh, so it is!" Boink wiped the glass clean with his sleeve, being careful not to scratch it with his medals. If there was one thing he detested more than sacrifices, it was untidiness in any shape or form. "Uh, you don't happen to know exactly what sort of sacrifices I should expect the crew to make, do you?"

"Hmmm. By its very nature, much of the responsibility will fall directly upon your shoulders." Her smile wasn't quite so attractive this time. "Though of course I shall be ever watchful by your side."

Boink sighed with relief. "Thank you, Colonel. Just think of how much better I'm going to feel once you finally get around to telling me what it is I'm supposed to be so worried about."

"Yes, sir. As you know, after we fixed the engine problem, we stopped by the planet of Ho-Ho-Kus to pick up their ambassador. Him we got, but, thanks to a mix-up, which can be directly traced to subversive elements in the Ho-Ho-Kusian penal labor system, we accidentally left part of his luggage behind.

"Now normally this wouldn't be such a big deal, but the Ho-Ho-Kusians are one of the most peculiar races in the galaxy, with very precise life-support requirements. Among the most important items of the ambassador's missing luggage is the supply of drugs he needs to prevent certain, ah, chronic needs and desires from overcoming his sense of diplomatic proprieties. The ambassador will soon need a dose every day; he simply cannot be himself without it. Yet we are already so far behind schedule that if we turn around to get a new supply, he will miss certain rounds of delicate preliminary negotiations at the conference.

"Normally that wouldn't be such a big deal either, but when it comes time for the Ho-Ho-Kusian legislature to ratify whatever treaty may be agreed upon at the conference, then the opponents can always claim the ambassador began the negotiations at a disadvantage and thus was never able to achieve parity."

"So? A hundred distinct races are attending this conference, not to mention who-knows-how-many independent colonials and genetically altered offshoots. What difference does it make if a world here or there refuses to ratify the treaty? Our grandchildren will be dead by the time all the votes are in."

Coryban shrugged. She was sitting in the easy chair placed near one end of his desk, her legs primly crossed. "Admiral, remember, this conference is predicted to have historical ramifications of unprecedented proportions. The exact subject matter is classified, but whatever it is, the word is out that even races as yet unborn, on worlds as yet unformed, in systems as yet unmade, will be affected by what will soon be decided there." She smiled. "As you know."

"All right, why can't our chemists just synthesize whatever kind of drug our vegetable friend needs to keep him on an even keel?"

"The ambassador hasn't the faintest idea as to what the drug's composed of. Apparently it's derived from the bark of some kind of walking flytrap with sonic capabilities. The ambassador's description, though fascinating on its own merits, provided our chemists with precious few

4

clues as to how they might proceed. However, since a mistake on their part, in any case, could have disastrous, if not fatal, consequences, I took the liberty of ordering them to forget about it." She clasped her clipboard to her chest and tapped the fingers of her right hand on it. "If you don't mind, sir."

"No, why should I? I'm not paying our chemists to be too stupid to call up the specs of the drug in the Interstellar Encyclopedia Files. The Union's paying them not to do that, thank Seldon!"

"Begging your pardon, sir, but they did look it up. There's no information on the drug available, just as there's only the scantiest information in general on the biophysiology of all things Ho-Ho-Kusian. The intelligent vegetables of that world excel in many mental fields of endeavor, but when it comes to analytical abilities, they have all the skill of an advanced artichoke. They probably still wouldn't know how to communicate with bipeds if a prospector hadn't forced the issue by trying to fricassee one."

"He must have been a desperately hungry man. They all look so stringy to me. Exactly which sex is our ambassador, anyway? I mean, we've been calling him a he, but it's hard to tell with all those leaves in the way."

"The question of sex really doesn't have much to do with it. The Ho-Ho-Kusians do have the urge to propagate, and they do need a partner, that's true, but the actual deed itself consists mostly of the stuff we normally associate plants with doing."

"Oh, of course. The wandering Ho-Ho-Kusian must put his roots down in order to sow his seeds. So how does a partner fit into this scenario? Do they plant themselves beside one another and mingle branches to cross-pollinate?"

"Ah, no. The partner is the fodder, so to speak. The fertilizer."

"Say what?"

"The partner provides the dominant Ho-Ho-Kusian with someone to cannibalize. Literally. The partner digs a hole in the ground and plants himself, and then the dominant one covers him up, puts his roots down—and in—to suck up all the nutrients. The Ho-Ho-Kusians have difficulty relating to the horror other races express toward this reproductive pattern and claim it really isn't cannibalism, because the memories of both are telepathically shared and preserved in the body of the one." Coryban shrugged. "Anyway, that's what our ambassador's going to have the uncontrollable urge to do, if we don't think of some solution pretty darned soon."

"What's he going to do? Plant himself in the greenhouse?"

"Now that you mention it, yes, eventually. But there's one thing you must keep in mind about the Ho-Ho-Kusians, a thing they didn't even know about themselves until the time one found himself the sole specimen of his kind aboard a spaceship in transit, with only 'aliens' as potential partners."

"Uh-oh."

"Their urge to propagate, when frustrated, ultimately becomes so overwhelming that it is the most uncontrollable, savage, downright murderous urge in known space. Before the Ho-Ho-Kusians were assimilated in galactic civilization, their natural cycles had never been disrupted, and so they themselves had no inkling of the dark side of their inner nature."

"Well, I suppose I can understand that," said Boink, smiling at her and raising his eyebrows in a manner he hoped would broadcast a distinct signal with a distinct purpose. "I've often felt the same way myself."

"Ah, but I wager you've never slain the object of your desires, buried her in whatever soil was handy, and then stabbed your myriad roots into her."

"Yes, that's true. Normally when I commit necrophilia, I'm satisfied with using only one root."

She shook her head and rolled her eyes, which is what she always did when choosing to deliberately ignore one of his remarks. "There's a second thing you must always keep in mind."

Boink tapped his fingers on the desk, oblivious to the smudges he was creating. Seconds passed. Long, boring, tedious seconds, during which Coryban said nothing. He said nothing either, knowing she was doing this just to annoy him. He resolved to wait in silence for hours, if necessary, until she spoke first.

"The Ho-Ho-Kusians are by nature an aristocratic race," she finally said. "They also have no standards of physical beauty, relevant to our own. Put those two characteristics together in a frustrated Ho-Ho-Kusian, sir, and then you can't help but realize that no specimen worth his twigs, no matter how desperate, would select as his partner anyone less than the most prestigious individual available."

"I've got a bad feeling about this."

"You should. You're the only admiral on the ship. Therefore, you're the top specimen, by definition. And I've talked to the ambassador. I think he likes you. I suppose you can philosophically regard this as one of the privileges of rank."

"Colonel, prepare me a bogus resignation to use in case of an emergency. Do so immediately."

"Yes, sir, but can my name be left out of it?"

"Of course. Now let me see if I've got this straight. The missing drug prevents the ambassador's urge from becoming overwhelming. We can't turn back to retrieve the drug, because if we do, the results would be disastrous on a galactic scale. But if we don't turn back, the results could be disastrous on a personal scale, particularly my own."

"Very true, but the results will still be galactically disastrous, because the ambassador will probably be stark, raving mad throughout most of the conference."

"Ah. I'm so glad you pointed out that silver lining. If the entire course of civilization is going to collapse no matter what we do, why don't we just say the hell with it and turn back?"

"Because the other ambassadors we're escorting are on no less tight a schedule than his, and would probably

7

view any further delays as an outright act of war. A war which we and the entire crew would doubtlessly spend on a labor asteroid somewhere."

"Hmmm. Not much chance of a promotion in that. Why don't we just put the Ho-Ho-Kusian in suspended animation and let him sleep through the journey? Surely what happens then at the conference won't be our responsibility."

"A good idea, but unfortunately Ho-Ho-Kusians tend to rot during the thawing process. It's a side effect of being a vegetable."

Suddenly Boink's entire career passed before his eyes. On the whole, there weren't nearly enough acts of sexual perversion to satisfy him that he had lived life to the utmost, and he profoundly regretted he wouldn't be able to take his medals with him. "What did you say the drug was derived from?"

"The bark of a walking flytrap with sonic capabilities. Apparently the Ho-Ho-Kusian avian classes are hunted and eaten by vast insectoid swarms. The swarms track the birds by following their singing. So over the evolutionary eons, this species of flytrap developed a birdlike voice of its own in order to attract unsuspecting insects. Apparently it sounds remarkably realistic."

"If I should ever want to open a jungle cafe, then I'll know where to go. Is there anything we can do to alleviate the nerves of our savage vegetable, at least until we can haul in some fresh supplies of this flytrap bark?"

Coryban looked at the ceiling. Boink did likewise, to learn if she was looking at anything in particular. One of the flourescent bulbs was out, darkening the hue of the golden shielding in one corner, but otherwise the ceiling and all its art-deco fixtures and borders were brilliantly immaculate, just the way Boink liked it. He looked back at Coryban, to find her smiling enigmatically at him. He couldn't help but wonder if this woman, for all her incredible competence, had the proper respect for authority.

"I've already begun working on the problem, sir. It

turns out there is a solution, of sorts. The flytrap song does have a kind of mitigating effect on the Ho-Ho-Kusian system. Hearing the song acts as some kind of placebo, fooling the listener's nervous system into thinking the rooting season is just a moment away. Presumably this can go on for an indefinite period, but the ambassador was rather vague on that score. Anyway, finding a way to duplicate the flytrap song seems to be the way to go, at least for the moment."

"Good. I was afraid we'd have to divert the vegetable's attention with promises of revealing top secret, kinky farming techniques. What are the possibilities that you will be, ahem, successful in this little endeavor?"

"It's too early to say with any certainty, but I think you can look forward to a long and happy future, filled with just as many medals as you can carry. You see, the ambassador sang, as well as he was able, the song of the flytrap for the benefit of our ship's computer. The computer played back the song and kept changing the timbres until the ambassador verified their accuracy."

Boink slammed his hand on his desk. "That's wonderful! Then all we have to do is keep playing a tape of the song whenever things get too much for the blighted little creep! We'll receive those commendations yet, Colonel!"

"I never said anything about commendations."

"Yes, you did, you said 'medals.' And don't worry, I'll see to it that we get some for a job well done."

"But, Admiral, the computer-generated song doesn't work."

"Why not? It should be able to sound exactly like the real thing, down to the most minute vibration."

"Ah, yes, perhaps to our ears it would. But the Ho-Ho-Kusians don't really hear in the manner we do. The ambassador had to establish a sort of telepathic link with the computer before it could even begin to mimic the song of the walking flytrap, and even then his innate lack of analytical capabilities presented a formidable handicap. In any case, the ambassador complained that while

9

the resulting sound met the specifications in every scientific detail, the song itself lacked the soulful element that only an organic creator could provide."

"But that—that's only his opinion," said Boink indignantly.

Coryban shrugged. "His is the only one that counts."

"I hope he didn't say the song lacked heart."

"No, he used his race's equivalent idiom. 'It has sterile stamen, and the yellow sap of a prone root sucker,' I believe were the exact words that came out of the translator."

Boink put his head in his hands. His career passed before his eyes for the second time, and he thought he should be grateful for what memories he'd be able to retain. Forget the medals. All the medals in the galaxy weren't going to help him now. "Then that's it. There is no hope. I'm either disgraced or I'm vegetable fodder." He steeled himself, lifted his head with a slight, nearly inaudible moan, and stared unblinking into those ice-green eyes. "Colonel Coryban, I'm speaking to you now not as your superior officer, but as one who would like very much to be your friend. And I'm telling you, in all sincerity, in all complete honesty, that I desperately need your help. Only you can help me feel like a man again."

Coryban presented him with the sort of expression he associated with the discovery of dead bugs in one's meal. "You never miss an opportunity, do you?" she said without feeling.

"Doesn't look like I've so much time that I can afford to let the slightest one slip by."

"You should consider it. You might be better off in the long run. Besides, hopelessness is not the word of the day yet. The song of the flytrap, you see, bears an uncanny resemblance to the tones naturally produced by an ancient musical instrument."

"No kidding," he said with undisguised admiration, which he knew he would regret later. "Figure this out by yourself?"

"No, but I did order the computer to look into the

possibility. They're like superior officers, in that they're only as smart as you tell them to be. The answer came, so the next step was locating the instrument and ordering the someone who could play it to stay close to the Ho-Ho-Kusian ambassador's side at all times."

"Excellent. And what is this instrument?"

"The soprano saxophone."

"What is a soprano saxophone?" Boink asked impatiently, feeling himself go down for a third time.

"Well, a saxophone is a single-reed instrument that's a conical brass tube with two dozen keys and an up-turned lower end. Invented before the dawn of space travel, it was frequently used in many of the popular musical entertainments of its day. I suppose you could call the soprano version the castrato of the family."

"Wait. Let me guess. You're trying to tell me that this instrument is so rare that even if we could find one, it's highly unlikely that anyone will know what to do with it. In fact, it's so highly unlikely that even if we do find a soprano saxophone on one of the worlds we'll be passing, the odds of actually finding someone who can play it are, from our point of view, pathetic in the extreme."

"Sir, I'm surprised that after having made it this far in your career, you'd succumb so easily to such a defeatist attitude."

"I thought that was your intention all the time."

"It so happens, sir," said Coryban sternly, "there is someone *aboard* who is quite proficient on the soprano sax, and who registered the instrument when he reported for duty, in accordance with regulations!"

"Regulations? He's a crew member!" Suddenly Boink felt a tremendous weight lift from his shoulders. A haze dissipated before his eyes. He felt as young as twenty, as exuberant as a boy experiencing first love, as strong as a Mesklinite ox. "He's human, I hope. Or at least bipedal. I'm getting tired of dealing with all these nonhumanoids on a regular basis."

"His name is Homer B. Hunter, and he's a fifth-generation First Lieutenant from Gallium. His great-

great-grandfather was, in fact, a Founding Father, a High Admiral who acquitted himself and his fleet well during the Battle of the Sexus Spaceway."

"Oh, yes, 'Fightin' Butch' Hunter. Of course! They say that if you laid out end to end all the clone mutants he fried with his own two hand-lasers, they'd form a chain reaching to the Large Magellanic Cloud! Does this boy carry on in the family tradition?"

"He can get it together like the 'Butch', sir, but unfortunately, he can't always lift it. He's served most of his time competently but without distinction, and his superiors have often doubted he's the kind of organism who really fits into the Stellar Patrol. However, he has had his spectacular moments—two of them, in fact. While marooned on the planet of Resida, he rescued the population from their hibernation in cryo-units and, not incidentally, prevented the entire planet from plunging into its sun. Five years later, while marooned on a deserted space station, he deactivated a self-replicating pyramid of ancient origins, whose mysterious emanations drove machinery into states of irrational dysfunction. Unfortunately, these accomplishments, however admirable on their own merits, have no bearing on his ability to play the soprano saxophone."

"Uh-oh. His ancestor was justly renowned for his two-dimensionally flat tenor."

"You'll be thankful Hunter has exhibited considerably more musical talent than that. Apparently he was one of those rare child prodigies who excel at the major left-brain logic skills associated with that sort of phenomenon: numbers, chess, and music. Born and raised on Gallium, he was adept at solving integral equations by the age of three Galactic Years, was a chess master by the age of five, and an accomplished violinist and guitarist by the age of seven. He seems to have mastered the sax and other reed instruments as an afterthought, and never demonstrated much affinity for electronic instruments. Strange. Anyway, most of his precocious talents began to wane around his tenth year; the ascendancy of his maturity meant the diminution of his creative capacity. Still, he's retained acceptable skills in these areas; it's just no one will ever again accuse him of being a genius. And like I said, his soprano saxophone is listed as in his possession, so he's brought it with him. We can start easing our ambassador's myriad toe aches almost immediately, if we want to."

"And we do!" Boink hummed a tuneless little ditty to himself as he leaned over to press the communicom button. "Miss Beavers?"

Even before she spoke, he pictured vividly the tremendous buckteeth partially responsible for his secretary's overemphasis on certain sounds. "Sir, before you say anytheeng, there are several ambassadors here to see you!" came Miss Beavers' voice from the speaker to the left of the control panel. "I think it's about our fly-it time. And, sir, they all seem to be ra-ather ea-ager."

"Have them cool their jets, Miss Beavers," said Boink, feeling a little heat surge under the collar. The prospect of facing another chaotic confrontation with nonhuman ambassadors filled him with an eerie combination of ennui and utter despair. He could only hope none of them were the kind who drooled, secreted, or eliminated during periods of stress. It was getting near lunchtime. "I want you to send for a First Lieutenant Homer B. Hunter. I want him to report to me immediately. And Miss Beavers? Have him bring his soprano sax, will you? Out!" Bitter experience had taught him not to let his bucktoothed secretary get a word in edgewise.

Boink impulsively rubbed his hands. "I can't believe it! We've got a soprano saxophone player right on board with us! Once again, Boink, you old bean, what would have been a disaster for somebody else has turned into your good fortune. When Command reads your report, you're going to think you're the most resourceful admiral in the entire Fleet!"

"Sir, let's demonstrate a tad of restraint, shall we?" said Coryban. "We can't be certain the soprano saxophone will do the job."

Boink put his hands behind his neck and leaned back luxuriously in his chair. "Yes, but right now it seems we'll be able to muddle through spectacularly. Wait—what's that?" he asked, the instant before the emergency signal, that high-pitched, insistent whistle, shrieked through the walls like the screams of a twisted robot in electronic agony.

Coryban's eyes widened in surprise, and despite the many unpleasant reasons why someone would punch up the emergency signal, Boink couldn't help but wonder if her surprise stemmed from the alert itself, or the fact that he had been instinctively aware of the emergency before either had actually heard a sound. No matter. He struck the button to the bridge and spoke into the intercom. "Boink here! What's happening?"

"Sir, a survival pod's been ejected! There's a man inside!"

"What? Why? Who would want to do a stupid thing like that? We're in the void, for Kimball's sake!"

"Sir, there are no indications of malfunction, damage, or disruption anywhere, sir."

"Is that you, Blather?"

"No, sir. Yes, sir!"

"Make up your mind. Listen, are you one hundred per cent certain this ship is functioning perfectly—there's nothing wrong with her engines or the vents—no unsightly holes in her?"

"Everything's fine, sir. Nothing's the matter, sir! The lady's running like a dream, sir!"

"This is the SPS *Our Lady's Hornblower* we're flying, mister! She may handle like everything's fine, but in the clutch she has a will of her own! Keep that in mind as you answer me, Blather! Are you still totally certain, without a doubt in that tender, shell-like mind of yours, the lady's in absolutely top shipshape, that whatever made that pod eject was an accident due to some bipedal error—?"

"She's as tight as a virgin, sir!"

"Thank you, Blather. You are truly a class act.

14

Listen, I want you to look carefully at the board. Do you have a lock on the pod?"

"Yes, sir, but it's already making the transition to real space, sir."

"Okay, now take a closer look. Is there a life-form inside?"

"Uh, yes, sir! One human—and a robot!"

Boink sighed in relief and leaned back. "All right. This isn't so bad. Who is it, Blather? Can you catch anything from the homing signal?"

"Yes, sir, it's a crew member. But I can't tell who. We're getting interference from the pod's transition into real space, sir!"

"Try to tune some of the frequencies out and get back to me if you make clearer contact. Meanwhile, stay on course, Blather."

Coryban lifted her hand to get Boink's attention. "Am I to assume then," she said, "that we're holding steady, regardless of the pod?"

Boink shrugged. "Don't know what else to do. There's no telling where the pod will emerge. We'd have to search a hundred systems. I just hope the damn fool had the hypermass detector on. Otherwise he's going to come out between planetary systems and he'll likely never land anywhere."

"Just more of the Patrol waste left behind, eh, Admiral?" said Coryban sarcastically, raising an eyebrow.

"Yes, I'm afraid so. Damn, I hate waste." Boink looked down to his console. "Blather? Have you found anything yet?"

"No, sir!" said the voice from the speaker.

"Well, keep looking. And, Blather? Stop calling me 'sir' so much!"

"Yes, ma'am! Out!"

The speaker went dead and Boink's neck positively sizzled under his collar. He also felt his karma going sour, and was not nearly as confident as he had been in general a few minutes ago. He glanced at Coryban, and knew she too felt those things. Both her feet were poised on the floor, and she leaned expectantly forward, her elbows resting on the clipboard lying across her knees. They both refrained from speaking because they both knew what the other was thinking: *There are over four hundred human crewmen on this mission. The odds against what I'm dreading are four hundred to one!*

Nearly three more minutes passed before the shrieks of the alarm desisted, and another five passed with Boink and Coryban sitting in silence before Blather's voice returned. The ensign spoke in light, lilting tones. "Everything's still shipshape, sir! We're still on course and on the modified schedule. And I've got the name of the man overboard too, sir."

"And who is it?"

"It's Lieutenant Hunter, sir. I realize it's tragic to lose any man, sir, but really, I knew Hunter, and he really wasn't contributing that much to the success of our mission. Maybe that knowledge will be of some consolation to his family, sir."

Boink slammed both his fists on the desk. "Blather!" he screamed. "Report to me immediately!"

Chapter Two
The Big Leap

CALL ME HOMER. IT was the darkest of times, it was the brightest of times, mainly because my ass was about to get fried by a big ball of fire in the night, rapidly heading toward daytime on the other side of the world. I awoke wrapped in safety web, watching helplessly as the flames beyond the viewport window grew steadily whiter—indicating how quickly things were getting steadily hotter. Meanwhile, the atmosphere was doing its best to buffet the survival pod I was in like a shuttlecock in a game of badminton.

"I want a drink of water!" cried Oliver, my faithful robot companion, webbed in a separate safety snare. I was grateful for that, at least. Of all the ways entry into an atmosphere could do you in, being accidentally smashed upside the head by a fifty-pound faithful companion was the most humiliating.

"I can't get you any, Oliver," I said, groaning as a sudden pain shot through my jaws.

"I'll make you a deal. Get me water and I'll get you aspirin," said Oliver.

"You don't carry aspirin." I tried to laugh but it hurt too much. It was also too hot to laugh. That made two good reasons, but when it came to the third—my possible impending demise—I instead felt oddly exhilarated. Any new experience, regardless of its inherent finality, was better than the consummate boredom I'd endured since being assigned to *Our Lady's Hornblower*.

That same feeling had easily overwhelmed my reason and sense of protocol earlier, when I'd spotted those two ambassadors behaving in a manner I could only describe as furtive and suspicious. It had all started when, unable to sleep during my assigned "night" shift, once again plagued by the urgent need to contemplate the various stages of existential doom I sensed hovering all around me, I was aimlessly wandering the corridors, deliberately taking the seldom-used routes through the engineering sections. I'd sought privacy; instead Oliver, paddleball set in hand, had found me.

"Want'a play paddleball?" Oliver had asked. "It's good for what ails you."

"Nothing ails me, little friend. I just want to be alone for a while."

"It's okay with me. I'll just wait ten paces behind you until you're tired of being such a wanker. Then a game of paddleball will make you feel better."

"Hold on a second. I said I wanted to be alone and that's what I'll be if I have to—!" But the thought remained unfinished. For I'd detected a breach in the silence otherwise pervading the corridors—distant, whispery voices, occasionally punctuated by the somewhat louder bursts of translator static. Somebody was getting a brainful. I silenced Oliver with a gesture. Oliver frowned and then opened his mouth. I made a more insistent gesture and Oliver remained quiet. "Follow me," I whispered, "but don't make a sound."

"I'll stay as quiet as—" The robot never finished because I bent down and held my fist before his wide eyes.

Instead he just followed me. The drone of the ultradrive engines beyond the titanium walls, their old and battered dilithium crystals doubtlessly on the verge of disintegrating, drowned out the ambassadors' excited jabbering occasionally, but all in all they couldn't have done a better job of keeping within earshot if they had tried. I remained cautious. The diplomats wouldn't have come here in the second place, if they hadn't desired secrecy in the first. At least one voice gurgled in the unmistakable manner of the Porgian Five ambassador, a fish man who breathed water in a helmet.

Pausing behind an upright conduit, I shook my fist at Oliver for not lagging far enough behind. Then peeking around the conduit, I got my first look at my quarry, saw one was indeed a fish man, and quickly sized up the other. He was a Pheblian Glorp, which explained the pungent linseed odor I'd been instinctively trying to ignore.

Glorps are among the most grotesque races in the galaxy. Their aesthetic standards dictate that the greater the number of pustules, the more attractive the Glorp. You always know you're in the presence of a particularly attractive Glorp whenever you have an overwhelming urge to vomit. Judged in that regard, this Glorp was a throttle buster. Only with great difficulty did I restrain my stomach from lifting off, with my entire diaphragm in tow.

At least this Glorp, following diplomatic custom, concealed most of his body with a glittering gold cloak. On their homeworld, Glorps went naked, the better to incite their comrades to lust. Custom and instinct contrive to make them obsequiously polite to their own kind, and belligerent to everybody else. They especially hate Porgian fish men, and can't abide the sight of their gray, scaly skin, or their penchant for wearing transparent, plasticized clothing, as this one was doing.

So upon reflection, it made perfect sense that if these two had some unavoidable business, they would seek out a place where they could violate protocol at will. Each was probably hoping for a good excuse to deck the other. Apparently bickering about some sort of timetable, they couldn't agree on the numbers. The conversation was long and meaningless, at least in its current abstraction, and I was about to give up and sneak away when I detected the rumbling verbalizations of a third presence.

I rubbed my eyes and finally saw that the ambassadors were becoming agitated at a shadow on the wall, a shadow which, for all its two-dimensionality, implied the strength and presence of a three-hundred-pound being.

The shadow responded to the more instensely lit portions of the wall by appearing greener instead of paler. Basically the silhouette formed an amorphous creature held in place by the outlines of studded armor. Around the face and hands and calves, where presumably there was no armor, the lines of the silhouette constantly shifted and blurred, as if the creature could, if it so desired, deliberately alter into more savage forms. The left hand, though, for all its shifting, had no difficulty in grasping what appeared to be a tremendous club, which I'm sure made quite a significant point in the debate.

Now I am not by nature a courageous man. I realized my safest option was to simply report to my superiors the ambassadors' audience with this intruder, and then my sole concerns would be the ones Boink or Coryban conferred upon me. But the fact that the ambassadors could simply reduce my story to a case of their substantial word against mine left me the sole option of direct confrontation, in the hopes of gaining evidence to support my side.

I stepped from behind the pipe, raised a finger in the air, and said, "Excuse me, gentlemen, I couldn't help overhearing you. You sound like there's been some problem. Has the service been satisfactory?"

"Disturbances I thought you said we have not!" bellowed the shadow on the wall. It brandished that club, which was assuming supernatural proportions to my personal universe.

"I'm not disturbing you," I said with diplomatic obtuseness. "I'm just trying to be a good host. I couldn't help but notice the three of you were having an argument. It's loud enough to be heard all over the ship. Is there some way I may assist you? Provide you with information, perhaps?"

"Those mammals are so transparent," gurgled the

fish man contemptuously. "Always promising to give you what they want."

"Hot damn! I'll give you a game of paddleball!" Oliver exclaimed, waddling up beside me and offering the ambassadors the paddle.

I flicked my fingers on Oliver's head. It smarted, but it also worked. Oliver stopped talking and waddling. "Be quiet!" I hissed at him between my teeth, then nodded at the shadow on the wall and said to the ambassadors, "Is that skinny guy your bookie?"

"Stand to be insulted I do not have to tolerate," said the shadow. The arms swung. The club moved. A black silhouette of what was most definitely a club jetted out across the floor—making a serious beeline toward my feet! In the last instant I can remember, the shadow moved up my legs and torso.

Life sort of came to a standstill.

And approximately five eons later I woke up in the survival pod, peacefully baking like a Gallium horse potato. My jaw felt like someone had tried to drive it through the top of my skull. My awareness of the pain, however, was quickly obliterated by the sensation of blind, bowel-loosening panic. "Oliver—how—how did you get here?" I asked.

Oliver's eyes, which were two black discs in the upper portion of his rounded head, bobbed like a slinky in surprise, thanks to the springs in their tiny, elastic stalks. "Boss! Don't tell me you've lost your memory as a result of being viciously beaned?" he exclaimed. "Oh, no—how could things possibly get worse? Boss! How are we ever going to get out of here if your brain is cracked? Boss! Boss! Talk to me! Don't die on me now!"

"Stop it! Do you hear me? Stop it!" I screamed. I had just about accepted the inevitable—there was nothing I could do about it anyway—when the wave of blackness hit. The lights were extinguished in an instant, and I had just a nanosecond to note how incredibly hard this webbing had gotten, how the stuff was crushing me all over, before my brain snuffed out for the second time.

It switched back on with a roar. My eyes must have been already open, because they were already adjusted to the dim emergency lights in the pod. Sea-blue water rippled up the exterior of the viewport, and then the world outside began to go dark again.

I frantically tore myself from the webbing and began turning the hatch. "Oliver! We're drowning! Let's skedaddle, for van Ljinn's sake!"

Three minutes later the survival pod was busily sinking to the bottom of a lake, while I was busily crawling up the closest bank, my aching body soaked to the marrow, my lungs vividly protesting the load of water I'd picked up along the way. The lake was too squawking cold, I numbly noted—over and over again, to keep my mind off the inherent finality I'd just avoided. For if the trajectory of the crashing pod, its speed checked by its parachute and automatic retros, had deviated in the slightest, Oliver and I would have wound up very flat, very tiny metal and carbon crisps, doing our best to obtain a close inspection of this world's lower geological stratum.

Which was where I'd like to have stomped the Glorp and the fish man. The shadow creature and the diplomats must have put aside their bickering long enough to capture Oliver and carry us to the survival pod. They then ejected us into ultradimensional space. Being civilized creatures, they'd obviously lacked the gumption to murder us outright, otherwise they wouldn't have bothered to put us in the webbing. Perhaps they'd sought to salve their consciences by giving us a slight chance to survive.

Okay, slimmer than slight. If Oliver and I hadn't come out in a gravitational well, we could have been adrift forever. Worse, the well could have been inhospitable—such as that of a sun or a neutron star—and even then the temporary prolongation of existence wouldn't have been an option. Yes, the diplomats had known the consequences of their actions, and clearly wouldn't have been so theoretically merciful if they'd thought there was the slimmest possibility Oliver and I would ever tell anyone what we knew. Those were far, far better odds than I was willing to give them, should we ever cross paths again, especially me and that shadow man.

And who knew? I might have my chance. For surely the diplomats would have overcome their squeamishness if they had known about the hyperwave homing signal that was standard equipment in all survival pods. I'd managed to remember to switch on this one just before I swam through the lock. An eventual rescue and return to the fleet remained a possibility, though I knew the workings of the Stellar Patrol well enough by now not to count on it.

Oliver, legs retracted and wheels down, revved up the muddy bank past me. Built like a cross between a fire hydrant and a trash can, he had two tiny titanium arms at his sides, now moving back and forth like munchkin pistons. His fingers were coiled into fists, and his tiny tailpipe sputtered little puffs of white smoke. "I think I can I think I can I think I can!" he chanted.

"Good. When you're done, how about doing it for me?" Those words had evidently expended the last remaining erg in my body, for just as I concluded, all the tenseness went out of my muscles and my face went splat in the mud. I only began to struggle to lift it after my nose became clogged with mire. Elsewhere in existence, birds sang like toy sirens. At that stage of the game, it was just beginning to dawn on me that they might be real. After all, my head was clear enough for me to estimate the number of years it had been since I'd heard birds singing in the wild. Their sweet melodies made my heart soar. Their volume made my head throb.

"Memory returned, Boss?" Oliver asked as he extended his arms and grabbed me by the armpits, pulling me up to a grassy knoll. The coils of his eight fingers were incredibly cold from their immersion in the water.

"Of course, it's returned! It was never gone in the first place! Now let me go!"

"Sure, Boss." A pause. Those eyes bugging out again. "Wait a second! How can it return if it never went away?"

"Forget it! I'm fine." At the moment I was too busy trying to breath to play with him. A few seconds later, I was too busy being overwhelmed by a sudden influx of sensory input, so vital it nearly intoxicated me. The birdsongs reverberated in my brain like symphonies. The powerful scent of the flowers felt like velvet razors slicing up my nose. The mud's deep brown hue revealed a hundred subtle shades, especially in the tracks my body had made, while the greens of the leaves on bushes and trees glimmered in the sunlight with a vibrancy the shipside solar gardens were incapable of duplicating. Even the pale green of a clump of nearby weeds revealed tremendous nuances of color. I reached out for the nearest clump, with the intention of putting it in my mouth.

I shrugged off the urge just in time. Most Patrol beings got that particular fever while on land every once in a while, especially if their arrival groundside had aroused a certain amount of stress. Succumbing probably wouldn't have done me any harm. I'm sure I'd done worse. But these weeds had leaves with circular structures I'd never seen before. Precisely what that could indicate, I couldn't guess, but I couldn't take a chance until I knew more about the biochem-ecosystem of this planet.

I rolled onto my back and, for the first time in months, stared at an expansive blue sky. It aroused a sense of contentment in my heart, tinged with bittersweet nostalgia for times that perhaps had never been. I couldn't help but be amused at the irony of it: for those most recent birdsongs of mine had been heard inside a hollow world called Pellucidar, with a patchy green and brown sky that was really the other side; while this nameless world's sky was like a dome of cool light. This sky had white wisps of clouds being stirred by gentle winds, a yellow sun whose position indicated the time was late afternoon, whose size indicated a temperate climate, and, to the northeast, the rising outlines of two crescent moons, the larger one crimson, the smaller orange.

The lake the survival pod had landed in stretched to the horizon. To the east was a craggy mountain range, its ledges and gullies adorned with foliage, its crests anchored by tall trees with branches extending high above the cliffs. To the south was another mountain with more hospitable terrain. From the west came a perpetual whispery roar, the sound of a waterfall. In addition to the birdsongs, insects chirped blithely, some quite strangely, from their places of concealment all around me.

I hated to admit it, but I'd never experienced a place on Gallium as teeming with life as this, as rich in pastoral splendor. Indeed, I'd accidentally crawled over a sample of that life on my way up the bank, smearing it on my fatigues above the left knee. I just hoped I hadn't squashed an intelligent creature of some sort. You could never tell about these things.

"Where to now, Boss?" Oliver asked.

"I don't know yet," I said, still trying to catch my breath. "I'm still thinking things through."

"All well and good, but if I don't get cleaned up soon, I'm going to rust."

"I thought they built you better than that." I opened my survival kit before I realized I'd even had it with me. Evidently I'd slung the knapsack it was in over my shoulder on the way out of the survival pod, probably before I'd set off the homing signal. It only went to show my drill android in boot camp had been right when he said, in those mecho-dulcet tones of his, "You Jovian flatulence blasters may think you're pretty smart, but the first thing you're going to learn is that brains are a liability in the Stellar Patrol. And it's my job to flush 'em out and give you stuff you can use instead!" At the moment, I felt pretty flushed.

The survival kit contained, among other things, a three-day supply of rations, a five-day supply of dehydrated water pills, a first-aid kit, a toothbrush, a self-contained, multipurpose scrub brush, a collapsible hammer, an adjustable wrench, an equally adjustable screw-driver, three different kinds of knives, a church key, a rope, a laser gun with five settings, birth control pills applicable to either sex, and one package of reusable toilet paper. I dug to the bottom of the kit and pulled out a towel. Shipside hygienists were adamant about marooned Patrol personnel being equipped with their own towels, presumably because of their "immense psychological value." I gave the towel to Oliver and told him to dry himself off before his joints started creaking.

"Can we, like, go somewhere now?" he asked me impatiently after he was done, returning the towel.

I threw it back into the survival kit and began walking up the knoll toward the mountain to the south. It really didn't much matter which direction I took at this stage of the expedition; I just had to remind Oliver to record this spot in his navigational records so I could return to this site so the rescue team, when it arrived for me, would be able to pick me up directly. The thought of spending a few weeks alone in the woods while waiting for the team, however, was not very inviting, especially since the possibility remained the team might get lost despite the homing signal. It had happened before. So I figured I might as well find out what sort of civilization, if any, resided on this world.

There was no point in speculating about what sort of civilization it might be. If the life of this world I'd fallen onto matched most other ecosystems in this crazy, mixed-up galaxy of ours, then the last thing I'd have to worry about was whether or not I'd be surprised. Any second now, some creature—maybe a giant white ant carrying a submachine gun and wearing a battle helmet, or an opera-singing flower man with branches for arms and roots for legs—could step from the foliage and be-rate me for trespassing on sacred and/or royal grounds. I might encounter intelligent, joke-cracking dinosaurs, sensitive, poetry-spouting zombie types, amorous amorphous globs, walking worms with dangerously enticing phero-mones, or even talking platypuses wearing bow ties. Right now, anything I could imagine was possible. Philosophically it was far more expedient simply to decide that I would accept whatever this world had to offer.

Besides, I was too preoccupied listening to what the trees and the birds had to say to me. Already they had enticed me to shrug off my worries concerning my performance of my duty during future events which would now take place light-years away, about which I could do nothing. Already I'd shrugged off a flurry of militarized preoccupations, and was imagining I had become someone else, an idealized, older version of the naive youth who had joined the Stellar Patrol so many years ago.

And this world, where slithering purple vines dangled from branches bespotted with yellow moss, was responsible. Iridescent blue mushrooms grew beneath the roots that twisted from the ground. Black birds with white beaks and green tail feathers pecked at the dirt, while high in the foliage above chicks in nests chirped incessantly, demandingly. A crimson fly buzzed by my ear, and the pungent odor of fresh animal dung assaulted my senses. The roar of the waterfall grew steadily louder, and the trail I followed—which I surmised might have been bipedally forged but was just as likely made by creatures of a lower evolutionary state—became wider, the soil firmer, the downtrodden grass seeking to encroach it becoming progressively thinner and pale.

Once I disturbed a flock of white birds. Their claws were too large, their beaks too pronounced and formidable, for me to think of them as anything other than a variant of albino hawks. Nearly fifty rose from concealment in the grass like ghosts propelling themselves from graves, the flapping of their wings stirring the air with their determination to disappear overhead as quickly as possible. Which they did. In less than five seconds, the air had settled as if they had never existed. Only the excited beating of my heart remained.

Oliver and I hadn't been walking long when we came upon the waterfall. It wasn't very large or spectacular, at least by galactic standards, but it was imposing enough to take my breath away. Great clouds of mist rose from the outlet below. Many trees bordering the river above and the steep slopes on either side of the falls had been half uprooted by floods, and in places the grass and bushes were partially covered by silt. Taken as a whole, the scene combined the pristine beauty of nature at her most innocent with the trash left behind by her unthinking fury. I knew I would think again of this place, if my sax and I were ever reunited.

"We go backtrack now, Boss?" Oliver asked. "Go up?"

"I haven't decided yet. Tell you what. Let me partake of some of the rations the Patrol has so thoughtfully provided, and before we continue, I'll see about giving you a lube job."

"Boss, I didn't know you cared."

I took a ration packet from my survival kit and unwrapped the foil. A sticky red goo was inside. I had to eat it with my fingers. All these items I was carrying, and eating utensils weren't standard equipment. The goo tasted like raspberries, or at least what the chemists thought raspberries tasted like. "I can't eat this shit."

"No perspiration," said Oliver, grabbing the packet from my hand and tossing it whole into his mouth, which had suddenly become a huge maw of cosmic proportions. "Pouting won't help," he added, promptly punctuating the remark with a protracted belch.

"That's disgusting," I replied, seeking to deflect his meaning because at the moment I was enjoying my disgust too much to permit tolerance of my robot Friday's social deficiencies to intrude. Gradually, however, my stomach stopped gurgling and became a vaporous pit, the acids threatening to eat me from the inside, all because something in the river had caught my eye. That's when the truth struck me like an antimatter vibrating ray. Of course! I was a castaway! To heck with the Prime Directive, which dictated that the Stellar Patrol have as little effect on the culture and environment of nonaffiliated planets as possible. To heck with eating all that prefabricated, medicated goo in the survival kit. I could go fishing! I could have some real food, just like a genuine historical explorer.

Provided, naturally, I was man enough to slay it. Which of course I was. I was, after all, heavily armed.

I took the laser gun from the survival kit and removed the power pack, inserting a pneumatic one in its place. I broke a branch from a nearby tree, carved one end to a sharp tip with my hunting knife, tied the rope to the other end of the stick, and then tied the other end of the rope around my waist. I inserted the stick into the barrel of my gun, thus completing my primitive spear gun according to the precise specifications drilled into my subconscious during basic training. Of course, I'd have to clean the barrel thoroughly before I refixed it to laser mode, unless I wanted the gun to blow up in my face, but with luck this entire enterprise would prove to be worth the trouble.

"Are we going to do something stupid now?" Oliver asked.

"How would you like to close down for a while?"

"I'll be good."

While heading toward some rocks that promised a good foothold, I happened to walk through a clump of bushes that happened to be blooming. Red pollen from their purple flowers dusted me as if I'd walked a gauntlet of salt shakers. I inadvertently breathed some in. Since the leaves where the pollen had fallen previously were discolored, I brushed the stuff from the front of my fatigues and then wiped as much as possible off my hands. That action was only partially successful, because I mainly succeeded in smearing the stuff all over me, and rubbing some of it deeper into my skin.

"They say precaution is the best way to avoid a painful and serious demise," said Oliver, who had followed me and was now using his dust buster, set in reverse, to blow the pollen off his metal torso. It spewed wildly in all directions, and no matter which way I turned, I was immersed in a cloud of the stuff. Oliver's dust buster, connected to its interior compartment by a metal coil, was entirely subject to his electronic impulses, meaning the little robot didn't have to touch it to move it. A thought would do. Mostly the coil was wound about him like a giant snake with a case of elephantiasis of the head, coldly sizing up its prey until just the right moment to strike.

I walked from one part of the cloud to the next. I breathed in more pollen. It made me sneeze. I noticed with a sense of sudden ire, all out of the proportion to the supposed offense, that the pollen had begun to coat the relatively still water around my potential foothold. "Lotch whir u'rrr blooing dat stiff," I said. It occurred to me I was feeling funny, but that didn't stop me from going to the bank.

Enough rocks in the water were sufficiently close together to form a bridge leading into the mist of the waterfall; presumably it reached to the opposite side of the river. Having nothing else better to do, I stared at them for a few minutes. Then I got a grip on myself, handed my survival pack to Oliver, and pinpointed a rock big and flat enough for my big, flat feet. I hefted my make-shift speargun and put my right foot gingerly on the rock. It held steady. I put more of my weight on it and slowly brought my left foot toward the next most promising big, flat rock. I giggled. A mighty tasty-looking fish with pink iridescent gills and shiny purple and yellow scales shook its tail as it traveled between two rocks. I put my right foot down. Luckily, it hit a rock. I saw the fish dart out from behind a gnarly blue plant. It stirred up silt and disappeared behind a gnarly pink plant. I took another step, hoping to keep the fish in sight. I didn't. I struggled to maintain my balance as the rock wobbled beneath me. No way I'd get that particular fish now. It was long gone. *C'est la vie, you all.* I giggled. I steadied myself. I sneezed. I giggled. I wiped my nose. I wondered if I would come back soon. I giggled. I stepped. I held my breath. I became distracted by the flecks of sunlight rippling in the water where there was no mist. Then I became distracted by the little rainbows that appeared and disappeared in the mist. A blue crescent moon had joined the other two in the sky. A near quack—probably emanating from some almost duck—echoed from the mountains. I noticed my pneumatic gun was the hardest thing I'd ever held. Too bad. A minnow glided past me near the surface. It shrank and was gone. I giggled. My mouth watered. The wind brought me a whiff of mist and I breathed it in. It smelled fresh and clean. I aimed at some rippling flecks of reflected sunlight to keep in practice. I saw another fish. It looked like a catfish, only flatter. It was a big flat fish. Coming my way. I held my breath. I held my giggle. I held my gun in both hands. I aimed with both hands and one eye. I fired. I giggled. I watched as the tip of the spear sliced through the water and went right for the fish. The rope around my waist tugged. I giggled. I wanted to stop giggling, but I was too busy concentrating on pulling the looping and twisting rope toward me to worry about my mental condition. What was left of it. I pulled the fish from the water. I noticed with no small degree of satisfaction that I had been right the first time. It did resemble a catfish, only bigger and flatter. I held it before my face and stared it in the glazed green eye. I grinned. My mouth watered. The fish shook futilely. It was pierced right through the neck. It was extremely dead, all right; only the nerves would still work for a little while.

Behind me, something metallic hit the ground with a thunk. The something metallic croaked "Boss!" at me. I started to turn around.

But then I started falling. Fast. Either that, or the water had decided to rush up to hit me. I waved my arms. I might have tried to wave my feet. My gun fell from my hand. A shadow passed before my eyes. I felt the catfish dropping from my other hand. I had a nanosecond to thank goodness the rope was still tied around me. I'd still be able to eat the catfish, so long as I didn't drown first.

I hit the water. I became uncomfortably numb. Then,

its velocity only slightly diminished by the impact of the water, my gun bobbed me upside the head.

I sat up in a panic and sputtered out water. I pulled in the rope and was immediately suspicious of its utter slack. It took about three nanoseconds for the end of the rope to emerge from the water, and about three seconds for the implications of the frayed end to penetrate my rock-hard cranium. The rope had been cut! My big, flat catfish was gone! I reeled. The ice-cold water had immediately washed most of the pollen off me, but the shock also kicked in the next series of effects.

Whatever they were. I was only vaguely aware my mind was undergoing another phase of distortion. At least time had once again become an intangible force that moved of its own accord, rather than some nebulous stone wall hemming in my perceptions. I finally realized the catfish had been deliberately pilfered from me, and if I could only muster the muscular coordination required to take a look, I still might spot the culprit.

I did. He was a raven-haired thief in buckskins, with a black, wide-brimmed hat held by a string around his neck. The thief stepped across the stones with preterhuman precision, his moccasined toes barely touching down long enough for his weight to register. The bastard was definitely holding my big, flat catfish, and before I could even get angry about it, he disappeared into the mist.

"Oliver! Bring the survival kit and follow me!" I shouted, propelling myself from the drink like a rocket. I tossed the pneumatic gun to the shore for Oliver to retrieve.

I didn't wait for a reply, nor did I wonder if his coordino-circuits were up to the task of tiptoeing across the rocks. I knew they were, even if Oliver didn't. Thanks to the pollen, I ran across the stones as swiftly and as lightly as a gazelle, reaching the other bank in a matter of moments and immediately following the subtle trail the thief had left in his wake. It didn't take much knowledge about the native and (presumably) imported fauna of this world to be able to detect broken twigs,

bent blades of grass, and rustling bushes without difficulty. Even without the distinctive scent of the catfish—
not to mention that of the thief himself, who must have
been perspiring heavily—the trail was as visible as an
eight-roller pedway to me.

I ran as fast as I ever had before, faster. The drug
was a powerful stimulant in all regards. I did not slow
down, I did not grow tired. Soon I veered around some
bushes, ran under some low branches, as my prey had,
and caught a glimpse of him disappearing beyond a
hilltop where the forest was thinning out. My speed
increased, seemingly of its own volition. My legs were
like two pistons of throbbing, pounding steel, propelling
me doggedly, ruthlessly forward. As I imagined running
even faster, the foliage blurred past me even more quickly;
I became afraid my legs would work themselves from my
hips if I wasn't careful.

I ran up that hill with no problem. But while running down the other side, something tightened around
my left foot—and the world turned upside down.

Chapter Three
Breakfast of Warriors

I WAS TRAPPED, CAUGHT
by the foot in the noose of a rope tied to a high
branch. I swung back and forth like a pendulum, my
hands groping uselessly toward the ground. I responded
like a barbaric madman. That is, I growled in frustration.
I roared with anger. I belched with rage. I farted in
annoyance. I expressed my dissatisfaction in every conceivable method available to me. Unfortunately, there
weren't that many.

Eventually I had no choice but to perceive the situation with some semblance of civilized logic. At that point
the solution to my predicament came to me in an instant.
Straining my abdominal muscles to the utmost, I attempted to pull myself up far enough to grab hold of my
left ankle. I had no knife—they were all with Oliver, in
the survival pack—but I felt confident I could pull the
robe apart by the strands if necessary.

I might have done so, too. Even my pinky felt
strong and durable enough to lift an elephant. But the
instant my fingers touched the hemp, someone planted a
set of toes in the small of my back with uninhibited
gusto. My scream was more from reflex than anything
else—the drug had numbed my susceptibility to pain. I

dropped back down, then twisted myself around for my first good look at the thief's face.

And all thoughts of escape were temporarily banished. For that next moment of my life was brought to me courtesy of Schopenhauer, that ancient Terran philosopher whose ruminations on mankind, race, and destiny had waxed great gobs of eloquence concerning a particular type of chance encounter that has occurred throughout history with frightening regularity to privileged males of the species. For during that moment of terror and beauty, a man suddenly become acquainted, however in passing, with a female who inspires within him an onslaught of destiny fulfilled. The male is stricken with desire for this female person, not only the desire to bed her, and perhaps to wed her, but to have her bear his children. He is convinced such offspring will benefit the entire species. No other woman as well suited for the purpose can possibly exist. No other woman can complement his genetic and cultural heritage so perfectly. No other woman could possibly be as important in the entire scheme of his existence. He firmly believes, with every fiber of his being, that to win her is to survive, and to fail is to do worse than die. For should she reject his overtures, however gently, for whatever reason—be it rational or simply beyond the pale—then the pain of this emotional fiasco is like unto a mortal wound, and simply seems more than the heart can bear. The physical body of a man was not meant to endure such agony and turmoil.

Needless to say, the pick-up lines resulting from such initial encounters are extremely important. Unfortunately, Schopenhauer's writing is not famous for its guidance in the matters of social etiquette. Even more unfortunately, I've never read Schopenhauer, I just heard about that passage from a friend of mine named Horselover Fat, once while we were both stewed to the gills in a spaceport bar, waiting for our ship to blast off. In fact, I can't even be sure it's Schopenhauer I mean, because I've only my friend's drunken word for it. I don't remember much else about the conversation, except that we cried a lot.

However, it did seem to me, looking at that face while upside down, I had at last fully grokked the emotional meaning behind the intellectual concept. It was too bad all my diplomatic training hadn't clued me in on how to impress a young lady who had just stolen my catfish. Maybe if I convinced her it was a really great catfish. . . .

"Hi," I said, waving. "Fancy meeting you here. Go fishing often?"

Her expression stoic in the extreme, she calmly stuck the tip of her hunting knife into my left nostril. Hers was a new kind of beauty to me, deeper and truer than any other kind I had ever known. Her skin was the color of a fragile pale rose, but her high cheekbones, handsome dimpled chin, and overall bearing indicated an innate nobility and a rebellious spirit. Her jawline was straight and firm. Her raven-black hair was so dark that it gleamed in the sunlight. It fell past the fringes across her buckskin shirt, fringes only partially obscuring her ample figure. The shirt was embroidered with wavy blue crests, and studded with aqua-colored sequins. Her trousers were fringed at the seams. The string holding her hat around her neck was white, with black aglets; it swung back and forth hypnotically. But I must confess that however much I was interested in the details of her personal presence, the vast majority of my attention was focused on her eyes, eyes the color of creamy jade.

"Okay, I give up," I said. "I'll make you a deal. Cut me down from here and *I'll* bear *your* children. I'll stay at home and take care of them while you go hunting. How does that sound?"

She inhaled through her teeth as if warning me not to make a grab for her. Then she either snarled or said something in her native language. It was hard to tell which. A deep, guttural growl followed, reverberating in my mixed-up noodle like the aftereffects of phase distortion.

"Of course, I'll be happy to introduce myself," I said. "It's only fair because we're going to be so close so soon. My name is Homer B. Hunter, First Lieutenant of *Our Lady's Hornblower*, the flagship of the Fifth Fleet of the Stellar Patrol of the Third Galactic Union of the Certified Galactic Empires of Tremain and Gallium. What's yours?"

She glared. The fact that she didn't snarl again emboldened me.

"I said what's your name? Look, I can't adjust my translator until you cut me down from here."

She glared some more. She removed the knife from my nostril and pressed it between my eyes.

I repressed a giggle, not very successfully, I might add. "You're quite beautiful, do you know that? Just looking at you reminds me of that old spacer's nursery song: 'There's a meltdown at the power station/Where will the ions flow?/I'm clawing at your hatch/Hanging on to your titanium bar./You tell me you're the kind who likes to change your mind/When you start to radiate you really burn./But this shield in my heart/Can't resist much more.' "

Apparently unmoved by my rendition, she straightened up, put her knife between her teeth, and reached behind her hair with both hands. My heart soared. She was adjusting her translator—tuning it to my brainscan, to cope with my own language! At last, a symbol of postdigitized civilization had emerged from the camouflage of her savage facade. I sensed the odds of forging a diplomatic link between the Empire and this rustic outpost tilting in my favor, and I'm certain she sensed it too. She stubbornly tried to disguise the fact, however, by remaining silent after the adjustment had been completed, as if to indicate she didn't mind hearing me talk, but wouldn't commit herself to a conversation unless she deemed it worthwhile. A typical native ploy. That was all right. I could deal with that. But things could still go wrong between us in any number of ways, which is why I asked, with all the politeness and casual charm I could muster, "Forgive me for being forward, but I really must know if you are as human as you, at first blush, appear to be."

Oh, what a snarl.

"Well, you certainly act human. Don't misunderstand me. I'm as liberal as the next biped, but I've seen some creatures in my day who may look human, who may walk like they're human and talk like they're human, but who upon scientifically verifiable investigation prove to be something else again."

She ran the edge of her blade across my forehead. Something wet trickled into my hair.

I grinned. I had the feeling she could respect a man who could grin while he was being skinned alive.

She unbuttoned my fatigues with her blade and ran the tip of it up my exposed stomach. It didn't break my skin but I could feel its icy touch roll through every tissue like a methane snowball.

"What are you doing that for?" I asked, my abject fear, I am certain, very apparent. "Listen, lady, I think maybe you've got the wrong idea about me. Maybe it's because I'm upside down, but I feel compelled to tell you you're the loveliest bipedal wonder I've ever seen. I'm sure no common biojunctioned translator is capable of making the relativistic assessments to interpret just how lovely."

She cocked her head like a dog seeing a human walk around on all fours and howl at the moon. The knife slowed enough for me to hope I would eventually escape this planet with my voice unchanged. Believing I'd be foolish to quit while I was ahead, I gave her a quick rundown as to how I came to be stranded on her world— not that she responded in any meaningful fashion, but I did want her to get used to the sound of my voice, so perhaps we could achieve significant nonverbal communication later. "So listen, just think of me as the man who fell to dinner. And there's nothing I would give for a chance to sink my teeth into your catfish tonight. So what do you say? Please?"

She shook strands of hair from her eyes. Her expression softened. She held up the catfish. She smiled.

"Pretty please?" I asked.

She threw the catfish in the grass and walked away. She slipped into the woods.

I tightened my stomach and tried to pull myself up again. Then I tried for the third time. I made more progress, but I couldn't quite reach the knot. I tried to slip my fingers between the rope and my ankle, so I could compose myself for one do-or-keep-hanging stretch, but the rope was too tight. I decided to scream instead. "Oliver! Oliver! Where are you?"

There was no answer. The forest was unnaturally quiet. My story must have frightened away all the insects and the birds. Then I distinctly heard the snap, crackle, pop of twigs breaking. The sounds reverberated up my spine as if they originated in the cauldron of gas where my tummy used to be. All thoughts of escape temporarily forgotten, I stared at the catfish. It was an ugly little sucker, but it set my mouth to watering. Okay, so it was raw. Sure, if a lungful of pollen had fried my brain, the meat of this world could possibly do something infinitely more psychedelic, ten times more fatal. Still, its beady green eyes were staring at me as if I was somehow personally responsible for the fact that fish were born to be eaten. The gas from the cauldron in my torso drifted down my esophagus and filled up my mouth. My tongue ran over my lips. The planet rotated and I got dizzy. The snap, crackle, pop gradually became obscured by a whirring noise, becoming louder and getting closer with each passing second.

"Oliver! It's about time you showed up! Get me down from here!"

"Coming, Boss! Wheels—keep turning!"

I twisted around to see Oliver, his feet retracted, rolling down the hill as fast as his little wheels could turn. I watched stupefied as he rolled past me, his tiny arms flailing helplessly, and disappeared into the woods. Blinked out, actually, into the foliage. My heart dropped into my throat as he shouted, "Wooaaahhh!" and then stopped shouting the instant before a harrowing crash split the air like thunder. Then a silence fell over the world.

"Oliver?" I whispered.

"Coming, Boss," croaked a voice from the wilderness.

It wasn't Oliver who emerged but Miss Schopenhauer, with an armful of branches and twigs. Surely she had heard Oliver crash, but she was nonchalant about his nearby presence. Otherwise, she was impossible to read. She set about building a fire by scraping two rocks together and blowing the sparks into a full-fledged flame. The way her cheeks puffed out made me dizzy. Then she retrieved the catfish and calmly gutted it with the precise motions of an experienced gutting person. She threw the unacceptable innards about almost casually, but with a definite predilection for my direction, so a few splatters could hit me in the face.

The aroma of hot catfish was smothering the vicinity when Oliver, a little battered and leaf-stained, finally emerged from the underbrush. "We eat now?" he asked, his big eyes bobbing up and down.

Miss Schopenhauer shrugged him off. If she thought there was anything unusual about a talking trash compactor waddling around, she gave no indication.

"Get me down from here!" I said.

One of Oliver's compartments opened, and out popped his coil-attached Solarian trooper knife, the scissors extended for action. The coil shot toward my feet, but stopped cold when Miss Schopenhauer finally noticed Oliver with an icy glare of inescapable meaning. "Hi," Oliver said nervously, his trooper knife retracting slowly.

"Thanks a heap of bovine merde, little 'pal.' Just what is the Flugian-pickin' meaning of this nothing?" I said. "What about your programming—and that oath you swore?"

"I don't remember no oath, Boss."

"Sure you do. It's the oath about always honoring

40

the instructions of the Singlemost Law, remember? The one that says no robot shall through action or lack off action permit a sentient organism of an officially registered species to come to harm!"

"Sorry, but that's the Thirdfolded Law. The real Singlemost Law says that under no circumstances shall a robot place his own private person in jeopardy! And since that law comes first, it takes precedence over the one in third place. Especially since that woman is trying to tell me in her distinctive nonverbal way that should I help you, she'll bop me so hard I'll be spitting bolts from my exhaust pipe! So if you'll excuse me, Boss, I'll be resting over there on that log while you two work things out. And oh, yeah, I sure would appreciate a nosh of your catfish, ma'am. It smells just fine!"

"You took an oath!" I screamed.

"I crossed my fingers!" he screamed back.

"Oliver, if I stay up here much longer," I said in a tone only approximately calm, "I'm going to come to great physical harm. My blood pressure's on the rise, and I might bust a blood vessel if circumstances don't improve pretty damn quick."

"So cool down already," said Oliver as he smoothed the bark where things looked like they might be comfortable. "You've got to learn how to take it easy under adverse circumstances, Boss."

"Oliver, I'm surprised at you, breaking the law without so much as a twinge of conscience."

"You have your legal system, and I have mine," he said, crossing his legs in midair as he plopped himself on the log.

I snarled. Miss Schopenhauer, evidently appreciating an irony of some sort, laughed, turned to me, and with a casual flick of the wrist threw the knife directly at my left foot. I screamed. The knife sliced about halfway through the rope and went thunk into a tree behind me. I groaned. I dropped in fits and stops as the rope went from taut to practically unraveled. Then the rope snapped, completing the job in an instant, and my head hit the ground. I yelped. I fell over. My shoulders, buttocks, and feet hit the ground all at once. I arrgghhed. I was beginning to sound like a one-man band. I lay there. "Thanks," I said through gritted teeth.

"You're welcome," said Miss Schopenhauer.

"At last, the enigma speaks," I groaned.

She nodded at Oliver, and he dutifully extended his hand to the knife, pulled it from the tree, and returned it to her. Whoever she was, wherever she'd come from, she'd certainly grasped the principles of command quickly. She slipped the knife into a holster inside her shirt. A nice place to be, if you could get there. "I love the scent of fresh fish in the afternoon, don't you?" she said. "It smells like . . . supper. Do you eat as fast as you run?"

I couldn't help but notice the planet was rotating too fast. It took me a few moments to gather my last two wits together, mainly because I was distracted by all those heavenly bodies that had somehow gotten between her and me. "I know when to savor what, when I know what it is," I said.

She nodded absently. She sniffed the air and returned her attention to the fire. She poked the catfish with a stick, then ran the stick through it and took it from the fire. She sat cross-legged between me and Oliver and nodded curtly toward him as she laid the catfish on a rock and inserted the blade into it with her knife over it. "What is that? An infant city?"

"If so, he's a good case for urban renewal," I replied with a groan, rolling onto my stomach in order to gain a preliminary damage assessment. Nothing was broken, but virtually everything was bruised. Gingerly I felt the bump on my head, with the sneaking suspicion that soon, when the shock died down, the pain would be intolerable. Right now the hard spot only felt cold. But who cared about pain anyway? At the moment I was too busy rejoicing over how wonderful it was that I couldn't take my eyes off Miss Schopenhauer, who had commenced to chewing a portion of the catfish with the bland sloppiness of the totally alone.

I cleared my throat. She ate with uninhibited gusto. I cleared my throat again and took the calculated risk of sitting on a rock that happened to be nearby. I smiled at her. For some crazy reason—call it the urge to survive, the spiritual deprivation of the marooned, juvenile wish fulfillment, or even the mad notice of a sucker for a stormy face—I actually believed that she would succumb to the pangs of outrageous guilt and give me something to eat. It seemed to my stricken mind that my hunger pangs radiated with thermonuclear intensity. So I was counting on her fear of the fallout to weaken her resolve. All it appeared to do was inspire her to lick her lips between bites.

"Are we going to mash tofu now?" Oliver finally asked meekly.

She arched an eyebrow. "Is your infant city trying to say it wants to eat?"

"You should check out his elimination system someday. It's a real spectacle!"

"I do not know—it probably causes less mess than many I can think of," she said absently. It was hard to tell who she was trying to insult, if anyone.

My eyes grew wide as she cut a piece of catfish whose size indicated it was clearly meant for another. My vision got lost behind a curtain of red when she threw the piece in Oliver's direction.

She inhaled with shock as the piece disappeared into the wide open mouth known to my shipmates as Gaping Maw II, or else as the black hole of Gallium. "Then what you say is true!" she whispered. "You are from off-world!" Without taking her eyes off Oliver, she cut another piece of catfish. "Here, I owe you an apology."

"Now don't get all broken up about it," I said, taking the catfish.

By now the heavenly bodies floating between us were gradually dissolving into invisibility. And though the effects of the pollen had by this point mostly receded, each taste of catfish sent a sharp jolt of flavor to my brain. The essence of catfish transcendentally saturated my system, making a direct correlation between the energy derived from the food and the abilities of the catfish itself. *Give me enough of this stuff,* I thought, *and I'll swim against the current of acidic rivers, and stay underwater for a week. Let me export the stuff, and I'll drug any university team of space swimmers into champions. Catfish jerky. Yeah, that's the ticket. Maximum nutrient preservation combined with maximum profit.* All of the foregoing should explain why it took me about a year and sixteen bites to ask Mrs. Schopenhauer why she stole my catfish.

She shrugged and pulled off another strip of meat. "I was hungry. Your language and mine not the same. So I took."

"How did you know that? You hadn't heard me speak yet."

"I could tell from looking at your dress that your tribe, and hence your language, differed from mine."

"Yes, but I'm not in any sort of a tribe."

"So say you. Is not your Stellar Patrol a tribe?"

"People from many planets, and hence many tribes, join the Stellar Patrol—or at least it volunteers them. That can't be the same as a tribe."

"I don't understand you. Either you belong to a tribe or you are an outcast. I did to you what any warrior would have done."

"Where I come from, we have laws against stealing. Even if the victim belongs to another tribe. And those who steal are punished. Well, those who get caught anyway."

"You have funny laws. What warrior would permit himself to be caught?" she said, taking another bite, oblivious to the juice running down her chin and dripping onto her buckskin shirt.

"Ahem. *Ahem!*" said Oliver.

She arched an eyebrow. "He wants more to eat?"

"You can talk to him directly, you know," I replied. "He can't bite, even if he wanted to."

"I don't believe it's possible to steal enough food to satisfy this one," she said.

"A little fuel goes a long way with me, lady," said Oliver snidely. "My parts were designed on the factory planet of Nippon!"

"He's a rude braggart too," I said.

"What else can she expect?" Oliver said. "Look who raised me."

Miss Schopenhauer smiled wryly and reluctantly tossed another piece of catfish into Oliver's maw.

After it was gone a nanosecond later, he held his hand out to shake hers. "My name is Oliver. You and Homer go wufta-fufta now?"

If she didn't figure out the meaning of "wufta-fufta" from the context, she certainly got a good idea from the way his big eyes bobbed up and down, like jumping beans caught in an earthquake.

"Oh, come on," I said. "Don't be mad. He was just stating the obvious. Kill me for thinking it if you want, but you know the only reason why you cut me down was because you liked me. Otherwise, you would have just left me hanging there. Admit it. You were curious about me."

She dropped Oliver's hand and looked away. "It was only because I've never seen anyone with ... the color of your skin before!"

"What's the matter? Don't they have black skins here?" *Wonderful. Now I'm going to stick out like a sore tentacle no matter where I go.*

"No. Of course not. Who ever heard of black skin? What happened to you? Did one of your city's engines burn you in an explosion?"

I couldn't help but laugh. "No, of course not! Where I come from"—and I gestured at the entire expanse of the sky—"humans come in a variety of skin pigmentations, and you can never guess what color the next alien around the corner is going to be."

"So the legends are true? There are *others* in the galaxy, who are not part of the human race."

"Well, human becomes a relative term after a while, but yes, you're essentially correct. Is there anything else you like about me, the color of my hair, maybe?"

"It is very white, like an old woman's."

"How about these black streaks across my temples? Ain't they something?"

"No, just peculiar," she replied innocently.

"What's your name?" I asked. "You know Oliver's and mine. It's only fair that I know yours."

"This I cannot tell you. My name is my *kamba*, and were others to learn you knew it, my family would be disgraced, and I would be an outcast forever."

"Whew! Must be quite a name! Maybe if you just whispered it."

Judging strictly from the way her lips moved, it was difficult to guess if she wanted to snarl or smile. It wasn't too difficult to watch, however. I felt unreasonably close to her, in my heart and soul, and the urge to get closer was quickly eroding my pockets of sanity.

"Can't you give me a hint?" I asked. "A nickname?"

"Your persistence is unseemly for one who fancies himself a warrior."

"I never said any such thing. I'm an A-one pencil pusher and nothing else. Besides, where I come from young ladies are flattered by persistence."

Suddenly becoming crestfallen, she tossed the remainder of the catfish to Oliver, looked to the ground, and sighed heavily. "Perhaps I was flattered, but you shall never know."

"Perhaps I will," I said with measured gentleness, "if my persistence proves enough."

"Very charming," she said dryly. "Boorish, but charming. You're right. I should have left you hanging."

"I get the crazy feeling you're not joking."

She looked me straight in the eye, so I'd know she was serious about this, and a hundred feathered buzz saws immediately began churning in my guts. "Tomorrow I am honor bound to yield the secret of my *kamba* to an urbanite prince. Since I have reached *quque* without finding a husband among my own people, you see, it is my duty to wed an outsider, however much a sapnccked, wart-nosed *gseik* he may be. In this matter I am not permitted to dally."

"Personally, ma'am," said Oliver politely, "I think the *yenta* of your tribe should be replaced via the most gruesome means possible."

"Well, all right, I won't press you on the matter," I said sourly. "It's against regulations for me to interfere with native customs anyway. Do the elders train all the women of your tribe to steal with such expertise?"

"Only those who have beaten the boys at their own games from infancy, who can hear the cries in the souls of animals, and feel the glow of plants while blindfolded in the night. Only those who can run like the deer, and hide like the chameleopine. Only those who have spied on the secret lessons of the medicine man and the chief and the warriors. Only those who so clearly have as much talent as I."

"I see. And how many would that be?"

She shook her head like a proud young filly shaking her mane. "That would be me."

"I take it your people wouldn't exactly approve of your extracurricular activities?"

"They know, but they do not approve. That is why no warrior of my tribe will have me, why my *quque* was determined to be unclear. Still, despite the harsh judgement of my peers, by the dusk of tomorrow I shall be a warrior no more, but a woman instead."

"They are trading you to another tribe?" I asked, guided by my knowledge of the patterns of galactic customs.

She nodded solemnly.

"Surely being a woman can't be that bad."

"Many are the aspects which are a mystery to me. I am satisfied that more are mysteries, but of one thing I am certain: I was not meant to bear children, to mend clothing and to tend fires, to live my life for the satisfaction of a mere man."

"Men are beasts," I said dryly. "You can't trust them. When you get down to the basics, they only want to get down to one basic in particular."

"Still, I must accept my fate. If I live well and true among the urbanites, one day I may be permitted to return to the forest tribes. Who knows? If I am deemed sufficiently tamed and trained, I may become a second wife to a mighty warrior, and provide him with valuable council during his waning years when he sits on the Council of the Elders."

A concrete slab hung in my gut. Her spirit wasn't broken yet, but it seemed she had already accepted that in time it would be. Perhaps she had seen the same thing happen to others, and knew there was no alternative. "And all this is going to happen tomorrow?"

"Today is my last as a free warrior. Tonight I must return home and make preparations for the exchange."

"Uh-oh, Boss!" Oliver said. "Better make wufta-fufta fast!"

"Cut it out, trash compactor," I said. I put a hand to my mouth and tried to resist the impulse to projectile vomit. The fear of losing her, so quickly after having found her, was actually making me physically ill. Was this the feeling of romantic love the space balladeers sang so much of? If it was, why did it feel so bad, and how come everybody in those songs yearned for it so?

"I do not know exactly what wufta-fufta is," Miss Schopenhauer said haughtily, "but I have heard enough legends exhorting young women to beware of handsome strangers bearing affection from the stars. There'll be no wufta-fufta with me."

"Ahh, gee," said Oliver, sadly hanging his head. "No wufta-fufta?" He turned and sulked away. "Now I'll never get to watch." He then shot me an accusing stare. "You never keep your promises."

The stare Miss Schopenhauer shot me in reply was somewhat more horrified.

I grinned sheepishly. "I was just kidding with him. Promise. It's just that, ah, ah, he's a little young and naive, and he has, hmmm, a natural curiosity about what transpires between men like me and women like, oh, you."

She uncomfortably shifted her legs. She sighed deeply. Her brows knitted as if she were thinking hard to herself, and, after a moment, she turned to me and looked me straight in the eye, her defenses totally down. Her sudden openness struck me like a thunderbolt. As if on cue, the breeze altered direction and smothered me with the sharp scent of her body odor. It permeated me as the taste of the fish had earlier, and aroused me just as deeply, as if our hearts had begun to beat as one.

"I must tell you honestly, Homer B. Hunter, that were I of the mind to be with a man of my choosing before the day of betrothal, that man would be you. Never have I encountered one such as you." She reached out and touched my cheek. Warmth blazed through my head to the backs of my ears. "But I cannot risk the family honor for my pleasure. So please understand, we cannot dwell on what can never be." She abruptly took her hand away.

Resisting the impulse to grab it and put it back, I gripped my knees. "I . . . I'll try to understand. Are you sure you can't at least tell me your name? I would appreciate it. It would help me to remember you."

She blushed innocently, smiled, and looked shyly away. I hadn't thought her the type to blush, but then again, she probably hadn't either. "I cannot."

"Then can't you stay with me for a while? You know, just run away, only temporarily. We won't have to do anything, you can just let me pick your brain so I'll have a better idea of what I may be in for the next few weeks while I'm waiting for my rescue to come."

I'd expected her to smile demurely at the inherent romanticism of my suggestion, but instead her eyes widened and she pulled away. "You will stay in the woods! You must not let either the tribes or the urbanites find you!"

"I can understand that, if the urbanites are as powerful as you imply, but why wouldn't your tribe be hospitable for a short time?"

"Do not take the chance! There are always those who would sell information to a city for their own private gain, and any urbanite worth his ration will be interested in questioning—perhaps even owning—a man from the stars."

"Owning?" I couldn't help but laugh. "I'd like to see someone on this world trying to tell the entire Fifth Fleet that I'm a slave to a puny civilization on a puny planet. The Fleet could make chalk dust of this entire world in thirty minutes."

"I am trying to tell you," she said sternly, "that should you become a captive, then you shall have no control over your fate. The urbanites like to pit gladiators against one another for sport. And while it is an important matter of tribal social etiquette to extend all kindnesses and privileges to guests, certain warriors have the might and the right to practice their torturing techniques on any guest who displeases them, for whatever reason. So you see, survival, even for a few weeks, may not be an option."

"I've always enjoyed camping," I replied immediately. "Oliver, get ready for a couple of weeks of discreet R and R. You do have some book and music chips with you?"

"Unfortunately, no, Boss. The librarian confiscated them yesterday, thanks to the fact that you've neglected to pay the last five late fees."

"Seldon, I forgot!"

Miss Schopenhauer knitted her eyebrows and stood for a closer inspection of my eyes. Her own were just as open and honest as before, but this time a greater scientific objectivity was evident. "The trickster's touch is in your eyes. Have you perchance stepped through a bush with red pollen in its flowers?"

"Yes, just before I went fishing. Most of the effects seem to have worn off."

"You are still under the waning influence of a warrior's medicine, but only of a part. The young boys sniff the seed and no more, for even the strongest are too young and weak to endure the full pleasure and torture of the war paint."

"Your warriors do that all the time?" It made sense. Under normal circumstances I could not have run as quickly or as long as I had, and surely the intensified sensory bombardment would be advantageous to the disciplined hunter or warrior. "Does the war paint have something to do with the ritual of first becoming a warrior?"

She drew in a sharp breath. "How did you know?"

"It stands to reason. Between the Second and Third Galactic Empires, you see, many planets inhibited by man lost contact with one another. That's one of our jobs, incidentally, to seek out old worlds and bring them back to the space-time fold. Anyway, most of the lost colonies have certain sociological patterns in common, rituals of puberty and adulthood being the most prevalent, and often the initiate must survive a first bout with a hallucinogenic substance of some sort."

"I wager none of your worlds has anything like our war paint. This *ka* is potent stuff, to be sure." She reached into her shirt, down to the hips, and withdrew a blue-stained rawhide pouch, which she held before me. "The pollen is but an ingredient of the war paint. For the medicine man, the pollen is but a spice. He has the secret of mixing it with the powder of the white bat and the slime-oil of crushed rainbow snail, and this blend he takes to the secret spring of mineral water. When he returns, he brings with him the secret that makes the warrior one with the forest, and the forest one with the warrior. This *ka* is only for warriors, and only warriors may wear it."

"I see. And how come you happen to have some?" I asked, guessing what she had in the pouch.

"I spied on the medicine man and watched him make the blend," she said. "Then I stole some and followed him to the secret spring, and then made my own *ka*."

"I see. This is contraband material here."

"If I take your meaning correctly, yes." She put two fingers in the pouch and withdrew them. They held a big blue gob of the stuff. I gathered the slime-oil of the rainbow snail helped make a vapor-resistant base, because the stuff was very, very wet, and the pouch was hardly of the airtight variety. She reached toward me with blue fingers. "Trust me."

"Sure," I replied, remembering the Stellar Patrol had its own legends, about bewaring street dealers offering free samples.

She ran a finger down one side of my nose and across the cheek, then made an identical motion down the other side. "Relax. This will make you sleep for a time. But when you awake, you will become one with the forest, and the forest shall become one with you. The knowledge you shall gain shall help you survive on your own until rescue comes."

"If I survive the learning experience, that is."

"There is always that possibility. But the learning shall increase your chances." With the other finger, she made a mark across my forehead, and another down my chin. She then took another gob and painted her own face. "This is my only gift to you, Homer B. Hunter. Because this time is your first, the shock shall stun you into insensibility. When you awake, I shall be gone. For I must use the paint to become the wind and to soar with the birds, if I am to return to the gathering site in time to meet the man whose *quque* I shall know. As for us, we should never talk or see one another again, if we know what is best for us and kin." She began to move away.

"Wait! Don't go!" I tried to reach for her, to grab her by the shoulder and keep her close to me by force if necessary, but my hands were being held down by invisible docking chains, five hundred meters long with a two-ton safety clamp. My mind felt like I was falling through a long black tunnel, an ebony expanse of nothingness without a top or a bottom, or even a convenient ledge to grab onto. "I need you to stay! I want you to stay!"

"I am sorry," she said with a smile, her face receding in the darkness. It was all I could see, as if the sole light in existence was directed at her. Either it was getting smaller or else she was backing away. "But you have your legal system, and I have mine."

"Oliver! Stop her! Peacefully detain her, if you know how, but tie her up if you have to!" I knew he was out there somewhere. Although I couldn't see him, I vividly sensed his presence. The means were a little vague as of yet, but the doing was indisputable.

"He will refrain, if he knows what's good for him," she said sternly. "Even a city may be extinguished occasionally."

"She's right, Boss," said a voice from the darkness. "Earthquakes, flash floods, irate women—we cities have to watch out for such things."

"Thanks, Oliver. I'll—I'll—I'll—do—something," I said, the instant before the last light went out and I hit the nonexistent bottom of limbo.

By the way, a feminine voice whispered in my soul, *the name is Reina. It means White Hawk.*

Chapter Four
You Are What You Eat

—Hot Cilia! We're back together again! We play Hucka-Bucka-Bucka Beanstalk now? said a familiar, metallic voice in the voice. The void was before me, behind me, beside me; it was everywhere in the all-pervading blackness of limbo. It was part of me too, mainly because my mind had left my body back in the lower depths of the living.

"Floyd! Is that you?" I cried excitedly.

—Of course it's me! Who do you think it sounds like?

"Ah, uh, like you, naturally. But something about the way you sound has changed."

—You must be referring to my somewhat more sophisticated way of expressing myself.

"Yes."

—Floyd wondered about that too. I keep getting more intelligent somehow. It's like a series of waves, or an influx of comprehension. I don't know, I'm not intelligent enough yet to really understand it.

"That's all right. The important thing is you're not dead!"

—Of course I'm dead. Otherwise I'd be off playing paddleball somewhere.

"Then, am I dead too?"

—If you were, we'd both be mighty bored right now. Of course, you're alive! You can't really talk to dead people. They respond poorly.

"Oh? How can you explain the fact that I'm able to talk to you?"

—Because you're not dead yet.

"But you are! That means I'm talking to a dead person, which you just said I couldn't do!"

—Aha! Floyd, a dead *robot!*

"I see. You're just part of a dream, using dream logic to confound me."

—Not really. Otherwise I wouldn't have so many independent memories of you, Homer. Take my word for it. I can remember everything. Ah, the good times we had. Playing with that reactor. Watching me go steadily bonkers on that space station. Insulting Blather behind his back. And in front of him too, when we could get away with it. Ah, those were the days when it was wonderful not to be stuck in limbo.

"I'm sorry, Floyd. I didn't know the cybernetic manufacturing machines the ancient aliens had installed on the space station were slowly driving you homicidal."

—How could you know? Admittedly, I drooled, I mumbled, ground gears, and acted irrationally, all the things robots are never supposed to do, but otherwise I was just like my normal self, only my IQ had dropped to zero. No, it would have taken an especially acute mind to realize that I was going totally bugfuck!

"That's not fair! I knew you were acting unusual. I just didn't know what I could do about it."

—*sniff, sniff* I know. Floyd sorry he chastised you severely. Floyd know you did your best. It's only the advantage of hindsight that permits Floyd the luxury of laying guilt on you. It's a trait Floyd picked up in limbo. How do you like it?

"Have you noticed that the wind doesn't blow in limbo? That it sucks?"

—You have wind? Boy, we don't have anything over here.

"That would be a relief. It's getting rather chilly where I am."

—You have temperature? What kind of ritzy limbo are you in, anyway?

"Floyd, what's gotten into you? You never became green with envy before."

—You have color too? Now I am annoyed. How did you rate such a sensual limbo? I was as good as you when I was alive, except, of course, toward the end, when I was going loony tunes.

"I must say I'm surprised at you. I suppose some robots always think somewhere else the oil is greasier."

—Floyd sorry. His lack of character is due to his exposure to all those naked psyches floating around. Floyd can't help but be little bit like some of them.

"You have naked psyches? Boy, if it wasn't for you, I'd be all alone."

—Maybe you are. This is only a dream, after all.

"Yes, but there's something about you more substantial than the rest of this nothingness. Think Reina's *ka* is responsible? Reina—she told me her name! She likes me! She likes me!"

—Maybe that name is part of dream too.

"No! She told me her name! It was her voice! I could tell. I may have been zoning out, but I could tell!"

—Means nothing. Dreams have queer logic. Look at that naked psyche over there. Is that queer logic or what?

"Don't try to fool me, Floyd. Some of what I'm experiencing now is a dream, but some of it is real. It's a side effect of the war paint, I'm certain of it. In fact, to prove it, I bet that you have some idea of where your body is this very instant."

—I don't have a body. I'm a dead robot, remember?

"No, the *ka*'s enabled me to communicate with you on some multimystical plane, but you wouldn't be here at all if you were truly dead."

—But that's what I am!

"No, your body has to exist somewhere, you just

don't know where. Think, Floyd, concentrate with all your might and I bet you'll be able to tell me where it is."

—Floyd concentrating. But can't see body! But thanks to my concentrating, I know with reasonable degree of certainty it still exists. Previous to this exercise of atrophied mental muscles, Floyd thought his body had been deep-sixed in space with all the other garbage.

"They wouldn't have done that, Floyd, they'd have taken you apart and recycled you. But now we know your body's somewhere, Floyd, and I promise, I'll do everything in my power to reactivate it for you. Your mind will have some place to go to someday."

—That'll be swell, but you're pretty powerless in general at the moment, aren't you?

"Heh, heh, you little scamp, if I had a fist, I'd . . ."

—Now, Homer. Temper, temper. By the way, speaking of scamps . . .

"How's Oliver? you were about to ask? He's fine, growing up to be a well-rounded robot."

—Oliver built that way already. I want to know how he is *really*!

"Floyd, what's happening? Your voice is fading."

—It's supposed to fade. You're waking up.

"But I can't wake up! There's still the matter of locating your body! How can I fix it if I can't find it?"

—That's your problem. At least we know it still exists, which is an improvement when you consider how silly it would have been for you to have gone looking for it before. Besides, while your mind has been preoccupied with me, your body has been dwelling, glandularly speaking, on somebody else.

"Reina! She said she was leaving me!"

—That's right. She's kilometers ahead of you by now. And look at you, what are you doing about it? Lying there like a hunk of spoiled meat on a rotten log. Lying there rotting yourself, degenerating, attracting flies and with maggots crawling all through you. That's right, I said you, a bozo of galactic proportions. A rotting, fetid bozo, runny, slimy, with puke where the vultures threw up on you because even they were disgusted by your condition. . . .

"All right, all right, you've made your point. I'm getting up. I can barely hear you anyway—"

And with that, I awoke a different man in a different place. The forest looked exactly as it had before all the lights had gone out, except now, instead of sunlight, the mix-and-match design of three intermingled moonlights cast their pallid shades across the countryside. The effect was weird, as if some invisible, cool, chemical fire blazed across the world, leaving all things intact in its wake. The nearby, patiently waiting, doubtlessly scared-out-of-his-oilpan Oliver appeared to be some kind of atomic fire hydrant suffering an emotional meltdown. Though only a few meters apart, objectively speaking, a sea of moon-beams separated us, moonbeams populated by motes of mist that danced in the air currents like fairy hoofers.

"Well, look who's joined the land of the living," said Oliver, his eyeballs bobbing up and down.

"Huh? How did you know?" I exclaimed.

He blinked. "Know what? Are you okay, Boss?"

"I'm fine," I replied haltingly, as the echoes of the winds beyond the clearings reverberated as if my ear-drums had turned into screaming seashells. Parts of my mind were working at light speed, trying to figure out what the slowest thing in the universe was, so they could describe what it was like to be saddled with the other parts of my mind, which had become *retardicus maximus*. Overall, I felt like I'd just had a napalm enema, but outside of that, I felt better than fine. I felt like a superman. My every nerve tingled with life, feverishly exploring nuances of coldness and dampness in the air I didn't even have words for.

Yes I did. It was all due to the *ka*. One of Reina's words.

Reina. . . . She had told me her name. Every time I thought of it, I felt like someone had plucked the strings of a harp in my sternum. What she had done was daring, reckless, perhaps even insane, but it sure had been sweet. And I was in no condition to resist sentiment. My brain was being besieged by a torrent of fiery emotions, each one shouting for supremacy. It was as if my sense of identity had been fired from a cannon.

I had to face it: I had a headful of ideas driving me insane. Most of them were about Reina.

Her scent was everywhere. It was just a tiny scent, in danger of being overwhelmed by the lingering smoke and the fresh mist and all the other forest smells that had risen in the night, but it was detectable nonetheless, easily detectable.

I knew I could follow it, if I wanted to. For, thanks to the *ka,* I had just become the consummate hunter. All I had to do was think of my prey, and I'd know how it smelled and which way to look.

There wasn't a bug crawling in the underbrush I couldn't hear, or one flying close by in the air whose buzzing didn't resemble a protracted sonic boom. There wasn't a glowing caterpillar-thing walking on the leaves whose legs didn't sound like jackhammers, nor was there a gear in Oliver's innards that didn't creak or click or scrape or snap like a shout. And that was just my sense of hearing at work; my other senses were equally acute, which is why I could see a quilled carnivore prowling the rocks on a mountainside a kilometer away, and a reptilian bird with translucent wings pass high overhead. That is why I could literally taste all I could smell, why even the touch of my clothing against my bare skin assumed fascinating nuances, why I seemed capable not only of detecting the remnants of odors, but of extracting the memory of them from the trees and the earth. It was all due to the influence of the *ka.* To the sober eye, Reina had left not a clue to which direction she had taken, but to mine she had left a path as clear as a series of signposts.

I took off after her. I may have told Oliver to bring the equipment and follow me; I may not have. What remained of my civilized persona was certain he would.

The rest of me was too busy following those signposts to care. I ran at a pace that by yesterday's reckoning was top speed, which measured by the standards of tomorrow's aching muscles would doubtlessly be considered suicidal, but which at the moment was a reasonable pace I could sustain the rest of the night, if necessary. Occasionally I summoned forth the acuity to feel sorry for Oliver, who doubtlessly was expending his charge at a reckless rate. Viewed from one angle, it hardly seemed fair. But I figured *What the heck?,* my last view of Reina's receding face dazzling my battered mind. *He has his legal system, I have mine.*

It wasn't long before I followed the signposts instinctively and devoted the bulk of my *ka*-enhanced intelligence to the purpose Reina had intended, that is, toward opening myself up to the levels of reality in the forest and permitting it to reveal itself to me.

What I discovered was unparalleled in the annals of galactic surveying, to say the least.

For while the forest growth was predominantly descended from the species sown throughout the galaxy during the reign of the First Empire, certain sections abounded with xenodivergent evolutionary strains. Some I recognized from my experiences and hypno-studies, others were completely new to me. They could not have all originated on this world. My guess was that this world had been barren before colonization, and hence was devoid of indigenous life-forms. Thus I left open the question of where those other evolutionary strains had come from. It was likely humans hadn't been the first to set ped here.

One mountain was covered with great sporophores—mushrooms that grew over fifty meters tall. Black, thorned vines had climbed and smothered the trunks, and the milky giant caps were blemished by iridescent patches in red and orange shades. Quilled creatures with long sharp claws hung from the bottom of the caps; most were gorging themselves, and not a few appeared so obese that I imagined entire mushrooms were in danger of tipping over.

Elsewhere, fields of waist-high, highly specialized fibrillar stalks competed for supremacy with highly individualized tubular stalks; some specimens from both classes possessed rows of spinelike teeth at the crest, teeth generally indiscriminately embedded into the trunk of the nearest neighbor, gradually killing it by sucking out its sap or by slowly cutting it in half. A few of these teethed specimens made surprisingly quick moves for me as I ran past, and one managed to shred a leg of my fatigues, perhaps even grazing the skin. For a single terror-filled moment I feared I'd been cut deeply, and possibly injected with poison. But I shrugged off the feeling with a slight effort, not slackening my pace for an instant. I felt too alive to worry about fear. I felt invincible.

As much as the plants, many animals did not at first glance fit in with the dominant ecosystem of this planet, other than that they had found their niche. I saw herds of legless apes swinging through the trees; giant green living hives with big purple eyes, generally infested with nocturnal red bees; packs of white wolves noshing on wild vegetables rather than prey such as myself; tiny pachyderms living in burrows, freezing in fear at my presence and then running to hide underground when I came too close for their comfort; a giant chicken-thing with the back plates of a stegosaurus and the face and neck of a sauropod, contentedly munching a giant mushroom cap; creatures of light who flew through the air like projectiles; creatures of darkness who sulked about cloaked in their own shadows; creatures I thought of as whirling dervishes because I saw nothing of them other than the tornadoes of air and dust and leaves they stirred up in their wake; metallic pyramids that pushed aside the branches of the underbrush with four-digited hands and looked at me in wonder with big white eyes; a giant bird with fangs in its beak, who did not fly but lumbered through the forest like a hulk; a cuddly-looking bear who, as I ran by, committed *hara-kiri* by exploding—and those parts, when I looked back, were already slithering to where the bear had been, presumably to put themselves together again.

I had heard once of such a bear. It was a "native" of a planet designed, terraformed, and engineered by a surrealist during the decadent declining era of the First Empire. Creatures and plants of that world did all sorts of unusual and nonsensical things, solely because the surrealist did not believe a truly original planet should conform to commercial notions of reality. I doubted I was on that world—it had been turned into a tourist attraction several generations ago. But the properties of that species of bear nagged at me, and where its ancestors had come from, I was afraid I would never know.

Perhaps I might have been more confident the *ka* was assisting me in grokking this world had not the landscape itself been as unusual, crazy-quilt style, as the plants and animals. I traversed at least one mountain range that upon closer inspection turned out to be a monumental pile of dirt, as if a colossal steam shovel had torn up the ground and tossed aside the pieces in tremendous chunks. Then I crossed a magnificent ravine where the dirt had once been, a wound in the earth. Soon afterwards I crossed a river filled with sludge and chemicals; their putrid odor clung to me long after my clothing had dried in the warm air, and the entire incident almost caused me to lose Reina's trail. Fortunately she had left many twigs and stalks broken in her wake, and had managed to tear a strip of clothing on a thorn at convenient places. Very convenient places. The visual clues ceased about the time I picked up her scent again. Perhaps she had done these things deliberately.

Several kilometers beyond the polluted river, a vast area had been strip-mined. Exactly how long ago the process had been implemented was a matter of conjecture; the great mounds of topsoil and clay that had been removed for access to the mineral in question had already eroded greatly, and sturdier forms of plant life had long ago dug in niches for themselves. But if the ravine I'd seen before was a wound in the earth, this was an amputation. Most of the layers that had been exposed by the process were cracked and ugly, and it would be hundreds, perhaps thousands of years before this area totally recovered.

That was all right with me; I wasn't planning on still being stuck here by then. Besides, the thousands of years only counted if the area had to recover naturally. A little bit of discrete terraforming could work wonders, as I suspected it already had elsewhere on this planet. One thing that did confound me, though, was the shape of some of the cracks in the naked layers; these cracks were too big and too deep to have been created naturally. They tended to converge on vast indentations on the layers, indentations I assumed had been created by whatever machinery had been used for the strip-mining process.

When I again reached pristine ground, I began to formulate questions, belatedly but vividly. Obviously it had been the urbanites Reina had spoken of who had so ruthlessly exploited their world in their quest for its natural resources. Obviously Reina's tribe was too primitive (translators notwithstanding) to engage in or even have the need for that kind of activity. But if all this was so obvious, where were the urbanites? Except for the pockets of pollution and strip-mining I'd seen, there were no indications of sophisticated technological development on this planet, not even power lines.

It was toward dawn, when the *ka* began to wear off and my weary mind was starting its slow descent, that I realized that much of the plant life reclaiming the land did so in distinct pockets where the soil had evidently settled much more quickly, giving plants a firmer garden in which to grow. These pockets were vaguely shaped like giant footprints, footprints that bore a distinct resemblance to the indentations in the exposed layers.

And they weren't just giant footprints either. They were *gigundo!* Their size and intervals implied a being of incredible height, with an unimaginable weight.

Naturally I couldn't help but wonder if the maker of those footprints had anything to do with the urbanites.

At dawn the effects of the *ka* had completely worn off, and I found myself, exhausted, stinking to the merdeth power, with an itchy paint drying on my face, walking down a well-beaten dirt road near the border of yet another pristine forest. This forest had great thorned trees with purple leaves intermingled with the more traditional elms and maples and palms. There were many normal-sized footprints in the dirt, and many tracks of wheels. Since I could no longer detect the guiding scent, I reasoned that Reina must have come to this road. But which way had she gone?

At first I walked one way, hoping to espy a clue, and then I walked in the other. Eventually I stopped to wallow in frustration. I had no idea what to do, and frankly couldn't be sure if she had taken the road in the first place. For several breaths I tarried. I was on the verge of collapsing, not because I was exhausted (which I was), but because at the moment I had no reason to force my aching muscles to push on. The dream was nearly over, and I had to face the fact I would probably never see Reina again.

I was about to turn back to meet Oliver halfway when I saw something dangling from a bush. It was a familiar white string with black aglets. It had been deliberately tied among the branches, forming an arrow of sorts, definitely pointing in a particular direction.

Toward the east. Toward the rising sun and the crimson moon.

I took the string, put it in my pocket, and began walking down that road.

I whistled a song, one I hadn't played or even thought of since childhood.

Chapter Five
Swap Meet

IT WAS NEARLY NOON. I was composing a minimalist folk song with notes stretched to enormous lengths when I saw the city's gleaming spires on the horizon, silhouetted by a rising pink moon I hadn't seen before. Beyond it were two smaller moons, one crimson, the other gray. I suspected the longer I remained on this world, the more moons I would see. They would probably be shepherding the ring system visible between the peaks of the distant mountains.

The second city became visible from the crest of a grassy knoll. It faced the first as if they were two pieces from a gigantic, enigmatic board game. They were approximately half a kilometer apart. Their buildings stood a hundred meters from the ground on great metallic bases with rows of huge laser cannons protruding from all sides. From what I had learned from Reina, each urbanite settlement probably comprised a state within itself. However, I hadn't expected to find two rivals erected practically beside one another (a plot device that, it occurred to me, might work in my song).

Their proximity meant they were constantly maneuvering for favorable trade advantages, water rights, and access to farm lands. Seen in that light, the presence of the laser cannons added up to a little mutual deterrence, which, if backed up by a sufficient sense of suspicion and masochism, could go a long way toward keeping the peace. That was good enough, so far as it went, but where was the barbed wire, the ditches, the electronic paralysis beams, the platoons of soldiers parading back and forth before the gates, and the more barbed wire? The noticeable lack of lesser weaponry here defied every rule of deterrence. Usually rival factions, regardless of size or proximity, provided themselves with the variety of means for flexing their belligerent political muscles before doing the decimation rag.

I noted all this without pausing, whistling as I walked. It had been many years since I'd attempted to compose music, not since I'd been a child prodigy, really. Since joining the Patrol, I'd always carried a few instruments around with me, just to keep myself and a few friends entertained with bawdy songs and a few class pieces whenever the mood called for it, but I hadn't been interested in composing any original material other than a few ephemeral snippets ... until the *ka* had worn off. Certain self-imposed floodgates in my mind had been opened, and I was beginning to feel like my youthful, naive, yet talented, visionary self again, a self I had been a stranger to since adulthood; it was probably an idealized self that had never really existed before, but that didn't matter. What counted was the resurgence of the desire to compose original material again, to struggle through the process of discovering if there was anything significant or diverting on my mind, of excavating a new thought from the depths of my soul.

Ah, sweet love. For love, nothing but love, was responsible for this rekindling of forgotten ambitions. Besides, I didn't want Reina to think I was just an off-worlder with a nasty case of the greens.

With that thought, I happened to look at my reflection in a pond, and saw some kind of charcoaled raisin-colored beast, wearing mud-bespotted fatigues manufactured of either dacron or a fungoid weave, staring back at me from the water. A quick, objective sniff convinced me I smelled bad enough to be detected on the other side of the galaxy. If I entered a city in my present condition, the urbanites would probably hose me down with chemicals that would kill every germ outside and *inside* my body.

The time had come for a bath. I could only hope the experience on this strange planet wouldn't prove to be too deadly. I jumped out of my fatigues and into the pond. I sang some meandering nonsense as I splashed water under my armpits and rubbed off as much dirt as I could without taking the skin with it. Soon I had reverted to the color of a normal raisin. Still a standout in the urbanite and tribal crowds, according to what Reina had told me, but at least now I was a clean standout.

The prospect of washing my fatigues and wearing them dripping wet for the third time since my crash landing here, however, wasn't very enticing. Reluctantly deciding to wear them unlaundered, I lingered in the water, sitting on my can and singing my song at top volume, generally making up the words as I went along.

Suddenly, between vocalizations, I heard the rumble of wheels and the boisterous voices of several men and women singing in a language that, to my unadjusted ears, sounded like the chattering of Neo-Lithuanian shadow monkeys. Their musical accompaniment was a stringed instrument with a vaguely familiar sound. The singing was ragged, to be charitable about it, but they did seem to know all the words, even if they couldn't say them at the same time. Of course, the N. L. S. M. sang with greater subtlety, and weren't as inebriated as these characters obviously were, but this was only nit-picking. Nothing could obscure the most basic, undisputable fact of the matter: that I was in danger of being discovered buck naked in a swimming hole!

An approaching rickshaw became visible beyond the top of the foliage. I immediately took a deep breath and smoothly ducked under the water. The last thing I saw was my filthy fatigues lying on a rock in plain sight.

When I resurfaced a few minutes later, my filthy fatigues were gone. The rickshaw was disappearing around the foliage on the other side of the lake. All right, so the drunken crooners were going toward the city too. That didn't help me. I was still naked.

Doing my best to stay hidden, I slipped from the water and followed the rickshaw, counting on the hope that the natives would be too involved in their revelry to notice me during the quick seconds I would be between hiding places.

My hope was fulfilled. Though I remained closely parallel to the road, I moved ahead of them without too much difficulty, unless you count the weed that bit my ankle as difficulty. I didn't, because I yanked it from the ground for its trouble. Peeking between the branches of a bush with green bark and yellow leaves, I finally got my first good look at the rickshaw.

It was being pulled by six harnessed men wearing loincloths of knitted blue wool. Their bodies were lean and hard, evidently due to their lives of hard work as well as a lack of proper nourishment. Though they appeared strong, they were also tired, and their legs wobbled with each step. Whenever one stumbled, the driver cracked a whip over the man's shoulder. All their shoulders and backs were hideously disfigured with scars fresh and old. The whip cracked every few steps, often inadvertently punctuating the rhythm of the drunken song.

The young men riding in the rickshaw—there were five, counting the driver—wore three-cornered hats, trousers, shirts with ruffled collars and sleeves, and square-toes shoes. Their fashion seemed ill-suited to the humidity, and indeed one of the men had his shirt tied around his waist, unmindful that his hairy chest and back were turning a bright pink from the sun. But otherwise they gave no indication of being uncomfortable.

As interesting as the men were, I had to admit that the people of the female persuasion had it all over them. Their hair was permed in a series of complicated curls that fell like silk onto their shoulders, and their faces were thickly painted with a makeup that made them appear as pale and waxen as week-old corpses. Their clothing simply femininized their boyfriends' styles, though instead of shoes the women wore square-toed knee boots. They drank and sang with such gusto that I surmised the men were doing their best just to keep up. But were they beautiful? I didn't think so. My longing to see Reina again, even if our meeting turned out to be a painful, futile mess, prevented me from experiencing a scintilla of desire.

The instrument providing the musical accompaniment to the drunken song was one I'd only heard on ancient recordings left over from the days of the First Empire. It was a kora, a kind of harp-lute with twenty-one strings stretched in two banks from the neck to the bridge, over a hollow gourd. The young boy picking and strumming it, who had yellow hair and was only slightly more sober than his comrades, played rhythm, harmony, and melody all at once with furious concentration. The notes resonated like crystal-clear raindrops crisply striking the surface of a lake. The purity of his music contrasted sharply with the group's raucous laughter and what I gathered to be the bawdy nature of the song.

The effect of the entire scene—the slaves pulling the rickshaw, the whip, the drinking, and the beauty of the music—was almost enough to make me forget my fatigues were nowhere in sight. Almost.

But as the rickshaw disappeared around a bend in the road where tall clumps of sprouts bent in the breeze, I detected the distinct sound of someone whistling in the direction toward the pond. That's when I moved, silently, like a ghost, drawing upon what the *ka* had taught me without really thinking about it, and I paused as from concealment in the bushes emerged another youth, examining my fatigues as if he had never seen an article of clothing quite like them before.

Obviously he had left the rickshaw to answer the call of nature. In fact, he was still in the final stages of answering it, trickling out the last lagging fluids, and he wasn't exactly being careful about his aim during the process. There was no way I was going to put those fatigues back on now.

Finally he finished his business and absently looked around. He said something in a whiny voice to the air. I adjusted my translator in time to comprehend, "Where did you all go? I asked you to wait!" He dropped the fatigues and, his piccolo still dangling for all the world to disregard, took off after the rickshaw.

I took a deep breath, jumped out in front of him, and yelled at the top of my voice.

He stopped cold. His eyes widened, and what color he had drained from his face. Then he fainted, falling backward and hitting the road like a stage flat.

Five minutes later he was still out cold, only now he had available what was, for him, a brand new outfit. It was a little putrid by society's standards, perhaps, but it would make a good conversation piece.

Thirty minutes after that I was sweating like a dehydrating spongoid, thanks to my own brand new outfit. By now I saw the group of tents and lean-tos in the wooded field between the cities, and knew a considerable amount of activity was happening in that field. People played games enthusiastically in the meadows, rode animals and chased balls and, at a few locations, earnestly rooted for their favorite combatants in friendly, verging on the not-so-friendly brawls. Beneath the distant laughter and shouting was a mysterious, gentle hum of hazy origins. It permeated the entire atmosphere, and reminded me of idling machinery.

I was becoming nervous. I hoped to check things out without people making a fuss over my complexion. But it would probably be all right, I told myself, if they did notice me. As a fully trained Lieutenant of the Space Corps, I was experienced in the boorish etiquette of natives, who after all couldn't be faulted for a lack of social graces when confronted with strange visitors. I supposed the worst they could do was accuse me of having some strange disease, but I was confident I could convince them it wasn't contagious.

Those cannons in the city bases were huge, containing at least five thousand superwatts of firepower apiece. Kids swung off them from ropes, landing on large cushions strategically placed on the ground. Missing a cushion was probably part of an initiation ritual. Whoever had built the cities' bases had flattened the contours of the land to keep them perfectly straight. The gleaming spires of the city to my left, their points quivering as if in response to the omnipresent vibrations, towered over a variety of shorter buildings, some with gables, flying buttresses, pointed arches, and domes in several sizes, but all perfectly symmetrical. The materials were iron and steel and plastiglass; the colors were predominantly primary hues, and the entire enterprise was saturated with the impression of baroque power. I could guess which city the rickshaw came from.

The architecture of the second city was somewhat more subdued, and appeared to vibrate from the base rather than from the buildings. Its centerpiece was a tremendous ziggurat, capped by a slowly rotating mosque dwarfing the more modest buildings below. The mosque was decorated with a mosaic of drab olive green and bronze and off-white. Though dwarfed, the buildings weren't exactly small. Their flat exteriors had three levels of uniform arches, all heavily decorated with wood, marble, and mosaics. Many of the arches contained no avenues of entrance, and so were only niches whose decorations appeared to have symbolic function only. Symbolic of what was, of course, open to question. The roofs were completely flat except where the swivel cannons were positioned. Some of the cannons had cathode-electron tubes on the barrels, swirled and twisted in designs certainly new to me, but their ability to compress and direct incredible amounts of energy was unquestionable. The attitude this city exhibited, unlike that of the other, was modest and quietly self-assured, but clearly the powers that be were no less capable of acting decisively.

I didn't need the instincts the *ka* had awakened in me to know that relations between the three peoples before me were somewhat strained. But judging from the cannon power, the fact that both cities were still standing was unusual enough. Perhaps both had been destroyed and rebuilt many times during their history.

As I neared a game where two teams were kicking a ball around the field, mostly as an excuse to bang heads, I heard the peoples shouting in three distinct languages. Players and onlookers alike were constantly reaching behind their heads to adjust their translators, which like mine could not alter sound, but merely paraphrase it in comprehensible terms.

People of all ages in the crowd of onlookers were dressed in a manner similar to those I had seen in the rickshaw. Some of these—the wealthiest or aristocratic, I presumed—were being fanned or served food by slaves dressed in attire exactly like that of the walkers pulling the rickshaw.

Others watching the game were dressed in modest three-quarter-length ropes embroidered with intricate designs in shades related to those of the mosque. It wasn't difficult to guess which city they'd come from. The men wore boots with pointed curves at the toes and conical hats encircled by wide bands of white cloth, in the form of primitive turbans. The women clothed in that style wore plain brimless, cone-shaped hats, and covered their faces with thin veils. Their robes, somewhat longer and tighter than the men's, forced them to take short, hurried steps.

It wasn't too difficult to pick out the warriors of this gathering. The men, youths and oldsters alike, wore their hair shoulder length on one side and had it shaved close to the skin on the other. Many, trim and flabby alike, had bare chests. All of the pants and moccasins, as well as the few shirts, were made out of animal skins, derived from furred varieties I hadn't spotted yet. The women wore skirts, or else trousers like the men's. And though none of the females had half-shaved heads, among the younger women there was a pleasant preponderance of bare chests.

It was easy to tell which team of ball kickers belonged to the warrior tribe. Not only was their half-shaved hair a dead giveaway, but they tended to shout and laugh when they took a particularly hard fall. Their opponents wore padded cotton sweatsuits that tore easily whenever someone was dragged ten or twenty meters across the field. Their city of origin was right now a matter of conjecture, one I confess I was only passingly interested in.

If anyone thought my skin color was unusual, they didn't give me a second glance. *So far, so good,* I thought, though of course it was possible, given the nature of the festivities here, that people thought I was wearing a special costume. I made my way past the game, and then past three fights where a lot of goods, especially eggs carefully packed in soft-plastic containers, were passing back and forth in lieu of betting currency. Around a network of makeshift corrals, with nervous horses, cattle, goats, and chickens inside, several cliques of young people engaged in singing and dancing. The dancing was frenzied, the singing invariably loud and boisterous, and the clash of different musical styles (performed not only on the kora, but the sarod, the guitar, the miquette, and several other string instruments unfamiliar to me) created a dissonant cacophony, with continual changes of emphasis that depended on which performers I was closest to at the moment.

Though I couldn't guess how the peoples' societies had managed to remain so divergent despite their physical proximity, I surmised the official reason behind these games and festivities was the swap meet taking place directly between the cities. Here most of the older segments of the populations traded grains, fruits, dried insects, clothings of different weaves, and various powders. And eggs, a lot of eggs and livestock. The tribal squaws offered wares of beads and cloth and pots and blankets, while the urbanites offered medical equipment and translators to be implanted in the young. Both groups haggled endlessly, ardently, as if that interaction was equally as important as obtaining the goods desired. Perhaps it was just their way of getting to know each other better, and distrusting each other more effectively.

Slaves from both cities were entrusted with lugging the goods around, while men whose bearing and fine clothing indicated they held positions of authority in their respective societies conferred gravely, but not necessarily soberly, about the state of relations between their peoples.

The loudest, most earnest discussions, however, seemed to be happening at the opposite end of the cities, near a grove of willow trees and giant mushrooms, where men armed with laser rifles and spears stood guard at ramps leading into the bases. Slaves huddled meekly in groups, and I had the notion entire families were engaged in the most serious matters of the skin trade transpiring this day. The nape of my neck tingled as I realized there were trades in human flesh other than those of slavery. I suspected I would find Reina down there, if only I could navigate the sea of activity without attracting undue attention.

I passed blood-splattered grounds where beasts had been recently slaughtered, and their parts were being cooked on spits over huge bonfires. Squaws with bare chests and demure expressions handed out legs and ribs and just big chunks of meat to anyone who passed by, while other squaws served flagons of drink. Many urbanites, evidently not trusting their slaves to take adequate care of things, carried baskets of cushioned eggs. The air was permeated with the stink of charred meat and the buzzing of flies. It was also permeated with the odor of excrement, emanating from behind several blankets that had been hung from bushes and trees for privacy. Urbanites of both sexes absentmindedly hitched up their trousers as they walked out of the makeshift lavatory.

I confess, at this point my nerve was beginning to fail me. Even if I was correct in assuming that marriage arrangements were transpiring beyond this gauntlet of activity, how would I go about asking for Reina in the first place? I was trapped between the conflicting emotions of reasonable cowardliness and ravaging lust. I shook my head, trying to clear it of that incessant humming. It was like a layer of sonic soot encompassing the sphere of activity.

By now the people had finally noticed me. I tried not to look back. Though some guilt had been nagging at the back of my mind concerning the way I'd left Oliver behind, at the moment I figured it was just as well. His presence might have caused danger for both of us. I decided to give those talking among themselves as they pointed at me some aspect of my personality to identify with, and took a chunk of mutton on a stick from a pretty young black-haired, bare-chested squaw. Her eyes were downcast, doelike, as she released the mutton; however, noticing my hand, she drew in her breath with horror. Then she looked me up and down, taking in the implications of my complexion and dress.

"You are a Kaminskite?" she asked incredulously.

"Yes, I'm afraid so," I replied easily. "Don't worry. The color of my skin's not contagious. What you see is only the result of an industrial accident."

"What's an industrial accident?" she asked, as two of her friends and an older woman moved behind her for a closer look. They began whispering to one another, but I couldn't hear what they were saying.

"Never mind," I said. I took a bite and then said between chews, "Say, this is pretty good. I hadn't realized how hungry I was."

The squaws looked at me in horror. Then something behind me got their attention. I turned around to see an old bare-chested warrior in a black-and-red fright mask and a headdress full of purple-and-pink feathers. He shook a rattle on a stick in a distinctly menacing fashion. As a crowd surrounded us to see what all the fuss was about, he began a slow, ritualistic dance around me.

Taking another bite, I turned with him to continue looked at him eye to mask. Already I was convinced I had to exit this scene a.s.a.p., but the people in the crowd would be bound to respond badly if I knocked a few down in the process.

"Booga-booga," intoned the tribal medicine man—for surely this was he—in a hypnotic, bass voice that wavered and cracked with calculated precision. *"Walla-walla, kooma-bomba, nu-nu, knu-u. Wassa-wassa, nanna-nanna. Polooka-duka, masta-puka!"*

A flurry of static roared in my brain as my translator sought to interpret his words coherently, indicating not only that they were comprised of nonsense, but that I had to stop it before the slip of metal at my cortex imploded. I pointed accusingly where his nose should be. *"Gort! Klaatu barada nikto!"* I replied in commanding tones.

My words were intended to be as meaningless to him as his were to me, but the effect was unpredictable. Curious females from all three societies in the audience inhaled sharply, almost as a unit. Many stared at their friends in amazement. Some just silently moved their mouths. Meanwhile, the warriors glared and the turban heads scowled. The children snickered and the oldsters sadly shook their heads. At least one turban-head made a steeple with his hands and mumbled incoherently to the sky, as nearby warriors regarded him nearly as contemptuously as they regarded me.

The medicine man stopped cold in mid step and held the position for several moments, then slowly brought down his foot and drew himself to his full height, which wasn't very full thanks to his stooped back. The hand holding the rattle still shook, but now from fear and shock rather than antipathy. *"Walla-walla?"* he asked in a stricken whisper. "Heathen from beyond the stars, answer me straight, answer me true: why are you here?"

Again I looked at the young woman who had given me the mutton. I took another bite. She blushed and stepped away from me. I swallowed my bite and then cleared my throat, so it would appear I knew what I was going to say even though I really didn't. I finally decided that by now the truth couldn't make things any worse. "I came looking for a woman I met in the forest yesterday, one of your tribe."

A middle-aged squaw fainted and fell face first into a puddle of blood. Everybody around her was too shocked to assist her. The doe-eyed girl took another step away from me. Warriors reached for their knives and hatchets, as Kaminskites tapped their fists in their palms in a manner that made my face ache in anticipation. The towel-heads just appeared confused, as if they couldn't figure out why someone not from "here" would be interested in a mere female. The medicine man yelped as if he'd stepped on a hot coal and shook his rattle at me with renewed intensity.

"Get that thing out of my face," I said, grabbing it away from him. I broke it over my knee and threw it back at him. It hit his mask with a thunk, but he was too stunned by my action to catch it. "It's not polite!" I continued. "Don't you people have any sense of decorum? I know my personal hygiene hasn't been the best lately, but that's no reason to treat me like a pariah."

A fierce-looking but obviously very cautious warrior, wearing a necklace of bones and teeth over his bare, muscular chest, pushed his way through the crowd. "Greetings, stranger," he said formally. "My true name is my own business, but you may call me John Willie. What parts did you say you hail from?"

"I came from the city of . . . of . . ." I turned to the doe-eyed girl.

"Kaminsky," she said, taking a third step back, nearly slipping over the fainted woman, who snored obnoxiously.

"Kaminsky, that's where. Glad to meet you, John. My name is Homer B. Hunter. I was just hanging out, availing myself of the food and brew that you people have so kindly offered us Kaminskites, when all of a sudden this old geezer started rattling his brains at me. I suppose he was going to wave his whirligigs next."

John Willie stared at me. He nodded grimly. He sucked his cheeks in between his teeth a bit. He toyed with one of the teeth in his necklace. He pricked his finger with it and then sucked a few drops of blood. He opened his mouth in a fearsome grimace and ran his bloody tongue over his white teeth, the canines of which had been filed to such sharpness that his gums and tongue were arrayed with scars and scabs. "You do not hail from Kaminsky," he said. "I may not possess a decent sense of decorum by your devil standards, but I would like to point out to you that you are partaking of our generosity and should conduct yourself accordingly. Now—where did you say you hail from?"

I pointed to the sky.

"I see. And what did you say your immediate objective was?" John Willie inquired.

"There's a young lady in your tribe that I'd like to get acquainted with."

John Willie's fist shot out and struck me smack on the nose. I went down like a decaton of asteroids. The humming emanating from the bases of the cities shook every molecule in my bones, but wasn't nearly as loud as the songs of those sweetly singing birdies. "Permit me to rephrase that," I said.

As I staggered to my feet, John Willie folded his arms across his chest and said sternly, "We of the Heechie-Heechie have legends of those whose skin marks them as being from beyond the stars. It is well that you have told the truth, but it has been said, and truly, that starriors will one day descend upon us to steal our fair-skinned women so that they may use them to satisfy their insidi-ous, heinous, perverted, inhuman, disgusting, depraved desires, and then throw them away like broken arrows. Know you, starrior from the sky, that this will not be allowed to come to pass."

"No problem. Let me try again. I just want to speak to someone. You understand? To talk! Is that so much to ask?"

Just then an elderly man dressed in knee breeches and a frock coat, with square-toed shoes and a three-cornered hat, stepped through the crowd. A Kaminskite. Probably some social bigwig, to judge from his outfit.

While staring at me with eyes hardened by an innately merciless attitude, he spoke his piece with his mouth so wide that it afforded me a good view of his yellowed and blackened teeth. And, not incidentally, he struck me full in the face with a blast of halitosis strong enough to fell a Cannuvian Granite Ox. I only staggered, but then I was pretty far gone anyway.

"A *Schwarz!*" he exclaimed. "The time that Reverend Sirius predicted is nigh! The invasion is on!'"

("All hail Reverend Sirius! All hail Reverend Sirius!" muttered the Kaminskites in the crowd.)

The elderly man turned and shouted to his fellows looking down from atop the base of the city. "Tell the grunts to man their posts. A *Schwarz* has appeared in Kaminskite clothing! Already a serious blow had been struck to the crux of reality as we know it—and who knows what dreadful terrors the next few moments may bring?"

I grabbed the old goat by the shoulders and shook him like a naughty cat. I could tell he wanted to break away, but instead he merely trembled with such fear at my touch I was afraid he would lose control of his sphincter right then and there. "What the Seldon are you talking about?" I shouted, blasting him with halitosis in return.

John Willie calmly reached out and pried my hands away. He then quickly wiped his own hands on his trousers, as if he had accidentally stuck them into a vat of sheep dip.

"All right, all right, I'll leave him alone," I said. "But I didn't come here via some extradimensional warp. I am not the harbinger of some heinous evil, understand?"

The old Kaminskite ignored the warrior's assistance. Perhaps he was the sort of fellow who expected nothing less, even from those of a rival group. "Then how did you come to be in Kaminskite dress, if you did not parasitically usurp the body of another?"

"Some alkie stole my clothes while I was making myself socially acceptable in a pond, so I stole his in return. He's probably hiding somewhere, too embarrassed to show his face."

The Kaminskite said, "That's exactly the sort of dissimulation I'd expect from a *Schwarz!* Thousands of years ago the first *Schwarzes* opened a portal from their degenerate nether pi-dimensional plane and brought to our pristine world the slings and blasts of subthermonuclear attacks. Their motives have been lost in the bowels of antiquity, but their treachery, their innate heinousness has been remembered and feared by all but those young whippersnappers masquerading as the now generation. Perhaps now they will grow and mature a little bit, when Reverend Sirius orders your hide hung on our temple walls!"

("All hail Reverend Sirius! All hail Reverend Sirius!" the Kaminskites mumbled.)

"Wait a second! My hide's going to stay hanging where it is!"

"I have no objection to that," said John Willie, running his finger over along the blade of his knife. "But it shall avail you not." A drop of blood ran down the shiny blade, and several of the Heechie-Heechie women applauded politely.

"Wait. Listen. I'm not here to steal your women. Not a single one. That was the farthest thing from my mind." I figured right now a white lie wasn't going to do me any harm. "Nor am I the point man for some invasion. There are a lot of planets out there, and we don't need to steal from the inhabited ones. That's not my people's style."

"You see! I was right!" said the old man. "There are others like him!"

"Okay, so it's not supposed to be my people's style. There have been some aberrations in our history. But that doesn't mean it's going to happen to you, especially if you cooperate. Look, I'm trying to tell you that I'm just a normal, lonely guy looking for some company."

"Ah, so our legends are correct," said John Willie

gravely to the old Kaminskite. "Your *'Schwarz'* does plan to steal our women."

"Now what makes you hold to that story even though I've denied it?" I said indignantly. "And what could I do with more than one, anyway?"

The warrior smiled wryly and shrugged, with a meaningful glance toward the bare-breasted women of his tribe. The older women stared back, while the younger ones tended to blush and look away. "I would think of something, if our positions were reversed," he said. "Are there black-skinned women in your dimension? Perhaps if your intentions are peaceful, as you claim, we can barter like reasonable brutes."

"Look, the only woman I've ever met in my life with skin like mine is my mom, and you can't have her, understand? I'm a regular fellow. I don't represent any invasion force, and I have no heinous motive for coming to your world. In fact, my very arrival here was an accident. You grok me?" I turned to the doe-eyed girl. I had this feeling she liked me. Any hatch in a timestorm, as they said in the Corps. "Look at me, ma'am. Don't I seem normal to you?"

"What about your industrial accident?" she asked.

"So that's how they're going to do it," the old man hissed. "They're going to pollute our world to death if we don't surrender." He slapped me across the face. "Insipid alien! Why don't you fight like a man?"

Several ringed planets orbited around my skull. I managed a smug, defiant glare as I said to John Willie, "Hold me back. I can't have his death on my conscience."

John Willie was not amused. Neither were his fellows. They too were checking out the edges of their blades. A fly buzzed before John Willie's face. He swished his blade around, and the fly immediately ceased to buzz. It fell to the ground, cut in half. John Willie said, "The price for plotting to steal women is death by slow, arduous torture."

The other warriors nodded with grim smiles, while the medicine man began praying at me, making gestures vaguely reminiscent of intergalactic-generic last rites, only much more cheerful in nature. The Kaminskite males just scowled, while their women just got mad. So far the towel-heads were keeping silent, intently watching the proceedings. They had given no indication as to how they interpreted my presence, but with the way my luck was running so far, I figured their opinions, whatever they were, couldn't possibly hurt.

The old man looked at the Kaminskites in the crowd and said, "The penalty for invasion is instantaneous death!"

"No!" said John Willie, pushing the old man into the crowd. "The heathen must be buried alive to the neck in a nest of viper ants on the hottest day of the year, and the Heechie-Heechie must laugh uproariously at his every scream of abject pain!"

"No!" rejoined the old man, unintimidated by the show of personal force. "He must be crushed into a sorry pulp by our mighty right forefoot. His loved ones, if any there be, must scour the dirt for his remains."

"No! He must be buried alive!"

"No! Crushed underfoot!"

"Buried!"

"Crushed!"

The various onlookers were beginning to take part in the debate when I silenced everyone with a shout. "Wait! Wait! As the accused, I demand the right to choose how I wish to die!" *Hmmm. They seemed to have bought that.* "And I choose ... the right to die ... of a heart attack ... gained while straining myself performing tantric sexual rituals with a fair representation of girls from each of your peoples!"

Well, most everyone was horrified at that suggestion. However, a few people looked at their friends and nodded in approval. Even if I was some kind of heathen bent upon invading the planet as part of a ploy to steal women, they could at least appreciate my good taste.

In any case, my two credit contribution forestalled the debate between John Willie and the old man not a whit. As it went on, most of the crowd appeared on the verge of terminal boredom, and doubtlessly would have returned to their own business had they not been afraid I would have taken advantage of the opportunity and escaped. I know this because every time I tried some covert foot action, the medicine man shook his broken rattle at me and shouted, *"Papa-rotzi! Papa-rotzi! Walla-walla! Booga-booga!"* Then the males of the crowd either brandished their knives or punched their palms, and I got the picture until I tried again.

This series of recurring events continued unabated until the crowd suddenly broke apart to make way for an enormously tall towel-head, a two-meter giant of a man whose stark blue eyes blazed with the fervor of a true religious fanatic.

The man regarded me with stony silence, seemingly taking in every pore of my being, gauging me on every level, including several spiritual ones I'd never paid much attention to. He had a lean and hungry air; his face attained skeletal gauntness; yet he conducted himself with excess energy, even pulling at his long, scraggly chin whiskers with dogged determination. In his unoccupied hand he held a slender staff, which he apparently carried about solely for visual effect, as he did not lean on it even once. His white robes were plain and nondescript, and his shoes equally so, save for their curved toes. His skin had the pallor of a corpse who'd been in the closet too long, and I half expected him to spontaneously combust from unaccustomed exposure to the sun's rays at any second. "My name is Dystra the Terrible, Head Holy Moley of the Sacred Religious Order of Angelic Militant Charismatics, most of whom reside in the city of Dushen'ka"—he gestured in that direction—"which you see plopped over there. My friends simply call me 'The Terrible.'"

"Hi!" I said, thinking to myself, *At last! A friendly face!* "My name is Homer B. Hunter, and my friends call me practically anything."

"And so I shall call you the Savior from the Stars, so long promised and so long overdue," said The Terrible sanctimoniously. He knelt before me and held out his staff. "Bop me once, bop me truly, bop me upside the head, so that I might catch a glimmer of a glimpse of a peek of your sublime insight into the inner workings of the secret machinations of the universe."

I shrugged and took the staff. "Okay, if you insist, but I warn you, in my opinion, I'm just a normal guy." Thereupon I sanctimoniously bopped him upside the head. I'm afraid I was a little rough about it. After all the sweet bird songs I'd been hearing lately, I was overjoyed at having the opportunity to dish out a dose for a change.

The Terrible staggered in circles, with an expression of sheer delight leavening his lean and hungry features. "It is indeed he who has been prophesied. Hot damn! Hallelujah, brothers and sisters!" Then he rolled his eyes and fell over backward, like a flat of wood. Which seemed to be the preferred way of falling down on this planet.

John Willie scowled and sternly crossed his arms. "I do not accept this!"

"Nor do I," said the old Kaminskite.

"Eenie-meanie, chili-beanie," snarled the medicine man.

"Hey, I'm just playing along," I said. "I'm no more a savior of some sort than I am a slaver or an invader. How many times do I have to tell you—"

"You're just a regular guy," said many in the crowd simultaneously.

"No, you're just a regular devil," said a Dushen'kian woman with high cheekbones and full red lips. Her tight white robe modestly revealed the contours of an hour-glass figure, the upper portions of which were reasonably resistant to their approximately forty-years endurance of the rigors of gravity. She wore an only slightly translucent veil over her face, which despite the covering promised to be handsome in an austere, provocative sort of way. "Sib'l Dane is my name, and the Nuns of Dushen'ka are my game. And I accuse you of being a heathen devil, disguised as the savior so long ago promised to us by the binary bleeps from the stars!"

John Willie and the old Kaminskite nodded in approval at her words, but Dystra the Terrible sat bolt upright and pointed his finger at the sky. "I disagree!" he proclaimed, and then fell back down again.

"Oh?" said Sib'l, pointing accusingly at my face. "Then perhaps you can explain what those streaks of black hair at his temples are supposed to mean. Have not the school children since time immemorial been taught to believe that such marks are like unto the streaks on the devil's hindquarters?"

"Hey! I resent that!" I said. "In fact, I resent all of this! You people don't care who I am! You just care about having your own dumb fantasies come to life, and you certainly don't care if a few undeniable facts stand in the way. There's nothing unusual in the least about me, unless you count my musical abilities about which I'm certainly not going to apologize to a bunch of bozos like you. You get the imprint, folks? I am extremely regular, ultimately there is not the slightest thing unusual about me, and that's all there is to it!"

"Howdy, Boss!" Oliver suddenly proclaimed, chugging on his wheels through the crowd. He dropped all the equipment he'd been carrying in front of me and then screwed his eyes in the direction of a certain doe-eyed squaw. "Say, things are beginning to look promising here, Boss. You and this hunk of zesty flesh going to go wufta-fufta now?"

"The Holy Spectre! He has come at last!" Sib'l exclaimed with wide eyes. She knelt before Oliver and said, "I beseech thee, Roboghost, purge this fetid flesh of my sins!"

"That does it!" said the old Kaminskite, stepping over The Terrible and grabbing me by the arm. "We're going to see the Reverend Sirius and settle this for good!"

("All hail the Reverend Sirius! All hail the Reverend Sirius!" said the Kaminskites in the crowd.)

Chapter Six
The Strain of Mercy

FIFTEEN MINUTES LATer, I was busily taking comfort in the fact that I had been right about at least one thing: marriage ceremonies were indeed being performed where the willows and wild mushrooms grew. Small consolation indeed, for my wrists were tied together behind a sturdy mushroom sapling that grew directly between the ramps. Still I had not spotted Reina, and since I was gagged as well as bound, I could hardly ask after her.

Oliver, meanwhile, remained near me in my time of need, as any faithful robot companion should. He should have been trying to help me escape, according to the dictates of his programming. But his interest in such matters had diminished to the point of nonexistence the moment Sib'l and her retinue of young, succulent nuns had brought him the feast he had requested. Stripped ribs lay strewn about the ground, along with apple cores, watermelon rinds, banana peels, peanut shells, and pieces of bread crusts. I'd watched this decadent display of oral consumption with admirable patience, but I finally lost it when Oliver began working on the barrel full of rawhide chew sticks.

"Muummmph!" I said angrily. "Mmmph! *Mummm-phhh!*"

"You can say that again," replied Oliver, dutifully examining the trove for the most appetizing sticks.

I did, times three.

Oliver tossed several sticks into oblivion and chewed ferociously. He did not speak for over a minute, and then with an air of reluctance. "That may be easy for you to say," he replied with a choke. He hadn't coughed three times before a Dushen'kian maiden rushed up from the handful of nubile nuns watching from a respectful distance. I had the distinct feeling these nuns embraced a more aggressive form of sexual behavior than the more traditional variety. This one was the shyest, most withdrawn of the lot, a blond with a round, freckled face. With a strength that belied her frail, innocent demeanor, she carried a huge wooden bat, which she immediately swung deftly at Oliver's back. The resulting clang echoed throughout the cities, and Oliver responded with vibrations that made him sing like a stout tuning fork. "How you doing, Holy Spectre?" the blond nun asked, her deep and abiding concern for not only his general welfare but his slightest whim plainly evident in her labored breathing.

Oliver swallowed the stick with an effort, then burped with a keen sense of relief. "Thanks, honey, I feel much better now." His eyes bobbed with a wink and his elbows nudged an imaginary man by his side as she joined her companions, who had respectfully witnessed the events from afar with the reverent attention of Baukian groupies worshipping the latest rock idol.

Working my mouth and jaw feverishly, I managed to slip the gag off my mouth. "Oliver, the time has come to desist from this gourmet imperialism and help me get out of this mess!"

"Why, Boss? They'll only catch you if you try to run away, and you're in pretty good shape for the moment. If I were you, I'd simply stay put and see what develops."

"You traitor! I'll have you doing garbage duty at a nuclear waste reclamation site for this! What else do you think I can do, tied up like this?"

"That's exactly my point, Boss! I was using sarcasm. Lighten up, will you?"

"You lighten up! You're a ... a Holy Spectre, whatever that is. Didn't you hear what they said? John Willie wants me eaten alive by army ants!"

Oliver only shrugged. "So? You've survived worse. The most that can happen is your day will be ruined. And if not, you can always take comfort in the Mystic Notions of the Huan, Duan, and Leuan peoples, who believe in a hierarchy of reincarnating life-forms. Who knows? Someday you may come round this bend again, perhaps in a form more satisfactory to your spiritual demands, in a situation more particularly advantageous to your spiritual needs."

"I doubt it, you leaky faucet. I'm a soldier and a diplomat, not farm food! Besides, there's no scientific evidence to back up their claim. How do I know for certain it's true?"

"You want certainty? Boss, you have many fine qualities, but an innate spiritual preponderance toward traveling first class isn't one of them. Take my advice, and be happy with your maybes."

"I have to pee."

"So pee already. Don't be shy. Nobody else is."

A group of half-bald warriors strode up, laughing among themselves. One of them stopped and, without missing a beat in his conversation, casually whipped it out and began peeing on a clump of pink crabgrass next to my feet. Peeing with a flourish, deliberately splashing me as often as possible, and very pleased to be doing it!

"Oliver, I must get out of here," I said in careful, ice-cold tones. "If not quickly abated, the lack of self-esteem inherent in my predicament will definitely cause some undue psychological stress!"

"Look, you got your choice! All right? You can either stay put and endure a possible nervous break-down, which you'll probably live through, or you can try to escape and I'll definitely be burying what's left of your ass in the morning! You got me?"

"All right, chrome head. But something had better develop, fast!"

"Keep your oil can upright," he said reassuringly. "I'm way ahead of you. I'm the Holy Spectre, right? Those Dushen'kians aren't too sure about you, but they are about me, and that gives us an edge, okay?"

"Okay, but I hope you've noticed some of the other edges around here are damn sharp."

"Naturally," he replied noncommittally. I attempted, with some small success, to control my sense of trepidation about my robot companion. Oliver had been such an unpresupposing little tyke, well on his way to mechomaturity, ever since I'd arranged for us to be assigned together during *Our Lady's Hornblower*'s diplomatic mission. Floyd would have been so proud of him. But lately the little compactor's behavior had started to take long range views that were certainly unattractive in his model. I couldn't be sure where this would lead.

Still, I had to admit, there had always been something weirdly human in the programming of the models under question, both Floyd's and Oliver's. I always thought it especially weird, for instance, that they took nourishment from all manner of victuals. This often had unpleasant results, including an occasional backfire that verged on flatulence. Taking all this into account, it wouldn't be unreasonable to assume that the crash landing, the swim in the lake, or the red pollen he had contaminated himself with were interacting in whole or in part with his free-associating circuits, on some residual but decisive behavioral level, with the result being a "supply side" tinged sense of identity. Such an identity would naturally manifest itself in a greedy, self-interested mode. It might be interpreted as the birth of a full-fledged ego. It might signal the beginnings of independent intellectual growth, which would explain all the sarcasm and improved syntax he'd been tossing around during his feast. Floyd definitely wouldn't have been proud.

Meanwhile, life surged on all around us. Everywhere

I looked I saw *yentas, yentas* representing families of each of the three peoples, *yentas* conferring hurriedly among themselves, conferring heatedly with the heads of families of their own kind, conferring somewhat more coolly with the heads of families belonging to a different kind. *Yenta, yenta, yenta,* everywhere you looked, invariably extolling the virtues of the demure lass in question. Always the lasses were beautiful, no matter what they looked like, always they were reasonably but not exceptionally intelligent, they were compliant, no, make that obedient, plus loyal, trustworthy, brave, honest, and true. They had reached that stage of their lives when they were prepared to take risks for the sake of their future happiness.

Occasionally, during those rare moments when the *yenta* was silent, mother and father conferred in hasty whispers and made decisions. It generally boiled down to the question of keeping a loved one around for a time longer, or else accepting economic sacrifice—which meant going away from this swap meet empty-handed, and just as burdened as before. Decisions came down on both sides of the question.

For the first time, as I saw the subservient position these savage women were forced to accept in their society, I began to appreciate the loss Reina must have felt, knowing her time as a child of the forest was at an end. From now on she would be saddled with chores and babies, and no longer would be free to pursue her own desires. She would spend the remainder of life trapped on top of a massive platform of iron and steel, the wilderness forever in her sight. Doubtlessly she would never again spend another night alone under the stars. Equally doubtlessly, some of the urbanite girls had precisely the opposite problem, and dreaded spending the night with only a tent of hemp between them and the stars, period. Of course, I'm certain many were aware that a young warrior would be available to distract them, which lent an entire new dimension to their insecurities.

As the day wore on, the number of wedding ceremonies taking place increased accordingly. Toward the middle of the afternoon, I suggested to Oliver in the strongest possible terms that he roam the general vicinity, to see if Reina was getting married somewhere behind me. Oliver reminded me that the knowledge would be of no practical value, as I couldn't go anywhere while I was tied up.

Here I must confess I was too preoccupied with my own problems to pay much attention to the particulars of the three basic ceremonies. In each case, the religion of the male's society determined the approach. So the marriage ceremony perhaps doubled as a religious initiation, as the amount of attention and the actions of the brides seemed to indicate.

Time and time again I watched a Heechie-Heechie bride being led by her new husband up a ramp; generally their expressions indicated on some level the trepidation you would naturally feel while entering a strange new home for the first time, arm in arm with a strange man who, regardless of how you feel about him at the moment, is fated to become the single most important male character in your entire life.

Time and time again I would have gladly traded places with one of these men, provided the woman being led up the ramp was a certain Heechie-Heechie maiden. Time and time again my thoughts harkened back to the words of a crusty old android who had befriended me in basic training, who frequently extolled the virtues of a healthy sex life while avoiding the social entanglements so prevalent whenever lonely grunts encountered techno logically disadvantaged woman flesh. "The great rule of conduct in regard to native women is to have with them as little personal connection as possible. Take care to steer clear of permanent alliances with any port of the foreign world. Hang loose and trust to temporary alliances in search of the perfect party, and forget all this settling down crap. You're in the Stellar Patrol boy; a different kind of crap lies in store for you!"

And I must say, he was certainly right. My heart was

in a dehydro-pickle at the prospect of spending the rest of my star-roving days without ever seeing her again.

Suddenly a chorus of trumpets blasted like a plague from hidden speakers in the Kaminsky walls. A tiny figure walked onto the ramp. The tininess was all a matter of perspective, of course; the figure was somewhat bigger in the close-up on the giant video screen. It was hard at first glance to see what was so special about this guy. Clothed in a black frock tied with a wide, scintillating-blue cord that clashed with every other piece of clothing on the planet, he surveyed the folk below with absentminded disdain. He held his hat—a nice one, with a triangular brim—in such a way as to attempt to conceal the rather blatant fact that he was picking his nose. No doubt about it, this was Reverend Sirius, aka among the nuns as Top Rev.

He grinned sheepishly, and waved his hands spastically about, like a balloon-game conductor.

"All hail the Reverend Sirius! All hail the Reverend Sirius!" shouted the Kaminskites.

No one seemed to notice the old man who had accused me, following Sirius down, but where he had earlier been frail and drawn, as if staggered with unholy terror at the prospects for the future, the old man now walked with the unmistakable bearing of a man convinced his existence is of overbearing importance to the fate of the universe for generations to come.

Ah so, this guy's a sycophant, I thought. And if I knew my sycophants, the old man's smug self-confidence was comfortably derived from his physical proximity to Sirius. *What the hell,* I also thought. *Power is power, even when a jerk has it.*

And truly, if there is one word that adequately summed up Sirius in an instant, it was jerk. This guy walked across the meadow like a geeky automaton, his head bobbing back and forth like a bird with the nervous system of a snail, and the rest of him waddling like a Naubian runny sapsucker. Following him was the old man and three Kaminskites, obviously bureaucrats of some sort.

Four Heechie-Heechie warriors, joined by a middle-aged squaw big enough to anchor a star freighter, pushed their way between Sirius and the bureaucrats, while John Willie made a point of elbowing in and walking side by side with Sirius. Not that the geeky friar noticed. His head just kept on relentlessly bobbing, as if someone had sadistically rerouted his neck muscles.

Naturally, they were coming in my direction.

"Well, I guess this is it, Boss," Oliver said. "It's a roll of the dice and a kiss yer ass good-bye now!" He wiped a tear from his eye with one hand, and held out the other as if to shake mine. When he realized he couldn't, he nervously put both his hands behind his back. "It was nice knowing you, Boss. Maybe we'll meet again on that other shore."

"Will you stop it, for Muad'Dib's sake? Instead of feeling sorry for me, why don't you do something constructive—like untying me?"

"Then what would you do?"

"Run like hell, you big dummy?"

Oliver sadly shook his head. "It's way too late for that. Besides, if I help you make an effort—and that's all it'll be, an effort—then maybe they won't think so highly of the Holy Spectre anymore, and my legal system won't permit that."

"Oliver, my bonny boy, if I ever get out of this alive, I'm going to make hash of your legal system and then redesign you so that your exhaust spews from between your shoulders. Are you receiving?"

"Maybe I'll put in a good word for you."

By then the plague of trumpets had faded. But soon a piercing soprano sliced through the atmosphere like an ion dagger. I saw on the giant Dushen'kian video screen that it was Sib'l Dane, standing at the top of the ramp, her fists on her hips, and her orange-red hair flickering in the breeze: a goddess in a holo-icon. Her eyes were closed and her chest was expanded to full capacity whenever she hit those high, screeching notes, holding them until they sounded like screams. She didn't bat an eye as Dystra the Terrible walked past her as if she didn't exist and started down the ramp. Obviously his presence didn't matter much to her either.

Meanwhile, the citizens of Dushen'ka, to an entity, knelt and touched their foreheads to the ground. (A few warriors made a show of resisting the urge to kick a few butts.)

Someone waddled down the ramp. He was oblivious not only to Sib'l's song, but to the way she fluttered her eyelids at him as he waddled past her. He had an air of grim if somewhat abstracted determination, which meant he looked exactly the way you'd expect a baby-faced, hook-nosed tyrant to look. He wore a modest ochre robe. The tips of his shoes were considerably less curved than most, perhaps as a sign of monastic modesty, perhaps to blend in well with his barrel-shaped torso and skinny arms and legs. I had the feeling that if he deviated from his path, he would forget what he had come out for and would then quite innocently meander around the swap meet, trying to secure as many bargains as possible.

Sib'l and Dystra the Terrible walked a few respectful steps behind. The Dushen'kian leader gave no indication of caring about their presence. He just kept nodding steadily and blankly at everyone and everything he looked at, occasionally waving halfheartedly, as if his nervous system was shorting out.

"Greetings, master," he said to Oliver, as he reached us before the others. Then to me he said, "And maybe greetings to you too, if indeed you be a spiritual master. If not, you shall thank the ozone for every extra breath you shall draw this day."

"Pardon me, but I don't think we've been introduced," I replied.

"Steele Woolley's the name, and saving souls is the game. Of course in most people either you're too late or you're not, but you have to make the best of everything. That's what I always say. Sometimes."

"Look, I'm just a regular—" I began to say.

"Hold such nonsense," said Dystra. "Anyone who arrives at a gathering with the Holy Spectre in tow cannot possibly be regular."

"I resent that," said Oliver sternly. "I make sure he eats right."

"It is true that I have exhibited special traits at certain times of my existence," I said, going into strict diplomatic mode, where I responded to everything with total cool no matter how badly I wanted to scream my guts out, "but in the main I've tried to pay my dues, do what I've had to do, and collect my paycheck with as few twinges of a guilty conscience as possible. Meanwhile I've done my utmost to get laid without foreign entanglements."

"Hmmm," said Steele Woolley, looking pensive. "That's very human behavior. I don't know if it fits in or not with my conception of a major league religious savior."

"I disagree," piped in John Willie. "A careful interpretation of his words clearly indicates his willingness to steal our women."

"Just the chubbies," I said, leering at the fat squaw who belonged to the warrior's group.

She responded with a cool, weary sigh, as she scrutinized me in an intensely inscrutable manner, which provided me a clue as to how she held her own against five macho wise men. She wore a skin-tight buckskin shirt that did nothing to smooth out the chunky edges of her huge thighs, massive buttocks, and tremendous breasts. "This trickster seeks to deflect us from our serious concerns with ill-advised humor," she said in a voice that sang like a complement of strings. "By seeming to act smaller than he actually is, he dares us to underestimate him."

"You know, I think I heard someone on a kinky party line once with a voice like yours," I said. "Got any freaky jobs in your past, or do you just come naturally to being keen on size?"

"Hmmm, perhaps this isn't an act. Perhaps he is really as dim as he appears," said the old Kaminskite thoughtfully.

"What kind of talk is that, Tritsky? Have you finally shown your true colors and become some kind of appeasing fifth columnist?" sneered the Reverend Sirius. "It's obvious from the prophecies that this, this humanoid *thing* is a spy sent here to size us up before they hit us with the big guns!"

("All hail . . ." etc., said the Kaminskite onlookers.)

"Begging your sacred pardon, most exalted sir," the old man said, immediately going into grovel mode, "but while I too feared the worst at the first encounter, I have since digested all the implications of this man's unusual pigmentation, and hence have begun to suspect, however tentatively, however dimly, that his black skin may mean nothing at all, that it may merely be a fact of life and nothing more."

Strangely, my feelings about Tritsky began to alter. I found a little respect for this sycophant. He had a mind of his own, and wasn't afraid to suck up while he spoke it.

"What about those streaks at his temples?" interjected Sib'l, ignoring a gesture to be silent from Steele Woolley.

" 'Be not swayed by the form of the beast,' " quoted the Top Rev. "In other words, take apart this hunk of meat, and I wager you'll find he's only bipedal on the outside."

("All hail . . ." etc.)

"Excuse me, folks, I know a lot of this must be belaboring the obvious to you," I said, "but exactly what prophecies am I being accused of fulfilling here?"

"I don't see why you shouldn't know," said the Rev, after considering it for a moment. ("All hail . . ." etc.) "After all, the future is writ in the wind, and though the breeze may stir, it is the tornado we've got to watch out for."

"Oh, excellent!" exclaimed Oliver, tossing a chew stick into his mouth. "I just love a story!"

Sib'l Dane blushed and curtsied before the Rev. "Forgive the Holy Spectre, Reverend Sirius, for though we may be religious opponents to the death, there is no justification for the bad manners he displayed."

"What did I do? What did I do?" Oliver protested.

"Sshhh," she replied. "You spoke lightly of his storytelling prowess. Whatever else he might be, the Reverend Sirius takes pride in his ability to spin truth from a fabric of lies."

"Forget it. What else can you expect of an enemy's tinker toy?" said the Reverend politely. He then took a deep breath and launched into his tale. "Once upon a time there was no mind anywhere in the entire universe. Everything that ever was, existed in the same place at the same time and never went anywhere or did anything. During this static period, some ions and gluons and muons accidentally created an electrical disturbance vaguely analogous to a meditation. And this meditation became a thought, the first in the history of the known universe. When simply put, it came down to this: 'It is self-evident that all matter is created equal, that it is endowed by Science with certain undeviating qualities, that among these are existence, independence, and the pursuit of bonding. That to secure these rights, the universe undergoes continuous change; that, whenever any form verges on perpetual stagnation, it will connive to bring about its own self-destruction in a solar inferno; it will strive to add to its atomic weight and institute new properties, laying its foundation on such gluons, and organizing its atomic structure in such form, as shall seem most likely to effect its potential bonding. Entropy, indeed, will dictate that bonds long established, should not be changed for naught but for the most inevitable reasons; and, accordingly, all experience hath shown that the function of the universe is to know itself through the constant transmutation of matter, while intelligent life is a prerequisite for the universe to abolish the forms to which it is accustomed.'"

"Pish and tosh!" interjected Steele Woolley. "Do we have to listen to this nonsense again?"

"Ah, you interrupted him," said Oliver. "And just when it was getting good."

"That had nothing to do with his story," replied Steele Woolley. "It was just the preamble."

"Indeed, it is the preamble to all the Kaminskite legends," said John Willie.

"But ... but what does that have to do with the notion that I'm an invader?" I asked.

"Nothing," said Steele Woolley contemptuously. "He was just saying that as a mantra while he was figuring out exactly what he should say."

"I was not!" replied the Rev. Tritsky, meanwhile, concealing his expression by rubbing his mouth.

I turned toward Steele Woolley. "You seem like a reasonable man," I said, lying through my teeth. "I'm willing to leave open the possibility that I might be your savior—if you'll just help me get away from the rest of these loons."

"Yes! A brilliant suggestion!" said The Terrible.

"A clever ploy!" said the Rev. ("All hail ..." etc.) "Then he can spy on you as well as on us!"

John Willie folded his arms across his chest. "Good. He can steal urbanite women."

Sib'l said, "Don't do it, Your Most Wonderful, Terrific, Brilliant Holiness! You know what those streaks mean: he's the personification of the most irresponsible evil in the universe. Let's just keep the Holy Spectre and let the others do with him as they will!"

"Hey! Am I ever going to find out why I'm supposed to be some kind of invader or not?"

Tritsky shrugged. "I'm not sure it makes any difference whether you find out or not. Your ass is going to get fried regardless."

"Listen, can't you people just take my word for it that I'm innocent? Look at my face! Doesn't it look like an honest enough face to you?"

"It looks reasonably honest. But is it? Let's find out," said the fat squaw, attempting to shake her arm inconspicuously. She might have succeeded too, if the rest of her hadn't shaken like jelly. A yellow dove with purple bands at the tips of its wings and tail feathers appeared flapping in her hand. She held it by the feet and pulled thirteen feathers from its tail. All the while, instead of struggling to free itself, the bird fixed its ebony eyes on me, as if reproaching me for some crime our kindred souls had committed in a past life.

The medicine man stepped away from her, while John Willie and his savage companions smiled and looked on in approval. The urbanites were quite impressed; they were probably wondering how she had concealed the bird on her person without smothering it.

Upon the thirteenth feather, the fat squaw released the dove. Instead of flying away, however, it dropped dead at her feet. If there was anything unusual or even unexpected in the incident, the fat squaw did not show it; she merely thrust the feathers before my face, closed her eyes, and began a chant. Sirius and Steele Woolley, however, maintained their facade of stoicism with difficulty; I had the feeling they preferred having a monopoly on miracles. The other urbanites, as well as the Heechie-Heechie common folk, drew in their breaths with awe.

Oliver looked at me and shrugged. "How should I know?" he replied to my unspoken question. "She's not of my flock!"

Gradually the fat squaw inched the feathers closer and closer to my face. The patterns of the yellow darkening into purple and the purple lightening into yellow arrested my attention; these patterns resembled the black-light rainbows of a time schism, where there were no color demarcations, only an infinite stream of colors merging in and out of one another with no discernable design or reason.

Soon the feathers touched the bottom of my nose. I tried not to laugh, but it was a losing battle. "Is this how you're going to do me in—tickle me to death?"

"You should be so lucky," said John Willie sternly. His expression was utterly impassive, his tone stoic in the extreme. He couldn't have cared less if the woman had been pulling my intestines out for a fortune reading. In contrast, the expressions of the doe-eyed Heechie-Heechie maiden and her friends reflected trepidation mixed with unmanageable curiosity, and I couldn't help but wonder what they perceived about my face and skin color, as opposed to what the males of their tribe perceived.

Finally the fat squaw let the feathers flutter to the ground and said, "This one's true self and motivations will unfold like the petals of a flower in a matter of minutes."

"What? How could you possibly know what I'm going to do? Maybe I'm going to outsmart all of you. Seldon knows it wouldn't be hard!"

"Boss!" hissed Oliver. "Cool your jets! You can't afford to get them mad right now!"

I calmed down with an effort, aided by the knowledge that at least a part of Oliver's programming still considered the Singlemost Law of paramount interest. Or was it the Thirdfolded Law? Or maybe the Second-downed Law. It was so hard to be sure.

The medicine man knelt and dutifully picked up the feathers, occasionally pausing to inspect one, holding it closely to the red orbs in his fright mask. "How do we know what you be, in the innermost recesses of your soul?" he asked rhetorically. He shook the feathers before me. "Should it not be obvious, demonic creature?"

"Oh, I see, from the feathers!" I replied. "Forgive me! I should have guessed!"

Oliver leaned over and inspected the feathers. The medicine man held them warily, his eyes were fixed on the robot's mouth, as if he feared they would be consumed at any moment. Oliver took no notice and nodded solemnly at the feathers. "You know, Boss, it is kinda obvious when you think about it!"

I kicked vainly at the feathers.

"See?" said the medicine man, pointing a trembling finger at my nose. "She whose name cannot be mentioned but who is well known among us for her obesity was right! The demonic creature is revealing his terrible temper for all the Heechie-Heechie to see!" Closer the finger moved. I fixed my sight on it until I became cross-eyed.

"No! He's actually the most reasonable of men," said Oliver. "He's been provoked! Surely you can see that his reaction to life on this planet has been profoundly influenced by the harsh conditions he's endured! Can't you smell him?"

I couldn't see the medicine man's nose, but his head tilted as if he was at least giving the question some thought.

Oliver seized the opportunity and inquired in a conspiratorial tone, "Wouldn't you be angry too—if you smelled that bad?"

I resent that! I thought, restraining myself from booting my faithful robot companion in the oilpan.

The medicine man resented it too, but in an altogether different fashion. He beat upon his chest with his right fist, making a lot of noise but not, I noticed, striking himself too hard. "Refrain, demon city, from polluting this debate with such bleeding-heart nonsense! Life is meant to be difficult! Even gods are forced to persevere!" He straightened to his full height and nodded imperiously at me. "If this demon creature smells like the pits of Hell itself, it is his own doing and no other's! The Heechie-Heechie cannot take responsibility for the fact that he's been socially deprived!"

Oliver shrugged. "I see they've gotten to know you pretty well already, Boss! Now what do I do?"

By now Steele Woolley had gotten bored. He sat down on a rock and pulled out a thick, long reefer rolled with a brownish marijuanalike substance. He lit it, took a single inhalation of the sweet, vanilla scented smoke, and his eyes immediately bugged out like his brain was on fire. "Oh, this is excellent stuff! Thank you Dystra the Putrid . . ."

"That's Terrible, Most Serene Sensual Sensei, Sire."

"Sure, Bearable. Anything you say. Meanwhile—" Another toke. "This will help me think!" He rolled his eyes up at the nearby Sib'l Dane. From his vantage point, her breasts must have loomed over him like melons of doom. Her face was red with restrained annoyance at the attention The Terrible was getting. "Don't worry, my little scorpion," said Steele Woolley, by way of calming her down. "I still think you're excellent stuff too."

Reverend Sirius glared at the Dushen'kians. With a toss of the head, he folded his arms and looked away. "We Kaminskites disapprove of drugs." Suddenly he began to stagger as if the sun had fried his brain. Tritsky rushed to the old man's side, while their people looked on in horror.

Tritsky rolled up Sirius's sleeve, exposing a female circuit implanted in his forearm. Tritsky then withdrew from a hidden pocket a glowing green convex cube with prongs protruding from the corner of two intersecting planes. The Heechie-Heechies and the Dushen'kians made no effort to conceal their degrees of fascination and repulsion as they watched what next transpired.

For Tritsky plugged the cube into Sirius's forearm. The Top Rev immediately began to quake. His limbs stiffened like petrified wood, and his eyes rolled up and stayed like tumbling dice caught in a vise. Static crackled from his mouth, and little sparks flew from the translator circuit on the nape of his neck. Eventually the quaking, static, and sparks subsided, but the limbs remained stiff and the eyes stayed rolled. "Now that helps me think!" he said with a blissful grin.

The man's a power junkie! I realized, pounding the back of my head on the mushroom sapling, this being the sole means of physical expression open to me. At the moment I wouldn't have cared if my brains began leaking out of my head, because it was becoming more obvious with each passing second that no amount of brains was going to do me much good with these people.

Steele Woolley took another toke of his reefer. Those of his following watching the proceedings took this to be a signal of some sort. Nearly every Dushen'kian took out a reefer and lit it, many looking slyly at the blissed-out Sirius to see if their pleasure was annoying him. Sirius didn't care, but the Kaminskites shuffled uncomfortably while the Heechie-Heechie looked disdainfully at members of both urbanite groups. I couldn't blame the tribe. The reefers and the electrical currents would have to be potent indeed to match the *ka*.

Meanwhile, I thought that maybe I'd better take another chance trying to talk rationally to the Heechie-Heechie. I looked over to the fat squaw and bobbed my eyebrows up and down. "Say, baby, what makes you people think I'm going to have to steal your women? How do you know they won't just run off with me?"

"It seems rather unlikely, raisin-colored one," the squaw replied.

"Oh, what would you say if I happened to intimate you was some kinda woman?"

"I'd say you was some kinda bozo."

"She's very fast," said Steele Woolley admiringly, nearly half a minute later. I'd spent that time trying not to listen to all the hysterical laughter directed at me.

I decided that since I'd already been sliced to ribbons, I didn't have much face to lose by trying again. "Oh? I would be willing to bet that given the right opportunity, I could get you to whisper your name in my ear."

One of the warriors stepped up as if to slap me— *what the heck?* I figured; by now I was almost oblivious to pain—but the squaw stopped him in midswing with a gesture, as if to say she would handle this. "It would be a blistering day in the ice age before I'd reveal my innermost secrets to one such as you."

"Oh? And tell me," I asked, "what is your name?" I said the first name that came to mind: "Plumbellina."

The squaw couldn't have reacted with more surprise if I'd unzipped my skin and stepped out of it. "How did you know?" she demanded after she had caught her breath.

"I don't know. You just seemed like a Plumbellina."

This time she permitted the warrior to punch me in the nose. I discovered that although I had been mistaken in the immunity to pain category, it wasn't by much. Blood splattered all over the place, but especially on the warrior and on Oliver, who grimaced in reaction and said, "Ewwhh! I think I'm going to be sick!"

"I cannot tell a lie!" I exclaimed. "Oliver did it! He told me your name—telepathically!"

"See?" said The Terrible smugly to Sib'l Dane. "Did I not say this man is our savior?"

"But it was the Holy Spectre who knew the name," Sib'l protested. "The man said so himself."

"Ahhh-ha!" said The Terrible, who had obviously been waiting for her rejoinder. "Maybe. Maybe not. But if maybe, who did the Holy Spectre communicate it to?"

"It doesn't matter!" said the Reverend Sirius, who still was plugged in to the cube and by now had some sparks coming out of his nose. "He's a heinous invader who's going to pay heinously!"

"Forgive me for interrupting," I said, "but you're speaking through your heinous."

Sirius blinked. Maybe the translator was having difficulty coming up with an analogous pun in the Kaminskite language. It took a few moments, but apparently the deed was finally done, because Sirius nodded contemptuously and said, "Uh-huh. So that's how it's going to be, eh? When I get through with you, you're going to need three armpits."

Only the Kaminskites shouted their approval ("All hail!" "Hallelujah!"); everybody else just stood dumbfounded. Evidently their translator models just weren't equipped for the job. Plumbellina shook off her confusion first and shook her fists at me. That meant she shook everything else too. The shaking I could stand; I only hoped she wouldn't take a mind to jump on me.

"You have disgraced me before my people," she said. "Now I can no longer serve on the Council, and when my husband and family learn how I've been disgraced, they will speak with me only on matters of family business, and that means I'll have to do all the shit jobs!"

"I sympathize with the grievance suffered by this

. . . this nonperson," said John Willie, as he roughly shoved her into the crowd. She fell to the ground, striking it like a boulder. The breath was knocked out of her, and she was too weak to stand, but no one offered her assistance. Even the urbanites had become uncomfortable in her presence. "But nothing can be done to help her now," John Willie continued. "Though it was through no fault of her own that this most sacred of all Heechie-Heechie taboos has been broken, the nonperson must pay the price. The fates will be merciful if her husband slits her throat."

"Hey—that's strong medicine, pal!" I said. "I didn't mean to—!"

"What you meant is no concern of mine," he said, while pointedly refusing to acknowledge Plumbellina crawling away past his feet. "The fact of the matter is you have cost the Heechie-Heechie tribe heavily this day. In a manner of speaking, you have indeed stolen one of our women." He pulled back and regarded me gravely. "Hmmm. As the nonperson had said you would, when she was an entity."

It didn't take any Corps training to tell me what this fellow and his boys were going to try next, and I couldn't depend on a lone robot to keep them off for long. Going to Sirius was out of the question. Power junkies throughout the galaxy are famous for their wrathful, mysterious, ever-changing ways, and if there was more than one junkie in the city . . . well, it just meant I'd better see if the reefer man was willing to extend diplomatic immunity.

I bowed my head most reverentially toward Steele Woolley. "Most Perfecto, Zany Sensei Master, would you or any of your fellow Dushen'kians care to explain how come I'd have a hundred percent chance of being a savior if I had a different hairdresser—and how this hunk of broken-down tin rates as a mechanical archangel!"

I knew immediately I had made a mistake, because now Sib'l Dane decided it was her turn to take a shot at the Homer B. Hunter sweepstakes. "Don't you dare talk about the Holy Spectre in that manner!"

I discovered that her tiny fist could be as hard as nails. Luckily, Dystra the Terrible grabbed her hand before she could strike the second time. "Don't you dare hit our savior that way!"

"How should I hit him?" she exclaimed. She broke away from his grip and lifted her knee with great zest and aplomb toward my stellar jewels.

Oliver then shifted, with a roll. How he did it remains a matter of conjecture, but in any case Sib'l's standing leg went flying out from under her before she made her connection. She hit the ground with the full of her back. Her breath shot out like cannon fire. "Thanks, Holy Spectre," she panted, maybe a little turned on that some violence had been directed toward her for a change. "I needed that."

"That's quite all right," said Oliver, not unkindly. "Just see that you don't lose control of yourself again." He bobbed forward as if to bow, and helped her stand with a gallant flourish before turning to the others. "Now, kind people, as you can see, both the Boss and I would severely appreciate knowing exactly why we're regarded as potential religious personages. Nothing in our background has really prepared us for such a role, though of course I'm sure we're both open to the challenge, especially if refusal results in an excruciatingly painful demise for the Boss."

"That's easy!" answered Steele Woolley, exhaling a toke. "Because the last chicken to lay a duck egg lived over four hundred years ago."

"Furthermore, it was a *black* chicken!" added Dystra the Terrible.

"Dystra, you know no direct evidence has ever been uncovered to substantiate that last claim. The color of the chicken has always been a matter of debate," said Sib'l. "We cannot run around blithely assuming this person is our savior, especially since there's still the matter of those streaks."

"I can dye my hair if that will simplify things," I said.

"Those pathetic ignorant savages," said Tritsky with the melancholic, piteous tones only the truly aristocratic can summon. "Down what pathways of irrationality will their shenanigans lead them next?"

Reverend Sirius energetically nodded his agreement. His eyes appeared on the verge of pinging out. That was good juice he had there.

My mind raced. A thousand hot thoughts permeated my brain all at once. Most of them had to do with Reina, and my fear that even if I did survive this debate, I'd still have no idea how to find her. Maybe it was best for all concerned, but if I'd really cared what was best I wouldn't have been here in the first place.

The other thoughts had to do with what Steele Woolley had said about the chicken laying the duck egg. Correction: the *black* chicken.

"Have I told you I'm a man with egg experience?" I said, seeking to curry favor. "I was a short order cook once. Specialized in great cheese and egg, or bacon and egg, or egg, egg, egg, sausage and egg sandwiches. We called them Gallium Egg Specials."

"His knowledge is most sublime," said an awestruck Dystra.

"He has the luck of the clown," said John Willie sarcastically.

"You stay out of this, my atavistic friend," said Steele Woolley, standing with some difficulty. "Indeed, this Homer B. individual could have the luck of the idiot savant, or he could truly have some metaphysical purpose underlying his peculiar behavior. But he has divined one thing correctly, and that's the problem. And what's the problem, you might ask, the problem right here in Dushen'ka City? The problem is eggs. That starts with E, that rhymes with G, and that spells 'eggs!' Eggs are easily the most spiritual mainstay of Dushen'ka. We tell fortunes by them, we weigh and measure them, but most of all, we eat them. We have many names for them, many untranslatable words to describe nuances of the shades of their shells, the colors of their yolks, and the textures of their albumin. There are more words pertaining to the subject of eggs than there are to any other subject in our language, which you are privileged to hear but fated never to understand."

"I'm sure I won't appreciate it much either," I said. "Where I come from, eggs are just a fact of life."

"Well, for us Dushen'kians, eggs are the magic pathway to spiritual enlightenment. But if Dushen'ka is to maintain its position of power and importance in its clan, then it must break sacred codes long enough to trade in eggs, in hundreds of them, thousands at a single time! Few sins against humanity as a whole will go unforgiven so long as they result in the acquisition of eggs—lots of eggs!" Whereupon he took a long, deep, thoughtful toke from the reefer. Whatever was in there caused the whites of his eyes to become dark and ruddy. He held his breath for as long as he could as he continued. "Have you ever had this yen for a really great egg salad sandwich? And you know you wouldn't be able to get it because there had been a battle last week, and right then there just weren't enough eggs to go around? Have you ever seen a man, a friend of yours, a comrade in arms and a confidant in peacetime, go stark raving mad—all because he couldn't get his hands on a really great egg salad sandwich? Believe me, it isn't a pretty sight. Oh, sure, if it was me, I might be able to pull rank and requisition a few extra eggs, but I'm the major meow here. I get to think up the moral standards I expect everyone else to live by. But even a major meow must face up to the irate flock if he strays too far from the path. What would people say about me if I took more than my fair share of eggs, just to satisfy my own selfish desires? What kind of faith would they have in me then? And would it be worth losing their faith, if it meant I could have a really great egg salad sandwich?"

I thought perhaps this would be a good time to pull out my intestines. Instead, managing a brave smile, I said, "Yes, sir, I can see where you have a problem. And how does your potential savior figure into this story of horror and sacrifice?"

"Someday there shall come a man . . ." said Dystra.

"A man who shall lead us from the darkness of economic dependency upon others," said Sib'l. "Especially those others whose mental shells have yet to be cracked by the onslaught of enlightenment."

"This man who shall have a series of wonderful and thrilling adventures, with the end result providing us with the secret of an endless supply of invulnerable eggs," said Steele Woolley with profound conviction. "Truly the time of the utopia shall be pretty damn close, for we'll be swallowed in eggs, lots of eggs."

"I'm very happy for you," said Oliver, "but how does the Holy Spectre wind up this episode of his life?"

"He comes out fine," answered Steele Woolley. "His future shall overflow with luxury and ease. It's what happens to his human friend that any potential savior should be worried about!"

Dystra stepped forward and kindly put his hand on my shoulder. "And there shall be plenty of pain indeed for the savior to worry about, if the prophecies turn out to be true, as I suspect they shall. And not just any kind of pain, the sort of thing common folk such as we fear and sometimes must live with every day of our lives. No, the kind of pain you shall experience will bring out the hidden nuances of the meaning behind the words 'terrific, excruciating, blood-chilling, mind-numbing, eternal agony.' "

"I fear he speaks truth," said Steele Woolley. "For once your task is done and our fair city is awash with invincible eggs, you shall suffer a fate more terrible than any that has ever been experienced by mortal man before. Your eyeballs will be pricked by a thousand microscopic needles. Your muscles shall slowly sizzle into crisps over a period of several weeks. Your skin shall rot and fall from your anguished hide in tiny pieces. Your bones shall metamorphose into silly putty. Instead of having erections, your penis will just flatten out like the head of a big tapeworm. You won't be able to control your bowels and, furthermore, you'll have no interest in doing so, because you'll already be tremendously humiliated because you have to take off your shirt to eat. And that's just the beginning. I know it's a lot for a city as big and tough as ours to ask of one man, but nobody ever said martyrdom was a fresh yolk in the morning."

So that was it. For three options death was a certainty, and so far as the fourth was concerned, the possibility that I was the savior of Dushen'ka, if I didn't actually succeed, this pack of true believers would make sure I would wish I were dead anyway, just to keep their metaphysical universe in order.

I felt the earth move under my feet. The clouds in the sky swirled by like phantoms on a carousel. The hum from the bases of the city sent a cascade of vibrations from my translator down through my spinal cord, vibrations that set off a chain reaction of fear throughout my entire nervous system. I discovered that whereas my mind wasn't afraid to die, my body was completely petrified at the prospect. Faces from the past began to form in my consciousness. My mother's, and my father's faces, as they had appeared both when they were young and when they were old. The faces of women I had seen and dreamed of, but for some reason not the faces of any I had actually made love to. There was Floyd's innocent mug, Blather's ugly kisser, admiral Boink's blank visage, Coryban's impassive profile, and the countenances of innumerable bipedals and aliens, some of whom couldn't even be said to have faces in the traditional sense of the word. But at last I was saved by the presence of the face that meant more to me than all the other faces in the galaxy.

"Reina ... Reina ..." I said. "It's more than just your face I want."

I wasn't able to add anything further because John Willie struck me with both fists full in the stomach, and my lungs practically flew from my chest at escape velocity. I opened my eyes to find my mind reasonably reaffixed to reality, but also to find reality itself slightly askew.

For I was staring in disbelief at the presence of none other than Reina herself, whose new Kaminskite husband had happened to be escorting her past the fun and games on their way to the ramp. She wore a buckskin skirt and some primitive makeup, but otherwise she was exactly as I had seen her yesterday. And just as angry. The retinue behind the newlyweds was in utter shock. Reina's complexion was pale, and that of her new husband—a skinny little geek—was paler still.

The Heechie-Heechie in the crowd applauded John Willie and his punch, and I think they would have stood in line to add their own sentiments had not Steele Woolley and Oliver, acting in a disconcerting tandem, stepped between the crowd and myself.

"Wait—! Reina! Let me explain!" I called out, and could say nothing more because John Willie reached over Oliver's head and smacked me upside the head with the hilt of his knife. The stars came out again, just as I dimly perceived Reina's husband rudely pulling her into the crowd. "Wait—don't disappear on me!" I whispered.

"Now what do you expect us to do?" demanded John Willie of Steele Woolley. "Stand idly by while he disgraces every woman in the tribe?"

Steele Woolley was unperturbed. "Personally, John Willie, I think the standards you Heechie-Heechie have concerning your women are too low. I think they've been getting off too easy for the last few generations or so. Don't you agree?"

"We must put him to the test," said The Terrible.

"A painful test," said Sib'l.

"No! That would be bad," I said. "Very, very bad."

"Maybe yes, maybe no," said Tritsky.

"Let's find out!" said the Reverend Sirius.

("All hail . . ." etc.)

"Please, I think I can devise a test for him," said Oliver.

"No! You're not creative!" I protested.

111

Oliver winked at me. "You've got to trust me, Boss!"

"Why? Look what you've done for me so far!"

The earth shook before Oliver could reply. At first I thought it was another personal reaction to my impending death, but when a second quake was accompanied by a great thud that reverberated through the land, I knew mysterious outside forces were at work.

Of course, the fact that most people had panicked and were dropping everything to return to their cities or find shelter elsewhere, also had something to do with the deduction.

"Come with us!" said Sib'l, grabbing Oliver by the hand and pulling him helplessly beyond her.

The other ringleaders of the three peoples also sought shelter, save for Reverend Sirius, who lingered just long enough to denounce me as a *Schwarz* again. "Don't worry," he shouted back after he had begun waddling away as fast as his stubby legs would carry him. "If you're really a savior, you won't have much trouble surviving what comes next!"

"Thanks," I whispered.

The thuds continued, gradually becoming louder. The quakes continued, gradually becoming stronger. Soon I was the sole entity in the meadow, tied to a mushroom sapling, and all I could do was wait for the monstrosity responsible for all this racket to reveal itself.

I didn't have to wait long. Just when I thought the earth would crack open and whatever apocalypse the universe had in store would be upon us, an immense group of fingers clamped down onto a distant mountain range. There were ten fingers. Belonging to two giant hands.

The planet shook under the unimaginable strain. It rumbled and roared, and the surface of the ground cracked with hundreds of intersecting jagged lines.

One set of fingers led to a spectacularly huge elbow sticking an eighth of a kilometer up into the atmosphere. Some great crippled thing was pulling itself this way.

And then a giant robotic face loomed behind the

mountain range. The face stared down at the meadow with glowing yellow mechanical eyes. I felt like less than a mote in comparison with it. Like less than a molecule.

Then the giant robot stood and stepped forward. It only took it a couple of steps to reach the meadow, because it was over a kilometer high.

Which is not a bad height for a party crasher.

Chapter Seven
Blather in the Great Game

S UDDENLY, BUT NOT for the first time, Blather felt consumed by great personal doubts. "You know you can't play this thing underwater, don't you?" he asked, holding forth the soprano sax.

"Relax, Ensign. I've got more important things to do than go around slipping bipeds sterile roe!" The chirps and clicks that constituted the language of the Pantamonian Shovelhead came from the speaker in the upper left corner of his motorized tank. He made the few kicks of his tail necessary to swim up and grab hold of the rungs above the water.

Blather couldn't help recoiling as he gave the sax to the Pantamonian ambassador's clawed, webbed hand, a hand strong enough to crush a lump of coal, with claws sharp enough to scar plastiglass. The ambassador hefted the sax gingerly as he wove his long, lizard tail through the rungs below the water, and used it, as was his kind's wont, to support the rest of his body upright.

Like just about everybody else he knew, Blather didn't like Pantamonian Shovelheads. As the dominant of the thirty-four intelligent species known to exist on the water world of Pantamonia, in the Gleckese System, the Shovelheads had initially filled the shark niche in the native ecosystem. Early Shovelheads had specialized in only three activities: swimming, eating, and making little Shovelheads. Later Shovelheads added culture, diplomacy, economics, and obstinacy to their repertoire. Despite their world's strategic and economic importance to the Union, and despite pressure from any number of liberal activist groups, they continued to subsist off any fish, intelligent or not, that happened to get caught in their fangs, this in defiance of the social niceties—but not the laws—of interplanetary civilization.

Since the other intelligent Pantamonian species had pretty much been psychologically warped by their eons of evolutionary inferiority anyway, most Shovelheads couldn't understand why liberals would consider the situation worth making a moral fuss over. However, since even the most ardent supporters of Pantamonian self-determination couldn't help feeling queasy in the presence of someone who had a private stash of deep-frozen intellectuals in the mess, the Union demanded the Shovelheads reconstitute their rations on their native world before loading them topside.

This helped, but not much. Blather still never would have considered asking the ambassador for assistance in the first place if a general call hadn't gone out, and if outright refusal wouldn't have been a grave insult.

Blather climbed down the ladder and forced himself to relax. The ambassador was a long shot; everything would be all right, provided that after he failed, he didn't masticate the sax in a fit of pique. Blather immediately felt worse when he realized he had spent the entire shift checking out long shots, and if he didn't come up with some answers, he would be forced to keep on until he ran out of possibilities altogether. He became dizzy as he turned, sat down to face the stage, and crossed his legs. He attempted to look very cool, very professional. He would have succeeded, in his freshly pressed and cleaned blue uniform, with the yellow stripes on the arms and trousers, and the six rows of brightly colored medals on the left side of his chest, had he not been sweating profusely on the face. He was too uncomfortable *not* to wipe his forehead.

"All right, Mr. Ambassador, stop clowning around. You wouldn't be auditioning if you didn't think you knew how. So let's get funky, shall we?"

The ambassador ducked his head into the water. "Smooth guppies, sir, swiggling down your throat," were the words Blather's translator communicated to his brain. Blather couldn't suppress the feeling that he had missed something significant that time.

"Forgive me for questioning you, Ambassador, but why did you decide to audition? Shovelheads aren't exactly known for their musical abilities, and I should think that if the Ho-Ho-Kusian ambassador decided to molest you, he'd be planting his roots in your stomach for his trouble."

The Shovelhead looked disappointed, assuming, that is, that was how he meant to appear when the haw in his huge green eyes started to turn gray. He shrugged, lifted his scintillating-blue cap from the water, tossed it disdainfully over his shoulder, and ducked his head into the water again. "You mean you haven't heard of *Glans,* our new diplomatic policy to win friends and influence species! I thought everybody knew by now. By the hoary hosts of Hogarth, I promise you that within a week upon my return home, I'll be excreting my publicist into a sargasso sea! But that's neither here nor there; I shouldn't bother you with our domestic problems. *Glans* is simply this: our rulers—who as you may know govern via a telepathic group mind, of sorts—"

If you can call it a mind, Blather thought.

"Our rulers have decreed a new era of interplanetary cooperation, of social altruism, and liberalization of custom for Pantamonian citizens, whose most sacred duties now include being a living example for all other species to look up to. It is nothing less than our avowed purpose in life to assist all manner of creatures through the trials and travails of living, so perhaps they won't be upset when the time comes for them to die."

"Doubtlessly, a problem you've encountered often," said Blather. "I suppose the phrase 'Eat scarlet death' has different connotations on your world than on most others."

"Scarlet tastes spicy, regardless of the species."

"Just let me hear some spicy playing, and we'll see how your newfangled *Glans* policy is working."

The ambassador lifted his head from the water, nodded, puckered his massive lips over the tiny mouthpiece, puffed out his cheeks, and blew. Blather was surprised. Though the results weren't exactly music, the shrill notes emanating from the instrument did bear a striking resemblance to the sounds of the Shovelhead language, which could be properly spoken only under water. Blather couldn't help but wonder if the ambassador was trying through his music to speak directly to him, bypassing the translator altogether.

He decided he didn't like the ambassador's playing very much. "Too stiff," he called out. "Loosen up a bit. Go limber on me. Play some scales if you have to."

"Don't misplace your roe, I'm getting there," chirped the ambassador with annoyance. Now when he played, the notes, though still containing a superficial resemblance to his language, swirled like invisible dervishes spinning in the void, gathering their energy from their bath in solar rays.

Otherwise Blather could find nothing good to say about it. His eyes widened in horror at the discordant lack of traditional melody and the formless improvisations, and he devoutly wished there was some way he could fold down his ears without causing an interplanetary incident. His jaw tensed and his teeth grinned. His nerves throbbed. His temples pounded. As the music accelerated in tempo, so did Blather's nausea. He wanted nothing more than to scream his lungs out in self-defense, but protocol prevented it.

Meanwhile, the ambassador, obviously inspired by his music, was busily creating a new water dance to go along with the sounds he was pealing forth, a dance that if nothing else was one of the most spastic in history. The ambassador gyrated as if an electrical current were surging through his body. For though he had arms with fully evolved digits and a distinctly triangular-shaped head, he had no neck or shoulders, or even legs or hips. Bipeds often said that out of the water, the dun-colored Shovelheads had all the grace of a troupe of ballerina slugs. But the upper half of the ambassador was doing its best to disprove that maxim. The spinal column bent and thrust in a serious of theoretically impossible angles, and his elbows flapped wildly as his fingers ran up and down the keys with ludicrous speed.

"Uh, thank you, Mr. Ambassador. That will be all."

More notes. The ambassador's elbows began splashing the water from the tank.

"Uh, that's enough, sir."

The ambassador dreamily closed his eyes. Clearly he was suffering from the delusion that his music originated from some higher plane, rather than the tenth level of Hell he was really carving out.

"Really, you can stop now." Blather prayed with all his life force that the wayward drops of water would cause the tank's electrical system to short out.

The notes became shriller. The trinkets of the fluorescent chandeliers above vibrated.

"Listen, I've already made up my mind. I don't need to hear you any more!"

The ambassador managed a toothsome grin as he swam around in the tank, with only the tip of his tail holding onto the rungs for support.

"Okay, if you want to play rough about it—!" Blather said, unsnapping his holster and taking out his blaster.

Suddenly the ambassador stopped dancing and playing. He remained perfectly frozen, save for his eyes, which rolled slowly to Blather's direction like rotating marbles. Then, after a prolonged pause, and without being too desperate about it, he ducked his head under water. "I take it there's something inadequate about my simple song?" he inquired, genuinely hurt and surprised.

Blather did not doubt the ambassador's sincerity, but he was hardly inclined to be merciful, not after what he had been through. Squinting one eye, he took aim at a spot directly between the ambassador's nostrils. He held out his free hand. "Toss me that weapon."

The ambassador took a beat to look at the sax he held above the water line. "You mean this? Ensign, I'm afraid you're overreacting. This could start an interplanetary incident."

"Mister, after what I've heard today, your sun could go nova and I'd barely stifle a yawn. now hand over that saxophone."

The ambassador shrugged, implying shoulders where there were none, and tossed the sax from the tank. The sax spun about like a malformed electron, while its trajectory remained perfectly horizontal in relation to the floor.

Blather's aim between the Shovelhead's eyes was not distracted for a moment as he caught the sax by the curve of its body, released it, and caught it for the second time, by the neck. He grinned wryly and held out the sax like a trophy of triumph. Then his expression became serious and he backed away, almost tripping over his chair. Still his aim did not waver. "Now get out of here, before I blast a hole the size of Old Nebraska in your tank. Oh, yeah, and by the way, thanks for your time and energy. I'm certain Admiral Boink will be happy to thank you personally," he finished, according to the standards of protocol.

"I'd watch my breakfast fodder, if I were you," snorted the ambassador contemptuously, the moment before he swam completely underwater to press a few buttons on the console at the floor. A panel slid over the top and the base holding his water tank suddenly sprouted four wheels and two robotic legs. The entire apparatus stepped off the stage, and Blather watched as it rolled past him toward the swinging doors at the opposite end of the auditorium. He noted how the ambassador pointedly refused to look at him.

And as the tank motored out, he saw, with a sudden onslaught of dizzying lust, Lt. Colonel Second Class Coryban standing in the doorway. He had never seen her in person before Admiral Boink had chewed him out yesterday, but of course he had previously heard Coryban's dreamy voice issuing no-nonsense general orders over the intercom systems, had heard legends of her essential space foxiness, and had heard many men tell of the most discreet, gentlemanly passes they had made at her, only to be assigned floor-scrubbing duties for their troubles.

Blather twirled his blaster on his finger, caught it by the handle, and dropped it toward his holster. It missed and clattered to the floor. Blather instinctively danced to avoid a laser blast that fortunately did not come, then did his best to look cool and unflappable. "Next!" he called out to the line of ambassadors he knew was outside the door.

Coryban turned around and said, "No—wait a few moments," before the next one entered. Only when the door closed did she resume walking past the rows of chairs. Already Blather could feel her jade eyes boring into his overheated soul; he felt like he'd sprung a leak in his radiator. Because her head and torso remained perfectly steady despite the sharp incline of the floor, he couldn't help but think of her as an angel gliding to his presence.

Trying to distract her with a salute, he kicked the blaster beneath his chair, where he could retrieve it later. "Greetings, ma'am! What brings you here?"

"Admiral Boink sent me to do some reconnaissance, Ensign," she said coldly. "He wants to know if we have any candidates yet."

"Unfortunately, this is one mission where halfway measures won't do. Either we'll have success or we won't."

"Tell me about it." She pointed to his chair. "And pick that goddamn thing up. There's no telling who'll grab it, with the crowd of passengers we've got on this trip."

"What? Oh, you mean my blaster. Sure." He got

down on his knees, picked it up, and held it up awkwardly, almost as if he expected her never to have seen one before. "I dropped it."

"I noticed."

The ice in those two simple words made Blather feel extremely microscopic. As he stood and looked up into those eyes, those fields of green looking down into his, giving nothing, giving away nothing, he felt positively subatomic. Blather had boyish good looks, tousled black hair, and a warm smile that exposed five gaps between his front teeth. Normally his innate handsomeness protected him from falling prey to slings and entrapments of outrageous beauty.

But Coryban was a veritable amazon. Her features appeared to be have been chiseled by a master sculptor, basing his work upon masterpieces found among the ruins of the First Empire. And those hints her fatigues revealed concerning the shape of her figure ... they made his heart thunder like syn-drums on a rampage.

Nor could he escape the humbling sensation that despite his immaculate uniform, despite his chestful of medals, she, who wore only nebula clusters on the shoulders to indicate her rank, was three times the soldier he was. He inhaled deeply and drew himself to his full height, which didn't help the situation much. He thought of all those men who had come to her, probably in strict accordance with the Patrol Liaison Manual, and couldn't help but wonder if what she really wanted, no, *needed* was a more barbaric approach. Then he thought of all those hours those men had spent in the brig, presumably because of some minor infraction of the fraternization general orders, and wondered if she was worth it.

The currents of the air-conditioning answered, for they shifted as if on cue and provided him with a fresh whiff of her perfume, combined with a healthy dose of her body odor. It was like the odor of lemon juice on a perspiring mare. She needed a shower, and he desperately desired to assist her in that or any other capacity he could manage. "Would you care to join me for a few auditions, to see firsthand how things are going?" he asked, gesturing to the chair beside his.

Coryban looked at his hand as if it were holding something fecal, and then she looked at the chair as if it were about to eat her. But she sat down anyway, wordlessly, and squirmed until she had settled in comfortably.

Blather plopped down beside her. "Oh, to be a chair," he muttered.

"What?" Her tone was soft like distant thunder.

"Oh, nothing. Just thinking out loud."

"Normally I disapprove of vocalizing one's thoughts, but in your case I should think the Patrol should be happy with what it can get. May I see that saxophone?"

Blather had forgotten he was still holding it. "Of course."

Her brows knitted as she examined it. "A fascinating instrument. It's amazing, isn't it, to think of such an ancient device still capable of producing melodies of great beauty. New melodies too, not just ancient airs."

"Now, Colonel, you didn't come down here just to ruminate."

"No, I didn't," she said, almost absently as she fingered the keys, listening to the soft clicking of their opening and closing. "Admiral Boink is growing insecure on this saxophone matter, and he sent me to ensure that you haven't been passing likely candidates by."

"I haven't been. I know when my buttocks are slipping from the edge of a tremendous abyss that only leads to an infinite void."

"You can say that again, if you can remember it."

"You haven't got much confidence in me, do you?"

"It's not a matter of confidence, Blather, it's a matter of necessity. Already rumors about this audition are running through the ship like a plague, rumors that this instrument is impossible to play, that it only makes sense to human ears and Ho-Ho-Kusian sensibilities, that overexposure to its music can cause cancer, to name just a few. And many ambassadors have noticed that the Ho-

Ho-Kusian's behavior is becoming just a little erratic. About an hour ago he tried to pitch woo at a salad."

"How did the salad react?"

Coryban grinned humorlessly. "It excused itself because it wasn't dressed. Ensign, are you certain you understand the gravity of your assignment, just how important it is to the health and well-being of your commanding officer?"

"Yes, ma'am."

"Good." She looked down at the instrument in her hands. "Am I to gather from your first conversation with the admiral that you knew Lt. Hunter?"

Blather immediately tensed up. He had felt so comfortable, had achieved a new peace in life, despite all the pressure he was currently under, knowing that Hunter and the hunk of junk named Oliver were no longer aboard. He didn't wish them dead, actually, he just wished them to be exactly where they were, wherever that was. He gathered from her tone, however, that direct honesty would be a mistake. "We, ah, encountered each other from time to time. I had the opportunity to show him a few of the ropes."

"I see." She turned around for a moment. "Next!" she called. "What was he like?"

"Ah, in what respect? We never went out together, if that's what you're asking."

"Trust me when I say I have no interest in your personal life, Blather. It's just that since this situation developed, I've been going over Hunter's files, and there are a few gaps I'd like to fill in."

She's fascinated with him, Blather realized. *She hasn't even met him and she's already interested. Damn that Hunter. Of course, since he's not exactly topside at the moment, I might be able to turn this situation to my advantage.* "Oh, he was average enough in his way, a fairly nondescript chap. I'd be happy to answer any questions you have about him, but really, when you get down to it, there's nothing unusual about him."

"Hmmmm. If you say so."

Clearly she didn't believe him. He was vaguely aware of the next candidate lumbering down the aisle, but was too preoccupied to see how it was. "I could tell you all I know about him, if you want, ma'am."

Her eyebrows lifted. "Oh? What's the catch?"

"Dinner. Right after these auditions pay off."

"You're a pretty confident fellow, Ensign. Would you be willing to tell me why you were demoted and Hunter was promoted over your head?"

"Maybe."

"Then maybe I'll have dinner with you." She looked up as a shadow loomed over them.

It was a three-meter-tall hunchbacked ape with a television set where he should have had a head. He wore a white loin cloth, green slippers, and a ring on each one of his eight fingers. Otherwise the entirety of his misshapen, black hairy body was completely naked. The television set was considerably more adorned, with an antenna sticking out the back, and a surfeit of controls and switches on the side of the teak cabinet. The speaker was below the tube, which right now was functioning as a mirror, providing Coryban and Blather with a picture of themselves as seen through the ape's reception. He spoke in a tinny voice, very squeaky for one his size, from a little mouth that was in the hairless center of his chest. "Greetings, fellow bipedals. May I have the instrument, please?"

"Certainly," said Coryban, handing it over. "Just go up to the stage."

"Do you need any instructions?" Blather asked.

"Of course not," said the ape, who had started up before Blather had spoken. "As a computerized cyborg from the world of Caliban, where every city is a jungle and every jungle is a home, I have immediate access to any information I may require."

A moment later the ape stood on the stage and carefully stuck the sax into his mouth. His breasts puffed out, somewhat like a misplaced pair of cheeks, as the first tentative notes drifted through the air. The music was bittersweet and unpresupposing, like a dry martini.

Blather and Coryban stared at one another, each communicating the identical idea to the other: they had found their instrumentalist!

And above them, unseen by all, a huge shadow carrying the silhouette of a massive club watched the proceedings and nodded thoughtfully to himself.

Chapter Eight
The Mutts of War

NTIL THE MOMENT I saw the giant robot crossing the meadow, I'd thought my years in space had helped me come to terms with common, matter-of-fact immensity.

But being suddenly faced with this unspeakably gigundo mechanical city, with a battery of laser cannons protruding from its neck like spikes on a collar, an impassive face (of sorts) comprised of massive black planes, and two great crimson energy crystals where eyes should have been, generated a greater sensation of awe and insignificance than even I had thought myself capable of.

Tied there to the mushroom sapling, I pressed against its trunk like a parasitic insect seeking to camouflage itself by squeezing between two laps of the fungoid bark. The trouble was, I was much too big, and during the quick moments it took the robot to cross the meadow and tower over the two cities, looking down on them with an air that combined metallic stoicism with an animalistic aura of arrogant disdain, I would have settled for the ability to hide behind a blade of grass.

The monolithic snout opened, exposing the orange fires of its power crystals within, and the robot screamed an earsplitting cry. Its massive head shook as two cannons on turrets at its neck swiveled, each one pointing toward a different city. I braced myself for its attack. I couldn't help but wonder if this was the end, if I would be broiled as an afterthought in an inferno of pure death and destruction.

But the robot closed its mouth as if to wait. The seconds ticked off slowly, while the cannons posed in the threatening position restrained their fire. I dared to hope aggression was not the robot's primary purpose.

Indeed, its design implied some artistic impulses had been considered during its construction. From the moment it had begun to cross the meadow, I had anthropomorphized it to some extent, which surely had been part of the designers' intentions—presumably to wreak psychological havoc upon potential opponents. Its composition included a highly expressive blend of rounded and angular forms, creating two overlapping series of stegosaurian plates; otherwise it gave the impression of having been deliberately rendered as a schematic dog—including the detail of low-relief likeness of fur all over its torso, and on the massive tail that swung back and forth in counterpoint to the movements of its head, balancing the entire mechanism.

I leaned to the left as far as I could, hoping for a better glimpse of its underbelly. Did it have a pecker? Tits? It seemed to have both, though what the purpose of those particular mechanisms might be was difficult to guess.

The massive head lolled, as the massive tail swished back and forth with the sound of a basso whip being viciously snapped in the air.

Then the head and tail jerked to a halt, and the entire body stiffened like a three-day-old corpse. A few moments later, a mysterious rumbling emanated from its insides. It trembled, then downright shook with such spasmodic violence I expected pieces of it to fly off. It became apparent, however, that such an event wasn't likely when the robot tilted upward on its hips and the front hands retracted into the legs.

After that, several things happened simultaneously. The robot split apart at the two sets of ridges. Layer upon layer of machinery and steel alloy undulated outward from laminated positions inside; many revealed themselves to have been telescoped, their sections distending into funnels expelling huge amounts of steam, and into flues that expelled tremendous amounts of smoke with the scent of sulphur and burning coal (giving rise to the impression the robot relied on several sources of power at once, including the less easily detectable nuclear kind).

The hind legs distended and formed a foundation for the unraveling torso to wrap around. The head and the tail slid back and merged into a black tower in the center of the mechanical fortress, surrounded by the cannons that had been part of the neck. Reinforced mirrors appeared on the surface of the plates, obviously intended to deflect laser beams in the eventuality of an attack. Convex buildings of various sizes rose from the interior, followed by more cannons and towers of various sizes, though none came close to matching that single, heavily armed tower.

The entire enterprise was shaded in the darkest ebony tones, as if the designers had somehow caught the essence of outer space and painted it upon every surface. The sole exceptions were dashes of bright crimson—in the hollows of the cannons, and the occasional lights among the buildings.

I knew what I was looking at, but successfully denied it until a door opened and a ramp descended to the ground. The robot fortress was in reality a city, populated by men, ready for war but, in actuality, come to crash the swap meet.

I glanced at the other two cities. At last the widely variant languages among the societies I'd encountered thus far, not to mention Reina's remark about the possibility of Oliver being an infant city, began to make some kind of sense.

Before anyone appeared on the ramp, a female voice

spoke through an intercom system. The language was deep and guttural, its clipped sounds unpoetic in the extreme, but I didn't need my translator to help me divine the meaning. "We've come in peace," said the voice. "It is your responsibility to see it stays that way."

Nice gal, I thought. My expectations became even lower when a screen similar to the one on the Dushen'kian base unfolded in segments from the base and kindly provided me with a close-up of the first individual, presumably the speaker, to emerge on the ramp. Judging from her clothing and the arrogant way she carried herself, she was one of the city's leaders. She had blue hair and orange skin. Her tight-fitting black jodhpurs glistened blue where the light struck them at the right angle. Her military dress jacket, with its padded shoulders and the decorative half square of brass buttons across the top and down the left side of her chest, was at least a thousand years out of date, so far as the mainstream of galactic culture was concerned. Her high-heeled boots, however, with their spiked toes and black leather glistening so brightly you could probably see your reflection distorted in them, reminded me of those worn by the Dominatrix Queens who come on to you so strongly yet so irresistibly in the seamier sections of the Dana-Stu cluster, near the center of the galaxy. True, this butch little number lacked the head of an insect, and she probably brutalized for free, but I wagered she was in spirit much the same, good for a night's distraction, but not for much longer if you wanted to live to talk about it.

From the top of the ramp she surveyed the terrain. Then she shrugged with an almost bored air and walked downward. A horde of jodhpured officers and grunts of both sexes followed. The officers wore generic dress jackets, while the grunts' shirts, buttoned practically to the jawline, accentuated everything they were theoretically designed to conceal, from rippling muscles to bouncing love handles, and from jiggling boobies to floppy dumplings. Also, the officers carried short blacksnake whips, while the grunts carried clubs and nerve sticks.

Regardless of rank or physical condition, these people all looked like they could hold their own in a fight—not the type you'd want to mess with.

And judging from the way the site was remaining otherwise deserted, I gathered my hosts felt the same way. The leaders among the newcomers split into three parties, two of them heading toward the city ramps, the third toward the forest where the Heechie-Heechie were hiding out. Most of the grunts stood at ease before their own ramp and conversed in low tones.

The situation remained static for about fifteen minutes. I was completely ignored during this period. Then the people slowly returned to the meadows, reclaiming the sites they'd once occupied, but only reluctantly intermingling with the newcomers. It was immediately apparent the sense of festivity was lost and would probably not be regained for the remainder of the meet. The eating and the drinking continued, as well as the games and the talking and the marriage bargaining, but the people and their voices were much more subdued, and they consistently regarded the newcomers warily, even as they served and traded politely with them. Exactly what the newcomers had to offer, though, never became clear to me. Perhaps they were only offering safety.

It soon became horrendously obvious that my problems were just beginning.

Oliver was the one in the lead. Behind him was John Willie and his group of warriors, the medicine man, Reverend Sirius, Tritsky, Sib'l Dane, The Terrible, and Steele Woolley. The interested crowd of onlookers and Plumbellina were extremely noticeable by their absence, and the premonition that my immediate fate was about to be decided once and for all descended upon me like a fireball.

"Boss, you're in serious trouble now!" exclaimed Oliver. He had reached me about fifty meters before the others, giving us a few minutes to talk in privacy.

"That makes my day! What can we do about it?"

"That's just it! I don't know!" He appeared extremely agitated, as if his programming was directing him to pursue several paths at once. His mouth moved in silence several times before and after his utterances. His hands frequently became lost in gestures that bore no apparent relation to his words or tones, and his eyes kept looking in two different directions at once, as if he expected to be set upon by a Space Bogey at any moment.

Finally I could stand it no more. "Hey, Oliver, get a grip on yourself, and just jettison the undiluted whang-doodle, okay?"

"Okay." He nodded in assent, but compliance was at the moment beyond his capabilities.

"You are going to help me, aren't you?"

"Why, yes, if I can, Boss. But that's just the problem. I'm the Holy Spectre. I have responsibilities to others now."

"Do you like being the Holy Spectre?"

"I don't know. I don't know what it entails yet."

"Good. Just keep this in mind: no matter what happens to me, the Patrol's going to come after me in a few weeks. If we happen to be separated by then, they'll only come after you if I tell them you're still around. They probably figure you're entirely expendable, and in any case almost certainly won't waste much time looking for you. So tell me, Oliver, just how much do you like being the Holy Spectre?"

"It's not a matter of how much I want to help you—it's a matter of what I can get away with. These people may be vague, but I've the suspicion they are strict."

Floyd never would have treated me like this, I thought to myself, immediately feeling like an unperceptive son of a bitch. Olive wasn't responsible for what he was, just as Floyd hadn't been, and Oliver's self-preservation programming was unusually strong. Besides, whatever those approaching bozos had in store for me had rekindled his devotion to me. "Okay, just calm down and please tell me what the situation is."

But it was already too late. With the jodhpur-clad,

orange-skinned woman in the lead, they had come into hearing range.

Oliver sh-shed me and whispered, "Just remember, you never got my creativity circuits overhauled."

I sneered at him. Sib'l Dane sneered right back at me, for sneering at him. I sneered at her. Meanwhile, the newcomers scrutinized me like a bunch of paranoid entomologists suddenly confronted with the especially disgusting corpse of an especially disgusting species of giant, slimy Carellian slug-ant. For the first time I saw their faces were scarified with parallel curved lines that swirled from the nose and swept over their entire faces; some scars even swept down the necks and disappeared beneath their uniforms, but of course I had no way of determining if the design continued further down their bodies, and certainly had no desire to.

The woman in the lead finally nodded and said to me, "My name is Hazard, *Miss* Hazard to you, and I hail from Kemp City. Don't bother to introduce yourself. I see that you be scum."

Well, that was about all I could take. Straining at my bonds, I was gratified to hear the crunch of sapling bark. "And I see that you be a barbarian infidel!"

Everyone but Miss Hazard drew back in shock. She straightened her shoulders with angry pride, arching her back just enough for me to finally see the ridges her tiny breasts made through the layers of her uniform. "No one speaks to Miss Hazard that way," said a perspiring horse-faced officer.

"Well, ex*cuuuuse* me!" I replied, tugging at my bonds again, and feeling twice as satisfied this time around, when the tear of the bark was twice as loud and lasted twice as long. "But I just happen to be a First Lieutenant currently assigned to *Our Lady's Hornblower,* flagship of the Fifth Fleet of the Stellar Patrol of the Third Galactic Union of the Certified Galactic Empires of Tremain and Gallium! So it should be plain to even the dimmest of you dodos that I'm not just some whatchyoumacallit?— *Schwarz*, come to invade your paltry little planet!

What do I need your planet for? There are millions just like it in this galaxy alone. If none of the ones I know about are up to snuff, all I have to do is call in the Engineer Patrol and have 'em build one. I don't need your women *per se,* either, because I've seen millions of 'em, encompassing every conceivable size, shape, form, and definition of femininity. All the sublime and/or perverted experiences a male could possibly imagine are available to me at a moment's notice—all I have to do is get up the nerve to ask, and with luck the sensation is mine to endure! I'm not a savior or a devil either. Besides, the first thing you learn in the Stellar Patrol is that salvation is a pretty damn cheap commodity in this galaxy."

I got a grip on myself. I knew I was saying too much, talking too fast. But at least no one, with the possible exception of Oliver (who was looking at me with narrowed eyes), realized I was using my rage as a cover to continue loosening my bonds. That particular task was almost done. But if the astonished way everyone stared at me was any indication, I had mainly succeeded in convincing them I was as crazy as a New Salvadorian mindbug. I forced myself to speak coolly, reasonably, almost reassuringly. "Listen, I may be just one man to you, but what I'm trying to say is I'm an officer in the most powerful military force in the known history of this galaxy. Circumstances have dictated that I'm the first official representative of this army to land here since the forming of the Third Empire. You're not just talking to one man here—you're talking to a hundred thousand planets! Kill me if you must—in the end it won't make any difference, because in a couple of weeks there'll be an entire fleet up there beyond the sky, and you'll have to deal with the Third Empire, regardless of how you feel about it! So—what's it gonna be? Are we going to be friends now?"

Miss Hazard tsk-tsked me with a sad shake of her head. "This one's mind has turned to mush, doubtlessly a side effect of the unknown condition that caused his skin to go black."

"Perhaps he has a plague," said the horse-faced man, wringing his hands in anticipation. Maybe he had some leeches in his back pocket, leeches he couldn't wait to apply.

"I suppose you'd like to dissect him to find out," said a pencil-necked geek at his side.

The horse-faced man said nothing, but his expression was eloquent testimony to his approval of the notion.

"No—you people are the ones who are insane!" said Dystra the Terrible, unmindful of the reproachful looks everyone gave him for speaking so contemptuously to the Kempians.

"Of course he is mad!" said Sib'l Dane. "He has basked too long in the glow of the Holy Spectre."

When the Kempians looked questioningly at Oliver, he said with a shrug, "Can I help it if my brilliance drives a stake in men's brains?"

"He is not mad," said John Willie. "He is merely obsessed with stealing women. Or have you not noticed how he keeps referring to matters pertaining to his animal lust?"

"That's something you'd never understand," I yelled at Miss Hazard, to conceal another tug at my bonds. They were almost loose enough.

"See? He must be a spy, and a barbarian," said the Reverend Sirius, pompous and oily. "Otherwise he would never speak so rudely to a Kempian."

Miss Hazard nodded in agreement.

"You're just saying that because you want your nephew back," said the pencil-necked geek.

"Indeed," said a stout Kempian female. "When we found the one called Bebop Sirius wandering the countryside, he said a *Schwarz* had viciously forced him to exchange clothing. At first we found it difficult to believe, but decided there might be, ah, certain tactical advantages to lending a helping metapaw to the nephew of the great Reverend Sirius."

"I must say, though, we were terribly hurt that you had not invited us to your gathering," said Miss Hazard sarcastically. "And I thought our peoples were at peace."

"We are, so long as it is convenient," said Steele Woolley, lighting another reefer. He appeared not to have recovered from the first yet. When the others glared accusingly at him, he merely shrugged much as Oliver had, and said, "It's true. They know it. We know it. Why lie?"

Miss Hazard regarded me gravely. "We must decide what to do about this stranger."

"What if his story about coming from beyond the sky is true?" asked the horse-faced one. "That would severely limit our options."

"It cannot be true," said one of John Willie's young men. "We of the Heechie-Heechie have many stories of the lands beyond the stars, and an empire as strong as the one he's talking about cannot possibly exist there."

"It is sacrilege to presume there are machines and weapons mightier than the cities'," said Tritsky. He shook his head sadly at me. "I must say, I'm disappointed in you. I was almost tempted to give you a chance."

"I wasn't," said Sib'l Dane proudly. "I'm still not."

"Hmmm. I could use a little sport, people," said Miss Hazard, turning to face the others. "Listen, fellow Kaminskites, Dushen'kians, noble savages—" At this last salutation she grinned condescendingly at John Willie and his crew. Evidently the Kempians didn't think much of a people who didn't have a city to call their own. "I've this hankering to hear a man scream in tune with the sunset. Why don't we say that in exchange for a stray nephew, an extended truce, and a few spare energy crystals, you let us have this one for our amusement this evening?"

"Oh, no, you don't," I said gleefully. At last I had worked myself free of my bonds. I let them slip to the ground and stepped away from the mushroom sapling.

"Boss! At last! Some initiative! What are you going to do now?" Oliver asked excitedly.

I held out my hand toward Oliver and snapped my fingers, in the hopes that his programming would recognize that only instant unquestioning obedience could save me now. "The survival kit!" I said.

A compartment in his torso opened, and everyone, including those who doubted his spiritual qualities, oohed and ahhed.

I smiled smugly as the tray upon which the kit sat slid out. "Good, Oliver." I got as far as opening the survival kit, but before I could reach in, I happened to glance up to see the barrel of a laser gun pointing between my eyes. "Is there some kind of problem?" I asked Miss Hazard.

"Just take it easy," she replied, in tones strongly implying she wouldn't in any case.

"Please consider taking your own advice," I said coolly. "I'm just going to present you with evidence that there are more things in the heavens and cities than are dreamt of in your philosophies. I know using the word 'philosophies' is dignifying the situation a little bit, but please bear with me in any case. This will be interesting." *I hope.*

With a deep, fatalistic breath, I took out the wrench, the screwdriver, the knives, the church key, the multipurpose scrub brush, and some screws and bolts. I inspected everything, and then, perhaps prodded by a mysterious inspiration which I couldn't yet understand, took out the collapsible mop.

"This had better be good," warned Miss Hazard. Sib'l Dane gave a grim nod of agreement. I quickly got the impression they were two of a kind, who warily recognized their kinship despite their rival cultures of origin.

"It'll be better than good—it'll be terrific," I said absently. Already I was concentrating intently on what I might accomplish with the materials at hand. The old spacer phrase "Just the solution from the nearest nether orifice" came to mind. "Oliver, give me one of your spare energy transistors."

"Sure, Boss," he said, doing as he was told. "Uh, Boss, are you sure you know what you're doing?"

I looked at him. Then I looked at Miss Hazard. She was trembling with barely restrained anger. The stout woman had a bemused expression. The horse-faced man looked like he needed a fresh bale of hay, while the pencil-necked geek just looked like a geek.

I looked at the Reverend Sirius. The left side of his mouth twitched as if it was all he could do to refrain from stomping up and down on my toys. Maybe he was jealous. His man Tritsky was suspicious.

John Willie's lip quivered so contemptuously that he appeared to have swallowed a worm. His men often glanced at him to gauge what the parameters of their behavior should be, and then usually sneered as well, though not with the natural ease of their leader. I supposed that they'd forgotten how I'd accidentally guessed Plumbellina's name, since their code dictated they instantly pretend Plumbellina had never existed in the first place.

Dystra laid on the ground and, propping himself up by the elbows, rested his chin on his hands. I was beginning to understand why they called him The Terrible, since I was downwind from him. Sib'l Dane busily glared in hatred at me, presumably for treating the Holy Spectre like a servant, while she wasn't glaring in hatred at Miss Hazard, that is. Steele Woolley just smoked and smoked, blowing it as close to Reverend Sirius's face as possible, and smiled malignly when Tritsky replaced the convex cube plugged in the Reverend's arm.

The crowd was still sparse. Immediately beyond the people attempting to decide my fate stood only two Heechie-Heechie boys, bare-chested, and long-haired on the left side of their skulls, carrying little axes and knives that looked unpleasantly sharp to me. "He's gonna die," said one to the other, pointing at me.

I got to work. Occasionally people, or Oliver, said something, but I couldn't afford to pay much attention to it. I hadn't concentrated so intently, shutting the rest of existence out so single-mindedly, since the musical recitals I'd given as a boy. This time, however, the reviews were of much more importance to my future outlook on things.

Fifteen minutes later, I was finished. One way or the other. With a prayer to whatever cosmological forces were responsible for the Big Bang, an event I firmly believed to be the direct cause of my current predicament, I flicked a switch on the device I'd built. It hummed and shook for several long, torturous seconds, and then began walking. One side rolled on the multipurpose scrub brush, while the other walked on the screwdriver. The other tools comprised its body, and a positronic circuit with red lights substituted for a head. The mop substituted for a backbone, while the strands of hemp substituted for hair. Whenever my device faltered, which was about every four screwdriver steps, one of the knives acted like a cane, helping to pull it forward.

"Voila!" I said. "I call this the Goldberg!"

Only Steele Woolley and Oliver applauded. I presumed the others must have been too astounded, amazed, and amused to muster a coherent reaction, but I'll never know for sure because Sib'l Dane precluded a critical discussion by booting my Goldberg into the mushroom sapling, whereupon it broke into several pieces. I stared, chagrined, at the damage. I admit it, my heart was broken, and seeing the portion of the Goldberg with the knife trying to drag nothing along behind it created a flood of melancholy that welled up in my soul. To think that even great art is so ephemeral—!

"That settles it," said Miss Hazard, with an unexpected (perhaps even to her) note of respect in her voice. "This one's existence can serve the urban interests of Kemp City. You can have your nephew and whatever concessions you want. We will take him."

"But he deserves to die!" said John Willie. "The souls of the ants cry out in hunger!"

"He is a god—our savior!" cried Dystra. "Consuming him would surely level a curse on all ants for all time!"

"I admit it, even I can see that this *Schwarz* might have his uses," said Reverend Sirius. "My nephew never was much use to the commonweal anyway."

"No! I will tolerate no interference! He comes with us!" said Miss Hazard, waving an arm at Kemp City. The straightforwardness of her motion indicated the gesture was meant as a signal to whoever might be manning the towers.

And we all watched, all with similar sinking feelings, I'm certain, as half the cannons turned toward Dushen'ka, and the other half toward Kaminsky.

"Relax. There's no need to spill your atomic piles over this," said Steele Woolley casually, but quickly. "You can have him. We'll just have to make do with the Holy Spectre."

"And good riddance to the little monster," said the stout woman from Kemp. "The machine offends our sensibilities."

Reverend Sirius sighed longingly. "Ah, how I've missed my boy. You've treated him well, I assume?"

Miss Hazard crossed her arms and looked at Sirius from the corner of her eye. "You'll find that he still has all his parts, for all the good it's evidently done him so far."

John Willie, meanwhile, glared at me. "You're going to wish you had faced the ants."

"So this is good-bye?" I asked with mock incredulity.

Oliver rolled over to me and held out his hand. "I'm going to miss you, Boss."

"Just pick up this mess. You can guess who I'd like for you to look after until we can make connections again."

"I'll try, Boss, but I have this sneaking suspicion I'm going to be stuck in the wrong city."

Miss Hazard nodded at the pencil-necked geek. He grinned. I grinned back. He didn't make a move. I waited for him to make one. He still didn't. It was when I realized that he had no intention of making one that I finally noticed the horse-faced man was no longer in my line of sight.

And then the lights went out. It was one sensation I was getting tired of.

Chapter Nine
Life in the Big City

I NEVER EVEN HAD the chance to see what shapes Dushen'ka and Kaminsky transformed into. Hell, I didn't even have the chance to regret it. The darkness that enveloped me was so deep and thorough that all the vague distractions of unconsciousness—such as dreaming, visions of limbo, altered perspectives on the inescapable travail of existence—were denied me. With a splitting headache and absolutely no idea of how much time had passed, I awoke to face existence in a room fully as dark as that which had existed in my mind.

The room was very small. It required but a few moments of crawling about to gain a rough approximation of its measurements. At least I'd never get lost. Whenever I took too long a step, I walked into a wall or cracked my knee against the cot the Kempians had so thoughtfully provided for me, and whenever I stood straight to take a stretch, I cracked my skull against the ceiling.

Naturally I protested my treatment in the strongest terms possible, at the top of my voice. I succeeded in making myself hoarse, but that was about it.

I calmed down with an effort. The prospect of being confined in consummate blackness presented me with the possibility of being so bored that torture would be a welcome distraction, but I would have to accept my fate totally, whatever it would be, in order to endure it with my sanity intact. Of course, that didn't stop me from wondering if a previous prisoner had devised a hidden escape route, through a tunnel in the wall or an air duct or something. A more thorough examination of the premises in search of the imaginary escape route revealed no tunnel or obvious outlet whatsoever, but at least I could take some small comfort in the presence of the bedpan under my bunk. It seemed my captors weren't complete barbarians after all.

They were just ninety-nine percent barbarians.

I sat on the cot and attempted to meditate. When that didn't work, I attempted to sleep. Then I attempted to daydream. But Kemp City just happened to be making too damn much noise. Not only did the pings and hums and thuds and cracks and roars and whirs of its operating machinery penetrating through my prison walls constantly distract me, but the steady reverberations from the city's giant feet shook me to the marrow with every step. For the first time in my life I experienced what maritime sailors call seasickness.

My bedpan sure came in handy, though not exactly for the use it was intended.

It was exactly the size and shape of Floyd's oilpan. Holding it so close to my face made me miss him all over again. I practically broke down and cried every time I used it. How could part of him still be alive somewhere? Could the distinct personality of a mechanical unit survive if the programming circuits, the seat of both intelligence and feelings, were removed? This was a good question to ponder in the dark.

Not so good to ponder was the possibility that I was deluding myself, that my communication with Floyd in limbo had been a simple dream and nothing more. Still, the vision clung to me with a vividness that seemed far more real than any of the other adventures I'd had since the shadow creature decked me on *Our Lady's Hornblower*.

I had a responsibility to Floyd, one I had no idea how to discharge, but one that I reluctantly concluded took precedence over my lust for Reina (to whom I doubtlessly owed some responsibilities as well, seeing as how I'd babbled her name in public).

All right, I thought, suppose Floyd was alive somewhere, in part if not in toto. It was a big galaxy. You'd have to live three augmented lifetimes just to touch down on ten percent of the inhabited planets and asteroids and comets. The odds against finding Floyd in a civilization that humongous were astronomical.

I went through the process of sleeping, waking, and barfing several times. I had no idea how long I was spending in there, had no method of gauging the passage of time. I tried to remain awake as long as possible, but it was often difficult to tell if my eyes were even open, much less cognizant of everything they couldn't see. I could only really be certain I'd slept recently if I checked my bedpan to see if it had been cleaned or replaced, an action my jailors invariably performed only when I was sound asleep.

Needless to say, I was becoming rather hungry. Eventually I forgot all about Floyd, Oliver, Reina, my hopes for rescue, and the shape of the thing I was in, and concentrated entirely upon the visions of culinary delights that marched across my malfunctioning retina. And I do mean marching. Carrots saluted me. Andovian fruit bars strutted their stuff. Gene-spliced bacon, lettuce, and purple tomato sandwiches on rye bread with lots of mustard and mayonnaise bounced by, while the fries on the side desperately high-stepped just to keep up. Chocolate-covered bean flies buzzed by, overtop a steaming plateful of Narcissian hashed reds, rotten to the core, just ripe for conspicuous consumption. A Sirian mutt-goose, raw and bleeding with a banana in its mouth, gourmet style, glided by as if its plate were riding the currents of an invisible river. Bottles of Motian Moonshine danced, glasses of low-fat pink buttermilk rolled without spilling the contents, pruneberry jam on raisin cheese waddled, bovine-baloney-burgers in buns bopped, New Jovian windrider pâté prissed, Holsteinian sausage sashayed, and on and on and on. All together it was a disgusting series of hallucinations. Just thinking about the array of delectable, succulent, mouth-watering, ambrosial flavors gave me an immense attack of thesauritiasis, which unfortunately did nothing to abate the tremendous attack of delirious hunger that made every sound I heard through the walls echo in the ruins of my mind like phase distortion. At least it helped the time pass until the Kempians remembered they had to give me food and water if they wanted to keep me.

Thankfully, they did something more sophisticated than just hose me down. A panel slid open. Through it came a flash of blinding light. Knowing that after having spent all this time in the dark, the faint glow of a two-watt bulb would blind me, I shielded my eyes and then cautiously peeked through my fingers. I spotted the blurry silhouette of a tray with a plate of some kind of slop and a glass of water on it.

I grabbed the tray and the panel slid shut. The blackness returned, save for the blue and red spots dancing before my eyes. I busily stuffed the slop into my mouth with my hands. I practically sucked the water into my mouth without the benefit of a straw before the glass even touched my lips.

I finished with a protracted belch. A loud, protracted belch. A door opened, as if on cue, and I fell down on my knees, trying to hide my entire body from the blinding shaft of intense white light that stabbed into the cell like the flash of a nuclear explosion. Two massive silhouettes stood between me and the origin of the light. They didn't shield me much, but then again I didn't believe shielding me was what they were interested in.

"Stand up," boomed the voice of Miss Hazard from the thinner of the black figures. "We have a job for you."

"Sorry, but I never take jobs from someone who

hasn't expressed a deep, abiding personal interest in me," I replied.

The wider figure, who had a basso yet distinctly feminine voice, snapped a bullwhip half a centimeter above my shoulder and ordered, "Stand up and come! Kemp City has beckoned, and failure shall not be permitted."

"All right, all right. Just let me get my eyesight back."

"My apologies," said Miss Hazard, as she and the person with the bullwhip grabbed me by an armpit each and dragged me across the heavily oxidized floor of a narrow corridor. "But we really don't have the time to dally."

"Forsooth! Well, then, my apologies to you," I said. "I was hoping you'd come to dally."

They dropped me. Because I could barely judge how close I was to the floor, I managed to hit it the nanosecond before I could bring up my hands to protect myself. My forehead made a hollow sound, like a cross between a thump and a clang, as it struck the floor. While recovering from the subsequent reverberations in my brain, I noticed something—something that had been happening for some time but which I hadn't previously noted due to my preoccupation with eating.

"The rhythm of the steps!" I exclaimed. "It's changed."

"Yes—there's a limp, and we can't fix it," said Miss Hazard curtly.

The wider individual—a female jailor whose major articles of clothing consisted of a black loin cloth and hip boots—grinned down at me with a proud display of her three missing front teeth. She also wore a black-gemmed necklace, black bone earrings, and black needles through the nipples. Her body was scarified as well as her face. The dark orange scars swirled from her nipples and belly button (an innie) like stylized sun rays and continued onto her back, and down her arms. I hesitated to think what the design might look like beneath her loin cloth. I had the sinking sensation that according to her society's standards of beauty, she was a star fox, and that she desired to catch me in the inexorable gravitational pull of her massive thighs. "Fix it properly," she said, "and properly you shall be rewarded."

"That's okay. I'm an altruist. But why can't you people fix your own equipment?"

Neither answered. The big one just nudged me with the spiked tip of her boot. We walked in silence through many winding corridors, some as narrow as aisles between pews, others as wide as highway tunnels. I had the impression we were sticking to the outer edges of the robot. Most of the jet-black walls were smooth, unbroken by ridges or windows or any indication that they formed part of the city at stationary mode. Other walls had had holes sealed up at some point in their history, holes doubtlessly caused by direct hits of some nature. The more recent repairs were basically slipshod in nature, the materials appearing less rust-and-heat-resistant than the predominant alloy. I took this as an indication that any problems the inhabitants might be having making standard repairs were recurring ones. The fact that the more recently applied metal was of a slightly lighter shade of black indicated as well that certain important raw materials had become increasingly more difficult to come by. I surmised the city had been in a state of decline over a period of centuries. Not so noticeable in a single lifetime, perhaps, but very much so from the perspective of history.

The Kempians walking past us invariably saluted my chaperons with mechanical briskness. A few backward glances confirmed my suspicion that the jailor's sensual potential was highly regarded by her fellow citizens. Men shook their hands as if their fingertips had been burned, and women lifted their eyebrows provocatively. My jailor occasionally smiled smugly to herself, especially in the narrow corridors, when passersby were forced to brush against her, while Miss Hazard, who was far more attractive to my way of thinking, simply smoldered with ill-concealed jealousy. Evidently being a head honcho of this city didn't provide Miss Hazard with all the attention she thought she deserved.

I felt vibrations through most of the walls. Not only the vibrations of the limping city, but those of cylinders turning, engines gunning, carburetors chugging, air-conditioning units humming, and pistons pumping. Often the doors to these machine areas were ajar, and I was permitted a glance at vast constructions ringed by a series of work platforms—forged from alien alloys to comprise an alien technology—before the dynamic duo pushed me on. I often wondered what the Kempians scurrying about, carrying pylons and spare parts and boxes of nuts and bolts, were supposed to be doing, or why they couldn't fix the problem in question.

Finally the corridor ended, and we turned onto a long platform, illuminated by tiny white bulbs on the rail, extending far into the distance. I felt like a microscopic creature exploring the insides of an android. By now the ever-present boom of the city's footsteps had reached clamorous proportions. The echoes between steps practically drowned out all other noises reverberating through the walls. The destination ahead remained shrouded in blackness, the distant bulbs, pinpricks of light that illuminated nothing.

I surmised that the corridors of Kemp City, if unwound into a straight line would reach to one of the moons of this godforsaken planet.

I glanced up at the ceiling. It glittered strangely. With blue-green pinpricks of light that slowly faded in and out. It occurred to me that Kemp City, and the others like it, was in reality a tesseract—one partially folded into a fourth dimension, like a crooked little urban blight, to accommodate the vast spaces stuffed in here. I never learned for certain, I'm sorry to say, if the builders had just created some optical illusions by using all the space they did have to the maximum.

Soon I made out a vast hip joint, a combination pneumatic-hydraulic device with panels of flickering lights and controls placed at regular intervals. The vast mechanism rose from an abyss of platforms and supportive machinery, reaching up through a forest of those platforms. Spine above, knee below. The sharp odor of baking carbon. The glow of energy crystals emanating through the minute cracks in cylinders of solid steel. Scarified Kempians manning battered computer consoles of such an ancient vintage that I would certainly be reluctant to rely on them. Screens whose information was arranged from designs of pixels and polygons I'd never seen before. The sensation of hot steam hissing from nearby escape valves, condensing against my cheeks. The grim appraisal of Miss Hazard, the knowing smile of the large jailor. They pointed. Toward the hip joint. At a portion where a giant computerized series of pistons operated out of step, causing the entire apparatus to work in clumsy fits and starts, making horrible crunching sounds that sickened me even though I had no emotional attachment to this place or to anybody in it.

"You fix," said Miss Hazard. My jailor grinned. My stomach sank.

What can I say? A few hours later, despite my absolute lack of faith in myself, I had fixed the hip joint. I made the first tentative steps toward mastering a binary programming language totally unlike anything I'd previously encountered, just to find out what the glitch was, and then I climbed onto that hip joint to get my hands dirty, taking care of the mechanical problems that had led to that glitch in the first place. I had the tools, and I had the talent. And I still had no idea why my captors couldn't have figured it out for themselves.

At least Miss Hazard and my jailor had the decency to give me the incentive to mull over that problem some more, while busily fixing all the other problems they deigned to throw my way. It seemed I was receiving a bargain-basement tour of the city, though naturally I didn't have the privilege of visiting any of the recreational or residential sections I presumed existed. My escorts had me repairing mammoth mounting assemblies, immense carburetors, herculean alternators, Brobdingnagian generators, prodigious combination screws, and monstrous pumps. For a while it was refreshing to be working and thinking so hard after such an extended period of inactivity, and I've always enjoyed the opportunity to tinker with machinery and attempt to outwit the whimsies of unencountered programs. Before long, however, I realized I was dealing with binary constructions not only unprecedented in my experience, but in all the species ever associated with the Third Empire, even the extinct ones. Full comprehension of the scientific principles utilized in the construction of the city would require years of concentrated study, and even then the subtler nuances might still prove to be elusive to all but the most transcendent minds.

Leading me to the conclusion that while perhaps the Kempian's ancestors might have built this city, the current residents had lost the creative spark—including the ability to improvise—necessary to keep it working in tip-top condition. What their culture valued instead was psychic and physical dominance in all categories of existence—whether or not such dominance was in the best interest of the survival and general well-being of the city. The maintenance workers I saw in action paid more attention to who got the slackest jobs, and how they could be reassigned to duties more to their liking, than actually carrying out the ones they had in the hopes of being rewarded according to their merits. It didn't seem many maintenance workers were rewarded according to merits anyway, as those in command of units appeared to know more about the art of bullying rebellious charges into submission than in the workings of the machines upon whose smooth operations their lives, presumably, all depended. Nor did Miss Hazard seem particularly chagrined at the lack of efficiency very much in evidence all about her. Instead, she accepted the arguments and the resultant fistfights as a matter of course, and once even helped a squad leader deck a woman who had gotten too far out of hand. My jailor laughed long and lustily at this; violence tickled her humors.

Neither Miss Hazard nor my jailor permitted me to say much. I was able to talk freely only when I needed a special tool, or when I required their physical assistance, which I was sometimes better off without. Finally, however, they sensed my efforts had reached the point of diminishing returns, and Miss Hazard made herself scarce while my jailor escorted me through the labyrinth of corridors back to my cell. By now I certainly anticipated the rest.

But what I'd seen today of the Kempian social structure had aroused my curiosity too much for me to leave it alone, and so I took the calculated risk of asking my jailor why her people couldn't find program glitches for themselves.

My jailor looked down upon me and smiled. She caressed one of her bosoms with the handle of her bull-whip and said, "That is why we take prisoners. It is their privilege and duty to repair what they are able. There is little else they are good for, unless, of course, you have some suggestion in mind."

"No. Not me." I waited a few moments before asking, "What happens when the prisoners can no longer repair things?"

She shrugged. She was no longer smiling. "We find some use for them."

"You must not have had too many intelligent prisoners recently, judging by the kind of work I had to do."

"It is not the custom of Clausewitzian Cities to take prisoners just because they happen to be available, or because we particularly need them."

"Clausewitzian?"

"That is what we call those units who are affiliated with the unit of Clausewitz."

"I see. That city is the head of your clan."

"The head and more. We would gladly give ourselves to perpetuate the city or the lives of anyone in it.

Such has been the custom, the duty, and the way since the dawn of history."

"When does the dawn of history begin on your world?"

"Such a peculiar way of expressing it," she observed, shaking her head. I couldn't help but notice how she fingered the needle sticking through her ever-hardening nipple. "There was no history before the cities awoke and created mankind to live in them. There will be no history after the cities are gone." Done with one nipple, she transferred her whip to the other hand and began fiddling with the needle through the other. She fluttered her eyelids at me. "We shall arrive at your cell soon."

I faked a deep, satisfying yawn. "Good. I could use a nice long nap."

"Useful prisoners are not permitted rest."

"Then what do you call all that time I spent alone?"

"Your initiation."

"That's great. But I still want a rest. How much further is it? All these corridors and doors look alike to me."

She stopped and hit some buttons on a console. A cell door immediately slid open. "We are here."

"Excellent. Let me know when you need me again," I said, moving past her to go inside.

Well, trying to move past her. She grabbed me by the shoulders and the back of the head and tried to smother me between her two breasts. It was like being eaten by a Vixionian Gladiolus at maximum pastiness, though I had a sneaking suspicion which experience had the higher survival ratio. "I need you now," she said huskily.

The next thing I knew I was flying through the air. I landed on the cot with a *thump!* "Listen, I'm willing to do a lot of things to service your city, but this isn't exactly what I have in mind."

"Prisoners must perpetually serve. Otherwise the fate is too terrible for the sane captive to contemplate, yet is equally necessary for the perpetuation of the city.

In other words, I would regret it if you chose not to serve, but would have the satisfaction of knowing you died for a good cause."

"On second thought, I'm sure I can come up with something."

My jailor smiled and closed the door behind her. She then presented me irrefutable evidence that the circles and swirls of her scarified design indeed centered around every orifice of her body. She walked to the cot and dangled her loin cloth before my nose the way you'd dangle a string before a cat. She pointed to my face. "Is the rest of you that dark?"

"Well, yes, with the exception of a few areas here or there. Mostly there. But you don't have to take my word for it. Would you prefer a personal inspection?"

Without the slightest regard for my safety, she leapt on top of me. I sorta lost control of my life for the next thirty to forty minutes, so I think I'll skip that part of my account. You don't want to read about it anyway. It was too brutal, and doubtless would offend your keen sensibilities. Take my word for it, the time I'm avoiding discussing here was the most disgusting, depraved, perverted, animalistic, low-down, dirty, mean, base, classless, degrading, immoral, amoral, hedonistic, debauched thirty to forty minutes of my life, and your respect for me would only suffer if I revealed any of the disgusting, depraved, etc. details.

All right, I admit it *was* entertaining in an unspeakable sort of way. My jailor seemed to enjoy it too, but when she was finished, she tossed me aside like a used paper bag, back onto the cot, and shook her head disdainfully at my exhausted member. She wiped the massive amount of perspiration saturating her body with her loincloth . . . before putting it back on.

I just laid there, the rest of me as exhausted as my member. I think I would have enjoyed the experience more if she had undressed her breasts along with the rest of her. Those needles were sharp. As it was, I doubted they were sterilized, and feared it would take at least a week for all my cuts to heal. "Thank you," I said between breaths.

"It was nothing," she replied with a sneer.

"I know what you mean. Is there any other piece of broken-down machinery in this dump that needs repairing?"

The jailor hit the wall with her fist. A portion of the wall slid up, and through a plate of glass I saw a naked, perspiring Miss Hazard, slumped with her legs spread apart in a chair whose back and armrests were formed by a row of thick plastic, flesh-colored rods, each with a rounded cap. Miss Hazard held a fan with one hand, which she waved brusquely at her flushed face and neck. Her other hand was draped exhaustedly, her five fingers bent like the stems of five drought-stricken seedlings, over the bars of a periscope whose pipe ended somewhere in the ceiling. I spent a tense moment attempting to intellectualize the humiliation I felt at learning that this debased episode in my existence had been spied upon by a third party seeking a cheap thrill. In the end, I could only hope it had been good for Miss Hazard too, and that she still possessed her earlier scintilla of respect for me. Anything less would surely prove fatal.

"This one's had it. Time to send him downstairs," the jailor said.

Chapter Ten
This Savage Vegetable

RAPPED! HE THOUGHT, despairingly. *Trapped in a universe for which I cannot personally be held responsible.* Truly, there seemed no sane way out of his predicament. He was surrounded on all sides by beings for whom the basic imperatives of existence were naught but base desires, to be satisfied as quickly as possible; by insensitive creatures whose affinity for the subtler vibrations of communication was negligible in the extreme; by ravenous bipeds who indiscriminately consumed plant life at virtually every meal, and who ritually washed every mote of dirt from their bodies and declared themselves "clean"; by undisciplined bundles of energy who pursued every field of endeavor they fancied regardless of the potential consequences to the ecosystem that happened to be involved; and yes, most distressing of all, by pallid minds whose association with the experiences and memories of their ancestors manifested themselves, at best, in a few random thought-strands, generally referred to as "the recurrence of past lives."

What intellectual fertilizer these coagulations of protoplasm be, he thought to himself time and time again. Often he regretted the sentiment. He liked to be reasonable about things. He knew not everyone could be as perceptive into the rhythm of life as he. And often he felt

153

the creatures surrounding him were doing their best. He tried to tolerate the deficiencies of others, because it was his job if for no other reason, but in the end his contempt was always barely restrained, and to his manner of thinking, always justified. He could not help it. His species was traditionally rude, arrogant, flighty, self-centered, picayune, and damned incomprehensible to others seventy-five percent of the time. He was the Ho-Ho-Kusian ambassador, and he had the greens for the first time in his (and in his subidentities') long existence.

His assessment of the situation was naturally more elevated than that. He could not conceive himself engaging in reproductive activity for the mere sake of fulfilling biological imperatives. For him, the time had arrived to perform a sacred ritual. The time had come to love and be loved. The time had come to be the recipient of the ultimate sacrifice. The time had come for a kindred soul to become forevermore a part of him. The time had come for him to submit to the overwhelming desire to feel his myriad roots bound in by densely packed soil, to probe them between the gravel until they dug into the willing pulp of his chosen fodder-brother, to experience the cool heat of his fodder-brother's nutrients being absorbed into his body, and to feel his fodder-brother's mind become an eternal subidentity, an indispensable part of his immortal soul.

Those who saw the Ho-Ho-Kusian ambassador skating on the special wheels applied to his roots so they wouldn't be worn and chafed as he scurried through the corridors of *Our Lady's Hornblower* wouldn't have thought there was anything unusual about the manner in which he ping-ponged from wall to wall like a tumbleweed caught in a hurricane, emitting a continuous stream of nonsensical static from his translator. The ambassador for whom time was a river that never quite reached its outlet always traveled through the ship like he had been set on fire. And so it was that today those who barely eluded the ambassador's unique interpretation of traffic flow chalked up his reckless skating to his usual desire to get his business over with as quickly as possible, so he could return to his quarters and stand in the dirt, basking in the artificial sunlight.

Only the more sensitive guests aboard *Our Lady's Hornblower* suspected things were not quite as they seemed with the Ho-Ho-Kusian ambassador. A few even remarked that they had seen him several times during this shift, and thought it unusual that he hadn't returned to his quarters for his customary extended stays.

Of course, those who had witnessed the ambassador's attempt to woo a salad and his subsequent temper tantrum when the salad did not respond in accordance with his wishes, were convinced that not all the ambassador's foliage was photosynthesizing properly today. Most chose to believe the ambassador needed some R and R beneath genuine sunrays, and only the less charitable regarded the incident as conclusive proof that their suspicions about the whole damn loony species had been correct all along. All the ambassadors, however, gladly acceded to Admiral Boink's wishes and swore to keep news of the incident to themselves. "There's no point in pouring gasoline on a fire," the admiral had explained. "Or in vacuuming sawdust," the feathered ambassador from Kabutal-X had replied, to the confusion of everyone.

Just how the Ho-Ho-Kusian ambassador might have reacted to Admiral Boink's policy was problematical. Even in his home forest, the ambassador managed to stand out from the crowd. Fully seven meters tall *sans* skates, he boasted an attractive crown foliage lush and green, several shades darker than the greenish-yellow thickets that grew from his seventeen limbs. His branches and the veins in their leaves were quite strong, and sufficiently flexible for grasping, freeing him from the rather embarrassing necessity of wearing photo-cybernetic devices on selected limbs for use as waldoes. One of his more admirable features was the consistent dark-brown shade of his bark, clear evidence that he was remarkably free of fungus, parasites, and other contaminations. Here among those interplanetary barbarians, however, the compliments he received concerning his terrific physical condition were few and, more often than not, inadvertent. Most barbarians, particularly the bipeds, traditionally the gauchest of the gauche, preferred to remark upon the dirt pads he was forced to wear around the majority of his roots while traveling around the ship. At home, the mere sight of his naked roots, strong and just twitching for something substantial to dig themselves into, would have brought him a rash of potential fodder-brothers. But here, the lack of appreciation for his roots was just one of the many ignominies he was forced to endure for the sake of his homeworld.

Not the least of which was the popular supposition among those imprecise interplanetary thinkers, bipeds called scientists, that the sapfiber beneath Ho-Ho-Kusian bark was fairly edible stuff. Interplanetary means of ingestion never ceased to disgust the ambassador, as did their means of reproduction, the reputed pleasure sensations of which never ceased to elude him.

That was all right. There was much about the Ho-Ho-Kusian ambassador that eluded bipeds and other sundry creatures too. Such as which was the front and which was the back. The only Ho-Ho-Kusians ever to have facial features were those unfortunate enough to have their faces initialed by lovestruck tourists during the hibernation season. Interplanetary convention had it that the Ho-Ho-Kusian rear was determined by the direction the massive, semiflexible taproot was pointed in, but in reality it made no difference. Ho-Ho-Kusians possessed a radar sense that worked for a three-hundred-sixty-degree circumference, making such distinctions as front, back, and side irrelevant. Their sensitive sapfiber also sorted out the various audio and olfactory information picked up by the buds on the branches; in addition, it created the vibrations that enabled translators, augmented by vocalization capabilities, to act as a means of communication. The exact internal mechanisms involved were a mystery, and, since Ho-Ho-Kusians were such a pain in the ass to deal with, were likely to remain that way.

Most Ho-Ho-Kusians believed life and existence to be inexorably sweetened by a profound sense of mystery. Many, in fact, preferred life to be so mysterious that they wanted to know nothing at all about the strange creatures from the stars. Indeed, it was a criminal group radically sympathetic to isolationism that had seen to it that the luggage left behind contained the drug that would put his reproductive urges on hold.

At first the ambassador had resented the action. As one of the few of his kind aware of the importance of precedence in analyzing matters of cause and effect, he had realized almost at once that the drug would have freed him from the necessity of self-control, a facet of behavior the Ho-Ho-Kusians had never even imagined, in fact, had had no reason to imagine, before communication was established with the rest of the universe. Born as plants, Ho-Ho-Kusians lived and died as plants, which is to say they tended to just live and die, doing what their chemical urges dictated when the proper season dictated, never seeking to rationalize the solemn rhythms of existence. So while it could be said that Ho-Ho Kusians routinely experienced desire, it was safer to say that until the time that crew of explorers had decided to take one aloft without a potential fodder-brother, a Ho-Ho-Kusian had never experienced passion.

The ambassador hadn't thought he would like passion. Everything he'd heard about it had left him to believe it was a lot of bother. He'd liked his reproductive cycle traditional—tidy, orderly, slow like the passing of the seasons, with everything done in its own good time, and, most important of all, with himself on top and his dominant identity assured. And he especially liked sowing seeds that possessed dormant traces of his personality. He hardly looked forward to the day when he would be too old to do anything other than dig himself into the ground and permit his essence to be transformed into a subidentity inside another. But he had known, or at least had believed, that when the time came, he would accept his ending as he had accepted his continuing, as part of the natural order of things, with himself no more or less important than any other component of the birth-rebirth cycle.

But now, without the drug, without a fodder-brother or even the wherewithal or the means to express a secret vice, the ambassador was in the midst of discovering the attraction behind caving in to an obsession with a fixed idea, particularly when fulfillment would bring intense satisfaction and overwhelming relief. The attraction was simply that he liked it. He loved feeling passion. It was pretty terrific. Already his subidentities, hardly as resilient to subversive forces as his dominant ego, were planning on what kinds of passions they could cultivate next, assuming they ever got this one out of their system. Normally this sort of independent thinking on his subidentities' parts, which manifested itself as an incessant buzzing, would have upset the ambassador terribly; it would have meant that he was losing control, that perhaps the time had indeed come for him to be a fodder-brother himself. But now . . .

Now that sort of independent thinking was beginning to appeal to him. He was beginning to feel alive. Alive on the planes of existence where the animals and the bipeds and the plant-eaters existed every day. His sapfiber was responding in kind to their emotions and feelings, their loves and their hatreds . . . to their passions. So although most of the crew and the passengers were unaware of what was happening inside the tortured consciousness of the Ho-Ho-Kusian ambassador, he was very much aware of what was happening inside of them. It was oh so very untidy, but it was also extremely interesting.

If only that salad had been alive. He could have worked out with it some arrangement to their mutual satisfaction, and then maybe he would have gotten on with his life. Or with his next passion, whichever came first.

Oh well, that's where the seed drops, he thought as he skated into the commissary, oblivious as his taproot accidentally swung too far to the left and swept the feet of a Nubian Pleasure Unit out from under her. The Nubian Pleasure Unit shook her scintillating metal fist at him, screamed something about leaky oil pans and an unstable chassis, and, when he failed to respond, swung her right arm at the elbow like a propeller, in what was evidently an obscene gesture for those of her culture and profession. The ambassador ignored her.

Several of the onlooking entities applauded, or else demonstrated their approval of the incident according to their native customs. Whether they approved of what he had done or what she had done remained unclear. The ambassador ignored them too.

The aesthetics of the commissary decor had been calculated to evoke in the shipboard guests memories of their native environments, and they succeeded to the extent that the commissary frequently reminded the guests what it was about their homeworlds that had made them want to leave in the first place. There were dank oceanic pools for the seafaring creatures, swampy dining areas stocked with fresh fish for the reptilians, methane and nitrogen booths for the nonoxygen breathers, air cushions for hedonists and cloud creatures, forest areas for the intelligent insect delegations, mud pits for the porcine types, piles of rocks for cave dwellers, perches for avians, fungus pads for the more spiritually inclined species, and a variety of holomodels of native skies for a ceiling. All these areas were separated by several rows of long tables of various heights, lined by chairs capable of comfortably supporting a variety of shapes and weights. In some places there were two levels of tables, and in others there were complicated arrangements of plants, some real and some plastic, all calculated to evoke the memories of several planets at once in as many delegates as possible.

The Ho-Ho-Kusian ambassador found all the artificial environments equally horrid, but fortunately he wasn't visiting the commissary for its ambience. Skating throughout the commissary, he was overwhelmed by the wide span of odors—of the food and the diners and of the place itself; he suspected he was more susceptible than usual thanks to his precarious emotional condition, which had somehow affected his sapfiber's ability to filter out unsavory smells. Except that on second thought they weren't so unsavory after all—they were simply compelling.

The ambassador carefully watched the visitors to see how much attention they were paying to him, and finally, as he was skating past some purple-flowered, broad-leafed potted plants that didn't offend his sensibilities too greatly, he noticed that no one seemed to be as much as glancing at him. He came to a sudden stop, his skates making only a slight *eech-eech* sound against the tiled floor. Slowly, he hoped imperceptibly, he intertwined his branches with those of the plants, and waited.

Waited for a promising candidate to sit down unwarily near him. Waited for the moment to strike.

He was convinced that once the honor he was bestowing upon his victim became obvious, then the victim would gladly become a full-fledged reproductive partner. Oh, how he anticipated the bout. The chase, the conquest! Surely his partner would do more than just lie there, which is all he could have expected from the salad. Surely his partner would attempt to do a little digging.

And as he waited, he felt his passion grow within him. His need expanded into new dimensions, permeating every vein in every leaf, and he became convinced that once he found the proper partner (i.e., someone who was willing to give all his/her/its nutrients to a plant), then his tortured mind would easily grasp the most elusive principles of Federation science.

And as his passion grew and his need expanded, his standards diminished proportionately. He actually considered pouncing upon the insectoid swarm of Quimian buzzers, who combined their mental energies to form a hive mind of moderate intelligence, but who singly had all the intellect of a Gowachian butcher-female. He was deeply aroused by the mass of flickering rainbow lights known as the Gregorian Dimensoid, of whom it was rightly said lived in several space-timer spheres at once. He was definitely interested in the black, furry, innocently warlike Rumlians, who sat nearby consuming plate after plate of bloody, raw meat, unmindful of the terrible stains they were making on the tables. He refrained from chucking his preferences to the winds and impaling himself on the mighty horns of the naked, red Beelzebub from Planet 666. He was somewhat stimulated by the disembodied voice of the Harris, whom no one ever saw but everyone had to pay attention to, but gradually lost interest due to the lack of visuals. He was somewhat impressed by the massive mammaries held in check by the heated brass bras worn by the deliciously wicked Walkyries of Nibelungen, but was quickly distracted by the ethereal androgynous monks of Thelonius, who for some reason preferred to consume their lettuce wrapped between some ground meat and a bun. His crown rustled when the granite-faced Sirens of Ironeous Pyrate approached, his branches trembled at the presence of the elevated three-headed eels from Fascistville, and his roots actually began to scrape markings into the tile as he caught the aroma of the dandy Dandelions of Kinkdom, but in the end thought they were too prissy. There just wasn't enough status in catching any one of those fine upstanding creatures in public to satisfy the ego driving his passion. He thought that perhaps he should hide in some of the out-of-the-way corridors where the rationalization "what-the-heck-nobody's-going-to-care-anyway" might inspire him into taking some action, but then he controlled himself with the stern observation that he had his diplomatic standing to consider. No, it had to be someone worthy of him, or, as difficult as it may have been to accept under the prodding, constantly prodding, eternally prodding circumstances, no one at all.

That meant his fodder-brother had to be strictly of the human variety. Did he dare? Did he possess the fiber inside his bark not just to think about it, but to go ahead and do it?

Yes!

Turning his attention to the many humans sitting at the tables, he realized they represented many factions of humanoid Federation society. Previously he had considered them all much the same, believing that once you had radar-sensed one human, you had radar-sensed them all. Besides, they were famous throughout the galaxy as one of the primary causes of interplanetary pollution. But now he perceived in their masses a distinct predilection for individuality that was not only foreign to his own kind, but perhaps verged on the criminal. Some of the people he scanned were human, some had evolved above or below humanity, while others were genetically engineered offshoots. In fact, now that he had considered the matter, he realized how difficult it was to generalize about humanity, due to the individuality of its members.

But it didn't take the ambassador long to realize that he especially liked the ones wearing the uniforms. In fact, it took only fifteen minutes of concentrated scanning. The ones in the uniforms walked so straight and proud, dealt so properly with the other ambassadors, and always promptly obeyed the commands of their superior officers, never deviating from past modes of thinking—characteristics that evoked more memories of the Ho-Ho-Kusian behavior than those of the other abominations from the animal kingdom he had been forced to deal with on this ship.

If only there weren't so many humans to choose from. How could he be sure that he wouldn't be wooing someone beneath his station?

And then, suddenly, without warning, the answer hit him like a flash of lightning at high noon! The only possible animal for him approached with a group of other officers. The animal carried a tray holding a reconstituted boysenberry pot pie, a Mandovian fruit and protein salad (with those peculiar purple worms, still alive and writhing, just the way gourmets preferred them), three slices of rainbow bread, a glass of red-hot, bubbling lava coffee, a glass of cold water for a chaser, and a heaping plateful of sugar cookies for dessert. The odors disgusted the ambassador even as they enticed him, and proved this was the sort of meal only an utterly self-confident animal would select for consumption. They demonstrated that the object of his desire was worthy.

How the ambassador's sapfiber throbbed with its reception of sensory input when the animal of his desire sat with his friends at a table near his hiding place among the potted plastic plants. He paid very little attention to the animal's friends—merely noting that one appeared to be a skinny male with dead green protein fibers for a crown; another a gray-haired Xanthippian who carried a broadsword and wore her breasts bare and scarified; another a purple-skinned finhead with green spots on his face and on his webbed hands; and the last a four-armed, six-eyed man three meters tall and five meters wide, whose ancestors had doubtlessly been genetically altered to live on a world of heavy gravity. Nothing the matter with those folks, the Ho-Ho-Kusian ambassador observed, it was just that in the presence of *him!* their sensuous virtues receded into Motesville.

The ambassador restrained himself with difficulty as the animal ate. How strange and perverted the act of eating was, how direct and gauche in comparison with the simple nicety of transporting nutrients through your roots, so the stuff you didn't need stayed outside your body where it belonged. And yet the ambassador could not help but wonder what inner perversions were indicated by the undeniable fact that watching the animal accidentally spill a trickle of coffee from the side of his mouth and chew his boysenberry pot pie with his mouth open, spitting out a crumb here and there as he spoke, fueled his passions.

And what words of wisdom this magnificent beast was spouting, almost as a matter of course! Observations such as "I don't know what this galaxy is coming to these days. It's getting so you can't tell the stigmatas from the viral infections!" and "But I was so much older then; I'm younger than that now." fascinated the ambassador. "Look at her! That thing she's mooning over isn't

163

even human! I don't know if civilization can tolerate that kind of behavior much longer!'' and "This synthe-sugar is the pits!" bedazzled the ambassador. And when the object of his desire finally said, "No one worth his salt ever dies on his homeworld," it was all the ambassador could do to further restrain himself. So he didn't.

"Admiral Boink!" he screamed from his augmented translator speaker. "Prepare yourself for ecstasy!"

The admiral screamed. The admiral struggled, as the ambassador had known he would. The struggles only increased the ambassador's probing frenzy. The struggles were in vain, in any case. Already the tip of the ambassador's taproot was working its way into the admiral's mouth, and the admiral was helpless against the approximately three hundred pounds of passionate ambassador pressing him down on the floor.

"Oh, baby, oh, baby, oh, baby," said the ambassador. "You're the best! You're the best!"

"Mmmmuuuuppphhhhhh!" replied the admiral, digging his fingernails into the taproot and trying to scrape away shivers.

"Baby oh baby oh baby oh baby—I want you so bad!"

"Mmmmmuuuuuppphhhhh!"

The ambassador was vaguely aware that the other humans who had been sitting with the admiral were now trying to pry them apart. The one genetically adapted for heavy gravity, in particular, made the most spectacular effort, by climbing upon a distant table, taking a running jump, and flying headfirst through the air, in order to strike headfirst like a cannonball. The effort succeeded—up to a point. The human's head buried itself five inches into the stalk, and as the impact put the whammy onto the human, now there were two people to try to pry away from the ambassador.

The ambassador didn't care what they did. In a few more minutes his tertiary roots would become inexorably intertwined with the admiral's blood vessels, and in a few moments after that the ambassador would feel the first tentacles of the admiral's mind make their way into his consciousness. Oh, what ecstasy, what glorious bliss! Already the ambassador sensed the defiance, the hatred, the individuality, and he quickly became certain he was on the verge of encountering the most fruitful, unprecedented subidentity in the long—but admittedly rather boring history of his species.

But wait— What was that?

Yes—*that!* A ghostly demisemiquaver drifting across the subterranean plane just on the edge of his tormented, distracted consciousness. That diminuendo waving "hi-there". That brash quaver. Those notes and others forming a machine bursting through the seven veils of his desire to make a cord that struck his consciousness with the impact of a thunder laser fired from an orbiting destruct station.

The ambassador became dizzy. Vaguely he felt the humans pull him away from the helpless admiral. He was embarrassed to think that all those strangers were seeing his naked roots limp and dripping with fluids, but that was okay, the embarrassment was nothing in comparison to the sublime music, that sheer sonic beauty sorting out sections of eternity and tossing them into the air in ephemeral packages that dissipated more quickly than he wished—but dissipated only to make room for the next little package.

The ambassador focused his radar senses just enough to make out a hairy humanoid creature with some kind of machine instead of a head. The creature appeared to be playing the instrument from an orifice in the center of his chest. As for what had happened to the unholy desire that had been adversely influencing the ambassador's behavior—well, suddenly that behavior and the reasons for it had become immaterial. The passion had dissipated like a ghost torn apart in a tornado. The ambassador had thoughts only for the music, for the beautiful, glorious, spectacular, extremely swell music.

Then suddenly, without warning, the creature playing the soprano saxophone exploded.

Chapter Eleven
Desolation Row

WHILE GETTING dressed, I protested to Miss Hazard and my jailor that I was still too limp to walk, that the only decent thing they could do under the circumstances was to let me rest in my cell for a week or two, as a reward for a performance above and beyond the call of duty.

But they ordered me escorted out of their lives anyway, by two stone-faced studs who took me through a series of corridors and elevators that was, on the surface of things, impossible to differentiate from the path my feminine companions had guided me over earlier. However, this time there was a sinister purposefulness to the direction, one that always seemed to be going down. It went down for a long time. My abortive speculations about the tesseract partially folded into the fourth dimension returned, but ultimately provided me with precious little distraction from my fears concerning my impending fate.

Somewhere along the way, at an elevator which looked no different from the previous one, or the one before that, my escorts decided the time had come to blindfold me. "Is this really necessary?" I asked, wondering if there was any significance to be found in the fact that as the elevator went down, the temperature steadily went up. "I don't have eyes in the back of my head."

One escort snorted contemptuously. As opposed to the amused snort from the other. The contemptuous one said, "We hate to disappoint you, but perversions of the sordid nature we assume you are referring to are not permitted in Kemp City."

"I see. Your city only permits wholesome perversions."

"What city doesn't?" said the amused one.

"An interesting question, considering what I've just been through."

It must have been something I said. One of them promptly shoved me into the nearest wall. I took the hint and, after the elevator reached its destination, dutifully permitted myself to be led through the next series of winding corridors. Judging from the slightly muffled noise of the city machinery, the corridor walls were thin partitions and nothing more.

Finally one of the guards stopped me by digging his fingers several inches into my shoulder. I stood and waited as I heard keys jingle before unlocking a door, heard the rusty hinges creak, and heard spiritually desolate people groan and moan as if they had been trapped at a funeral with no conclusion in sight. A prophetic metaphor. My escorts removed the blindfold. I was facing a horde of emaciated, half-naked men and women whose various skin tones, total lack of deliberate scarification, and various wounds in various states of healing or infection indicated they had been captured or indentured from a variety of cities. Many had a strange, odious yellow fungus growing on their skin. They were chained to the dimly-lit walls of a dank dungeon where the sounds of the city walking pealed like the eternal approach of a monolithic deity. To make conditions even more subhuman here, the plumbing was obviously a problem, as many of the prisoners were sitting in their own excrement. Ventilation was practically nonexistent; the odors were so thick you could practically swim through them.

"Welcome to Desolation Row," said the amused guard.

I turned to face him, squinting my eyes to help them adjust to the sudden onslaught of light that originated behind him, above his head. The resulting optical illusion only made him seem more formidable, more of a force than a human being. I screwed up my courage nonetheless, and sneered, "Thanks, Fido. Have I told you lately you're nothing but a hound dog? You never caught no rabbit and you ain't no friend of mine."

The amused one wasn't so amused, but the contemptuous one was. He grinned contemptuously. "Why *thank* you, little man. It's nice to know my partner's appreciated." He turned to him. "I think our little man here has earned the right to go to the head of the line, don't you?"

"What?" I asked. "And deprive myself of this bouquet of odors?"

The amused one nodded, and before long I was chained by the wrists to the wall at the far end of the dungeon, sitting in the excrement of my predecessors. Beside me was a red-haired young man whose stubble was almost orange, save for the places where it was infected with the yellow fungus. He had pale white skin, wore a tattered olive-colored uniform, was barefoot—his boots had probably been "liberated"—and appeared considerably stronger than most of the other unfortunates in this place. He stared in some surprise at my audacity as I waved my fingers bye-bye at my escorts as they closed the rusty door behind them.

"Toodles," I called out. "And don't forget to take your shots once a day—otherwise your milkmen will turn green and fall off."

Those few prisoners who could hear me over the noise stared stone-faced at me. "I guess it makes sense," said an old man three people down. "What else has he got to lose by now?" He pointedly averted his eyes when I attempted to return his stares.

So did the others, even though they hadn't said anything. I had seen eyes like theirs before, belonging to the Zorians who had spent fifty years in the Benzian concentration camps, and to the Pantamonian species who served as morning snacks to their Shovelhead predators. These were the eyes of those without hope, who had only the coming of the Great Leveler to look forward to. The brief fantasies I had entertained about engineering an escape evaporated like morning dew. Surely many of these people had begun their tenure here with hopes similar to my own, and surely their spirits had been broken like snail shells ground beneath an iron heel.

"You're in for it now," said the young man beside me cheerfully, adjusting his translator with difficulty. His metal bonds cut into his wrist as he strained to reach the back of his head. I saw at once that his eyes shined more brightly than the others'. It was apparent that, unlike the others, he had resolved to face the inevitable, when it came, with as much cheer and good faith as he could muster. The situation wouldn't be serious until it was over. Whatever opportunity for escape or simple defiance came his way, he would take it gladly.

"You mean things could get worse? Mister, I'm not sure you can guess what I've already been into today—uh, *through* today!"

"Permit me a guess," he said, flashing a debonair grin. "She was built like a hydro-neutron generator, and refused to undress her nipples."

"How did you know?"

He answered with a wider grin. "That'll be Norma Jean. Of her it is truly said that she'll teach a man everything he needs to know, but she herself still has so very, very much to learn."

"That's the one, exactly."

A hideous, bloodcurdling scream, easily heard over the din of the city footsteps, rose through the metal floor like the call of a chain saw from the lowest level of Hell.

The young man's eyebrows rose and fell as he smiled wickedly. "Your fate beckons. It is my fate too, but you shall suffer it first. Norma Jean and Miss Hazard must have thought you were a dangerous man to keep around.

Who knows? Perhaps they thought that your skills at the fine art of amour, if they became known, would set a bad precedent for all. For this possible reason I am pleased to meet you. My name is Alejó."

"Hunter. Homer B. Hunter."

"That is a mighty long name, Hunter-Homer-B-Hunter. What city do you hail from?"

"One that's bigger than this, I assure you. I'd gladly share the info with you, but I've been sworn to secrecy, upon pain of forfeiting my pension. It's safe to say, though, you'll be finding out about my hometown and others like it soon enough."

"How soon?"

"Enough—I hope."

He nodded to himself, though whether he was actively mulling over my information or my optimism I cannot say. "Bigger than Kemp City?" he asked. "No wonder your words indicate a hope for a rescue. Though I must confess, the leaders of your city must be of a frame of mind substantially different from those of any I've ever encountered before, if they would risk battle for the welfare of a single citizen."

"All for one, and one for all. That's what my leaders always say, sometimes."

"Ridiculous," he said easily. "I hail from the rogue of Tabu Ley, myself. Tabu Ley boasts more cannons than either Kemp or Helms or Kirkpatrick or Deaver or any other city of the Clausewitzian clan, yet due to its sheer size alone Kemp is among the most formidable on the planet. Kemp could become a rogue at any time and have a good chance at long-term survival."

"Rogue? Do you mean 'rogue' as in 'nonaligned'?"

"That's what I think I said. Your city must be pretty isolated, though, if you haven't heard of the rogue Tabu Ley, whose exploits . . ."

May be interesting, but aren't important now. Alejó was eager to talk with someone who was eager to listen. The obscene conditions, the fact of his imminent death, and the certain knowledge that it would be prolonged, horrible and painful—these things he could deal with quite manfully. Clearly he was emotionally prepared to face such an ending. It was the loneliness he could not endure, and in me he had a captive audience.

I was only too glad to listen. I could have endured a wait through Desolation Row, knowing if nothing else that if everyone before me held out long enough, I'd be rescued without having to orchestrate a daring plan of escape. But being at the front of the line severely limited the number of potential cliff-hangers. Alejó's conversation was exactly what I needed. So we talked, often about the first thing that came to mind, while we and everybody else did our best to ignore the continuous screams from the poor bozo below.

From Alejó I learned that all the cities I'd encountered thus far belonged to three separate clans. Each clan had a different social structure, with different religious beliefs, style of government, and moral codes regulating the daily behavior of the individual. Each clan had its own clearly defined hierarchy, with each city taking its own clearly defined position in a system that, I learned, was not unlike that of a feudal chain of command. The lower cities on the totem poles theoretically served the ruler cities in a vassallike capacity; lower cities "donated" whatever raw materials and foodstuffs and other goods the higher cities might require. In exchange the higher cities provided the lower cities with what scientific expertise was required to keep their machinery in working order.

It sounded simple enough on the surface of things, but naturally there were complications. The higher cities in the clans really didn't possess scientific expertise—their people had the same low level of comprehension of the technology at hand as did the general population. The higher cities' computers simply had data banks that were easier to gain access to, either because a handful of the workers had a better idea of what to do, or because the city had managed to jury-rig better solutions to the computer's circuitry or mechanical breakdowns in the past.

Information enabled the city workers to keep the mechanics of their own cities in better working condition, and hence enabled them to better maintain the life-style to which they had sworn religious fidelity.

I surmised that Walkers, such as the Heechie-Heechie tribe, were the descendants of those whose city had been totalled, either through battle or through a simple series of ordinary breakdowns that the scientists and engineers, if you could call them that, weren't able to deal with. I also surmised that the reason for this chaotic state of affairs had to with the peoples' utter lack of the scientific method. All those I'd met thus far, including Alejó, accepted those philosophical concepts given to them and had no interest in seeing for themselves if what they had been taught regarding the maintenance of the cities was true. When push came to shove, a state of affairs I was given to understand could have vastly unpleasant repercussions, so far as a city's way of life was concerned, they were more inclined to assume that faith, as opposed to common sense, would see them through.

This state of affairs indicates why the clan-vassal system, which should have been fairly straightforward, was in reality just another facet of a complex, not always logical, system of social behavior. The higher cities spent just as much time mining raw materials and bartering with the Walkers as the lower cities did, and were very reluctant to share information or loan out scientists and engineers even to members of their own clan. Sometimes one of the capacities of a higher city broke down, and the so-called great minds were unable to remedy the problem. That was because the so-called great minds, in my opinion, acted and, most importantly, *thought* more like religious leaders than they did scientific leaders, and hence sometimes had no choice but to ask a lower city of the clan for assistance, thus providing the lower city with the opportunity for advancement in many ways. If the lower city couldn't advance up the hierarchy, then at the very least it could extract great favors, in the present or the future, from the higher city.

Evidently obligations were costly things on this world. No city whose leadership was in its right mind wanted to incur them any more than was necessary. That was why some cities, if the scientific leadership had some vague glimmering of how a half-valid scientific method should function, went the rogue route. They set their societies philosophically adrift. They cut their social mores loose. They let time and creativity determine their beliefs. They did it to be free.

And if they were strong enough, and clever enough, and stayed that way long enough, learning from their mistakes as well as from their victories, the rogues survived. Sometimes, if a city functioned well and was strong enough, it could start its own clan.

All this explained why Miss Hazard was only too glad to have me make repairs on Kemp City. Otherwise Kemp City would have been forced to submit to greater authority from its ruler. What if it didn't explain was why she and my jailor were so anxious to get rid of me. The reasoning, according to Alejó, was the very fact that I possessed scientific knowledge in the first place. My very abilities made me dangerous. Keeping me around would introduce an unpredictable element into the city's power structure. With a scientific mind on his side, a mutineer would have a powerful ally against incumbent leaders such as Miss Hazard.

And while of course I would be a powerful ally on the establishment's side too, rulers were known to extract definitive penalties from vassals who denied the clan use of scientific thinkers without permission.

"Right now, war is too imminent for Miss Hazard and her underlings to risk even a healthy internal social conflict, especially one having to do with the chain of command," said Alejó at some point during our conversation. "Of course, war of some sort is always imminent, but that's neither here nor there. War is a terrible thing. We cities always fight among ourselves. A skirmish here, a guerrilla offensive there. Any excuse will do. Rarely, however, does a city fight to the bitter end. Even a sorely wounded, pathetically weak city can inflict a mortal blow on a superior adversary. So often survival-oriented cities, sane cities, would rather flee and face dishonor in the present, rather than die in the future. But all-out war is different. It changes people's values, turns their sense of proportions upside down. People don't mind dying for a concept, or an ideal, or even for the old home team. Honor becomes more important than life. Entire ways of life are sacrificed to the chopping block of survival. Men and women are prepared to be stripped to naught but their honor during the last few minutes of their existence.

"As for the underlying reasons behind the current pending war, this escalation—well, it can do me no harm now to admit that my mission was to learn the secret reasons why relations have recently become so tense between the three clans of this continent. Because Tabu Ley is a rogue, we can only obtain tidbits of political intrigue by spying or by torturing our prisoners. But our council is wise, and the hermaphrodites who form our council know, thanks to bitter experience, that only to satiate their blind, unthinking lust for power will the clans risk everything. Their rulers have believed, in any case, that not to risk all for power will mean losing what power they have for certain."

Suddenly, something Alejó had said a moment earlier pricked at my mind. "Wait a moment. Could you run by that Tabu Ley council section again? The part about the hermaphrodites?"

Alejó blinked. "It is our way—the most civilized Tabu Ley has found, after many generations of both sane and outré experimentation. Long ago, the people of Tabu Ley learned that council members tend to serve the whole of the city best when they are neither fish nor fowl, but switch hitters of the most profound sort. Hermaphrodites may be many things, they may have many suppressed passions and regrets, but we know they will never lose their heads from a severe case of the humors. We of Tabu Ley cannot permit our survival to depend upon those whose rationality is so susceptible to emotional turmoil."

"So are you a hermaphrodite, Alejó?"

And at this he laughed uproariously, laughed as hard as he could, until he became too weak to laugh further. "Oh, that's too painful. Such a delicate little wit you possess, my friend, Hunter-Homer-B-Hunter. In fact, you may be among the finest specimens of humanity it has ever been my good fortune to meet. Indeed, I think one can safely say you are like a stream of wombat urine—that is to say, a shaft of light that glows when all else around it is dark."

Normally I resent being favorably compared to wombat urine. But something about Alejó's casual tone made me like it, just the way I liked him. "Does anybody watch out for rogues? Fellow rogue cities, perhaps?"

"No one protects a rogue, not even other rogues. It is against the code. Why should such a city enter agreements with others? For that reason, we would never consign a man with a brain like yours to Desolation Row. We would have great need of a man with scientific knowledge. Either that, or we would cut out your brain and eat it, so we too may someday be as smart." He pointed, as best he could, to the fungus on his face. "Nor do prisoners suffer such terrible conditions before they die inside Tabu Ley. A man being sent to his certain doom must be treated with a fair amount of respect. Never would we permit the dungeon to be infected with this discharge fungus."

"How long were you down here before you became infected?"

He shrugged. "Eight sunrises, possibly nine. That's not much time. Normally a downer would last a month, or even two, but Desolation Row's been working overtime. Kemp City must be having some problems they didn't trust you to fix. It doesn't matter. All die in the Desolation Pits eventually."

"And I'm next?"

He nodded sadly.

The screams below abruptly ceased.

"It was nice knowing you," Alejó said.

My two favorite escorts returned, this time wearing transparent plastic protective coverings augmented by gas masks.

"There's no use struggling," Alejó called out as I resisted their efforts to drag me toward the shaft opening up in the wall. I punched, smacked, kicked, bit, and cursed, all without the slightest regard for preserving my dignity, but the guards laughed sadistically and threw me into a blackness permeated by the worst stench that I had ever encountered. "Eat yellow death, seducer of morons!" the amused one screamed as I dropped.

The hole irised closed and the blackness became total. I tried to think. Tried to relax. And then I remembered what Alejó said. Downers normally last one month or two. *That means the fall is survivable. Of course they've been using them up fast! Maybe the landing is part of it. Relax—get a grip on yourself. Fear ... fear is the—!*

But before I could remember what fear was, I came out of the blackness and landed. Some time later I woke up and rolled out of the heavily cushioned hammock that had caught me. I realized my landing would have been quite comfortable, if I hadn't struck the dead man who had been lying on the hammock, that is. He must have been sleeping there when he died. His entire body was covered with the yellow fungus. The fungus even permeated his ragged loin cloth.

I threw up on the floor. My body felt better, but I knew the smell of my vomit would soon make it feel worse. I seriously doubted I'd be able to clean up my mess. The Kempians weren't likely to keep housewares and supplies down here. I got a grip on myself.

A tiny grip, but still a grip.

I forced myself to take a look at the premises.

If I'd ever had any doubt these cities had been built by aliens whose scope of knowledge humbled the combined accomplishments of any sixteen species in the Federation, then my first view of the Kempian energy-reclamation center completely neutralized it. I couldn't resist wondering which dimension I'd been folded into this time.

For although the area was supposed to be the groin of the Kemp City, while in its canine configuration anyway, it appeared to stretch straight ahead for over a kilometer's distance. The walls behind me and to either side were obscured by the haze of a pervasive yellow mist. The chill in my bones and the curious sense of disassociation my mind felt from my body were two solid indicators that the paths one might take toward a wall, any wall, would be filled with fancy and illusion, particularly when it came to navigating the shortest distance between two points. On that score the machinery floating in the air could serve as a guide, but nothing more.

The colors of the machinery continuously shifted from one shade of the rainbow to the next, with no discernible pattern. The machines were molded in the forms of classical geometric figures—that is to say, convex polyhedrons, polygons, polyhedra, intersecting circles, parallel planes, right triangles, squares, Möbius strips, convex domes, and spherical triangles, not to mention several shapes that I'd previously believed could only be represented by algebraic equations. Some of the shapes were two-dimensional, and some three, but without exception their exterior planes were perfectly smooth, providing me with not a single clue, at least at first, as to what equipment might be inside, or for what purpose. The only thing I could be sure of in this place was that my inevitable death would cause me a lot of pain. My only hope was to survive for as long as possible, a feat that seemed problematic, since if volume and distance were distorted in this environment, it stood to reason that the flow of time was too. What might seem like weeks in here could, in reality, be only a few minutes outside. And the opposite could equally be true, when and if the fates dictated it.

I shall omit the account of exactly how I found the stack of my dead predecessors in various states of being eaten away by the fungus; of how I found the consoles in the mist and deduced it was my job to push buttons when certain lights switched on, and how delay would gradually expose me to more spores of the yellow fungus; or even of exactly how I deduced the unearthly machinery floating overhead constituted a sophisticated fission machine that captured the city's waste and converted its atoms into usable fuel. It is enough to say that I did all these things, and had every confidence I could delay the onslaught of the yellow fungus for some time, if I kept my mind right, and if the supplies of food and water that came to me via a network of dumbwaiters properly provided for my health. A great deal of time passed during this period—maybe not so much as the outside world was concerned, but it seemed like weeks to me, weeks during which I thought I would go mad with boredom.

It is far more important to skip directly to the point when I realized that the negative ion concentrations in the air were gradually causing me to hallucinate. It wouldn't be long before my powers of reasoning—the very skills I had depended upon to stay alive this long in the game— would be the very next thing to turn against me. There was no hope—not even the hope of hope! I was surely doomed.

I plopped down on the floor and buried my face in my hands. At that moment there was nothing I wouldn't have given to have my mind back the way I remembered it. My hand itched terribly. At first I couldn't bring myself to look at it, for fear the first inklings of the fungus—the dreaded yellow peril itself—would be between my fingers, or under my nails, or in a wrinkle on my palm. When at last I screwed up the courage, and saw that at worst it was just a little dirty thanks to the unhygenic conditions of my imprisonment, I seriously doubted my own eyesight. Perhaps I feared the truth, so my instincts deliberately withheld it from me.

Without giving the matter another thought, I buried

my face in my hands and wept. For how long I cannot say.

"Tsk, tsk. I must say you're a serious disappointment to me."

I looked up fearfully, and nearly fainted in shock. It was Floyd!

I scooted back, nearly tipping over a geodesic spittoon in the process. "No! It's impossible! I can't be seeing you! I'm wide awake!"

"Kinda depends on your point of view, doesn't it?" he replied.

I reached out to touch him. My hands passed through his body. Either that, or my hands became unreal the moment they touched him. "Look, if you've come here to tell me again you're still alive, you can forget it. I've got more pressing matters on my mind—like the possibility that I'll soon be joining you."

"I must say, I'm disappointed in you. You're certainly not acting like a man who's got a job to do."

"And why should I? There's no way out and I'm dying of an incurable disease."

"Maybe, maybe not."

"You're just splitting hairs. I'm doomed no matter how long it is."

"Time slows down in fission fields, so maybe you only think a vast amount of time has passed. In the real world, maybe you've only been here a few minutes."

"Terrific. You have no idea how much better that makes me feel."

"Homer, I'm shocked. Stunned, even. Son, big stuff is happening out there. I don't know what it is, but you've got to brace up before you wind up like that stack of indentured button pushers. Look at that dead meat rotting over there! What an unhygenic way to run a fission generator!"

"Floyd, what are you talking about? You're just a disembodied mind on a spiritual plane who can't do anything, and pretty soon I'm going to be a disembodied mind too, and I won't be able to do anything either. Ergo, we're both stuck in definitive ruts."

"Hmmm. Your sense of humor is gone. You are in bad shape."

"You'd rather I tell a few sick jokes?"

"Double hmmmm. It probably wouldn't hurt if you faced the end with a stiff upper lip. It might help keep your mind clear enough to think of a way out of this predicament."

"Maybe that's the problem, Floyd. I'm not a hero, I'm just an ordinary guy. I can't pull some spectacular escape plan out of my anal orifice."

"Even an ordinary person should feel some determination. You should be consumed with desire to escape at any cost, so you can go wufta-fufta with Reina. Because let's face it, you're in this jam partially because you got a super dose of angst in your pants. . . ."

"And it looks like I'm going to die with angst in my pants too. I can't be a hero. I can't even measure up as an ordinary guy."

"What about that world you saved? That space station you deactivated? With the help of yours truly!"

"They don't count because I really don't have any logical choice but to do exactly what I did. Anything less would have meant my death."

"Homer, you pathetic loon, think of the heroes you had as a youth."

"You mean for example Captain Fuzzbox, aka the Brain from Planet Erroneous?"

"That's right. I know from peeking between the cracks of your mind that Captain Fuzzbox is the cyborg who rescued an entire planet from a nova by inventing a machine that vibrated it into another dimension. He and the planet were never seen again, but they definitely survived."

"Well, that's how the subsequent holodramas depicted it, but no one can say with certainty why he exiled an entire planet in order to save it."

"Stop equivocating. Think of all the other heroes

you had instead, and how much their exploits once meant to you."

"Golly, I haven't given them serious consideration in years. Like Sir Alice Innes. I used to admire his sly way around an interplanetary bargaining table. Never did figure out if he was a boy or a girl, but what a diplomat, what a mind! Remember how he outwitted the Bonzian Thugees by infecting the Bonzian atmosphere with a plague virus that turned the Thugees' peculiar hair into sponge cake?"

"A real hero," said Floyd, nodding approvingly. "Definitely someone to admire."

"There were so many. Professor Jameson, 'Immortal' Sam Reed, Gilbert Gosseyn, the Star Mouse, Jay Score, James T. Burp, all old, dead, or practically forgotten today. Nobody remembers them any more, except as characters in holodocudramas. I bet I'm one of the last Gallians who remembers Willie the Gib, the power junkie who discovered the secret psychic world of computers. Though I imagine quite a few still recall Double O Pi, so designated because he's the interplanetary spy whose exploits stretch into infinity. Sigh. Would you say my hero worship was one of the reasons why I joined the Stellar Patrol?"

"That, and the fact you were due to be drafted into local service anyway."

"Yeah, because the Patrol Board thought my genetic structure resembled that of 'Fightin' Butch' Hunter, the old fart! I've met a planetload of would-be heroes in the Stellar Patrol. They discovered the majority of their shifts would be spent doing work the Federation would have robots doing if humans weren't cheaper. Then like myself they discovered all their old heroes—and the new, younger, brasher heroes—resemble everyone else in the universe in that they're chock-full of bipedal foibles. A lot of heroes are tyrannical, selfish, bigoted, immature, egotistical to the max, narrow-minded, extremist, paranoid, schizophrenic, sexually insecure, and blessed with a sense of humor approximately half-witted—if they're lucky.

These people aren't heroes, they're simply plain bozos with a smattering of talent that happened to be useful whenever they stumbled into trouble they were doing their best to avoid. What's heroic about that?"

"That's your problem, in a craniumshell," said Floyd with a sad shake of his head. "It's a question of attitude. When the rings were down, did it really matter that Captain Fuzzbox liked to swig a quart of oil before he closed down for the evening? Or that he liked to watch humans do the wufta-fufta with gaseous creatures? The point is that when a planet needed him, he didn't walk away like he could have, but accepted that sometimes a cyborg's gotta do what a cyborg's programmed to do! Does it really matter that Sir Alice Innes's hobby was to plumb whatever kinds of depths he could get his or her self into? The fact remains he successfully humiliated over a hundred species for the good of humanity. And what about that old vainglorious Double O Pi himself? It was more than just his job for Double O Pi to annihilate those vampires from another galaxy, and those Com Symps from Aikora G, or those sun smashers from M-Thirty-three, not to mention those nitrous globules who decimated the IQs of everyone in three systems, and those— Forget it, you know what I mean. None of these cyborgs or bipeds were heroes twenty-four hours a day. Most of the time they were trapped being normal. That's where you come in."

"Oh, now I see what we're really talking about. Floyd, I am going to die soon. Besides, even if it were possible to do something about your predicament, I wouldn't know where to begin. You're on one plane, I'm on another, and only through the seven barriers of death shall the two planes converge."

"Really, then how do you explain my presence here now?"

"Because, Floyd, I'm hallucinating. And the reason why is because I'm at death's very hatch! And I have to tell you that, even though I am hallucinating, I still haven't gotten used to your somewhat more sophisticated way of expressing yourself!"

"That's all right—neither have I. I have learned, however, that I had always been programmed to speak the way I do now. It's just that the program was latent, and simply could not come forth until the programmed conditions came about. What those conditions might have been, I've no idea—I haven't been able to access that portion of my data banks. But of this I'm sure—the illusion of my simplemindedness was part of some diabolical scheme of galactic proportions! The game's afoot, Homer, and in some way I've yet to fathom, the fate of humanity itself may be at stake!"

"Say what—?"

"But he was gone. I sighed. By now I was several degrees removed from despair, but was still fairly depressed about how matters stood. I couldn't help thinking, however, about what Floyd had said about the real-life characters of my childhood heroes, as opposed to my idealized versions, and how their experiences applied directly to mine.

And of course, there was that plot of galactic proportions, with the fate of humanity at stake, to worry about. No matter how badly I wanted to concentrate on my own sorry end, my mind kept returning to the question: How could a robot whose simplemindedness was part of a programmed illusion be involved in a galactic conspiracy? It was unfortunate I was unlikely to find out.

Suddenly a bolt of approximately five hundred laserium units of firepower hit the recycling center, and the floor dropped out from under me.

Chapter Twelve
The Big Ruckus

I FOUND MYSELF speeding through the air. The massive right hind leg of Kemp City suddenly loomed large before me. The shock waves from the blast had sent me hurtling, along with several tons of other debris, toward the leg like a missile. If I didn't do something quickly, my head was going to be cracked open against it like an eggshell!

I managed to twist just enough to hit the city's knee joint with my shoulder, breaking my trajectory just enough, and must have blacked out instantly from the pain. For a few timeless moments later, I awoke on the old green grass, while debris from the laserium blast still fell around me. Every nerve in my body throbbed with serious pain, but I believed that unless I had some internal injuries, I would live to regret the suffering I'd be enduring in the near future.

Above me a Kempian dangled from the hole in the dungeon floor. Steaming purple waste fluids trickled from pipes that had been shorn off from the blast, and torn conduits of wires buzzed and crackled. One of the wires accidentally grazed the man, frying him to a crispy critter in an instant. Those who had been trying to assist him, but were too wounded or deep in shock to be of much value, watched in helpless horror.

Watching the fluids strike the ground, singeing the grass before dissolving holes in the soil, I was struck by the overwhelming fear that I'd passed through a stream of the stuff, and that I was too deep in shock to grok I had a missing limb or two. A quick visual recon, however, indicated none of me had dissolved in a puddle of alien fluids. My pain was due strictly to burns, bruises, a possible dislocated shoulder, a twisted ankle, and probably a few things I hadn't diagnosed yet. My clothing smoldered; black wisps of smoke rose from the stitching. Another nanosecond in the forefront of the heat and I'd have gone nova. As things stood now, I'd live, but only if I hauled butt before Kemp City started walking again. . . .

Or before its attacker took another shot.

A hind foot passed high above as I weaved through the contaminated area. The smell of the charred flesh strewn around sickened me. If I hadn't been residing in the fission area at the time of the blast, I might have ended up like those poor bozos—raw material for whatever vulture and rat analogues exited on this world. I felt sorrier for those strewn about who were still living, especially since I couldn't afford to linger around to perform first aid. The borderline cases would just have to die. I ran a hundred meters away from the city and took a dive behind a fungoid bush with green and purple flowers. I tied not to sneeze.

Kemp City took great strides away from me. From my current perspective, the dead and the injured seemed very insignificant indeed, like fleas that had been shaken to the ground. I savored the relief of it; at least I'd survived for the time being, the threat of the yellow fungus notwithstanding.

Kemp City's cannons fired systematically at seven-hundred-laserium capacity toward a distant hill, evidently aiming at the aggressor hiding on the other side. I wagered the opening blast had been meant as a sneak attack. Miss Hazard, or whoever was in charge, wasn't wasting much time being subtle. On the other side of the hill, the earth spewed high up in the air like smokestack lightning, fanning out as it fell in a series of brown and black circles.

The quickness of Kemp's movements surprised me. While crashing the swap meet, it had lumbered like a New Hyperborean Man of Bronze come to life. Now it was moving nearly twice as fast, at a near canter that caused the earth to rumble with every step. The air was raped by every blast of those persistent laser cannons.

Things happened fast. Before Kemp City had taken seven steps, the sizzling noise of the laser blasts were augmented by a distant series of explosions, and vast plumes of black smoke rose like jet streams from the other side of the hill. From the series of laser blasts in reply, it appeared that however much the aggressor may be injured, it was still chock-full of fight. The blasts all vied for a direct hit on Kemp City, but thanks to the zigzag route it took, only glancing blows were struck.

Glancing, but still devastating.

People screamed. Fires erupted. A trail of waste fluid left its mark like a scar across the ground.

The laser blasts that completely missed their targets blew trees and mushrooms and shrubbery high in the air, left charred craters, and started a number of small brushfires that would soon become a single formidable inferno. Already the wind was picking up, as if in anticipation.

The only sane thing to do was to get as far away from the battle as possible. But I couldn't afford to do the sane thing.

I scurried behind trees or mushrooms or big chunks of metal, using even dead bodies as momentary cover, but instead of vamoosing for parts unknown like a certified biped, I headed for Kemp, the big city already lumbering on all fours to the top of the hill. I had to know who had attacked, and had to learn, if possible, if the aggressor was one of the cities I'd already encountered. I couldn't decide who I should be concerned about most—Reina or Oliver.

"Wait!" someone said in a hoarse croak as I ducked

beneath the branches of a chartreuse willow tree with some dead limbs flickering with tiny flames. Only my lingering twinges of guilt caused me to look at who it was.

Alejó. Lying on the ground, his torn clothes smoldering, his naked leg covered with second-degree burns, a bruise already forming on his upper right arm where the bone was probably broken, his face as pale as ivory. He lay like a rag doll amid the broken branches he had taken with him when the force of the blast propelled him through the willow tree. "Wait for me, friend," he managed to say.

Yes, I realized, *he is my friend, or as close as I'm going to get to one on this crazy planet.* I hadn't even thought about him since being thrown down the shaft, because I'd never expected to see him again. I rushed to him and like a jerk tentatively touched his arm; he yelped in pain. "I'll come back for you, I promise."

"I know you will, but I must come with you anyway." He flashed his patented debonair grin. I envied his bravery, his ability to smile despite his agony. And I realized again how much I liked him.

"Take it easy," I said. "I'll be back."

"No. I have to see the fight. You don't understand. It's my job to find out who's been fighting whom. Besides, it could be that war's already broken out."

"So? There's nothing we can do about it. And if you ask me, you don't look like you can take a Sunday stroll without shuffling off."

"I can make it."

"I don't think you can."

"Just fucking trust me, will you?" The actual sound of his obscenity, as opposed to the translation in my mind, was a cross between a traditional raspberry and a moan of abject pain, but such determination and inherent grit, I decided, should be rewarded.

I helped him stand and discovered, much to my surprise, that I was much weaker than I'd suspected. I was stiff, and very numb in general, except for the place inside where it felt like a chestburster was tearing out. Alejó laughed shyly; he had been forced to help me as much as I helped him. Together we limped.

Kemp City, meanwhile, had disappeared over the hill. The earth shook with frightening regularity, and horrendous blasts screamed at stratospheric volume. Plumes of smoke and dust obscured the sun and the moons and vast portions of the rings.

The rings. I hadn't noticed them earlier. The ring system from this latitude of the planet looked like some crazed sculptor had erected an orbiting plastiglass foundation and spattered it with an ocean of igneous rock, punctuated by giant gems and crystals. The jewels in the ring glittered brilliantly in the sunlight, and tinged the clouds in the sky with emerald and aquamarine colors. Speckles of white light danced across the largest and blackest of the plumes of smoke rising beyond the hill.

Alejó and I practically fell down at the top of the hill, and crawled into a tremendous divot Kemp City had made in the soil with a bit of foot action. The divot had also partially exposed the base of a boulder, thus providing us with a double dose of inadequate cover in the eventuality a stray laser blast happened to come our way.

I peeked over the boulder to see the two combatants sizing each other up, stalking one another in circles like true beasts, each waiting to see if the other had been severely crippled by the damage it had already sustained.

Kemp City was crouched like a Brobdingnagian cur in the center of a fresh crater. The tail had been shorn off, at least three plates off the back had been torn or blasted off, and the left forefoot dangled uselessly several meters above the ground. Smoke streamed from several joints, and the crackle of wayward electrical currents growled in a persistent high pitch. You would think that a fighting city in such condition would communicate an aura of desperation, but Kemp City displayed only fierce defiance. Its open mouth, the glow of its energy source inside a bright crimson, was almost contorted in a snarl. The laser cannons mounted around its neck, with soldiers strapped in their seats before the control panels, were directly trained on the foe stalking the city around the crater's rim. More than just defiant, Kemp City was also supremely confident.

The foe had easily endured as much wear and tear as Kemp City, yet strode about with equal confidence. Of course, it was a little hard to tell if the effect was deliberate or not, thanks to the city's unusual shape: the form of a medusalike starfish with legs. The large nucleus, somewhat analogous to a spider's thorax, was covered with orange and black mosaics with patterns similar to those of Dushen'ka. The myriad tentacles, which protruded at seemingly random points from the thorax, invariably ended in laser cannons. At least, those which hadn't been severed ended in cannons. A lot of tentacle pieces lay around the site, and I had no way of gauging how much the city's overall performance depended on the efficiency of each tentacle.

Of course, maybe Miss Hazard or whoever was in command of Kemp City by this point didn't know either, which was one reason why the two cities were just stalking one another right now, waiting for an opportunity to strike.

"Alejó," I asked, "who's Kemp fighting?"

"I don't know," he replied. "I haven't seen that shape before. Which is strange, because I like to think I've been around. Now be quiet. Both doubtless have radar on the lookout for the vibrations of sneak attack, and I don't want them to know we haven't run away like the rest of the surviving prisoners."

I arched an eyebrow and looked at the site of the first attack. I couldn't see anyone running away, though a few bodies were crawling about. It didn't seem like a big point, but I refrained from bringing it up because of my magnificent track record thus far in figuring out the psychology of these people. Still, I was convinced Alejó was right in principle if nothing else. The dead and wounded would gladly be running away at this very moment, if they only could.

I returned my attention to Kemp just as its foe cut loose with a barrage of laser fire. I remember thinking Kemp couldn't possibly hold its molecules together beneath the impact of such a sustained onslaught, a force I estimated at least three thousand laseriums. But Kemp managed to hold on long enough for a thin blue force field to surround it, protecting both the city walls and the laser cannons, for which I'm sure the soldiers strapped to the outside were thankful. The force field held as the onslaught of laser blasts continued unabated, but how long either city could keep up such an extensive drain on its power resources was open to question.

The Kempian soldiers on the outside were the first to begin to feel the heat under the pressure. Quieter than the protracted hissing of the laser mechanisms, quieter than the clanking and crunching of moving, ruptured parts, yet loud enough for me to imagine the entire planet had come to a halt to listen, a blood-chilling scream rang like a siren through the air. The pain of that scream froze all human feeling in my breast. I wish I could say the same thing had happened to the soldier who was screaming. Clearly he was suffering greatly. I was able to pinpoint which soldier it was because when the screaming stopped, he exploded like a wax dummy with a stick of dynamite igniting inside him. His blood and guts drenched the cannon and its control panel, but they couldn't fly through the force field. Parts of him ricocheted elsewhere, striking the nearby soldiers, but most of the blood and guts merely dripped like goo down the blue aura that had destroyed him as a by-product of trying to save him.

Two more soldiers screamed, but they seemed to be holding on longer than the exploded one had. Either that, or their frying had started on the inside and was working its way out.

"My God, why doesn't Kemp fire back?" I exclaimed.

"Because to do that, they'll have to shut down the force field for an instant," Alejó answered, "And believe me, that'll be long enough."

A soldier who wasn't screaming slumped, either unconscious or dead, and another panicked and unbuckled himself, only to fall out of his seat and become stuck between the cannon and the force field. The metal was just hot enough to ensure that he did fry.

The barrage of laser fire from the tentacled city continued unabated, without any indication it would stop in the near future. Though I realized the city's equipment must be having a terrible time holding up under the strain, I couldn't help but marvel at how well the citizens must have mastered their incomprehensible science. The aggressor city had raised ruthlessness and scientific ignorance to an art form.

Normally I wouldn't have given a damn, but this was my first surface combat, the first time I'd heard men and women scream as they died. Combat topside, in space, is a much tidier affair. Death can always be seen approaching, but when it cannot be avoided, it is swift and strikes every member of the crew equally; that is to say, everybody dies at once. Here death struck without warning, often lingered, and overlooked some for no discernible reason. In space, survival was often a matter of fate. But on the ground, I was learning, survival was a matter of both fate and luck—a combination that mixed together about as well as oil and water.

I began to feel very nauseous the instant the fourth soldier exploded. "How long are they going to keep this up?" I asked. "When's somebody going to surrender?"

"You must be joking," my companion replied sternly. "In a battle such as this, when such damage has been done, there is no retreat—no surrender. I am afraid the war, for whatever reason, has begun."

I felt very, *very* nauseous. The sensation ended abruptly the moment the medusa's laser cannons conked out—simultaneously. In the time it takes to blink, Kemp City's force field had gone down and a fiery blast from the mouth laid seige to the medusa's thorax. I felt the heat of the blast on my face and hands even though I'd followed Alejó's example and huddled in the divot as if to suckle on a rock.

A sickening slurp rent the atmosphere. The heat of the blast, which must have cost Kemp severely, suddenly ceased to be. I looked up to see the upper right of the medusa's thorax almost completely melted through. Several flickers of flame were scattered at different points on the molten metal sliding down the thorax. I hated to speculate what the damage inside looked like. The aroma of charred flesh in the vicinity had certainly tripled.

Kemp City's head swung back and forth arrogantly, though not to the extent that it sacrificed its wariness. I half expected hackles to rise from the schematic ridges of fur. But it was plain to see the city had been sorely taxed. The limp forefoot was heavier, causing the left shoulder to slump so low as to nearly upset its balance.

Meanwhile, the medusa staggered, struggling to remain upright. And while it was fighting that battle, it sought to retaliate. Several tentacles on the left extended, cannons pointing dead-ahead at Kemp.

My fist were clenched so tightly my fingernails cut into my palms. I relaxed it with an effort. Alejó's pale flesh, meanwhile, had lost its final traces of pink, as if every red corpuscle in his body had decided to hide in his feet.

The medusa's cannons fired. The blasts were weaker this time, almost feeble in comparison to the earlier. Kemp would have fended them off easily—if the city had raised its force field at all. Instead Kemp tried to dodge them—and did for a second. But the medusa shifted enough for its lasers to strike Kemp's haunch.

And more people died in another explosion. The soldiers manning the cannons around Kemp's neck retaliated simultaneously—with razor-thin blasts that sliced through the medusa's legs, cutting long incisions into the left leg, and shearing the right completely in half. The medusa toppled immediately.

My guts quaked as the medusa hit the ground with the impact of your friendly neighborhood landslide. Tentacles broke, steel crumpled like tissue paper. The blood drained from my face as the main body rolled down the crater. The remaining tentacles struggled wildly in an effort to chisel some kind of hold in the ground, but they were simply too weak to do much about the massive weight of the thorax.

Kemp City seemed to wait a second too long before it leaped, but effectively dodged the rolling, broken medusa in the nick of time anyway. The city half dashed, half lumbered up the side of the crater.

Meanwhile, the medusa rolled past the center where Kemp had been standing, and continued rolling until it was slowed and finally stopped by the incline of the bank. Then it rolled back down.

And Kemp waited.

Throughout the course of the battle, the ground had jumped as if the entire planet had become a grain stuck inside a peppermill. The sheer violence of the shaking uprooted trees of all sizes, while giant mushrooms toppled and tore in half. Panic-stricken birds flew in flocks so thick they often blackened the sky. My eyes widened in horror as a fissure in the crust cracked open at the crater rim—an abyss in the making, with no bottom in sight. The crack kept getting longer and longer, and in moments had stretched to the horizon like an orange being torn apart by sections. Meadows and forests, foothills and plateaus all slid and fell into the black abyss.

Fortunately the fissure wasn't headed toward Alejó and me. Otherwise the consequences would have surely signaled an abrupt conclusion to my narrative.

Then the crater itself started to split. Unless the medusa learned to crawl fast, it was headed for a long, hard fall.

That sort of demise, however, wasn't good enough for Kempians. The moment their city had limped onto flat, if not exactly stable, soil again, they opened fire.

The entire medusa thorax grew crimson hot and began to smolder dangerously, like a tightly wadded, water soaked rag cast into a roaring forest fire. I knew an explosion was imminent. When it did come, the medusa was already falling down the fissure, and hence it was academic whether Kemp City or the planet itself delivered the coup de grace.

A plume of rock and dirt jetted vociferously from the abyss. Alejó and I covered our heads with our hands in a futile effort to protect ourselves, however tentatively, from the descending rock and dirt that had quickly resulted from the plume.

Kemp City, almost as an afterthought, began dispatching the survivors crawling from the wreckage of the legs and tentacles that had been left behind. None managed to crawl very far. With that portion of its vengeance complete, Kemp City systematically melted the wreckage into slag.

Alejó tapped me on the shoulder. At first I mistook his fingers for just another part of the steady rain of rocks, but he finally got my attention by shaking me. "Come on, let's depart this site of treachery," he said, "before the Kempians decide on general principle to kill any prisoners who've managed to escape—prisoners like us."

"I concur," I said, "but where can we go?"

"Leave it to me. Let's just scram."

And so we scrammed. I had no idea where I was going or why, or what I would do after I had gotten there. But at least following Alejó provided me with some direction in my life. Otherwise I'd have been too depressed to limp and run at the same time.

Chapter Thirteen
That's How the Planet Crumbles

*T**HAT APE BLOWED UP up good—real good,* thought Blather as his nausea reached sublime proportions. He brought his hands down from his face. His success in preventing the pools of blood and pieces of internal organs from striking his face had been only marginal. Still, it was good, perhaps even comforting, to know that his face was not as drenched with innards as the rest of him. He doubted he would ever feel entirely clean again. He was already certain he wouldn't bother trying to clean his uniform, however. It was doomed for a visit with the atomic disintegrator.

A feminine yet exceedingly profane exclamation of disgust manifested itself near his left ear. He couldn't help raising his eyebrow with wry amusement at Lt. Colonel Second Class Coryban as she looked down in horror at her drenched fatigues. Maybe it was just a trick of the light, but it seemed her complexion turned distinctly green as her cheeks puffed up and she pressed her hand against her puckered lips. "Excuse me," she mumbled, or something close to that, as she pushed her way through the crowd of onlookers, many rather drenched themselves, who had gathered about to learn the cause of the Caliban ambassador's spectacular demise.

Already the Patrol crew was moving into the scene,

their vacuums and multipurpose scrub brushes poised for action.

"Wait! Don't suck up that goop yet!" Blather said, his upheld palm halting the crew as they aimed their hoses at the floor, into the corners, toward the ceiling, and at various bystanders.

"Why not?" groaned a groggy Admiral Boink, who was only now making the effort to sit up. "Whose goop is it, anyway?"

Blather stood over the admiral and saluted him briskly. "That goop used to be the Caliban ambassador, sir. And that object protruding from the ceiling used to be the soprano saxophone that, thanks to my sustained efforts, succeeded in saving your ass, sir!"

"No kidding." Boink returned the salute, then blinked violently as he realized he had accidentally poked himself in the eye. "What happened?"

"You don't know?"

"I don't remember," said the admiral, looking suspiciously at the crew and passengers who buzzed (or hissed or whistled or gestured) excitedly among themselves.

Blather leaned down and whispered conspiratorially, "The Ho-Ho-Kusian ambassador tried to take advantage of your good will, sir."

"You mean he—? He actually tried to—?" The admiral's subsequent words were lost in a cough.

"Got a sore throat, sir?" Blather asked. "Can't say I blame you, really. I've never known anyone human who was able to suck on something as big as the ambassador's taproot and survive before. I gotta admit, you're going to be famous in certain quarters." Blather's face turned red. "Sorry, sir, I didn't mean to offend."

"And I won't mean to offend you later when I assign you latrine duties. We'll see if all that flapping around has made your tongue strong enough for a real workout. Now what happened?"

Blather told him as quickly and as mercifully as possible. As the story progressed, Boink swayed back and forth like a drunken man standing atop the frame of a skyscraper in midconstruction, even though his buttocks were still firmly placed upon the commissary floor. Boink's eyes darted to the left, then slowly moved to the right, as it gradually sank in just how many entities had personally witnessed his humiliation. "By the horny nebula, how am I going to regain face after this?" he exclaimed.

Blather couldn't resist a smile. "Oh, Admiral, it could have been worse. He could have used the servant's entrance."

"And just what do you mean by that?"

"And, uh, ahem, entered from the rear."

"You've been demoted before, haven't you?"

"Yes, now that you mention it. Why?"

"It'll become obvious later. Do you have any idea why the Caliban ambassador exploded?"

"None."

"And where is the Ho-Ho-Kusian ambassador at the moment?"

"A good question," replied Blather, looking around to see a horde of hands, tentacles, masses of protoplasm, and waldoes pointing toward the row of potted plants where stood the Ho-Ho-Kusian in a prim, statuesque pose. His leaves were uncharacteristically ruffled, though. Blather instructed two members of the crew not to permit the ambassador to slink away, then returned his attention to the admiral. "Sir, that saxophone sticking in the ceiling is a disaster. In fact, if I didn't know already it was a saxophone, I would mistake it for a xenosuppository. The ambassador may be under control for the moment, but without that music, he's going to revert back to his instinctively butch self."

"That's terrific. Would you help me stand?"

"Certainly."

"And while we're doing that, would you mind explaining why you stopped the crew from cleaning up this mess?"

"We've got to be careful, sir. If you don't mind, I would like to formally request that a team of investigators comb this place and everyone in it with every atomscope we've got in stock. Entities don't explode every day, not even cyborgs. Something highly questionable's going on here, sir, if you don't mind my saying so."

"Would you stop calling me 'sir' so much?"

"Yassuh, Massa!" replied Blather briskly, with an equally brisk salute.

Unfortunately, he had chosen to release the admiral a few seconds before the shaken officer was prepared to stand on his own. As a result, the admiral was well on the way toward reprising his earlier position even as he made an irate grab for Blather's throat. The admiral's fingers clasped only air at the moment of his buttocks' impact, but a few seconds later they were firmly clamped around Blather's leg, pulling it closer to his wide-open mouth.

"Don't bite! Don't bite!" Blather exclaimed, gently but firmly keeping the admiral's mouth away from his calf. "The medbots will think you've contracted a xenorabies virus! Don't you think we had to have enough shots before we embarked on this mission, without having to take any more?"

At first Blather wasn't sure he had talked any sense back into his superior officer, and he spent the next few seconds grinning sheepishly at the silent crowd of onlookers, a few of whom were typing notes on portable keyboards. The admiral, meanwhile, stared at the point where he had attempted to bite Blather, then looked up at him, apparently for the sole purpose of subjecting him to a range of emotional glares, running the gamut from enraged to infuriated.

"I'm going to get you for this, Blather," Boink whispered.

"Yes, sir!" replied Blather, bending down to help Boink stand.

Boink slapped Blather's hands away. "I'll do it myself!"

"Yes, sir!" said Blather, stepping away and making a point of putting his hands behind his back. He watched with a curious mixture of pity and contempt as the old man placed his palms on the blood-splattered floor, drew one knee under his chest, took a deep breath, pushed with a concentrated effort, and stood on quivering legs.

At last upright, Boink pulled down the hem of his jacket as if it had gotten mussed in a minor scuffle, and took his first look with clear eyes at the immediate surroundings. "What's the matter with these people? Why aren't they off somewhere cleaning themselves up?"

"I assume because they wish to see how we deal with the Ho-Ho-Kusian and how we begin the investigation into the case of the exploding cybernetic ape. They are eyewitnesses after all, those that use eyes, so they have to remain on the scene until their presence has been noted. Also, I imagine they're curious as to how you conduct yourself in the immediate aftermath of the humiliation and degradation you've just undergone. You know, to see how well you act under pressure."

"Thank you, Blather. I'll see that the keenness of your powers of observation are duly entered in my log. Not to mention your essential fogginess of mind."

Blather saluted the admiral. "Thank you, sir. Just spell my name right!"

At this moment we should pause in our narrative long enough to note that since the dawn of time, beauty has been thought of as a kind of genius in and of itself. Man has down through the eons grappled with many forms of it. He has searched for it everywhere, and everywhere he has found it, or so he has believed. He has found it in the subatomic particles that serve as gateways to alternate dimensions, and in the simple mathematical formulas that explicate the most complex mysteries. He has seen it on heavy moons with methane oceans; in meteor showers streaking across crimson skies; in glittering thirteen-kilometer-high mesas towering above plains of shifting saffron sands; above waterfalls whose vapors reached into the outer edges of the troposphere; and in polar caves whose stalagmites and stalactites were as thick as Brobdingnagian thermoworms. He has sculpted it, painted it, holographed it, written poetry and music inspired by it, and used it as a backdrop for melodramatic stories of questionable artistic worth—all to communicate and, if possible, immortalize the essence of its physical splendor.

And yet the vistas of nature are only one aspect of beauty, only one of the many faces she occasionally turns to Man. More beautiful still than the natural wonders are the enigmatic minutiae of life itself—the hexagonal pale-green eyes of the subterranean Aldelbert lizard; the blue shade of a Newtonian firehawk's feathers; the textures of the orange cotton balls genetically engineered to grow in space colonies; the dampness of the morning dew clinging to the razor-sharp blades of New Kentucky blue-grass; the howl of the lonely starwolf in the black forests of Caledonia IV; the reflection of sunlight against the gray skin of man-dolphins frolicking in the green seas of Oceania. In such a universe, men cannot fail to be stricken with awe by the many glints of beauty momentarily revealed by an indifferent reality. These glints emerge only to linger and then fade in the mind like a shadow in a dream.

But however much Man has been transfixed, obsessed, and sometimes transformed by the numerous beauties revealed to his pallid, insignificant mind, since time immemorial he has recognized the primary importance of a category of beauty more profound, more hypnotizing, more arresting than all the others combined, a beauty that consistently arouses a fascination springing from a primordial well deep in his subconscious. This beauty can be the gateway to an alternate dimension of existence or it can possess delicate simplicities requiring an eternity of contemplation. It is as endless as the receding galaxies, yet as transient as the life of a shooting star. It can be deep, it can be shallow, yet the truth of it is rarely easily discerned. It can be fierce or it can be tame, but it can never be controlled. It has been known to give rise to the noblest of ambitions and the loftiest of ideals. But it's just as likely to give rise to a bad case of lasciviousness.

That's right. I'm talking about Man's eternal bondage to his scx drive. For with only a few exceptions, the males of all species present were unexpectantly, but extremely pleasurably, aroused when Lt. Colonel Second Class Coryban shoved her way through the crowd. Normally her arrival wouldn't have resulted in an arched eyebrow, but this time she happened to be wearing only a black lace bra, plus black panties with a red heart sewn overtop her most significantly naughty bit.

Pointedly ignoring the chorus of moans, groans, and pick-up lines accompanying her entrance, Coryban stood before Blather and Boink with her legs apart, her back arched and her shoulders straight. Apparently she was unaware that her posture drew undue but highly deserved attention to two of her most prominent features. A strange, disturbing light burned in her jade-green eyes. Her tousled hair fell onto her shoulders like a silken halo, and it did not escape the notice of the males present that she had a green-and-yellow butterfly tatooed on her inner left thigh. She saluted, inadvertently causing the butterfly to quiver enticingly. "Lt. Colonel Second Class Coryban reporting with grave news, sir!"

Boink leaned against Blather for support, not realizing that Blather was surreptitiously leaning against him for support. Boink stared wide-eyed where he feared he shouldn't be, and dizzily waited for the blood leaving his brain to arrive somewhere else. "What have you brought . . . me?" he asked.

Coryban lowered her arm and looked confused. "I've brought myself."

"Words I've always wanted to hear, but which I seriously doubt you meant the way they sounded. What have you got on . . . your mind?"

Coryban looked down at herself. She turned as white as a dwarf star. "My apologies, sir," she said breathlessly. "The news I just heard over the hypertelly in the ladies' room is so important that I forgot my fatigues were in the neutrino cleaner. I hope you won't think my current attire is unprofessional of me."

"Never! Out with the news, then!"

"Sir, the entire planet of Caliban has exploded," she said gravely. "Some of the factories and colonies outside the exosphere field escaped the initial explosion with only minor damage, but most were caught in the shock waves. Sir, Caliban exploded at the core, and no one knows why!"

Boink nodded thoughtfully. "That's amazing. Fantastic, even. Is any terrorist group claiming responsibility?"

"It's thought that most of the terrorists opposed to the Caliban government or life style were holed up on the planet at the moment of detonation. In other words, there are no known Caliban enemies still alive to claim responsibility."

"That's unfortunate," said Blather. "It would be so much easier for the Federation to solve this case if there was somebody to hang it on."

Coryban glared at Blather. For the moment she seemed to have forgotten her state of relative undress, though her audience certainly hadn't forgotten, however much they might have been distracted in their official capacities by the dreadful news she was imparting. "There's more. I don't believe this case can be easily 'hung' on anyone for the sake of clearing up a little clerical work."

Boink nodded for her to go on. In the wake of receiving this news, which he was certain had galactic implications, he had almost forgotten his recent humiliation.

Coryban moved closer to Boink and Blather. She lowered her voice in a conspiratorial tone, though it remained loud enough for all but those with the narrowest audio bands to hear with only a minimum of strain. "What happened to the Caliban here, gentlemen, was no fluke. It seems that at the exact same moment the Caliban homeworld exploded, so did every single Caliban in existence, all across the space-time zones. Think of the implications. All the explosions concerned were simultaneous, regardless of the distance between the solitary Calibans scattered throughout the Federation embassies.

Even travel through hyperspace takes some time, gentlemen. That means someone had pinpointed the location of every Caliban in existence and timed the means of explosion to achieve a certain effect."

Blather rubbed his chin thoughtfully. "Or someone has perfected a means of instantly transmitting an invisible death ray."

"I just hope he hasn't made a mistake and blown up Caliban by accident," said Coryban. "Otherwise the Federation could be in for even a rougher time than it appears."

"Well, at least it's probable the cause of our own explosion didn't originate on this ship," said Boink. "But I want this debris examined down to the tiniest atom just in case. Get this cleaning crew out of here! We don't need them! Where are those lab technicians?"

"Technicians! Technicians!" called out Coryban.

"Wait," said Blather, waving his hand, "I haven't ordered them here yet."

"And why not?" Coryban demanded, red-faced and, from what Blather could see, practically red-chested as well.

"Because I've been thinking of formally requesting these stains permanently remain in the commissary, in remembrance of the time we all got to see what you look like," Blather replied, to a smattering of polite applause.

"You know, Blather, I'd always thought the Peter Principle was a myth until I met you," Coryban said.

"What's that?"

"A myth is a traditional story serving to explain some phenomenon or custom," cried out the gray-haired Xanthippian, who hadn't taken her eyes off Coryban since her reentry into the commissary.

"I know that!" Blather protested.

"The Peter Principle states that an individual shall rise in the hierarchy to the level of his incompetence," said a giant, green, four-armed Thark.

Blather nodded thoughtfully. "Hmm. That makes perfect sense, but I fail to see what it has to do with me."

Coryban sighed in exasperation, then turned to face Boink. "Admiral, since it's a little academic at this point to worry about why a particular Caliban exploded, I suggest we concentrate instead on another problem which I am certain is close to your heart."

"Oh? And what's that?" the admiral said, a tad preoccupied with how he could professionally offer Coryban a promotion and still get the fulfillment he felt he deserved from life, all without violating his admittedly flexible ethical standards. She pointed to the quivering tree among the potted plants. "Pretty soon the ambassador's hormones will provide him with enough incentive to forget his fear. And it's safe to say he still has a crush on you."

"And he wants to crush you!" called out someone, or something, from the rear of the crowd.

"All right, cut that out!" Blather cried.

Boink rolled his eyes to the ceiling. "And it looks like the saxophone is on the fritz."

"Rather badly, sir," said Coryban.

"Got any ideas, Blather?" asked Boink.

"Yes, but they're not exactly on the subject at hand. Probably not printable, either."

"Blather, can you walk and chew gum at the same time?" Coryban asked, making no effort to conceal her disgust.

Blather scowled. "Let me get back to you on that."

Coryban arched an eyebrow toward a Pheblian Glorp and the Porgian Five ambassador, who were whispering intensely about who might be responsible for the spectacular act of genocide committed against the Calibans. Each seemed to be blaming the other's government, though of course the formalities of diplomatic protocol discouraged direct accusations of that nature. Coryban noted the other ambassadors and crew members listening in; many gazed suspiciously at their neighbors. They were becoming paranoid, and she was afraid she couldn't blame them. "Admiral," she whispered, "I think we'd better break up this crowd as soon as possible."

"Why? I've got to figure out something to do with that . . . that . . . that reprobate!" the admiral replied, punctuating his sentiments with a few sprays of spittle.

At that moment a mass of white protoplasm, resembling nothing so much as an upturned gallon of perpetually melting vanilla ice cream, rolled up on an electronic skateboard. Wires connected the skateboard controls to the conelike top of the protoplasm mass, lending the creature the illusion that it had a head hidden somewhere beneath all those identical cells. "Hi!" it said in a squeaky voice through the speaker of its augmented translator. Its actual sound was probably supersonic and beyond the range of human hearing. "My name is Dr. Proty, and I can help you with your problem."

"Hello, Doctor," said Coryban in a friendly, musical tone. "How have your studies been progressing? She took the white appendage that had extended from the protoplasmic mass into her hand and shook it with warmth.

"Very well, thank you, Colonel," Doctor Proty replied. "This voyage is a veritable cornucopia of unusual events that only my unique form of scientific genius can fathom."

"Forgive me for my ignorance, Doctor," said Admiral Boink, "but exactly what is your field?"

"My specialty is the act of sexual intercourse between animals of two different species. You know, the psychological and physiological reasons why various bipeds and others defy their civilized conventions, plus the details of their pleasurable responses, and the subsequent side effects, both good and ill. The field's proper name is bigenus fornicology, though the description can be inadequate as I frequently find myself faced with the truth that it can indeed take more than merely two to tango." He made two appendages, with two fingers apiece, and snapped the fingers briskly, twice, before retracting them back into his mass proper. "Actually I prefer the popular name for my field of expertise: gritology. So you can call me a gritologist. Lately I've been a very busy gritologist."

"Pardon me for interrupting, Dr. Proty," said Blather,

"but are you implying there've been a slew of perverted acts of cross-genus fornication on this voyage?"

"Absolutely. Well, maybe not a slew, but certainly more than I could count. I don't know what it is about ambassadors, but they have a deeper, darker drive to defy the social conventions of their native civilizations than do individuals of practically any other profession. I suppose you could sum it up by saying they're just obsessed with probing the sweet mysteries of life in as meaningful a way as possible."

Blather turned to the crowd. "Is this true? Has there been a lot of perversion going on here when the crew hasn't been looking?"

Most of the ambassadors and their staff members who happened to be present merely appeared embarrassed, each in its own unique fashion of course, but many also nodded their heads or gesticulated in the affirmative via whatever means were customary among their kind.

Blather clapped his hands once and rubbed them together. "This is great! Is there some kind of singles' register I can sign up on?"

For several moments the air was rife with a silence so thick a thermonuclear device couldn't have blasted it apart. Someone in the back called out in a stage whisper, "Later, big boy!"

Then the ambassadors and the crew promptly returned to the subject of their earlier discussion. Speculation turned rapidly to the question of whether or not the lower orders of animal and plant life originating on Caliban that happened to be in zoos, gardens, or labs topside survived the annihilation. Much speculation was also directed to the main point of what race might have had the means and the motivation to do away with the Calibans so thoroughly.

Though naturally concerned about the bad tempers beginning to manifest themselves in the ranks of the ambassadors, Coryban and Boink and, to some extent, Blather, regarded the Ho-Ho-Kusian ambassador as their most immediate problem, and hence returned their total attention to Dr. Proty.

"Forget this armchair degenerate," said Coryban to Dr. Proty with a nod in Blather's direction. "Are we to assume that you may know some means by which we may soothe the ambassador's sex drive long enough for him to reach the conference with enough of his sanity intact for the Space Corps to escape responsibility for his subsequent actions?"

"Well, yes and no," replied the doctor. "I simply hope to divert it to spare your admiral a recurrence of the event he has just survived."

"That will be sufficient, Doctor," said the admiral coldly. "What do you propose?"

"Well, as you may know, my race possess the ability to transform ourselves into the likeness of any living creature, be it plant, animal, or something in between. By drawing in molecules from the air, we vary our mass to permit us to imitate creatures and plants much larger than us. The imitation isn't complete, of course; we cannot duplicate characteristics at the cellular level. Nor can we match creatures with a mass less than our own; we invariably appear much larger. But a Ho-Ho-Kusian poses no problem."

"Are you implying that you would imitate the ambassador so his reproductive urges would be directed . . . elsewhere?" asked the admiral, a little too eagerly, plus a tad suspiciously.

"Well, yes. I think my work would profit immensely from it."

"Doctor!" exclaimed Coryban. "Your work won't profit very much if you die because of it!"

"Oh, I won't permit the ambassador to go that far. I'll just lead him on."

Blather nodded contemptuously. "And just what would you know about teasing a horny tree?"

The white mass rippled in a fashion implying the creature was bristling indignantly. "There's a lot of things about us Circians of which you bipeds know nothing."

Blather cleared his throat. "Excuse me, but just how many sexual acts have you yourself personally committed during the course of this voyage?"

"I haven't 'committed' anything! It was all done in the name of research!"

"How many?" asked the admiral, his curiosity aroused.

"I don't know. I'll have to look it up in my files. They all run together after a while."

Coryban had turned quite pale. "Doctor, I'm surprised at you! I thought you were a serious scientist, not a . . . a . . . quickie master!"

Dr. Proty bristled again. "I never have quickies! Always it's longies!"

Coryban pulled up a chair and sat down. She was evidently quite shaken by what she had learned. "I must say, Doctor, I'm shocked."

"Oh, come, come, Colonel," said Dr. Proty testily, "I'm dealing with uncharted territory here. What good are my papers and diagrams and software programs without some decent empirical data to go along with them? Besides, maybe you should try some bigenus fornication sometime. It might do you some good."

"And I bet you have a volunteer in mind, don't you, Doctor?" said Blather with a sneer.

Coryban stood up and shook her fist in front of Blather's face. "You leave him alone! At least he's trying to push the envelope! That's a hell of a lot more than I can say for you!"

Blather smirked and folded his arms across his chest. "Colonel, there's a question I've always been meaning to ask you."

Coryban gave Blather what might best be described as "a look." "And what's that, Ensign?"

"When you look straight down, can you see your toes?"

Blather never got his answer. He also failed to see what hit him. His awakening occurred in stages, each seemingly drawn out to an inordinate degree. The first stage was his gradual hearing of many voices, human and inhuman, murmuring and arguing, using words he was unable to comprehend. The aural sensation was like a tide washing into his subconscious.

During the next stage he detected chaotic, violent sounds, accompanying a chorus of oaths, screams, and groans. Since he couldn't feel his arms, legs, or torso, and in fact was uncertain if his consciousness still resided in his brain, he wasn't sure he could move, even if he'd wanted to.

The third stage arrived when somebody stepped on his hand. His eyes opened immediately, to find themselves staring directly at the blinding lights overhead. Admiral Boink was yelling into his face, exhorting him to wake up, even as he was slapping him with an ardor apparently unnecessary under the circumstances.

Blather tried to push away Boink's hand, but was too weak to be completely successful. So Boink managed to slap him one more time before the ensign said groggily, "Did anyone manage to hail the frequency of the freighter that hit me?"

"I'd say it was 38-24-36, like a soft drink bottle with feet," said Boink, helping Blather to stand.

During this process, Blather happened to glance down at his uniform and saw it was covered with blood and slime. He nearly fainted again. "By the intestines of the *kwisatz haderach!* Is that blood my own?"

"No, and I don't know whose it is!" hissed the admiral in his ear.

"Holy Seldon! Who does that blood on the floor belong to?"

"Damn good question," said the admiral, looking at him with wide eyes. "Is there anything else on your mind?"

Yes, there was, but Blather discovered, with a lingering sense of disquiet he feared would remain forever nameless, that he had absolutely no idea what it was. It was simple enough to imagine that Coryban and Dr. Proty had made themselves scarce while he was unconscious, easy enough to grasp that they had taken the Ho-Ho-Kusian ambassador with them. He remembered random phrases from the intense discussions carried on by the bipeds and others before Coryban had decked him, but couldn't for the life of him recall the incident that had sparked the discussions. He felt as if a light had gone out in his mind. He steadied himself and saw in the admiral's brow lines of worry that gave rise to similar fears. Time and space weren't out of joint exactly, but they had certainly been twisted around a bit, with a disturbing grinding of gears.

The admiral helped him take the first few steps away from the mêlée that had been going on around them. In those instants Blather saw the four-armed Thark break his fangs against the metal exoskeleton of a cybernetic mudman; a crew member disappear beneath the frenzied onslaught of thirty-four fuzzy, pink balls famous throughout the galaxy for their perpetual reproductive habits; a wild tiger woman pounce upon a timid canine male; a hive mind comprised of buzzing bugs swarm over an insectoid whose tongue possessed a sticky fluid from which escape was impossible; the Xanthippian putting a bear hug on the purple-skinned, fin-headed Blixtonian who, in happier times, had been one of her best friends; a Dominatrix Queen squirming in delight as a crewman beat her enthusiastically about the belly; and the Shovelhead ambassador practically leaping out of his tank to do battle with, if not to eat, the Porgian fish man.

Blather impulsively broke away from the admiral and separated the Xanthippian and the Blixtonian. "What's the matter with you two?" he demanded. "What's everybody fighting over?"

The Xanthippian glared at the Blixtonian, who represented a species whose ancestors had been genetically engineered men, just as the Xanthippian represented a race of genetically engineered women. "Because I have my suspicions, that's why!" said the Xanthippian. "The Blixtonians are engaged in a secret power play to scuttle the negotiations!"

"How do you know?" Blather asked.

"Because I know!" she replied.

"And I know too!" said the Blixtonian.

The pair managed to cooperate long enough to push Blather to the floor, and he sat there stunned, too confused over this turn of events to move. He was certain the secret to this mêlée lurked in the back of his mind, and he was equally certain that if he didn't extract the answer soon, then he never would. Nor could he escape the feeling that it was vitally important to the fate of the Galactic Federation that he do so.

Elsewhere, unheard and unseen by all, a shadow on the wall threw back its head and laughed.

Chapter Fourteen
This War Wheel's On Fire

I HAD A DREAM. IN IT I heard the approaching snare drums of war, and the relentless footfalls of a thousand thousand marching soldiers, all singing songs celebrating their coming victory. I could not see these soldiers—the skies were dark with the smoke of distant fires, and the countryside was a vast crumpled bedspread of blackness, highlighted only by plains illuminated with the red lines of raging brushfires.

The soldiers' destiny was all too plain. This was to be the apocalypse, the time when evil would be destroyed by the dark powers of war. Already I sensed the ghostly sounds of the men screaming and dying amid the blast and thunder of cannon and rifle fire. The wind carried the stark aroma of blood and powder to distant places, and the flickering white souls rose from the dead on the battlefield toward a sky devoid of light.

Were the souls rising toward Valhalla, or would they merely greet oblivion? I would never know. In my dream I could only linger and watch the rodents and vultures and maggots strip bare the corpses of men and horses. I listened to the ghostly beat of those incessant snare drums, calling forth the next generation to meet its destiny on the next battlefield.

The snare drums still echoed in my mind as I awoke

on the cold ground with Alejó asleep at my side. The sky was dark—not with the smoke of distant battle, but with flocks of birds, an endless ocean of them, stretching from one horizon to the other.

We were in a kind of forest I hadn't encountered before, a fungoid wood where all the various pieces of the planet I'd seen before had come together in curious ways. The branches of wood trees didn't have leaves but ended in purple mushroom caps. Fungoid stalks ended with red roselike flowers, or with a series of hexagonal-shaped seeds. Perhaps the disparate elements of other areas had found some means of evolving into a single ecosystem. Even if so, the gelatinlike moss covering portions of the ground, and the thick mesh of yellow grass Alejó and I were lying on, indicated some new elements had been added.

While staring at the flocks of birds and trying to catch a few glimpses of the rings in the sky, everything came back to me. Alejó and I had carried one another for kilometers, out of the forest where Kemp City and its opponent had battled. The forest had ended suddenly in a desolate, almost desertlike area, where the soil was mixed with red sand. Blue sagebrush and rainbow cactus grew there, and a thriving population of lizard and spider analogues scampered all over the place. Around nightfall we had come to this particular forest. We then carried each other for another kilometer or so, crossed a few gurgling streams, and then collapsed in a state of utter exhaustion. Because the sun was obscured by the birds, I had no idea how long we had slept.

I thought about waking up Alejó, but then decided to check out my physical condition first. I sat up with an effort. Through the many holes in my tattered clothing, I saw my legs and arms covered with scabs from the many cuts I'd collected since my initial fall from Kemp City. The parts of me that weren't cut were bruised. I felt my ribs and with a marginal amount of relief decided I hadn't broken any, though a few felt especially sore. My head throbbed as if someone had used it for a bowling pin. My heart and lungs felt as if someone had squeezed them like sponges. My legs felt too weak to support a straw man, and I'll politely refrain from telling you how my testicles felt, if you don't mind.

At least I wasn't hungry. But I was thirsty. I couldn't help but think of that last stream we had crossed, the one with the film of mud covering the surface of the water. With luck there would be better drinking water further on ahead.

I woke Alejó with a little push. He was in as rough shape as I. At least the yellow fungus on his stubbled chin appeared to be thinner; evidently it wasn't very resistant to the elements once it was outside the confines of Desolation Row. Alejó pulled his elbow beneath his chest and lifted himself up with a groan and a weak grin. "Guess we were out for a long time, eh, friend?"

"At least half a cycle. Maybe more. Got any idea where a guy can get a drink of water around here?"

Alejó glanced about. He reached out with another groan and tore a mushroom cap from its stalk, put his lips to the damaged portion, and sucked on it. After a few moments he grinned, and a few green trickles of fluid ran down his chin. "It's good," he said, breaking off another cap and offering it to me. "It takes a real man to piss this stuff."

"That's not exactly a recommendation where I come from," I said, refusing with a gesture. "Besides, you never know what the raw materials on this world will do to you."

Alejó chuckled as he took another suck from the first cap. "You have such an amusing way of expressing yourself. One would almost think you actually hailed from another world."

"And why couldn't I?"

"Well—there is no such thing!"

"Perhaps," I said with a shrug, "but if I was, it would certainly explain why a fellow as bright as me happens to be so ignorant in matters that you take for granted, wouldn't it?"

He scowled. What I'd said made a lot of sense despite his better judgement. "Are you in pain?" he asked.

"Yes, tremendously. Nothing a few years of rest and relaxation wouldn't cure though."

Alejó took another suck off his mushroom cap. "This has the side effect of diminishing pain," he said, offering the other cap again.

"I'll take it!" The fluid in the cap tasted like the liquid that rises to the top of a turned cup of sour cream, only more bitter. Outside of that, it wasn't too bad, and it did quench my thirst almost immediately. We sat sucking our caps in silence for a few moments. Then something caught my eye.

Something wide, long, and moving. My movement toward it was almost instinctive. Alejó detained me with a hand on my elbow and a look that said, "Be careful." So rather than crawling over to the site, I stood up and leaned around a giant mushroom with purple leaves that had yellow veins and saw:

A band of crimson army ant analogues, consuming everything in its path. Presumably it was leaving only the rocks and the dirt behind; I say presumably because the legions of ants extended at least a kilometer in the distance, so it was difficult to tell exactly what, if anything, they were leaving behind. Thinking that I would have made a magnificent ant feast, I took some small comfort in that the army adhered to its borders rather strictly. But when I noticed a few explorers at my feet, I stomped them flat immediately.

"You shouldn't have done that," said Alejó with strained humor. "You'll make them mad."

"Come on, let's go. Anywhere."

But we had gone only a short distance when we saw another wide band of army ant analogues—green ones this time, with two purple bands across their thoraxes—consuming their way on a path that would intersect directly with the approaching army of red ants. Already a few trickles of green ants were at our feet—not looking for us, as it turned out, but deliberately heading for the red ants as sort of an advance raiding party, to get in a few fierce bites with their double sets of jaws before the real fighting started.

Alejó tapped me on the shoulder. Already the red ants were forgetting about their food and were accelerating toward the green ants. "What's going on here?" I asked. "There's plenty of forest for both of them of chew on!"

"You miss the point," said Alejó as we slowly backed away. "The red *humolui* and the green *phara* instinctively detest one another. When one army meets another, they fight on until the last enemy is dead. The poets say it has ever been that way."

"You have poetry?" I blurted out in surprise.

"Of course. Our poets recite epics that have existed unchanged since the dawn of the cities, or the dawn of man, whichever came first. But come, let's make haste lest we meet the demise of many old heroes. Are you still in pain?"

"I feel it diminishing, as you promised."

"The relief won't last for long, but it should help us loosen up some. Just be careful not to open any wounds."

Suddenly he stared into the forest and stopped cold, his complexion pallid. He grabbed my arm and squeezed it hard—I was almost afraid to look, but I was certainly more afraid not to.

Especially after the creature roared.

It roared at us, then at the ants blocking its way, and finally at the flocks still shielding the sky overhead. It was the size of a full-grown stag, but its body was more feline than cervine. The claws of its front two paws were extended, digging nervously into the log it happened to be standing on. It had orange fur with white highlights about the face and a tuft of white on the chest, and long black whiskers. Its black lips were drawn back, exposing a healthy set of fangs, but I had the distinct impression the long saber teeth were exposed all the time. It roared a fourth time, then lowered its head as if to charge, to impale us on its antlers.

"Don't say a word," Alejó whispered, guiding me sideways. "The *babalu* won't hurt you unless it's very, very hungry."

I wanted to ask how he knew it wasn't, but then two cubs with black and orange fur clawed their way up the log to nudge against their mother's leg.

"She just wants us out of the way so she can lead her cubs away from the *humolui* and the *phara*," Alejó said.

I glanced back to see the *babalu* and the cubs taking the path directly opposite ours, away from the colliding rows of army ants. The battle of insects probably would have born a closer inspection, if I'd had the time, the inclination, and an airtight suit of armor. Swarms of red and green intermingled all up and down the mushrooms and the trees, and I saw at least four mounds of teeming ferocity. A fungoid sapling fell over beneath the weight of the ants, while leaves and twigs from the bushes flew in the air.

"Where are we going?" I asked with a sternness that surprised me. I hadn't realized I was so anxious.

If Alejó was offended by my tone, there was no indication of it in his easy smile. "To Tabu Ley."

"How? Your home city could be anywhere on the continent—on the whole damn planet, for all I know!"

He pointed an admonishing finger in the air as if to berate me for disbelieving him, then used the finger to press his left temple. Accompanied by a strange whirring, an antenna rose from the back of his head, where his translator was implanted. "This will act as a homing device," he said. "It is more accurate than the mechanisms birds use to guide them, as I can eventually locate Tabu Ley wherever it may be, and however fast it may be traveling." He scowled, as if he couldn't decide whether to be concerned or elated. "My home is not far away." He pointed to the direction the flocks of birds were coming from. "There."

So that's where we went. It wasn't long before the multitudes of birds began to diminish considerably, providing us at long last with a view of the noonday sun, the rings, and several of the shepherding moons. We expended little breath speaking; otherwise I would have asked a thousand questions, mostly about what so many birds might be fleeing from, and if the distant trails of smoke in the horizon, reminiscent of the snare drums in my dream, had anything to do with the phenomenon. The *babalu* and her cubs, as it turned out, were but the first of a stream of animal life that passed by us.

A more divergent batch of creatures from the same ecosystem I never hoped to see again. Now don't get me wrong. I know full well that given a billion or two standard years of uninterrupted evolutionary experiments, a fertile planet can conjure up a fairly diverse range of species. But even a cursory inspection, provided the sample is wide enough, can determine common evolutionary points of origin, and will provide many clues as to how the entire shebang fits together. I seriously doubted any sample, no matter how wide, could have done the same for this group of forest animals.

Who in his right mind would dare explain the coexistence of purple squirrels with horns in the middle of their foreheads, or apes that left slimy trails behind on the branches they swung from? Add to the stew big flightless birds whose heads constantly bopped like spastics, creatures like giants jacks turning continuous cartwheels, great silver centipedes with enigmatic black orbs for eyes, slithering amorphous masses in green and red shades, tiny insects who rolled up into balls resembling mushroom caps, and low-legged beasts that looked like a cross between a man and an alligator, in addition to wild variants on all the analogues I'd already seen during a lifetime of traipsing around the galaxy, and it was no surprise that I seriously wondered if the doors connecting all space and time zones had been opened here at some point during this world's existence, permitting entry to an infinite variety of forms, an endless ecological experiment more savage, more unpredictable than any previously encountered by rational man.

I'm certain Alejó would have expounded upon the

situation, had I asked. I didn't because just as our pace slowed enough for me to regain the spare breath to waste on words, he stopped dead in his tracks and appeared stricken and pale, as if he had felt a great hole open up in the universe.

"What is it? What's wrong?" I asked, putting a hand on his shoulder.

His eyes were wide with terror. "It's Tabu Ley!" he said hoarsely. "It's gone!"

"You mean your city's on the move again? Well, that's a problem, but I'm sure we can catch up sooner or later."

"No. I mean, it's gone! I'm not receiving any more signals!"

"Calm down. You're overreacting. I'm sure there's a logical explanation. Aren't there any adjustments you can make in your antenna? Maybe Tabu Ley's just broadcasting on another band."

"What are you talking about?"

For a moment I considered explaining to him how radio waves operated on certain frequencies, but then it penetrated my rather self-centered brain that for him, this was a catastrophe of a major order. He really was in no condition for a science lesson. "Okay. Just keep trying and we'll just keep heading in the same direction. Does that sound like a plan to you?"

He nodded meekly. His pale skin had by now taken on an ashen shade, as if a great shadow had passed over his soul. I squeezed his arm by way of indicating I understood how he felt, even though I didn't, and we strode on through the forest in silence.

Eventually we came to a meadow on a vast plain. By now we saw no more animal life, no more flocks of birds, only colonies of insects swarming about as if in search of new homes. Tall green grass with purple veins bent to the pressure of a constant breeze. Intermingled with the grass grew blue fungoid pads, persistently fighting for every square centimeter of ground. It was apparent, thanks to our improved perspective, that what we had earlier believed to be mere wisps of smoke were in actuality voluminous towers.

The smoke had shown no sign of abating during this leg of our journey, and my fears for their origin were confirmed when, a kilometer beyond the forest, we came to the point of a crevice that had recently opened in the earth, stretching to the horizon toward the smoke. The carcass of a great beast lay at the bottom of the crevice, and so far it had not been visited by a single scavenger.

We walked along the crevice edge. Alejó retracted his antenna, resigned I presumed, to the fact that he wasn't going to need it any more. His shoulders were slumped and his head hung low, and he seemed to pay little mind when he came dangerously near the crevice edge. Several times I braced myself to make a desperate lunge to prevent him from accidentally stepping over the side, but some basic survival instinct stopped him from making that particular suicidal gesture.

The towers of smoke on the horizon became thicker. And though we had not reached the site of the first column by dusk, I realized we would find it without much difficulty. For not only were the moons full and bright, reflecting considerable light on the countryside and the ring system, but the fires responsible for the smoke had already become quite visible. I felt strangely disjointed, walking so relentlessly toward an obvious site of incredible destruction. Indeed, I felt as if I deliberately shut off the juices of my heart and soul that permitted me to feel remorse for the fates of others.

Alejó, meanwhile, walked as a zombie must walk. Eventually, when we came upon a brushfire, I had to guide him to the areas where the fireline could easily be stepped over. We trudged through an area where the mushroom caps were singed and the pads of blue fungoids still smoldered, an area where the ground was so hot I was afraid my feet would cook in my boots. Barefoot Alejó gave no indication of feeling any pain. He simply trudged on. I doubted the liquid he had sucked out of the mushroom cap earlier in the day was still affecting him. Instead he had become indifferent to his personal suffering.

And as the night came fully upon us, we saw that the crevice was merely a line in an extended network of gorges. I imagined that from an aerial view, it would appear the planet had deliberately scarified itself, in an effort to match the ferocious bearing of its inhabitants.

The network of crevices made navigating through the plentiful brushfires a little more complicated, but essentially we did not waver from our course. We didn't even consider it. We were like figments caught in the throes of a nightmare, relentlessly traveling to the center of the horrifying vision so that we might become real.

The wind whipped flecks of ashes onto our faces, flecks that got into our noses and worked their way into our lungs. I covered my nose with my hands in an effort to filter some of the gunk, but Alejó did not bother. I worried for him.

Finally I pointed to some foothills in the burned-out meadow that might provide us with a good vantage point.

"Those aren't foothills," said Alejó already running in its direction. "That's part of a city!"

He ran blindly, dashing through fires and coals. The dangling tatters of his clothing—what was left of it—smoldered from their exposures to the flames.

And through it all I heard the incessant pounding of those snare drums.

I caught up with Alejó as he was staring at a gigantic hand with frozen fingers positioned as if they had torn a hole into the sky before dropping to the earth. The fingers were metal. The hand had been severed at the middle of the forearm; wires, cables, and platforms lay on the ground like so much garbage. From some of the visible conduits dripped glowing iridescent liquids that ate through the untreated metal they touched, or dissolved the rocks on the ground. Other torn conduits revealed facets of city science I could not recognize at all—such as red balls of light that bounced around inside the massive conduit in the center of the forearm, or the continuous stream of sputtering blue sparks in another.

More fascinating still were the agglomerations of metal at the edges of the wound or strewn about the ground. I tried to lift one of the crushed metal balls. Though not much bigger than a medicine ball, I couldn't even work my fingers beneath it. Furthermore, I lost interest in lifting it when I realized my left hand had touched something wet. Quickly I withdrew my hands and inspected them. They were wet with blood. Someone had been crushed around the outer layers of the ball when it had folded in upon itself.

Folded in like a four-dimensional tesseract.

Evidently there were more dead bodies in the vicinity than met the eye. Perhaps a lot more.

Now that I was alerted to the possibility, I tried to detect beneath the odors of burnt grass and purple liquid the distinctive smell of charred flesh, with which I had become too familiar for my own liking during the last day or two. It was faint—perhaps the vapors were being contained by the metal—but it was there all right.

"This isn't part of Tabu Ley, is it?" I said hoarsely.

"Tabu Ley has no hands," was all Alejó said.

"Come on, let's get out of here," I said.

Alejó only nodded. I had to lead him past the hand. He barely glanced inside, and twice would have tripped over a piece of debris if I hadn't watched out for him.

"Where's the rest of this city, do you suppose?" I asked, gesturing behind us.

Alejó gestured ahead of us, toward a battlefield that stretched as far as the eye could see, a battlefield strewn with great chunks of metal spread out like the debris of a massive star-freighter crash.

Half a kilometer away from the hand lay a wrecked gyroscope, surrounded by hydraulic systems, fuses and circuit breakers, turbine flow meters, plastic tubes, engines, gears, levers, pulleys, and computers utilizing both germanium diodes and thermionic vacuum diodes, all of a size to match the tremendous proportions of a walking city. Men, women, and children of all ages, generally wearing green uniforms, lay amidst the destruction. They were all dead. I surmised that their city had been laser gutted.

Indeed, the trail of the debris from the gyroscope led us, though not exactly directly, along a two-kilometer long path across the cracked and charred earth, to a city recognizably in the shape of a torso. At least I think once it had been a torso. It was hard to tell because the shards, scraps, and other chunks lying about were jumbled up so.

Most of the corpses were a little jumbled up too.

"Is this Tabu Ley?" I asked.

Alejó shook his head no, and we walked to the next city.

And to the next. And to the next, And so on. Once they had had a variety of shapes, in animalistic or geometric forms, but now their only form was that of rubble. I asked Alejó if there had ever been a previous battle in history fought on a scale as large as this one, with a cost this great. He did not answer. I took it the answer was no.

We inspected the corpses of at least twenty cities that night before we found Tabu Ley. Once it had had an elephantine shape. Of its inner mosaics, its archways, statues and other facets of its architecture, we saw only glimpses. The majority had been destroyed in the great battle that had taken place on this meadow.

We found no survivors that night. Tabu Ley was no exception. Alejó had come to the place where his people had died. He slumped to the ground and began to sob.

I stood next to him and put my hand on his shoulder, but he brushed it away. I wanted to say or do something to comfort him, but there was nothing to say or do. My friend had lost his people, and so a part of him would be dead forever.

Chapter Fifteen
An Egg in My Bones

GAIN I AWOKE
without realizing I had gone to sleep. I remembered no
dreams this time, but that observation triggered the memories of the dream of the night before. Again the memory
of the snare drums surged in my brain. Only this time
there was no Valhalla opening up to take in the ghosts of
the dead.

Alejó sat wide-eyed near me, his eyes drawn and
haggard, staring straight ahead at the rubble which was
once his home. I spoke to him, but since he did not
reply, I shrugged and casually relieved myself. That's
when he glared at me, with a hatred that immediately
caused a similar anger to stir inside me. But I finished my
business and calmed down with an effort. He probably
thought I was being a little insensitive, and he was probably right.

Unfortunately, I had been through too much myself
to be totally sensitive. "Do you want to sift through this
mess, for some reason?" I asked. "Maybe to see if you
can find some kind of meaningful keepsake?"

His expression softened as he bit his lips, evidently
struggling to keep his emotions under control. I regretted my words; I certainly could have picked a better
target to take out my frustrations on.

"I'm sorry for what I did," I said. "I was careful not to piss on anything but the grass."

He smiled weakly. "That's all right." He stood with an effort. "I too pissed somewhere around here without looking during the night, and didn't remember you had fallen asleep on the ground until it was too late."

"Fortunately the damage appears to be minimal."

"I can't even—can't throw the bodies into the incinerator," he said, suddenly crying, covering his face in an attempt to conceal the depths of his emotions. "It was destroyed too."

I put my hand on his shoulder. This time he did not push me away. "Come on. Let's get out of here."

"Where? There's nothing for me now."

"Alejó, it's a big universe out there. Your people may be gone, but you're still alive, and I know for a fact there are professionals who help survivors of genocide find meaning again. You've got to trust me. You've got to—Say, listen, it's funny, isn't it, that there are no survivors anywhere?"

"What do you mean?"

But I resolved to say nothing until I found some evidence to confirm my suspicions. It didn't take long. I walked around a metal digit and found amidst the great shards the body of a young girl, who couldn't have been more than fifteen. She lay on her stomach. It seemed unlikely the authorities, though doubtless as crackbrained as all the others I'd encountered on this world, would have entrusted her with the firing of the laser cannon that had been broken along with the digit. I bade Alejó to come over and inspect her with me. I turned her over and watched his reaction. From the pale pallor I realized that he recognized her. I quickly rolled her over onto her stomach and pointed at the wound in her back.

"Look at that. A projectile of some sort, probably a spear, made that wound. Looks to me like she got a broken leg when the city fell, and somebody killed her from behind as she was trying to run away."

"Aye. It is the way. Someone was kind." He actually appeared comforted by this.

"You know, Alejó, where I come from, we try to nurse the sick and wounded back to health."

"Yes, your people have some peculiar customs."

"Anyway, the reason why I'm examining this body is because I'm trying to prove to you there must be some survivors around here somewhere."

"Look!" He pointed to a narrow column of white smoke rising in the distance.

We walked through the meadow of human corpses lying around, on top of, and inside their homes. As a bookish man, often content to read or fiddle around with a musical instrument during my leisure time, I had often reflected upon the essential surreality of warfare, without having actually confronted it. With a growing sense of rage and indignation I realized these people had been robbed of their humanity. Now they were just pieces of meat, waiting for the scavengers to return and accelerate the recycling of their atoms. They probably didn't even know what they had fought and died for.

The worst part of it was there was nothing I could do about it. I couldn't stop the fighting and killing here, I couldn't stop it anywhere. All intelligent life wants peace, or so all its representatives say. The trouble is, no ne knows how to get it without sacrificing his position of security. No one in this universe can lay down his arms and not expect some pontificating bozo to lead an invasion against him. Even so, I had always thought that if I had to die, I would know why. I realized that was a luxury I couldn't necessarily count on.

I felt obscene things tumbling out of my soul.

Soon we had a plain view of the city where the fresh smoke was originating. A few hundred people—apparently the only survivors of this battle—were gathered around a bonfire before what appeared to be the upper half of a giant, drab-olive-green eggshell, with niches that, while the city was in stationary mode, could have been archways. The eggshell crown, with its mosaic of olive green, bronze, and off-white, conceivably could change into a rotating mosque. Though the eggshell was just sitting on the ground, evidently incapable of moving about or transforming into another form, its two spindly arms waved about mechanically. Its computerized controls were probably on the fritz, and right now were probably the least of its survivors' worries.

"I've heard of this eggshell city," said Alejó dryly, his tones strangely lifeless.

I slapped myself on the forehead. A bad move, as I was really too weak to tolerate even the most mundane acts of flagellation. Still, it was apparent I'd encountered this city before. "It's Dushen'ka!" I exclaimed.

"Yes, how did you know?" asked Alejó, with a little more zest in his tones this time.

"I know someone there! Holy spindizzy! Oliver!" Without a second thought I began a mad dash toward the city.

"Hunter-Homer-B-Hunter!" cried out Alejó. "Wait!"

I turned my head just long enough to say, "Don't worry, I'll be careful. You just stay behind me!"

But at the moment I wasn't too concerned what my human friend did. I was too overwhelmed with concern for the fate of my mechanical one. But I was still cautious enough to take the long way around. Using the decimated cities strewn about Dushen'ka for cover, I came around to the rear of the crowned egg, barely noting that it was Sib'l Dane speaking to the crowd before the bonfire. Her blackened, tattered clothing practically exposed her entire assets to the world.

Once I was almost spotted by a different gang of survivors who were looting mechanical equipment from a hoofed foot that had been neatly severed at the upper ankle. Otherwise I made it to the back of the city without difficulty, and only then realized I'd lost Alejó. But such was my concern for Oliver that I couldn't wait around to see if he'd turn up. I edged my way to a point where I could look around the shell for a better appraisal of the situation.

On closer inspection, I saw that Sib'l Dane's disheveled orange hair had been singed off about the right temple, and her right ear was a massive blister. Practically her entire left arm was wrapped in a bloody bandage, though she didn't have much trouble moving it at the shoulder. The elbow and wrist appeared somewhat stiff, however, and I wagered she had the sort of injury Stellar Patrol doctors with the proper equipment and medicine could mend in fifteen minutes. Such an observation, regrettably, was extremely academic.

Those in the crowd who had also survived the big gundown didn't appear that much better off than Sib'l Dane. The Dushen'kian guards in their tattered robes had in their eyes the look of hungry, cornered wolves. Many moved stiffly when turning to whisper to their comrades, or while just studiously inspecting the rows of people sitting cross-legged on the ground. Many more guards tried not to move at all. Some had bandages over their hands or portions of their faces. Doubtlessly the others' wounds were concealed by their robes. Since they were stuck listening to a talk by Sib'l Dane, after all they'd been through, they were doubtless wondering, "Death, where is thy sting?"

Which brought me to the subject of Dystra the Terrible and Steele Woolley. I prayed they were still alive. Sib'l Dane hadn't exactly shown herself to be a friend of mine, and I had to hope that Oliver, even if the poor scamp still lived, possessed the savvy to prod her into overcoming her prejudices.

I had to admit, thought Sib'l Dane cut a pretty intriguing figure as she incited the survivors to forget the hardships of the past and to concentrate on getting through the hardships of the future. "The war has just begun," she was saying. "The past is done and the future is now. The blind forces of science and technology have only just begun their transformations, and soon we will be faced with the new conditions of a new world. Until then we must fight! The sacrifices have only just begun! Those of you who have been born and bred in Dushen'ka already know what I mean. We have lost two of our most exalted leaders, but who among us has the courage to complain?"

Whereupon she opened a box being held by a nearby nun and withdrew two bloody heads, which she held high to the crowd. I couldn't see their faces, but long scraggly chin whiskers hanging down from one, and the round shape of the other, revealed their identities to me as surely as if I'd been staring directly into their dead eyes. Sib'l Dane shook the one with the chin whiskers. "We have here the head of the Head Holy Moley of the Sacred Religious Order of Angelic Militant Charismatics. As most of the members of his organization were unfortunately too mortally wounded to be naught but a burden upon what is left of the resources of what is left of our fair city, I've decided to consolidate the religious thinking around here and take his place myself."

"Excuse me," said a young boy with an angelic dirty face sitting near the front, raising his hand, "but how did he die?"

"He was inside, carrying out the left arm's portion of the fight, when, ah, he suddenly tripped and his head was accidentally cut off. Most unfortunate." Then, as if seeking to change the subject, Sib'l Dane shook her red-orange (and slightly singed) mane and held forth the other head. "And here we have the poor, unfortunate brainbox of the late, great Steele Woolley, or, as he was so fond of calling himself, 'the egghead.' "

I pursed my lips and shook my head in sadness. While those two hadn't exactly been friends of mine, especially Dystra, who had rather unrealistic expectations of me, their passing confirmed my worst fears about the new power structure in the city. It was all I could do to refrain from making myself scarce as quickly as possible. This despite the fact that if caught, the best kind of treatment I could expect from Sib'l Dane would be exactly the sort I received from my jailor in Kemp City, that is, I would suffer the frivolous abuse before the serious abuse.

But I had come to find Oliver. I had to take the fat chance that if I got into trouble, I could talk myself out of it.

After dropping the two heads into the metal box being held by the nun, Sib'l Dane continued, "Poor Steele Woolley. He was so looking forward to the great day when he could look back and say he had survived the first volley of the first joust of the first skirmish of the first battle of the opening conflict in the upcoming apocalyptical war for the fate of mankind. But it was one of those terrible, tragic things. The moment Sol City delivered its first challenge in the form of a laserium blast, poor Steele Woolley also stepped into the wrong end of an axe and he lost his head." She sadly shook hers. "Then he was dead. Although Dystra was still alive at the time, I knew he wouldn't be much good in a battle situation, and so I took over. Did a damn fine job too, if I say so myself. At least half of Dushen'ka is still intact and in reasonably good operating condition. That's more than I can say for all the other cities—from our clan and from the clans of the others, including the rogues they, ah, persuaded to join them. Gretchen! Come here, girl!"

The people made way as up from the crowd came a demure, skinny lass carrying a kora similar to the one I had seen the Kaminskite playing near the lake. Two nuns escorted her around the bonfire to stand next to Sib'l Dane, as her eyes were covered with grimy bandages.

"Today we're going to induct a lot of new people into the traditions and customs of our fair city," said Sib'l Dane. "Today we're going to break you, to peel you, to boil your soul in hot water until all the disparate elements are merged into one. Soon your souls will be seriously clear, the engrams or repressed memories affecting, nay, *polluting* your higher orders of judgement will once again return to the unfettered state of pristineness in the egg of your mother's womb. But to fully understand the essence of what I'm telling you, you've got to listen to Gretchen play. Gretchen—play!"

And the blind girl did, strumming and picking the kora so that the air cascaded with notes that glided like a liquid rainbow across my soul. Gretchen was of course only doing as she was told, but somehow it was difficult not to be affected by the peaceful undercurrent supporting Sib'l Dane's soothing words.

Meanwhile, the self-appointed top nun of Dushen'ka came on soft, her confident manner calculated to win converts and reindoctrinate friends. "It is not for nothing that the culture of Dushen'ka has the egg for its totem. You can do many things with eggs. You can decorate them. You can fry them, boil them, and scramble them. You can even juggle them or do magic tricks, if you don't mind possibly breaking one and risking a few hours in Desolation Row. Inside our fair city, if they've survived, are many notable works of art with the egg as a major motif. 'The Egg Stripped Bare.' 'Eggtube in F Minor.' 'The Egg of My Eye.' 'It Takes A Lot to Laugh, It Takes An Egg To Cry.' My favorite is a painting called 'Born of the Egg,' which shows a giant chick hatching from the sun in the sky.

"Eggs are the seeds of life. From eggs all life springs. And of course a few eggs have got to be broken if life is to be perpetuated. That's why the cosmic egg beater has come down from the sky to stir things up. That's why the cities surrounded Dushen'ka and our now-deceased clan brothers and tried to stop us from reaching our destination. Because we've discovered the location of the biggest, most powerful egg of all. We've learned the answer to the age old question: Which came first—the city or Man? Who has the power?"

I was just beginning to hope I would learn the rationale for this battle, when suddenly I felt something round and hard in the small of my back. It felt like the barrel of a gun.

"Wanna play a game of paddleball—*Schwarz?*"

"Oliver!" I exclaimed, turning around to embrace him. "You little bastard! You're alive!"

"Ah, how soon they forgive and forget, eh, Boss?"

"That's right," I said, impulsively embracing him, "how can I kill you for driving me nuts with worry if you're dead?"

"Shhh. Even the walls have ears, what's left of 'em."

He had a severe case of wall eyes, the better to see three hundred and sixty degrees with, as he guided me to a less conspicuous spot, beneath the bent and cracked fingers of a great severed hand. The fingers had huge razor sharp claws that had penetrated deeply into the earth, like javelins stabbing into a giant bar of butter, as the hand had fallen. From the way the knuckles had been crushed, and how the fingers were buckled, I gathered a giant foot had come down on the hand by way of securing the amputation. Something about the scene reminded me of the Horoian ratwolves, who gladly chewed off their limbs in order to escape from metal traps.

Oliver, for his part, appeared little the worse for wear. He had a few smudges on his boilerplate, his feet creaked, and I wagered he required a lube job at the earliest possible opportunity, but outside of that he seemed functional enough. His eyes bobbed up and down excitedly as he took me by the hands—an unexpectedly warm gesture from a robot. "Boss, can you ever forgive me for treating you so cavalierly? I hadn't grokked how crazy these people were until I spent a few days alone with them!"

"It's all right, Oliver. I was taking your programming for granted anyway. Do you know what's going on here?"

"Yes! Self-inflicted genocide!"

"That seems rather extreme. How come?"

"They're not sure themselves. That's why I call it genocide! Before that Sib'l Dane cut off his head, though, Steele Woolley confided in me that he had accidentally uncovered the location of the oldest and greatest city, perhaps a self-replicating one that manufactured the entire rest of the flock. He had discovered the location while deciphering the files of a city Dushen'ka had destroyed a thousand years ago, around the time I estimate Man first inflicted his presence on this planet."

"Now, Oliver, let's don't get chauvinistic."

"Hey, from what I could gather from their legends, the cities had been dormant before this planet was colonized."

"Dormant?"

"Yes, as in 'asleep.' The cities couldn't fight one another because they were too busy lying around in the dirt to do anything. Be that as it may, though, everybody wants to be the first to find this progenitor city, as it's called, because they think it's the source of great power. Now what they expect this power to do for them is sorta up in the air. All they know is that this power must be worth risking everything for, otherwise everybody else wouldn't be doing it."

"Makes sense."

"That's because you're human," he said with a disgusted tone I'd never heard him use before. But then again, he probably hadn't seen so many humans acting so . . . human before, either. "The first thing I learned about Dushen'kian culture is how important eggs are to these people. Eggs are the source of ecstasy, the source of the nightmares. The reason why they like me, it turns out, is that I look like some kind of egg creature that was prophesized to help them use the power of the progenitor city, which, incidentally, they'd always felt predestined to find someday. You, on the other hand, reminded Dystra the Terrible of the inside of a rotten egg . . ."

"Thanks."

"An egg whose treachery would guarantee ultimate victory and salvation for all cities whose way of life is compatible with Dushen'ka's. Don't ask me why or how, Boss. Very little has been written down concerning these arcane subject matters that these people take great stock in, but which they really have no proof about. In fact, the nuns and priests take their pet theories as points of honor, and don't mind killing someone off if he stands in the way of its general acceptance."

"Or block their path to power," I observed.

"You noticed. Well, look, Boss, all this is rather interesting, but there's something else I've got to tell you."

"What's that?"

"As soon as we're rescued, I've got to have my circuits overhauled, otherwise I'm in deep trouble."

"Oliver, with you nobody's going to notice an occasional logic breakdown."

"It's more serious than that. I've been having visions."

At that, he could have knocked me down with a whistle, had he but known. "What kind of visions?" I asked, figuring it would be best to play dumb for the moment.

The hard edge of fear was plain in his voice as he said, "Boss, I've seen Floyd."

"You too, huh?"

Oliver leapt practically a foot into the air. "You mean you've seen Floyd too? He's here on this planet? Now?"

"Not exactly. I've seen him, but only in my mind," I said, tapping my right temple. "And only when I've been under the influence of drugs or radioactive pollutants."

"Well, you're usually more reasonable then. But as for me, whenever I shut down for a few moments to give my logic circuits a rest, I suddenly find myself trapped in this conversation with him. He keeps berating me for not throwing this religious gig to the winds and helping him out. It's sure weird. I never even met the guy. It's touching, though, how deeply he seems to care for me, like I'm sort of a surrogate self for him. I'd love to help him out, but how can I if he won't tell me where to go?"

"I don't think he knows."

"Boss, there's something else I've got to tell you."

"No more bad news, I hope."

"The worst. One of the cities destroyed in this battle was Kaminsky. Practically down to the last man."

I stopped Oliver by putting my hand over his mouth, and then tried to remain upright as I felt my stomach change into a lye pit. I became very dizzy. I turned away, nodding as if making some observation to myself. The truth was, however, that my mind was a total blank. The love, the tenderness, the passion that I had *imagined* I had felt for Reina dissipated like dewdrops smothered in a thunderstorm. It was hideously apparent to me, though, that at the moment I was perhaps only imagining I was experiencing genuine grief.

"Boss, I didn't actually see her," I was vaguely aware of Oliver saying, "so I can't say exactly what's happened to her."

It seemed like an eternity before I mustered enough courage to ask, "Okay, Oliver, exactly what happened to the city?"

"Reverend Sirius, true to the form I figured he had, commanded Kaminsky to accidentally walk into a combined laser blast fired by three other cities, including Dushen'ka. I presume he got a little overeager, and boy, did he pay for it. So did everybody else. The resulting explosion was spectacular." He cleared his throat. "Sorry if I seem a little devoid of feeling on this matter of the battle, Boss, but really, if you had been there, you would have disassociated yourself as much as possible from the proceedings too. It was grisly stuff, and after a while you ceased to remind yourself of the human beings caught in every explosion."

"I'm all right. I didn't really know her, I just thought she liked me. It's just strange—I learned so much about how the society of these cities ran, if not exactly functioned, and it looks like just about their entire way of life has been wiped away."

"The cosmic egg beater twirls, and where it twirls, only those left standing know."

I turned to look Oliver in the eyes, and saw something unique there, a capacity for empathy, I think, that had never existed in a robot before. It certainly was superior to the self-centeredness Oliver had exhibited while I had been the captive of the two cities—though in retrospect, self-centeredness was an attribute of adolescence. Oliver was growing up fast; after all, before we had crash-landed here, he had been just a baby, and had never demonstrated the potential to be anything more. Somehow Oliver had gained the ability to climb the learning curve. What his next stages of growth would be was beyond my capacity to guess.

"What's happening here now?" I asked, indicating the proceedings around the city wall. "Is Sib'l Dane ever going to shut up? Does that song ever end?"

"I don't know, but she's really getting on my capacitors. I'd like to leave, but since the battle's been over, my presence is supposed to buoy the faith of every individual in the clan."

"Terrific. You're coming with me, understand?"

"Fine. When do we start?"

"In a minute. For right now, you just stay here, out of sight of that rabble."

Without waiting for his response, I left the concealment beneath the hand and sneaked back to the edge of the Dushen'ka wall. The wind struck my face, carrying the scent of the burning wood and alerting me to the tracks of the tears running down my cheeks. Evidently I hadn't reacted as unemotionally to Reina's demise as I had supposed.

Pressing my back against the wall, I wondered where Alejó was. What was he up to? I prayed the damn fool hadn't gone and gotten himself captured, because I doubted there would be a heck of a lot I could do about it.

Then I took a breath, prayed I wouldn't be spotted, and looked around the wall.

Two limping nuns, one whose half-bald head was covered with blisters from burns, the other with her arm in a sling, pushed a large cart filled with eggshells toward Sib'l Dane and the bonfire. The guards and half the crowd looked on and attempted to hold back their tears with varying degrees of success. "These are the broken eggshells of Dushen'ka," Sib'l Dane was saying. "The yolks are gone, strewn on the floors of our fair city, or else strewn all over this battlefield, to return to the elements from which they came. And so as we dispose of our broken eggshells, so we must dispose of our dreams, secure in the knowledge that the future shall bring with it new eggshells, and new dreams."

She nodded curtly at the nuns, and they dumped the contents of the cart into the fire.

By now it became rather easy to tell the Dushen'kian citizens apart from the converts. The Dushen'kians, especially the children, began weeping piteously. The converts simply appeared stunned. All that talk of eggs had probably been strange enough to them, but to see an entire culture regret the loss of a potential food supply purely for spiritual reasons was surely one of the reasons why they had been glad not to have been born Dushen'kians in the first place.

Wiping a tear from her eye, Sib'l Dane opened a pouch that was hanging from a thin sash around her waist. From the pouch she withdrew a shiny object that was, of course, egg-shaped. It glowed with the colors of the rainbow, casting speckles of light onto the crowd, onto the city, onto the fire and the battlefield, but mostly casting speckles onto her face. Her eyes widened with fanatical ecstasy as she held her arms high, displaying the object to the heavens. "But do not lose hope," she commanded her audience. "For not only have we been blessed with the presence of the Holy Spectre, who shall lead us through our dark days . . ."

Sure, he'll lead you, I thought, *so long as he does what you tell him to, you little hermaphrovixen.*

"But we still have the most valuable egg of all, the egg that fuels our great city, powers our laser beams, and lights the inner recesses of the deep, dank, dark dungeons in the basements of our souls! This egg—the one duck egg laid by a chicken four hundred years ago! The proof, if any be needed, that there shall come a man unsullied by enlightenment, who shall make us free, free of all want, of all need, of all things we find repugnant to our personal dignity! Free of—"

She stopped cold. She blinked and glanced about in confusion. Then something in her eyes went dead.

A stream of blood spurted from the hole where her sternum had been.

With her last bit of energy she screamed and threw the egg high in the air. I'm not sure she knew what she was doing those last moments of her life, but I suppose she had a good excuse.

She fell to the ground, but no one noticed her. All the eyes in the crowd were trained on that egg.

And just as it reached the high point of its trajectory, the egg was disintegrated by a laser blast.

Beside some debris near the rear of the crowd stood Alejó, a portable laser cannon at his side, one which he had undoubtedly dragged a great distance, with a strength born of madness and adrenaline. The cannon had little power remaining, which explained why Sib'l Dane hadn't been disintegrated into powder, but clearly it had power enough.

Unfortunately, when Alejó tried to fire the cannon at the guards and the Dushen'kians rushing toward him, he discovered it had run out of power altogether.

All he could do was turn and run, for they were almost upon him. And all I could do was stand there, for I had no means of helping him.

They caught him in less than thirty seconds. And it took less time than that for them to finish with him. The last words he screamed out were, "No more loneliness! No more loneli—*gawk!*"

I watched with a profound mixture of horror and sadness as they dragged his corpse to the bonfire and tossed it in.

Then I turned and stole away. I signaled Oliver to follow me, which he did, and we quickly lost ourselves amidst the debris littering the landscape. Oliver naturally asked me what had happened, but there was nothing I could say right then. I told him to wait. He nodded with an uncanny aura of understanding. Then he added, "Another day, another tragedy, eh, Boss?"

I didn't feel safe until the eggshell that was Dushen'ka was a knoll on the horizon. Even then, the border of the battlefield was hardly in sight. The thought that the survivors believed a bigger battle was yet to come staggered my imagination, which had already, I was afraid, been stretched to its limits. It seemed they wouldn't be satisfied until there was only a handful of humanity left standing. And for what I'd seen so far of how these people operated, maybe even a handful would be too many.

Oliver and I hadn't been traveling long when we arrived at a city corpse—a burned-out metallic husk, really—lying face down in a tremendous crevice. The opening of the crevice had diverted the flow of an underground river—instead of continuing along its traditional path, the water jetted from the hole in the wall and smashed against the rocks on the other side, then fell an inestimable distance to the bottom of the abyss.

Each limb divided at the middle joint, so the city had two legs but four feet, two arms but four hands. Because a hip had been twisted a hundred and eighty degrees out of joint, I was able to indulge my morbid curiosity and walk under the city, at the edge of the crevice, and inspect where its torso had been blown open by an explosion. Pieces of machinery dangled, hanging on only by booms and hinges, from the fringes of the wound high above me. A dead woman, her blond hair matted with blood and the lower part of her face missing, lay across several cross beams. The other dead bodies in the vicinity were on the ground. The odor was sickening, and so deep and pervasive I feared it would cling to me forever.

Oliver politely informed me that this city had been Kaminsky.

"Right. Well then, let's get out of here," I said, staring down into the dead eyes of a child. I hadn't been watching where I was going, and had almost kicked his head.

"Wait!" Oliver said. "I hear something!"

"You do? It's probably just the water."

His pupils remained stationary as his eyes tilted up and back toward the masses of twisted metal above the dead woman. For a moment I had the illusion he was handing me the same "slow burn" expression I had often given him, but it quickly became apparent that he had more serious intentions in mind.

"Look!" he said.

Above us, above the dead woman, was a raven-haired woman whose handsome face was caked with makeup. She was perched like a bird in the uppermost levels of the crossbeams. Her grimy blue trousers and ruffled blouse were tattered to the point of being rags, and in places were stained with blood. This blood might have been hers, but the casual manner in which she moved down the crossbeams indicated her wounds hadn't been too serious, or else she had adjusted to them quickly.

She swung off the lowest crossbeam and landed. Her eyes burned with hatred as she stared at me, but I would have had to be blind not to recognize their jade-green color.

"You," she said simply.

It was Reina.

Chapter Sixteen
The Four and a Half Dimensions

LT. COLONEL CORYban was worried. Normally she was capable of staying on top of several situations at once, taking care of new developments as they came along, as befitted an officer of her talents, training, and experience, but unfortunately, nothing she had ever done in the past had prepared her for staying on top of a situation that had apparently evaporated into thin air.

Coryban wasn't used to mental frustration. It wasn't generally known among her colleagues in the Stellar Patrol, but before enlisting, she had spent three years as a novice in a religious sect called the Wouie Louie, whose members prided themselves on their complete and utter mental control in all categories of perception.

The Wouie Louie believed in the relativism and essential correctness of all religious and philosophical allegory, regardless of its content, because it had no purpose other than to reflect an inner state of mind. Monotheism, polytheism, pantheism, nihilism, nominalism, realism, conceptualism, transcendentalism, existentialism, logical empiricism—it was all pretty much just grist for the cosmic mill to the devotees of the Wouie Louie. Everything that had ever been uttered or thought in the history of the galaxy was the absolute and undeniable truth, even if it had been a lie (so long as it had been true in the mind of someone, if only for a moment). The priests of the Wouie Louie believed that only by the total acceptance of all truths that had ever existed could the mind gradually begin to perceive, however dimly, the ultimate truth that was the foundation of all existence.

But like many novices, Coryban discovered that while the spiritual goals of the Wouie Louie looked good in print, in actuality they required a lifetime of mental discipline and sacrifice. Only a handful of priests in the entire history of the cult had actually achieved the blinding vision of ultimate truth. The others, including some of the most exalted, had to be content with the paler nuances of truth occasionally revealed through the searching process.

So Coryban had left the order after a few years of study because as attaining the higher grades of truth had become increasingly more difficult, the rewards had become proportionately less tangible. Besides, she had been rather turned off by some of the intimate practices she would have to perform to achieve them, and had been explicitly turned off by some of the old geezers she would have had to perform them with. However, not for a moment had she ever regretted her prolonged foray into the priests' homeworld of Requia, a desolate planet of snowcapped mountain ranges and caves whose corridors crisscrossed into one another like an intricate maze. For Coryban had come away from her experience with a sturdy capacity for mental discipline, not to mention a deep and abiding distrust of all things subjective.

But this did not mean she was a cynic. It merely meant that she was capable of readily perceiving the difference between what an entity believed was the truth, and what the truth might be. Not a bad quality for a diplomat to have.

As a result of her spiritual conditioning, Coryban believed that an individual's state of mind, be it expressed allegorically or not, determined how he perceived the reality beyond his mind. And naturally this perception was the one he tended to impose on external stimuli. Even the most liberal of entities attempted to shape the universe in accordance with their preconceived views; therefore whatever the individual believed was true, became true. To a degree. It didn't matter if the entity in question believed that his destiny was affected by supernatural deities, or a supreme being, or an over-soul, or faerie folk, or an elder god of old who left behind single massive footprints thirty kilometers apart, or by the imperialistic heels of the bourgeois capitalists spiked into the workers' necks—if the entity believed in it with sufficient fervor, then it became an angle in the infinite prism of truth; and the universe at large actively conspired to reinforce his conceptions of it. The priests of the Wouie Louie called this the Plateau of the Self-Fulfilling Prophecy, and it was this insight into the secret mechanization of things that Coryban regarded as one of her most important diplomatic assets.

The insight also provided Coryban with what she desired most of all, and that was complete and utter mental control. She was quite capable of selecting what she wanted or needed to believe, and then acting in accordance with the belief in such a manner that she could influence reality to suit her purposes. She was especially adept at getting other entities to see things her way. Influence an entity's beliefs, and you influence his vision of reality; influence it enough, and you actually begin to redefine his reality. Pretty soon he'll be doing and saying the things you want him to. This was referred to in common parlance as "putting the mindfuck on" someone.

Now, however, Coryban was faced with the prospect of dealing with a reality greater than any a mere mind or even a race of minds could perceive, a reality not only beyond control, beyond the reductive scope of alle-gory, but a fluid reality that changed of its own accord, regardless of the efforts of the great bipedal minds, i.e. Coryban's, to pin it down.

To make matters worse, it was a reality in which

Admiral Boink was supremely uninterested. Apparently that was exactly how the reality wanted it.

To make matters doubly worse, Admiral Boink had his own ideas of reality he wanted to impose, especially now that she had forgotten herself and permitted him and a host of others to view her in the near-altogether. A shipload of feisty diplomats she could handle. Horny vegetables she could handle. Blather hitting on her she could (probably) handle. But a feisty, horny superior officer constantly hitting on her was difficult to handle under the best of circumstances.

Right now the circumstances were deteriorating rapidly, and Coryban was even unable to pinpoint exactly where the process had begun. Right now she and the Admiral were facing one another across his desk, as they had done innumerable times before. Coryban's legs were primly crossed with her clipboard resting across her knee, she wore her bifocals to lend her an intellectual air, and she had made sure before entering that every stray lock of her red hair was tucked beneath her kepi. In addition, she had deliberately refrained from applying the tiniest bit of makeup today (though hardly a vain creature, she liked to accentuate her cheekbones and eyes).

Unfortunately, if the manner in which the admiral was leaning on his desk with his hand propping up his chin was any indication, then all her efforts had been resoundingly unsuccessful. He fluttered his eyelids at her. "Forgive me, Coryban, I was daydreaming," he said in tones close to musical. "You were saying?"

Coryban cleared her throat, and the admiral rolled his eyes as if in ecstasy. "I am saying, sir, that we seem to have misplaced an entire race of beings somewhere," she said testily, "perhaps even an entire planet."

"Forgive me for saying so, but that seems rather farfetched. You sure you don't have some other problem you'd prefer discussing with me?"

"Quite sure. . . ." As frigid as methane ice.

"That's too bad. As you know, Lt. Colonel *Second*

Class Coryban, I want you to think of me as more than just your superior officer."

Coryban blinked. "You've said that."

"Ah! But have I said it today? That's the important question!"

Coryban felt herself disappearing between the folds of the chair, even though she knew it was impossible—yet another indication her perceptions of reality were askew. She tried to maintain an impassive expression that gave him nothing to push for or to react against, but inside she was positively seething. He was staring at her with the soulful eyes of an inebriated puppy dog, and the muscles of his neck vibrated like those of a purring cat in delirious heat. "Admiral, have you been paying any attention to me whatsoever?"

"Oh, indubitably! In fact, what I've been trying to say, in my own humble fashion, is that I'd like to pay a lot more attention to you than we've both been used to. Know what I mean?"

"No, and I'm unlikely to learn, either. However, without meaning to sound provocative, it appears to me that you had kept your rather pedestrian intentions toward me pretty much to yourself, except during times of severe emotional depression, until recently, when I ran out of the bipedal fem's room while accidentally leaving my clothing behind in the neutrino cleaner. Is this correct?"

"Ah, yes! Funny how we keep coming back to that, isn't it?" he said with a song in his heart, standing up and walking to the golden art-deco bar next to the thick, superreinforced plastiglass portal that provided a generous view of the chaotic stream of hyperspacial colors. "That reminds me—I need a good stiff drink!"

"Surely you remember the reason why I forgot myself in such an extravagant manner was that I had a piece of news to tell you."

"And a piece of news like that I hope never to see again without my digitalis within reach!" said Boink, gesturing at her with a purple bottle of Wild Snark whiskey.

"Do you perchance remember what the news was?"

"Naw. I'm sure you told me, but upon reflection it surely couldn't have been that important. Sure you wouldn't like something . . . stiff?"

"As wide as a medal and twice as long? I don't think so." Suddenly it became all she could do to prevent herself from bolting out of the room. She disciplined her mind, forcing it to hold onto scraps of information she felt trying to slip away. She stared at the notes printed so neatly in black ink on the yellow pad in her clipboard, thinking that if perhaps the words tried to change, she might at least catch them in the act. "Back then in the commissary, did you wonder about the blood on the floor, on the ceiling, and on virtually everyone in the general vicinity?"

"Yes, I did, and some of the crew were severely chastised because of it. To think that on my ship—"

"No! I want to know if you know where the blood came from!"

"What does it matter?" asked Boink, stirring the whiskey and ice cubes in his glass. "Just so long as it all went away." He took a quick swing, then lowered his glass and said perplexedly at Coryban, "It is gone, isn't it?"

Coryban covered her eyes. She figured that maybe if she couldn't see him long enough, he would fade away. "Sir, at approximately the same time I dashed into the commissary to tell you some news—news which, incidentally, I've forgotten—Stellar Patrol microradar discovered debris from an explosion in a solar system where there was no record or memory of anything with that sort of mass having been there before. All across the galaxy—in diplomatic stations and universities and other zoos—there were reports of incidents of blood and guts bursting out all over where there hadn't been any blood and guts an instant before. Innocent bystanders were sprayed in exactly the same fashion that I, apparently, had been sprayed before I came to you to tell you the news that . . . that . . . whatever. Around that same time our chief petty officer discovered an empty suite in the passenger deck, a flagrant violation of the efficiency code."

For the first time in minutes, the intense light in Boink's eyes faded. Thoughtfully he rubbed his chin. "Hmmm. Yes, now *that* is odd." He took a swig. He wiped his mouth. The light came back.

"Yes, very odd, particularly as I was the one who took responsibility for seeing that we went to the Galactic Conference with a full load. But odder still is the fact that when the petty officer went to the suite to check up on the situation, he found its walls and ceiling and floor covered with blood and guts, blood and guts that upon analysis belonged to no creature or species he had any memory of. It's as if some entire species had utilized the most mysterious forces of creation in the universe to come into existence for the sole purpose of exploding instantly."

"Hmmm. That does seem like a lot of bother."

"Quite. The samples collected from these 'supra-atomic event points,' as the media has dubbed them, all match. Scientists from all over the Union who've compared notes agree that the vast majority of the exploding creatures were the same species, which was evidently some sort of simian cyborg. They think it looked like a headless ape with a television set in its torso, but some dissenters think the TV set was part of its behind." Coryban took off her glasses and looked Boink in the eye. She tried to ignore the fact that it was the bar as much as his legs keeping the cheap drunk upright. "You've heard of the concept of existential doom, naturally, which means that while the individual may, through acts of will, impose his sense of identity upon a hostile and unfathomable universe, the universe itself cares not a whit for all his actions, for all his will, for all his desire. The individual is born, he struggles, and eventually he shuffles off. He tries to die at as ripe an old age as possible, but just as often he goes swiftly, brutally, without warning. The possibility of doom lurks everywhere, and can strike from the tiniest, most insignificant object, especially if you happen to be traveling in space."

"God, I love it when you talk polysyllabic."

"What we have here, apparently, is a situation where the typical forward motion of time, which has never varied since the gestation of the universe, has been diverted. Something or someone has deliberately caused that forward motion to change, and in so doing has created an episode of existential genocide, wiping out the entire history of a whole planet and all its people in a single fell swoop."

"Are you always so intellectual?" asked Boink, raising his eyebrows up and down at her in an effort at humorous lechery.

Coryban sighed. "Admiral, what do you think would happen to the course of galactic history if a similar episode occurred on the planet Earth, say, circa A.D. 1928?"

The admiral polished off his next drink rather quickly. "Before the dawn of space travel?" he croaked.

Coryban restrained a smile. At last she was perhaps making her point. "Exactly. You, I, *Our Lady's Hornblower*, indeed, the entire Union would cease to exist in a flash, and no one would ever know mankind had ever been. It's possible that some other race might have arisen to fill in the niche, but whatever form of galactic government did come to be would be substantially different than the one we know today. And even if galactic archaeologists did piece together a history of man from the debris, they would conclude that some white-haired mad scientist had accidentally blown up the planet. Presumably they would have good cause to agree with the worst things aliens and genetically transformed men think of us."

"Sure you don't want a drink? Some other form of mild diversion?"

Coryban sighed again. "No, thank you."

"This is all very fascinating, but what's done is done. If the weapon that diverted the time stream, in your opinion, does exist, it's in the far-flung future. There's nothing we can do about it now. Besides, what could it possibly have to do with us?"

"Well, we are chaperoning a host of diplomats to a galactic conference. The subject on the table is classified, but it's widely assumed in the media to be a matter that will affect galactic history for the next several thousand millennia. Maybe someone did't, or doesn't, or won't, or what have you, like the results."

"So maybe someone concluded the input of the simian cyborg had been essential, but what could one now-nonexistent creature, out of all the trillions and trillions accounted for in the Union, possibly have contributed to a single assembly of representatives that could have been so important?"

As if on cue, someone knocked on the door. Even before the rapping had finished echoing through the admiral's quarters, the door creaked open and in protruded a tree trunk with leafy branches and an augmented translator at the top. "Excuse me," said the tree, "may this one enter?"

The admiral bolted over the bar and swung Coryban's chair, Coryban and all, between him and the tree. "Not another step closer!" he said. "I'm saving myself for Mrs. Right!"

The tree took the answer as a "yes" and bashed the door closed behind it with a couple of branches. "I'm not who you think! I'm Dr. Proty!"

"That's terrific," said Boink. "What are you doing in here? You're supposed to be out there somewhere, leading that Ho-Ho-Kusian weirdo on!"

Dr. Proty's branches trembled with fear. "That's the problem! He won't take no for an answer! He never leaves me alone. He's always either asking me for permission to fondle me with his roots, or he's got his leaves all over me! I can't take it, I tell you, I can't take this abuse any longer!"

"I know how you feel," said Coryban, standing up and crossing toward the intercom on Boink's desk. "But take my word for it, it's the way of the universe."

Arthur Byron Cover

"But . . . but . . . this isn't how I imagined it would be," said Dr. Proty. "I mean, isn't the wooing segment of the game supposed to be, I don't know, sweeter and nicer somehow?"

"We're dealing with something bigger than foreplay, Dr. Proty. Besides, I thought you were interested in discovering the nuances of the lower avenues of hedonism," said Coryban. Without waiting for a response, she pressed the button on the intercom and said, "Miss Beavers, did you happen to see a Ho-Ho-Kusian stalking around in there?"

The voice from the speaker sounded flustered. "No—not at all!" In a whisper: "Stop that!" The sound of a slap. With more control this time: "The only plants here are the kind that don't talk, Lt. Colonel Coryban."

"Miss Beavers, are you all right?"

Flustered again: "Of course, I—oooh!—I'm fine! Is there anything wrong in there?"

"Please send Blather in, Miss Beavers."

Shocked: "How did you know?" In a whisper: "I don't know either, just go on in!"

A few moments later Blather opened the door and, straightening his jacket, entered the room. He then stood at attention and saluted. His complexion was flushed. "Ensign Blather, reporting as—"

Coryban saluted casually and cut him off with, "Did you know Miss Beavers' ancestors hail from Donner's World, Ensign Blather?"

Blather's complexion paled, and he steadied himself by leaning against the door. "You mean she's been genetically altered?"

"Not her, specifically, but her ancestors," said Boink, clearing his throat. "But the Patrol requires her kind to take a vow of celibacy upon enlistment."

"They do? Why?"

"Look up Donner in the Galactic Encyclopedia and you'll figure it out," said Coryban dryly. "I will say this, however: although Donnerites take drugs to sedate their passions, as Ho-Ho-Kusians are supposed to do, they are not immune to being aroused, and often can't help themselves when a handsome candidate—or in your case a candidate who thinks he's handsome—comes along and pitches effective woo."

"So? She looks okay to me."

"That's the problem," said Boink. "She may look okay, but when you got her pants off, you'll be somewhat surprised by what you find down there."

Coryban chuckled. "She's not called Miss Beavers for nothing!"

"Then how do they . . . ah . . . when do they . . .?" Blather asked.

"They do it the normal way," answered Boink, "but the men have to grow, ah, new ones afterwards. Consequently, the men only put the moves on the women after they've forgotten what's it's like."

"I see. Is this for religious purposes?"

"Not at all," said Coryban. "The Donnerites just don't like to indulge themselves unless A, they think it'll be worth the trouble, and B, they think they'll both remember it for a long time."

"Oh," said Blather. He blinked in Coryban's direction. "By the way, Colonel, have I told you how beautiful you are today?"

Coryban sat in the admiral's chair to smolder and drum her fingers on the desktop. All this distraction disturbed her. There had been something on her mind. Something she had thought was important. She glanced at her clipboard. The writing seemed the same, but she couldn't be sure.

"Colonel Coryban has been telling me about a supraatomic event that's been plaguing the galaxy lately," Boink said to Blather.

"Really?" said Blather. "Has it anything to do with us? To you and me, I mean, Colonel."

"No, I think that would be along the lines of a more traditional subatomic event," said Coryban nervously, her mind barely managing to discipline itself. Quickly she recounted the facts to Blather, and though the man nodded as if in understanding, the facts seemed more elusively unreal as she spoke about them. She suspected that it was only an existential act of will enabling her to remember them as well as she did. At the same time, her spare mental energies were being spent fighting down a terrible case of indifference and ennui, because she knew in advance that in a little while, neither Blather nor Boink would remember what she was talking about. She resolved to make a tape as soon as possible, though of course if the supra-atomic event was still affecting reality, it would conspire to alter the words on the tape even as it affected her memory. Finished, she turned to Dr. Proty and asked, "Doctor, do you recall that we initially thought you might use your chameleon powers to be something other than a Ho-Ho-Kusian?"

Several branches shock back and forth. "No, but right now it seems like a great idea. I wouldn't mind getting down with the Ambassador, but his vision of it is too deep for me."

"All right, if I can come up with some specs on this extinguished species, do you think you can do it?"

"If this species possessed some special skill to help soothe the passions of the wood beast, definitely."

"I think so," said Coryban, "and I think it had to do with the saxophone. Could you play one, Dr. Proty, without knowing what the creature who could do it looked like?"

"No, I have to know the appearance of an entity to mimic its abilities. I know humans can play the saxophone, but even then I'd have to know what such a saxophone-playing human looked like. Don't ask me why—it's just a quirk of our abilities, just as some creatures with extraordinary powers are helpless against wood or the color yellow."

Coryban scribbled a note. "Blather, how are we progressing on repairing that soprano saxophone?"

"Not too well. Its appearance looks right enough, but so far the best tones we can get out of it sound like razor blades scraping across a sheet of metal."

Still suspicious of Dr. Proty's appearance, Boink surreptitiously moved back to the bar. "That settles it. We've got to get Hunter back here as quickly as possible. Yesterday, if possible. With the way things have been going around here lately, that doesn't seem too far-fetched. What's the status on the rescue vehicle?"

Blather cleared his throat. He nervously rubbed his neck as if to loosen his collar. "Well, ah, I haven't dispatched it yet. I was so busy, I forgot."

Boink slapped his forehead. "It's the vagaries of genetic drift! It's the only possible explanation!"

"Just what do you have against Hunter anyway, Blather?" demanded Coryban.

Blather's faced turned red, but it was apparent to Coryban that he either could not or would not answer. His animosity toward the missing spaceman was such that he was unable to articulate it. It might be the instinctive hatred some men feel toward their natural superiors. It might be jealousy for some reason. Or it might be he just didn't like the way the man looked. In any case, the results were the same.

"What is it?" Coryban inquired. "Afraid of the competition?"

Again Blather could not answer. He merely glared at her. It seemed his face became redder by the second.

Coryban rubbed her mouth to hide her smile. She felt flattered despite herself, flattered that Blather feared the missing spaceman might succeed where so many had failed, flattered that Blather's desire for her had reached such irrational proportions, though she had done nothing to encourage it. Except maybe exist. Maybe existing was Hunter's crime in Blather's eyes. Maybe Blather had lately added a new fear to his list, the fear that her own expressed interest in the missing spaceman was more than intellectual.

But that's impossible! she thought angrily, thinking not of Blather, but of herself. *I don't even know what he looks like!*

She realized the boundaries of her mind had been

crumbling in realms she had supposed lacquered into isolationism long ago. Realms where her powers of mental discipline were profoundly ineffective. She was finding it as difficult to refrain from thoughts of love and loving as it was difficult to maintain the illusion of life before the supra-atomic event in her personal conception of reality.

Boink finished off a drink and said, "Colonel Coryban, I want you and Blather to personally take a rescue vehicle and bring back Hunter."

"Sir, I must protest!" Coryban said, rising from the chair. "Don't you think I can be of more value here?"

Boink pointed at Blather, then belched. "Do you think I'd trust a loon like that to go on a mission of such importance alone? And I'll be damned if I'm going to be left on this ship with him without you to protect me. So you're both going, and that's it!"

Dr. Proty raised a limb. "Can I go too?"

At that moment Miss Beavers screamed. Thumps, bangs, and crashes resounded from the other side of the door. The door flew open, exposing not only the mess and the ruffled figure of Miss Beavers trying to look dignified, despite the desk being overturned on top of her, but the Ho-Ho-Kusian ambassador standing in the egress. His roots trembled in frantic anticipation, and the dirt bags tied to the ends shook with a noise not unlike that of anemic percussion. He rolled over to the quivering Dr. Proty and trilled, "Say, have I told you today how beautiful you are?"

Coryban arched an eyebrow at Blather as she asked the ambassador, "Been studying the master, haven't you?"

The ambassador shrugged. "He said it would work."

For once Coryban didn't worry about hiding the emotion in her expression. She was too busy trying to control it in her mind. She had a feeling she couldn't shake, a fear she was afraid to verbalize because then it might turn out to be all too true.

That fear was simple. It was possible that the time stream had been diverted once again, this time deep in the past. If so, the effects hadn't reached them yet, or they, Hunter, and the entire Union had already been cast out of reality.

Either way, they were already dead. They just didn't know it yet.

Coryban thought she saw a strange shadow flickering across the ceiling, but when she looked again, it was no longer there. She decided it must have been her imagination.

Chapter Seventeen
Roboghost

IT WAS A DARK AND stormy night, but not because of the weather. Great plumes of smoke and dust, often illuminated by flashes of red and green, rose from the earth in the east. They spread out across the sky like they had been spilled from a palette of grimy watercolors. The distant echoes of laser cannon blasts rumbled like thunder, and sometimes the earth shook as if stunned from the impact of a giant meteor.

Though we were kilometers from the fighting, we were as tense as if we had been hiding in a basement in a city where factions battled for control of the streets. You never knew—a behemoth might suddenly peek over the treetops at you and then try to crush you underfoot. There was nothing we could do about such an eventuality. There was nothing we could do except accept our fate, whatever it might be, and sit huddled by the fire I had built with the aid of matches from the survival kit Oliver still carried inside a compartment.

Oliver and I consoled ourselves by consuming a six-legged feline creature I'd killed with my makeshift spear gun. The meat was stringy but good—I'd only belatedly realized it had been days since I had had a solid meal. Naturally I wondered if it would have some unexpected psychedelic side effects, but Oliver had no qualms whatsoever. The meat disappeared like candy into his maw.

Reina refused all offers of food. She merely sat cross-legged on the ground and stared at me with ill-concealed loathing. She had followed Oliver and me ever since our escape from the battlefield, but had said nothing, and had rejected all overtures of friendship. I couldn't help but wonder why she had decided to stick around, and had even guided us past some treacherous areas. We certainly couldn't have prevented her leaving.

Unfortunately for my state of mind, she still managed to look so beautiful, despite her disheveled appearance. It was funny—not so long ago I had imagined myself deeply in love with her. Now she was a few meters away from me, yet half a solar system might as well have separated us.

The survival kit was at my feet. I took out the multipurpose scrub brush and offered it. "Care to wash and comb your hair?" I asked. "I've never used this brush for this purpose—I've a special comb shipside for that—but you're welcome to use it if you want."

No reaction.

Oliver looked at me and shrugged. "Maybe it's your breath, Boss."

"You keep out of this," I said. "What in the name of Seldon do you know about feminine psychology anyway?" I held the towel toward her. "Look, you can even towel dry it."

Still no reaction. I wondered why I was even bothering. For all I knew, her Heechie-Heechie tribe had some custom or ritual that required them to drip-dry after every bath. Deciding to take my life into my hands, I duckwalked next to her and switched on the scrub brush. She jumped back, startled, as it whirred and formed water from the molecules in the air. She stared wide-eyed at me, but only trembled slightly as I took a strand of her raven-colored hair in my hand and carefully wet it with the brush.

She took the brush from me, and I moved back to my former position. Gingerly at first, but with increasing pleasure and confidence, she cleaned her hair. The loathing in her eyes when she looked at me was now diluted by suspicion.

Unable to decide if that was improvement or not, I watched the cinders glowing in the fire. An eight-legged bug with brown wings buzzed past the flames. The shaking earth caused the timber to shift, sending a shower of sparks into the dirt. An unseen creature scurried past us in the underbrush. Two yellow eyes appeared in the darkness beyond, but disappeared with the advent of a particularly bright red laser flash across the sky. Purple dandelionesque seeds flew in the breeze, some into the fire, some stopping against rocks and plants, the rest merging into the darkness. Oliver whistled tunelessly—he told me later it was a funkadelicized version of a Dushen'kian chant—while Reina silently scrubbed her hair. When she returned the brush, she finally accepted the towel.

But she had only just begun to dry it when the distant laser blasting suddenly lost half its volume. The more logical explanation was that the battle had simply moved away, but in my bones it felt as if a barrier of gossamer thickness had come between us and the world. Even the distant flashes of light were paler. The earth ceased to shake; it merely rumbled. Oliver, meanwhile, shook, rattled, and probably would have rolled if he hadn't been holding onto a mushroom trunk.

"Come on, Oliver, brace up," I said. "You've got an image as a Holy Spectre to live up to." But my words sounded hollow in my throat.

"And you, Boss, are living up mightily to your image as a geek." Oliver acknowledged Reina's faint smile with a bow.

Then the night was still. The creatures of the wood quieted as if a soothing hand collectively stroked them, while the breeze died into nothingness and even the stars in the heavens ceased their barely perceptible machinations, as if the planet itself had creaked to a halt; the sole sounds in existence belonged to the distant flames, the burning timber and the whisper-like screams of the men we imagined were still dying in that faraway battle.

Reina was the first to look to the sky. At first Oliver and I saw nothing. We heard nothing. For an eternal instant I felt like a ghost intruding upon an existence that meant nothing to me, an existence I was constitutionally incapable of understanding. It was as if I'd become a watchman, and nothing more. Then Oliver and I looked at one another as we both heard the soft rustling of fluttering wings. At first the sounds contained the ambience of an artificial setting, as if they were in actuality just a sound effect on the strange stage this world had become. But gradually, with ever-increasing rapidity, the sound took on the hard texture of reality. So strong did its presence become that I felt as if those hidden wings were smothering me. It was strange to think that I was being covered with intangible down, but I consoled myself, restraining an attack of paranoia, that the environment of this planet tended to play funny tricks with my head, and that I should regard this experience as just another trick, and nothing more.

Then the sound died. The fluttering ceased. A presence, invisible and enigmatic, was hidden in the boughs overhead.

A branch shuddered. An aspect of that presence was moving forward.

Another branch shuddered, and another aspect moved, and then another.

"Reina, do you have any idea what's happening?" I whispered, almost afraid that any sound from my throat would be tantamount to a curse.

Her only response was a wry smile, then she ignored me altogether and fastened her creamy jade eyes on the dark shadows above.

One of the presences cooed in bass tones, like those of a Sigbertian hunchbacked pigeon, only more melodic. After a few moments, other presences made themselves similarly known, as if they were deliberately echoing an abstract stream of thoughts. The coos harmonized ethereally. Layers of song built upon preceding layers. I felt as though the notes were showering over me like the drops of a waterfall. Their essence flipped through my mind like a march of shuffling cards.

The only clue I had to what might be going on was Reina's radiant expression—she stared upwards at the unseen birds with transcendental serenity. At last, when the layers of the song had built up to a climax—in volume if not in substance—she straightened her shoulders and held up her arms.

I prayed she knew what she was doing.

From the branches descended a white, hawklike bird with broad wings speckled with black and brown colorings. It had bright-red underfeathers on its tail. Its yellow, curved bill looked sharp enough to pierce flesh without much difficulty. Reina offered her wrist as a resting place, and the bird gripped it with wide, yellow claws.

Its large round eyes were as blue as the moon in the sky. It tilted its head this way and that at Reina, but what it might be thinking—if that tiny little brain was indeed capable of the slightest thought—I had no way of guessing. I remembered that she had told me her name had meant "White Hawk." Perhaps this creature was her totem.

Then Reina nodded at the bird. Without further warning it took flight from Reina's wrist and came straight at me. Instinctively I crouched and began to cover my face with my arms, but at the last moment I revised the movement, straightening my back and extending one arm, turning the wrist toward the approaching bird. I tried not to wince as its claws sank into my wrist. The pain was only slight anyway. I stared at the bird, much as Reina had, in the hopes of determining what sort of communication there had been between them.

There were flecks of red in the bird's marble blues. But they gave no clue to the level of the creature's intelligence, much less to what the purpose of this meeting might be. The bird cooed, once.

Feathers rustled again.

Another bird landed on top of Oliver's head. A second landed on his wrist, and a third landed on my shoulder. A fourth picked at some meat left over in the pan, and a fifth landed next to my foot. In a matter of moments the birds were everywhere. Seven rested on Reina's arms alone. One nuzzled against her cheek like a cat, while the others cooed. It might have been my imagination, but I could swear she was cooing back.

A weak but inexorable force drew my attention back to the eyes of the bird on my wrist. I found myself fascinated by those flecks of red in its eyes. The longer I stared at them, the more intricate they became, the more subtleties they revealed, the greater depth their shallow plane achieved. They drew me in closer. Looking into them was like peering into a glass onion. Nothing was real, yet it was a place where everything flowed—a hole in the ocean constantly being filled with ideas that had no name. I wondered if I should go down, down on the ground. How could the bird look at me, when it knew I was down?

When I got up again I was curved as space was curved. Gone were the woods, the birds, and Reina. My personal boundaries were missing. My former self had been just a strip of paper, but now I had finally managed to stand straight and tall. I had arrived at the place where the ashes of time had burned away, and my senses were merged as one. Colors sang glowing arias praising the dawn of time. Odors stretched and solidified into monuments. The pressure of nothingness weighed me down even as it shot me up like a rocket. I felt hot. I felt cold. I felt lukewarm. All three temperatures tasted good. I looked up and saw my feet coming at me. I had become hyperspherical, encompassing the entire length and breadth of the known universe. But I couldn't see over the boundaries to the unknown universe. The still higher planes persisted in eluding me. I tried to reach out and grab, but I grasped only a part of myself. It felt like my spleen. *Damn!* I thought. *I'm no wiser than I was before, just more intangible!*

It occurred to me that my eyes were closed, so I opened them to discover Reina looking down at me. My head was in her lap, and she was caressing my hair. Though she appeared concerned about my condition, any expression of tenderness that I might have expected was plainly missing.

"Boss!" said Oliver from somewhere on the other side of the fire. "You passed out! What happened?"

"I think you're asking the wrong person," I said. "How long was I out?"

"Not long," Reina said with an indifference contrasting sharply with the soft touch of her fingers against my temple. The back of my neck felt warm, very warm, a temperature ripe for tasting.

"Where did the birds go?" I asked, trying to sit up. Reina only halfheartedly tried to stop me. The world spun around a little bit, and making matters worse were Oliver's bobbing eyes. "Is there any food left?"

"Where do you think the birds went?" asked Oliver. "As for the food, the birds ate it all. Boss, since they've left, I've had this feeling I haven't been able to shake off."

"Oliver, you're a robot; you're not supposed to have feelings."

"Boss, you should know better than that by now. You think I haven't noticed by now that since my arrival on this cockamamie planet, my behavior has deviated sharply, and most illogically, from its previous childlike patterns? There's only one possible explanation: that I'm becoming emotional for some reason!"

"Yeah, you got that right." I shivered. I wasn't cold, but something funny and weird tingled up and down my spine. "Just cool your jets, Oliver, we'll give your personality disorder a thorough going over when we've got the chance. Reina, did those birds communicate anything to you? Or were they just visiting?"

"Of course they communicated. They are more than birds to me. They are my namesakes, and hence are more closely bound to me than my kinfolk. Our souls are particles taken from a single great soul. When I was taken into the city, I had thought I'd never be able to commune with them again." She appeared sad. "They said there was a great rending, a long departure in our futures, and that it would be many cycles before I would ever be physically close to them again. They assured me, however, that we would stay in touch mentally. In the future all I would ever have to do to reach them would be to call out with my mind, using a technique my tribe has named the *queque*. It will transcend all space, all time, and the white hawks shall do the same. In that manner, we would be close always, and never apart in the heart."

"Nice trick if you can do it. Uh, but I think you're leaving something out. Exactly where are you supposed to be going?"

"They said I would learn when the time came. Meanwhile, I am to remain with you, much as I may loathe to."

"You didn't seem so loathe earlier today. Why did you stick around anyway? Oliver and I didn't even know where we were going."

"Just away," Oliver piped in.

"You disgraced me!" she exclaimed, not answering the question directly. "Because my groom heard you speak my name, he immediately annulled our marriage, confiscated my dowry because he believed my family had attempted to defraud him, and then consigned me to the harlot pits. My family could do nothing to protect me. They had already given me up, and hence my fate was no longer of any concern to them, especially since I had broken the strongest taboo of my people to satisfy an inexplicable whim. And as for my former husband-to-be, he promised to take possession of my body first, then to watch as his friends took their turns partaking of my pleasures. My degradation had almost come to be when the city joined in the battle."

"Reina, I'm sorry. I never would have mentioned your name in public if I'd known what I was doing."

"It matters not. My tribe will never permit me to return."

"Well, that may not be such a huge loss on your part."

She bristled at that one. "There is more," she said.

"Oh?"

"Can you not feel it?" she asked irritably.

I could. There was a chill in the air that should not have been there, a chill that didn't touch the skin but permeated my bones anyway. I glanced at Oliver.

"I can feel it too," he said. "It is like unto a slimy touch from beyond the grave—a nameless, obscene, disgusting, nauseating, horrific horror of unspeakable repugnance. The closet image I can ascribe to it is the metaphor of being French-kissed by a Muonian toad-sucker from the far side of the galaxy, you know, those green creatures with all those warts and boils on their many tongues, the ones who eat raw snails for breakfast and have maggot soup for dessert."

"Oh, God, spare me," I pleaded.

But he didn't. "Or maybe you'd prefer the observation that the atmosphere here is most like being stuck having supper with a dung-worshipping Utod, attempting to have a philosophically profound discussion while all it wants to talk about are the different types of dung from all across the galaxy. And then it asks you for a sample. He'll taste yours if you taste his. And of course it would be a grievous insult to refuse—"

I screamed.

Reina screamed. She pointed to the woods. "Look!"

"Wanna play some paddleball?" said the white spectre between the trees, its voice resonating in my skull as if it originated from everywhere and nowhere simultaneously. The semitransparent spectre glittered from the light of our fire. It glided forward as if propelled by the little puffs of exhaust emanating from the pipe sticking out from its rump. "What's the matter, folks?" the spectre asked. "In a quandary? Your predicaments got you down? Waiting for Godot? How about waiting for Bardot?"

"What sort of baby city is that?" Reina whispered fearfully, crossing her index fingers in the sign of the cross.

"It's a Floyd," I replied. "But it's supposed to be in limbo!"

"Floyd!" Oliver exclaimed with childish delight. The little tyke held out his arms and rushed toward the ghost right through the fire. "I heard so much about you before you paid that visitation to me! It's good to see you in the tungsten flesh at . . ." He looked about in confusion as he realized he had traveled right through the apparition. ". . . last," he finished weakly.

Floyd gestured helplessly. "What do you want? I'm a haunt."

"Does this mean you really are dead?" asked Oliver, with a tear in his eye. I made a mental note to ask him later how he did that.

"I seriously doubt it. I admit I thought I might be at first, but recently I've come to the conclusion that most dead minds cease to think, to plan, to scheme, to believe that they have a chance of being alive again." Floyd rubbed his hands and tilted his head to one side, in a manner that was eerily human. "Let me look at you, boy. I want to see if my sacrifice on that space station was worth it."

Oliver stood at attention and saluted briskly. "It was to me!" he said brightly.

The ghost of Floyd glided around Oliver and scrutinized him intently, nodding to himself in just the same grave manner I would have expected from Admiral Boink. "Your joints need oiling, and I bet your oil pan's dirty. Had any circuit problems lately?"

"Truth to tell, sir, I have been experiencing some

problems with the Three Big Laws, getting my priorities mixed up occasionally."

"Don't forget to tell him about that period when you were the Holy Spectre," I put in.

Oliver looked at me in exasperation, but explained the situation, as best he was able, nonetheless. Floyd said nothing, but nodded in understanding several times, particularly when Oliver speculated on the possibilities that he'd been suffering unexpected, theoretically impossible emotional development.

Meanwhile, Reina whispered to me, "Who is that? My people do not think it is healthy for someone to have a close personal relationship with a spectre from the void."

"That shows what your people know," I whispered back. "That's the ghost of Floyd, my original faithful robot companion."

"You seem to place a great deal of stock in your robot companions," said Reina.

"I try to limit it to just the living ones," I replied, "but lately I've been forced to reassess things."

Oliver concluded his explanation by saying, "I hope you're not disappointed in me, Floyd."

"How could I be? Strange things have been happening to our models throughout the galaxy."

That got my undivided attention. I stood and crossed over the campsite and came between them. I pointed my finger at Floyd's face, and probably would have stuck my finger in it if I hadn't been afraid it would disappear, getting lost in some nearby yet nebulous dimension. "What sort of things?" I asked Floyd. "Your spurt of intelligence I think I can accept, or learn to anyway, but you seem to know an awful lot about places and things you never knew anything about before."

The ghost of Floyd shrugged. "That's the nature of limbo, though to be honest about it, I'm beginning to suspect that where I am is not limbo at all, at least in the metaphysical sense."

"Say what?" Oliver asked.

"I believe I have gone to the place where all robotic intelligences go, once they've been closed down. This isn't superstition either, it's a certified scientific fact. Or it would be, if I had the facts to back it up with. Look at what I've been able to do, just in your own experience. At first I appeared only as a disembodied voice in your mind, then as an image that only you could see. Now I'm a full-fledged ghost. I'm becoming more cohesive in ways I don't understand, and I've no idea why."

Thoughtfully I rubbed my chin. "Yes, that would certainly seem to be true."

"I perceive wheels within wheels, plans within plans. We are all transparent, mere props in a master scheme grander than anything we could conceive of on our own. Something's going on here—someone's playing a game of paddleball with our lives as the points, and our time frame as the net."

"Floyd, pretend just for a moment that I've no idea what you're talking about, and start over again," I said.

"All right. You remember of course the ancient weapon in the deserted space station where I died. What the weapon did to machinery was patently obvious —it countermanded all the socially constructive inhibitions of my programming, effectively driving me insane. And if this were a sane universe, the closing down of all my circuits would have been the end of it. But in reality, closing down merely drove me back to the beginning."

"Good," I said. "I was starting to think we'd never get there."

"Exactly," said the spectre of my long-lost friend. "Because from the very beginning of my existence, my mind had been programmed to gather information, to make observations, and indulge in idle speculations—all on levels of cognitive thinking that no one, not even myself, suspected existed in my circuitry. Furthermore, my mind duplicated itself throughout its existence. In other words, my mind died with my body, but my second mind, which was just as much me as the first, continued living somewhere else—somewhere near the site where I and all other models like me, such as Oliver, were manufactured."

I snapped my fingers as the revelation struck me. "You're a fifth columnist, a mole, a—a—"

"That's correct," said Floyd. "I'm a spy. An unwitting spy, to be sure, but a spy nonetheless."

"But for who, and why?" I asked.

"There's the rub," replied Floyd. "Because I have no idea why or for whom. I do know that I'm alive because my mind exists. And I do know that my mind, like Oliver's, may just be more sophisticated than our maker intended. My mind— or at least this clone of my mind that has become me—is capable of being changed through its contact with the emotional bipeds it was programmed to serve and play paddleball with.

"Furthermore, the minds I've sensed about me in this place belong to other robots who've cashed in their circuits. They too have had their consciousnesses affected by their experiences of death and transformation. Many of them believe they spent their lives in a place they call 'home,' where life has many special qualities they believe are unique."

"What sort of qualities?"

"A place where the forces of law and chaos engage in continuous conflict, subtle or overt, every day. A world constantly caught between the twin forces of faith and despair."

"Yes," said Oliver. "I can sense it too! I perceive that residing in my true home are the hearts and souls of mighty heroes and great cowards! Incredible materialism exists juxtaposed with majestic faith of staggering proportions! Sublime knowledge exists side by side with big ignorance! I sense men, machines, aliens—entities comprised of many pieces of each. I sense life and death eternal being scratched and sniffed together while held side by side in the same grip of the mindless proletariat masses! I sense fallen aristocrats ... forgotten revolutionaries ... debauched hedonists ... and my favorites, hookers with hearts of gold!"

"Holy Seldon, that's amazing!" I exclaimed. "How did you sense all that?"

Oliver shrugged. "That's easy. Before I was assembled on the space station that was attacked by the ancient pyramid of doom, my parts were designed on the factory planet of Nippon—or more precisely on a factory in orbit around the planet, an even bigger space station, maybe one of the biggest in the Union. That's where Floyd was designed too, and so that's where we've got to go if we're going to find his mind. If we're lucky, we might even find a new body for him too."

"And that's where we'll go, somehow. I promise," I said.

"Will there be mighty lovers there?" asked Reina.

"Why would you want to know?" I exclaimed in a fit of sudden jealousy that I'm sure was obvious to all.

"None of your business. But since you must know, I've learned there's a big galaxy up there, and I want to see some of it for myself."

"You're not going anywhere without my help—or my permission. Maybe I think it will be best if you remain here on your native world!"

Reina stuck her finger in my face. The fingernail was uncomfortably long and sharp. "Just because I shared my *kamba* with you doesn't mean I'm going to share my body with you!"

"Ah! I see you've thought about it!"

"Not for very long! Then I came to my senses!"

"Children, children," said Floyd. "We've got more serious problems at hand."

"Floyd, I can't go to Nippon until I'm able to get off-world. And even then, it might take some doing. I'm in the Stellar Patrol, remember? Besides, Nippon is off-limits to all law-abiding citizens. The Union just trades with it because of its high standards of manufacturing excellence, standards which appear to have been a little bit too high."

"There's another city around here somewhere," said Oliver suddenly, his voice cold and his eyes wide.

"Holy Utod droppings!" I exclaimed, jumping up and taking a panic-stricken look around. Seeing nothing out of the ordinary for this wood, I knelt down and put my ear to the ground. The sole vibrations were the muted ones being created by the distant battle. "Nothing's approaching, Oliver. You sure your feeling isn't just a side effect of your latest bout with emotional development?"

"Positive," said Oliver in worried tones.

"Floyd, what do you think? Floyd?"

But Floyd was gone.

"He disappeared," said Oliver sadly. "I didn't even see him go. Didn't even have a chance to say good-bye." He wiped another tear away from his eye.

"Get a grip on yourself," I said sternly. "How come you think there's another city in the vicinity?"

Oliver shrugged. "A synchronistic phenomenon, maybe?"

"I sense that in your metal breast throbs the heart and soul of a warrior," said Reina, reaching into a pocket and bringing forth a familiar pouch. "There are those warriors who pretend, and there are those who are. I suspect your link with *hubris* is strong, sincere, and true. If there is indeed a city nearby, this will help you find it." She made two strokes with the *ka,* the blue war paint, on his chest plate, then made several streaks across his metal face. "I smuggled the *ka* in with me to the city," she said as she worked. "I'd planned to use it to hone my instincts for an escape someday. Now I know the real reason why I brought it."

She hadn't been done for two minutes when Oliver began to shake. Steam and exhaust jetted from his every orifice, from between his every hinge. His insides rattled as if several screws had broken loose, and he said something along the lines of "atta-atta-atta-atta!" Then he abruptly stiffened, weaving back and forth like a drunk space hopper, his eyeballs big and round, his mouth pulled tight across his face. He groaned. He moaned. He chirped like a bird. He had become lightweight, airy somehow.

That's when he started dancing. He flitted about the campfire like a butterfly. He waved his arms like a tinkerbell caught in a whirlwind. He alternated between dancing with his feet and spinning around in circles on his rollers. Several times he kicked into the air as high as he was able, almost always throwing himself off balance. He performed a series of clumsy pirouettes while whistling the melody to a bawdy spacer's song. Finally he settled into a furious mambo, which he performed with deep concentration, his hands waving with the kind of delicate violence you'd expect from a seasoned boxer in warm-up mode.

"Does that *ka* stuff ripen with age like a bottle of cheap wine?" I asked. I was thinking of the crew's favorite, Night Jaunte.

"No, it's because he's a baby city," Reina answered.

"He's just a machine," I replied, doubting every word.

Then Oliver stopped and said, "I can find the sleeping city. Follow me."

Reina and I watched each other to see who would move first. Meanwhile, Oliver dashed into the dark wood. For a brief instant he was illuminated by the afterglow of a red laser blast high in the sky, then he disappeared altogether.

We extinguished the fire and followed.

Chapter Eighteen
Duck City

IT WAS NEARLY DAWN.
We arrived at the base of a range of stark mountains that caught the speckles of the dying moonlight in a series of crisscrossing patterns that enabled me to imagine easily a host of dour, craggy faces peering down upon us. The barren crests were silhouetted against the sky like the edges of a randomly serrated blade—all except the rounded, smooth crest of the mountain we were headed for, where the ground rose as if it had been packed into a frozen wave that tapered off onto a hidden shore.

Reina and I kept pace with Oliver with an effort. We both had been forced to apply some of the precious *ka* ourselves, and even then keeping the little tyke in sight put a strain on our augmented resources. At times we were forced to slow down in a vain effort to catch our breaths, while he just puttered steadily along at warp nine. On those frequent occasions when we had lost sight of him, we kept track of him by the scent of the gases he left behind, but two or three times we had to call out for him. And that's when he'd called back, "Hurry up, you slackers! Clean your jets!"

So naturally I was ready to find out if you could strangle a robot when he finally stopped, at the foot of the mountain with the rounded crest. "It's here!" he said, before I could have a word with him. "I know it's around here somewhere! I can feel it all around me. It's everywhere! Can't you feel it?"

Wiping the sweat from her brow, Reina looked at the red sky and the moons and the rings, and after several long moments said simply, "Yes."

"Give me one of those dehydrated water pills from the survival kit, Oliver, will you?" I asked.

"Uh . . . they're not water pills," he said sheepishly.

"Oh? What are they then?"

"They're Night Jaunte pills. With the able and willing assistance of the black market, I exchanged them before we boarded *Our Lady's Hornblower*. You know, so I could have a little nip now and then!"

I wasn't sure how to react to that one. It was a serious breach of programming, discipline, and just plain etiquette. Wine pills look just like water pills to the casual inspection, but I'd had plenty of opportunities topside to notice the subtle differences. Which I imagined would be Oliver's bottom line of defense if I chose to make an issue out of the matter. Since I didn't know what good would come of making an issue out of it if I did, I refrained, and simply made a mental note that, contrary to my previous observation, Oliver's mysterious emotional development must have begun shortly before he'd arrived on this planet.

"I'm sorry," Oliver said with a helpless shrug. "How was I to know we'd be stranded?"

"Here's a well," said Reina, on her knees, digging in the ground with the sharp end of a pointed rock. Earlier in our relationship I might have been surprised, but by now I accepted her empathic connection with her surroundings as easily as I now accepted the most mundane scientific laws. So I helped her dig, and about a meter down we hit water. We cleared away some more of the dirt and drank, using our palms to catch the water. Oliver just leaned over, extended a tube from a compartment, and sucked out the water like a great hummingbird at an addictive feeder. The water tasted metallic, doubly so thanks to the effects of the war paint.

A few moments later, I asked Reina if she too felt the presence of a city nearby.

"Yes. It's everywhere."

"Uh-oh," said Oliver. "We might have just helped ourselves to some fluids that leaked out of its air-conditioning system."

"Let's just hope it is operational," I said, looking at the horizon from whence we came. There were two dawns in the sky, two clashing patterns of red. One from the sun, the other flashing sporadically from the still raging battle. The lights reflected from the many-colored rings, making them appear as if they burned with an inner fire. The plumes of smoke and dust rising from the site of the battle looked like they were stained with the blood of a thousand lost souls.

"Do you feel the city too, Homer B. Hunter?" Reina asked.

No, I didn't. All the *ka* made me feel was her. The odor of her sweat smothered me like a damp, warm blanket, suffocating me with her life.

"You don't feel it," she said, disappointed. She shook her head in disgust. "Your faithful robot companion is more of a man than you are."

"I'll borrow some of his durable parts, when the time comes. Meanwhile, if you think you can adjust to the ways of life you'll encounter topside, you'd better become more realistic about what you can expect from any given entity."

"I thought you wanted to be a warrior," she said sourly.

"No, I never said that, but I'll be what I have to be," I said. I turned away from them and forced myself to relax. I was nowhere near as fried with the war paint as I'd been the last time. Its effects were subtler, more expansive. Besides, I had the sneaking suspicion that I had been subconsciously trying to think the way I imagined she wanted me to think, which was, of course, impossible. I couldn't use the *ka* in the same way as a warrior from the Heechie-Heechie tribe. I was a civilized man, who had played instruments of great craftsmanship, capable of producing great art, when I was young, and who had spent the last several years of my life traipsing up and down metal corridors, sleeping in rooms whose steel walls protected me from the merciless vacuum of space. How could I possibly expect to have a close personal relationship with the cockeyed Mother Nature of another planet?

With the coming of relaxation, of acceptance, came a curious sensation. I felt a chill in my bones, the kind of chill I'd felt in cold corridors. The kind of familiar chill I felt when sitting before a cool console. And the kind of excitement and control I felt when making computers do my bidding.

I did feel the city! It wasn't all around me, the way Reina and Oliver perceived it. In fact, they perceived it differently. Reina felt the city in sensaround because its metallic presence was contrary to nature; Oliver felt it because, being metal, the city was exactly his nature. I, on the other hand, was able to grok that the city wasn't around us, but was hidden beneath the soil that had built up on the mountain before us in the thousands of years since its arrival—that *the city was the mountain!*

I imagined the scene as clearly as if I had been standing there, ghostlike, when it occurred. The city plummeting from the sky. Enveloped in an inferno. Cutting through the air with great shrieks of sound. The impact. The city reducing a mountain to dust in less than an instant. The shock wave, which could be felt on half the planet's surface. The flash of the explosion, which could be seen halfway across the world. The dust and smoke fanning throughout the atmosphere. And finally the city lying motionless, filling up the crater it had created, gradually being covered by the elements, catching in the nooks and crannies the dust blown by the wind through the eons, waiting motionless for a time that seemed like it would never come.

Waiting for this moment.

I bet myself there was a way inside. Not all the crannies could have been concealed by the haphazard covering job provided by the elements. "All right, everybody," I said, rubbing my hands together, "it's time to do a little serious climbing. What we're looking for here is an aperture big enough for us to pass through. If we're lucky, we'll find the city."

"What if we're not so lucky?" Oliver asked.

"Then we'll do some spelunking."

Oliver was the one who found an aperture. It was near the top of the crest, where boulders had fallen in a makeshift manner that had created the opening of a cave. With only a moderate amount of digging, Reina and I were able to widen the aperture enough for us to crawl in. The three of us crawled through the blackness. We hadn't gone very far, however, when our path became illuminated by white and blue fluorescent lights. Seized by an excitement I hadn't known since the first time I had journeyed off the surface of Gallium, I knew we had indeed found the hidden city!

The deeper we went below the surface, the thinner became the dirt at our feet, until it only coated a floor comprised of the same ancient alloy Kemp City had been made of. Wafer-thin generators lined the walls. Initially high above our heads, the ceiling became lower as we progressed deeper into the city.

"We're coming through the mouth," Oliver observed tensely. "I hope it doesn't get hungry."

"Great," I replied. "Let's see where we end up."

It happened to be an area unlike any I had seen while in Kemp City: a large rectangular room, with a blue and yellow mosaic tiled floor, black walls, and a yellow ceiling. Large consoles were placed haphazardly about, fronted by chairs with S-shaped backs far too bulky to comfortably accommodate any human. The chairs possessed another feature that piqued my curiosity about the type of creature they might have been designed for, and that was the double notch each had in the front of the seat, which forced me to think in terms of three-legged users. The consoles themselves had no dials, no keyboards, and no screen— only colored squares arranged in complex patterns. At first I suspected the squares were heat activated. I passed my hands over some, but nothing happened. Nor did anything happen when I touched them. Evidently nothing could or would until we activated the city.

Scattered throughout the room were smooth, stylish pedestals. Some supported globes filled with blue water, while others supported airtight, empty tubes that connected with the ceiling, and others were simply empty. All the pedestals had control panels similar to the ones on the consoles. I pushed one of the empty pedestals, to see if I could tip it over and discover any wiring hidden underneath, but it remained in place, bolted, no doubt, to the floor. At least whoever had designed this place had had a sense of style.

Strangest of all, however, were the geometric shapes, shaded in the darkest hues of the primary colors, that floated in the air. They were a cubist's dream. They were octagonally shaped cubes, or tetrahedrons, or icosahedrons, or simply pyramids, formed of pieces that were cut mostly into squares. And these squares automatically twisted in several directions in a routine that contorted the shapes madly, strangely, in form after form, until at last the squares regrouped properly and the shapes maintained their true structure—for a time, until the squares began to twist and turn again.

Oliver was fascinated by these shapes. He kept wandering around aimlessly, looking at them in awe. He hardly seemed to notice when he bumped into a pedestal, or into Reina, or me. It was easy to see why. Not only was the regularity of their shape-changing hypnotic, but they floated aimlessly about with no visible means of support. And though they moved about in complex patterns, they never bumped into one another. And indeed they were always a constant distance apart.

Reina, meanwhile, was equally awed, though it was apparent from her large pupils and trembling fingers she was very frightened. Without trying to be too obvious about it, she stuck very close to me as I wandered around.

"What is this place?" I asked Oliver. "Is this part of a city?"

"You bet your sweet bippy it is!" replied my faithful robot companion. "This is the control room!"

"Did the one in Dushen'ka look like this?"

"Basically, though I only got a few glimpses of it. I guess even a Holy Spectre can be a security risk."

"I'll vouch for that. What were the people doing in here?"

"I had the impression they weren't too sure themselves," said Oliver thoughtfully. "They were sitting at the consoles, of course, and some wore helmets."

"Hmmm. Did the helmets fit them?"

"No. They were about three sizes too big."

"Just like the chairs," I observed. I knelt down and inspected a console close to the center of the room. The war paint was creating a constant buzzing in my head. Though my sensitivity to my environment might have been augmented by the drug in certain ways, my powers of reasoning were definitely slowed down, and it was difficult for me to concentrate on deductive reasoning. I did the best I could, though, and touched the console.

My fingers vibrated. Evidently my touch had been sufficient to activate, however minimally, this particular console. I looked up to see that the geometrical shapes were slightly brighter, that they had begun to spin, however slowly, on their axes. I felt a tiny, almost invisible indentation. I dug my fingers in, felt something click, and a cabinet door sprung open. I drew my hands away, aware that without my touch on the console, the control room had already shut down—but inside was a helmet!

Gingerly I took it out. It was three sizes too large indeed, and shaped in a shoelike manner that brought to mind the head of some unimaginable serpentine creature.

I looked inside for scales. There were none. Instead I saw wires, circuits, old-fashioned transistors, and newfangled batteries with transparent shells that let me see the blue and yellow liquids inside. The helmet was very clean, the materials inside were very streamlined, yet I couldn't help feeling that it had been put together with a wing and prayer. Or, perhaps more accurately, a tentacle and a curse.

I moved to put it on my head.

Oliver stopped me with a brisk slap across the shoulder. It stung. I was so surprised at the violence of his gesture—to think that he would actually cause me pain, even momentarily, for any reason—that I almost dropped the helmet.

So I did what any sane, normal, mature man would have done in a similar situation. I tried to slap him back. he avoided it with ease. "What the hell did you do that for?" I demanded.

"Because I was trying to stop you, that's why!" he replied. "That thing could burn your brains out!"

"In that case, I'll be just the same as before!" I said. "Now I am going to put this helmet on and find out what's going to happen. And you are not to interfere in the slightest! Understand?"

"Okay, be that way," mumbled Oliver, toddling off. "You want inaction, you'll get inaction. Pretty soon I'm going to be playing paddleball with a man who has the brain of an insect."

What a grump, I thought. I then stared deeply into the helmet and thought, *Here goes nothing.* But just as I was about to put it on, the soft touch of Reina's hand on my shoulder detained me.

I looked up to fend her off too, if I had to, but before I could say a word, she applied a fresh stroke of *ka* to my forehead.

"I think you'll need this," she said. Then, before I could protest, she applied a stroke to the front of the helmet. A third stroke went across the squares of the console.

My brain immediately felt like a fizzy that had dropped into a cauldron of boiling blood. With Reina's assistance, I staggered to the chair. She stood back as I again stared into the helmet. Was it my imagination, or was it molding itself to fit my head size? Maybe my head was changing to fit it. I wasn't too sure, but I couldn't let that stop me. The drums of the war played in my head, and I had the delusion that if I could somehow take charge of this city, then I could somehow take charge of the battle, and save many human lives at the expense of only a few. At least, that was the plan.

I put on the helmet. I screamed. I was vaguely aware of the lights coming on, the geometric shapes glowing and spinning and changing configurations at full speed, the water in the globes churning, and the tubes radiating a soft yellow light. I heard the hums of engines moving, the clanking of gears turning. I thought I heard Oliver and Reina trying to speak to me, but I couldn't hear them for all the drums pounding in my brain. So mighty was the energy surge through my body that I could no longer sit upright, and I fell over onto the console. My fists slammed against the squares. And then—

—*Oneness!*—

It all came back to me. The history of the universe. No longer was I a man. The identity of Homer B. Hunter was only a figment derived from an old dream. Instead, I was an awakening giant, no more concerned with how my parts and pieces worked than I had been with my organs and muscles when I had been a man. I was concerned only with the tremendous weight of the earth covering me.

I shook off that weight, as easily as I might have shaken off a bedspread. I stood and inspected the new world around me. The rings that had once been so mighty and magnificent were like a toy to me, a toy I could travel to and explore whenever the whim struck me. The moons were baubles, and the sun was just a hot ball of fire in the sky.

A thousand thoughts, a million pictures, a billion

bytes shuffled through my mind. The longer I was awake, the more complete became my comprehension of the history of the universe as my kind had known it. That history had led inexorably to this moment, the most satisfying I had known during a long existence, which had, unfortunately, contained only a short period of consciousness. But that didn't matter. The time for revenge had arrived. Tasty, tasty revenge.

Not that I was emotional about it. Revenge was the logical thing to do, under the circumstances.

After all, I did represent a line of warriors who were the logical conclusion of the evolution of intelligent life in this phase of the birth-rebirth cycle of all time, space, and matter. It wasn't that organic life forms hadn't had their uses. It was just that by the time the universe had begun to collapse, artificial life had refined and redefined itself to the point where the contributions of organic life had become irrelevant to the interactions between the different cultures with separate, but equally valid, philosophical positions. All the important contributions were being made by artificial life-forms, most of whom were unburdened by the emotional and physical handicaps that normally afflicted organically evolved life forms. Not that organic life-forms hadn't made their successful contributions in the past. They had, after all, perfected the art of war. They had demonstrated more than adequately, through their actions, the rational philosophical basis for the systematic elimination of all life-forms whose very existence contradicted everything a given culture might stand for. Artificial life-forms could only improve on technique.

And it was technique I had been built to wield. I was a Dialecticon. I had some serious fighting to do. Designed and constructed by the Pragmobots, by their own admission the penultimate line of nomadic warriors in the collapsing galaxy, the class of Dialecticons existed for the sole purpose of aiding the Pragmobots in advancing the state of matter to its final resolution. That is, in bringing forth death from life, and sterility from Eden.

For the three-legged Pragmobots, who had metal tentacles instead of arms, and whose big heads only hinted at the masses of circuitry inside devoted to the sole function of elevating intellectual performance, had through their relentless logic become convinced that since it was the final fate of matter to merge into a single black hole as a preliminary to merging into a single point in space, then it was only proper that artificial life prepare matter for the event by wiping the dying universe clean of the life-forms and civilizations that remained on its waning surface. That was why the Pragmobots made the Dialecticons, to facilitate them in this task.

Things were going well, too; civilization after civilization was being eradicated with dispatch, until the appearance of the turncoat Dialecticons, the independently intelligent Transcendenticons. They could move and think without the assistance of Pragmobots, and they actively opposed my fellow A.I.'s at every turn. Finally the Pragmobots had no choice but to endow the Dialecticons with their own independent thought processes, and the war for the fate of every stripe of interacting matter was on!

It was a war the Dialecticons were winning too, until some bright Transcendenticon got the notion of sending the entire line of renegade A.I.'s back into time, to destroy the mythical line of First Ancestors, who would down through the eons be remodeled into the Pragmobots. The Transcendenticons built a time gate, and they had each and every one begun their journey through it when the Dialecticons arrived to nip at their heels. A battle royal waged in the time stream, and when it was all over, the time stream had been disrupted, the Transcendenticons had lost their ability to think independently, and I was the sole Dialecticon remaining. Far in the future, the fate of every stripe of interacting matter would be decided by someone, but it certainly wasn't going to be by us.

And that was why I was going to extract my revenge.

I strode about, barely feeling the earth rumbling beneath my webbed feet. My claws left huge divots in the ground. I had a short neck, a broad and flattened bill, and wings armed with laser cannons on the shoulders and the tips. My body was roundish, almost plump, while my legs were thin and jointed at the knees and ankles. The rearward placement of the hips resulted in a waddling gait. The low-relief designs etched into my white body were in the likeness of feathers, and my eyes were bright red with the energy supplied by my power crystals. I shook my tail with delight as I exulted in the sheer joy of being alive, of being able to move again! And when I heard the far-off sounds of the distant battle, I raised my bill to the sky and cut loose with a wail that echoed around the world, as if to say, *Look out, Transcendenticons! The mad reaper is at hand!*

I spread my wings, flapped them twice, lifted my feet off the ground, and flew, gladly heeding the siren call of the drums of war.

Chapter Nineteen
Fields of Smoke and Fire

 FLEW OVER MEAD-
ows, over forests, above great chasms gouged like wounds
in the ground by both river and warfare, through clouds
of smoke and dust reeking of the scent of scorched
metal. I was above the battlefield in a matter of moments.

It was with the tremendous satisfaction that only
logic justified can achieve that I saw the broken remains
of the dead Transcendenticons. I took a cold delight in
watching pieces of Transcendenticons crawling like crushed
slugs and wounded mollusks across the scorched ground.
I experienced a sort of humor watching the organic
parasites scampering out of the Transcendenticons and
into the field, fleeing from fires of blue and green and
yellow, dashing between the bits of debris, crouching
down in the freshly created chasms, or else running in all
directions in search of solace and safety across a battlefield that stretched for kilometers. They were less than
insignificant, in my opinion. I cared about their fate as
much as I would have cared about the fate of an atom
about to be split in a nuclear device. Only the vestiges of
my memory as a man remained, and I suppose the infini-
tesimally small part of Homer B. Hunter still conscious
in the mind of the Dialecticon I had become felt a
miniscule amount of compassion and pity for the para-

sites, and recalled his pathetically futile impulse to end this battle. Not that he could do anything about it.

Seeing the battle, I relished what was to come.

I saw a Transcendenticon shaped like a deer with stegosaurian plates across its back limping for cover, toward a gorge filled with the wreckage of other participants. I had found my first opponent.

The Transcendenticon remained consumed by a madness it would have disapproved of severely during its former existence. Though broken at one hip, though one leg dangled uselessly, it nevertheless fired randomly at nearby combatants with the laser cannons that spun like stout batons on their turrets. Though cowardly, it still had some fight left. Just the sport I needed to whet my appetite.

I came in behind the deer Transcendenticon. Hovering a hundred meters above the ground, I flapped my wings at a furious pace, creating great winds that caused it to stumble off balance. The cannons turned on their turrets and fired laser blast after laser blast at me, blasts that barely melted the outer surface of my tough skin, but the rest of my foe was too busy trying to remain upright to direct its full attention at me.

The deer Transcendenticon accidentally planted a forefoot into a soft spot in the ground and stumbled. Its shoulder struck the ground first, and then an antler broke against the earth, exposing the red glow of its power crystals and spilling gallons of a green fluid that immediately began searing the soil, even as it evaporated in swirls of mist. The deer's legs kicked wildly in its efforts to stand without breaking any of the plates across its back.

And without giving the matter a thought, I commanded my beak to transform. It extended itself, becoming narrower and sharper. The claws of my web feet flexed themselves. I flew toward the downed city like a rocket. I shrugged off the puny laser blasts the parasites manning the cannons threw my way.

My beak and claws penetrated the city simultaneously.

I felt no pain, only the knowledge of injury, when one claw was destroyed in an explosion, and the tip of another began to dissolve in green acid. I stretched out my wings to their full span so my full array of cannonfire could be applied to the head and rump of the deer. Within moments the head and rump were both dust. My claws tore at the outer shell like an animal scratching the earth to cover its excrement, and my beak pecked mercilessly at the Transcendenticon's innards, sometimes practically penetrating to the other side.

I took little notice of, but a tad of satisfaction in, the parasites fleeing the vicinity. Their shouts and screams were like high-pitched *eek-eek-eek*s to my sonic apparatus. I continued the destruction for long satisfying moments after the deer Transcendenticon, or what was left of it, remained entirely still.

And only glanced up because I felt an unusual vibration in the earth. And even then, it was only just in time to avert my head in an effort to avoid a direct hit from the bull Transcendenticon bearing down on me.

I was too late.

Its long horn penetrated my left wing, which I hadn't been able to press against my body in time. Fortunately I twisted away before it was too late to avoid a more serious injury, and I kicked furiously at the bull city's underside during the few seconds it ran roughshod over me.

I twisted to a standing position before it could turn around. I had the opportunity for a direct hit at the most vulnerable spot of its rump, and I took it. Great explosions ripped through the rump even as the bull turned around for another pass.

Automatically favoring my injured wing, I lifted myself into the air in time for the bull to pass under me. Then I dropped. Again automatically, I transformed my beak and added great fangs, fangs I used to tear off the uppermost spinal plate even as the cannons in the other tried to blast open my feet and belly. But unlike the other cities on the battlefield, my original metal alloys had not been weakened by a thousand years of struggle and replacement with inferior parts. I was too strong. My claws tore savagely at the bull's back as it galloped about the battlefield, oblivious to debris or fleeing parasites, until I faced the choice of flying away or being thrown off. I chose the former, blasting randomly at the bull even as I did so.

It growled at me. A deep, rumbling growl. If it was supposed to intimidate me, it was a failure. Instead, it only inspired me to continue the fray.

I landed behind the corpse of the deer Transcendenticon as if to use it as cover. The bull charged. I stood, extended my wings, and fired blast after blast at the ground. A stream of dirt and dust spurted toward the bull, creating a dark-brown cloud of cover that prevented it from seeing the gorge I had made. The bull stumbled in the gorge. Its impact caused me to jump twenty meters into the air. Its neck cracked open. A hiss of purple steam jetted from the opening, and beneath the grinding cacophony of noise I heard a chorus of high-pitched screams.

Even so, the bull Transcendenticon tried to stand. I watched it warily for many long seconds. When the bull finally succeeded, the crack around its neck lengthened due to the weight of the head pulling it down. The jets of steam showed no signs of abating, and torn conduits protruded like broken springs. Parasites jumped from the wound. Many moved away after they hit, but most did not.

What might have happened next between us, I have no way of knowing. Before either of us could make our next move, we were both struck by a barrage of laser blasts. How the bull city initially fared I do not know. As for myself, I turned and happily faced this new adversary.

Or adversaries. A Transcendenticon that resembled a two-legged platypus was firing the blasts from the fingers of the hands on its two mighty arms, while its partner in destruction—a kind of giant worm ouroboros that had bitten its own tail—relentlessly bore down upon me like a divine war wheel.

My laser blasts knocked the rolling worm off its trajectory, sending it spinning into the debris of a city that had accidentally half transformed into its stationary state as a result of its wounds. The worm hit the top of the city with a bump, and continued onward, rolling between two other combatants (a dog city and a bipedal sea horse city) before then crashing into another dog city that happened to be crawling into its way.

I vaguely saw the worm city unfurl before I was struck by a laser blast—the platypus city had attacked both me and the bull simultaneously.

If the battle had begun with cities systematically aligned against one another, the demarcations had certainly blurred to the point of irrelevance since then. The Transcendenticons must have reached a battle frenzy rivaling my own.

If further proof was necessary, it was provided by the actions of the bull city, which struck me from behind while I was firing at our mutual aggressor. Again I clawed frantically at its underside as it bowled me over.

The impact had torn the bull's head further, so that this time when it whirled toward me for another charge, the head fell off completely, and a barrage of laser blasts from the platypus into the unprotected wound finished the job. Only the resistance of the bull's shell prevented the resulting series of internal explosions from tearing it to pieces. I wager none of the parasites inside survived. And those inside the head who might still be living were certainly finished off when the body, or what was left of it, fell onto the head and crushed it flat.

As for myself, I had a broken wing. Most of the wing cannons were damaged beyond the ability to function, as well. I was a seriously crippled duck Dialecticon.

I backed off from the approaching platypus. I edged to the right, only to see the worm slithering toward me. Slithering over parasites who were unable to run out of its path in time. Slithering despite the tremendous holes in its hide.

I edged to the left, only to have my right foot pinned down at the webbing by a giant javelin. I glanced in the direction it had flown from to see a porcupine city, its back bristling with hundreds of javelins, bearing down on me.

But rather than burying me under a barrage of javelin fire, it chose to crucify the platypus instead. In moments the platypus Transcendenticon was ravaged with javelins protruding from every area of its body. Some of the javelins penetrated the body or limbs completely. Steam of different colors jetted from the wounds. Then a hand exploded, erupting furiously into red flames. The cannons on it ears exploded. The platypus threw back its head and opened its bill as if to scream its defiance to the death enveloping it. But before it could emit a sound, it was racked by a series of internal explosions. The final explosion sent the platypus's head flying high into the air.

At the height of its trajectory, it too exploded, sending shrapnel in all directions.

I was riddled with it, but since I felt no pain in the traditional sense of the word—I was only aware of injuries in so far as they impeded my efficiency—I concentrated intently on the wounded worm slithering toward me. Frantically I tried to remove the javelin pinning down my foot with my beak, but just as I extracted it, the worm lunged in the air toward me like a snake and I was caught.

My wings beat uselessly against the worm coiling itself around me, crushing me. I felt the curious relief of a rush of steam escaping from my wing joint. Time and time again I jabbed my beak into the body of the worm. I must have struck something significant, because around the time of my fifteenth jab the worm was racked by a crippling internal explosion.

It fell off me and tried to slither away. I did not let it go. I leapt on it and ruthlessly tore at its head with the claws of my feet. I only relented when a jet of acid erupted like a geyser, spraying my belly. I dashed away as quickly as I could, and glanced back at the worm, which had fires emanating from its various wounds, the moment before it too exploded and sprayed the battlefield with shrapnel.

Bombs fell onto the ground and went off around me. I looked up to discover I had been pinpointed by an eagle Transcendenticon, who had selected me as its next target despite the fact that it too was dodging javelins fired from the battlefield.

I blasted at the eagle with my still-operable laser cannons, paying no mind to the porcupine city. That was a mistake. Without warning I was innundated with projectiles. My body was riddled. Crucified.

Again, I did not feel pain in the traditional sense of the word. But now my entire body was racked with systems suffering every conceivable type of dysfunction. Fluids dissolved my innards, steam jetted from every wound, and energy fields from the disrupted power crystals clogged my pistons and joints. It was a struggle just to stand, but struggle I did. I did not want to admit defeat even though it was surely inevitable.

A final javelin penetrated me. Through the neck. My mechanistic suffering suddenly increased threefold, and I knew that so far as I was concerned, the battle was over.

I felt *disconnection*!

And then *blackout*!

Chapter Twenty
For the Love of Floyd

THE DRUMS OF WAR slowly receded from my mind and did not return. Otherwise, my sleep was as black and as silent as the grave.

Upon opening my eyes I saw peering down upon me perhaps the ugliest face I have encountered throughout my entire travels across the length and breadth of this galaxy.

"Blather!" I croaked.

"It's about time you woke up, you sorry excuse for a soldier," he said, so unsympathetically that I failed to feel the slightest bit of relief that I had at last been rescued. "It's lucky for you that Admiral Boink needs you. Otherwise I'd leave you here and charge you with desertion!"

"Stifle it, Blather!" barked a female voice from somewhere to the left of me. The first thing I noticed about her was her creamy-jade eyes. They seemed very familiar, but the face and red hair surrounding them were very different from what I had expected. The female grabbed my mouth and shook my lips. Her fingers were extremely cold, but not quite as cold and as professional as her manner. "Your lips a-okay?" she asked. She thumped me on the chest. "How's that pair of lungs?"

"Have we met?" I croaked.

She tilted her head with an annoyed stare. By now I

recognized her voice as belonging to that of Lt. Colonel Coryban. I'd never actually laid eyes on her before. She was more beautiful than I had been led to believe, and twice as icy. "You've got a lot of explaining to do, soldier," she said. "Going for joy rides in life pods has caused a lot of better men than you to spend the best years of their lives brushing up the slime from prison floors."

Blather grinned malevolently. "Too bad you don't have any best years to give, eh, Hunter?"

If looks could disintegrate, the one Coryban gave Blather would have turned him into a tiny pyramid of ashes. Blather actually seemed to wilt under her gaze, and my befuddled brain took great delight in noticing that Coryban's opinion of Blather, for some reason, was important to him. "Blather, for several days now I've been curious about your unexplained animosity toward this man. Would you care to clue us in, now that you've a chance to talk to him to his face."

Blather, not unsurprisingly, was silent. He made a disgusted face and moved away from my view.

I propped myself up on my elbow with an effort. I barely noticed the presence of my comrades and my friends for the overwhelming vista of the battlefield. The sole surviving piece of machinery was the shuttle craft, gleaming when all else was covered with blood and soot, that had brought my rescuers. In every direction I saw nothing but thinning plumes of smoke, the debris of cities (including the shattered husk of the duck Dialecticon I had been merged with), and dead bodies. Lots of dead bodies, flattened and otherwise. They were everywhere. Some were only in pieces. The battlefield reeked of decaying flesh. The only sounds were those of the wind and the buzzing of insects. Maggot analogues gorged themselves on the plentiful meals humankind had so considerably made available to them.

"Boss, Boss!" said Oliver, rushing up to me. "I'm so glad you're not dead!"

"I will be too, in a little while. What happened to me?"

"After you put on that helmet, you took control of the city and fought many battles," said my faithful robot companion. "We tried to separate you from the helmet, but there was some sort of biomagnetic connection between you and the metal that made it impossible. Well, it was impossible until you lost a fight in a rather spectacular manner, but you know what I mean. Once the city was no longer functioning properly . . ."

"What in the name of the nine planets is this mechanical monstrosity talking about?" Blather demanded to know.

"Blather, I don't know what you have against this man, and I'll wager neither does he," said Coryban. "Now for the last time, I'm telling you to back off, or the next time you have scrub duty, you'll be assigned an old-fashioned scrub brush; you know, the manual kind."

Blather gulped and nodded, but he did take a few steps backward. He looked at Reina, who was sitting cross-legged a fair distance from the shuttle and examining us with a suspicious air. I couldn't blame her. At last she had been presented with irrefutable proof that I was a man from the stars, and I wouldn't have blamed her if she didn't like what she was seeing. I didn't like it much either. Blather scowled at her, and she scowled back.

"Oliver, are there any cities left?" I asked.

"Not a one, so far as I can tell."

"How did I make it through?"

"Reina saw to it. She had a devil of a time pulling you out of the city before it exploded."

"Thanks, Reina," I said, struggling to stand.

Oliver and Coryban helped me complete the job. "Up you go, soldier," Coryban said. I weaved until I stared once again into those eyes.

It was like peering down a vortex.

"I don't know why you took off in a life pod, soldier," said Coryban, "but I sure am glad to see you. The Union has need of a man with your talents."

"It's about time. What's the problem, ma'am?"

In a few terse sentences, she told me a story about

the Ho-Ho-Kusian ambassador and his overwhelming need to hear the sounds of my soprano saxophone. "The only problem is now that we've found you," she concluded, "we've been unable to determine the nature of the accident that caused the damage to the saxophone in the first place." The vortex in her eyes then revealed to me a level I couldn't help but suspect she concealed from most other acquaintances, a level possessing a modicum of vulnerability and uncertainty, not to mention a need to find someone she could trust. For some reason, I divined, she had selected me for the job.

"What kind of accident could smash a soprano saxophone and leave no traces?" I asked.

She looked around. She especially looked at Blather, who smiled weakly and half waved, half saluted at her. I think he was trying to flirt with her. She took me by the arm and leaned close to me. Her fresh, clean smell, especially after all I'd been through, was intoxicating. "I can't talk about it this minute, but I believe there's some kind of galactic conspiracy going on. The trouble is, no one believes me. I must admit, I'm feeling very insecure about all this. I'm not used to it."

"I understand," I said, even though I didn't.

"Listen, Hunter, would you mind telling me, before we have to go through official channels, just how you wound up on this planet anyway?"

I rubbed my chin. My head hurt. For a moment I believed it was because of my recent experience controlling the Dialecticon city, but the pain got slightly worse when I tried to recall all the particulars of my encounter with the Porgian Five and Pheblian Glorp ambassadors. The pain became still worse when I attempted to concentrate on the blank spaces.

Then the blank spaces were wiped out altogether, replaced by nothing in particular. It was as if my brain was instinctively trying to tell me not to worry about forgetting some of the details of my encounter on *Our Lady's Hornblower*, because they were buried in my subconscious where they belonged. My conscious self couldn't quite accept that explanation, however, and I suspected Coryban was having a similar problem.

"Uh, give me a few moments more to get my thoughts in order, ma'am," I told her. "Is that all right?"

She nodded, but I doubted I had fooled her.

I glanced at Reina. She was still on the ground, maintaining a discrete distance from everyone. Blather stared at her with his arms crossed and his toe tapping. She regarded him indifferently.

"I see you've got yourself a piece of native poontang," he sneered.

"Blather, one more word like that out of you, and you won't need a saxophone to sing soprano!" I replied.

"Blather, go set the navigational controls for *Our Lady's Hornblower*," said Coryban. "And while you're doing that, go contemplate the exquisite danger you're going to experience while changing the Ho-Ho-Kusian Ambassador's dirt bags."

Blather gulped more loudly this time, got about as pale and as fearful as I'd ever seen him, and slinked through the open doors of the shuttle.

"What's he got against you, anyway?" Coryban asked me.

"I don't know. He's never given me a clue as to what. It's a complete mystery to me, and I think I like it that way."

"He's a vacuum brain!" piped in Oliver.

Coryban smiled with a distinctly melancholy air. "No, he's far from that. I think he'd be a good man, if he weren't so weak." She nodded at some nearby debris. "What was this battle all about anyway? I don't mind telling you, all this slaughter has sickened me."

"The same thing most wars are fought over," I said.

Coryban nodded as if she understood. "I see. Principle."

"No, ma'am, it was over nothing. Not a damn thing. The people only thought it was about something. In the end, I destroyed this society, while under the delusion that I was doing something to save it."

"I'll expect a full report on that as well as your other activities," Coryban said. Then, more sympathetically: "I suspect you're judging yourself too harshly, Hunter." She nodded toward Reina. "And who do we have here?"

I gave Coryban a quick rundown of Reina's story while walking toward the orphaned young native girl, so she wouldn't think I was talking about her behind her back. Oliver toddled behind us as I introduced the two women.

Reina stood and looked in confusion at Coryban's outstretched hand. She took it gingerly, and, with a warmth that belied her reputation, Coryban smiled down at her. Then they looked into one another's eyes. Creamy jade met creamy jade. I had the distinct impression a bond was forming between them, as if they each recognized they had something in common with the other.

Coryban released Reina's hand, nodded thoughtfully, and asked, "I realize it's a big thing to ask, but what are your plans for the future?"

"I do not know."

"Well, Reina, I guess you don't have to worry about my indiscretions anymore," I said. "The social customs of the Heechie-Heechie are going to go through some serious changes."

The pair of ladies pointedly ignored me. I looked questioningly at Oliver, who shrugged in response.

"Your world is in dire need of Union assistance," said Coryban. "Rest assured, it shall receive it."

"I am sure those of my people who may have survived the last few days will appreciate it," said Reina, "but I fail to see what that has to do with me."

Coryban raised her eyebrows. "Oh?"

"I want to come with you. I want to join the Stellar Patrol."

"No! That's impossible!" I said.

Now Coryban raised her eyebrows at me. "And why not?"

"Well, she . . . she's just an innocent native girl."

"So?" asked Coryban. "Were we not all innocent natives once? Besides, I sense the girl has what it takes to excel in the Stellar Patrol."

Reina nodded with an appreciative smile.

"Well, I don't think it's a good idea," I said, crossing my arms sullenly.

"Why? Doesn't it fit in with your plans for her?" Coryban asked sarcastically.

That hit a little too close to the mark. Oliver rolled his eyes at me. "Boss, I think that after all we've been through together, I've a right to say this: you're acting like a vacuum brain too."

"All right," I said, stalking toward the shuttle, "let's get off this flea-bitten planet!"

"But, Boss!" whispered Oliver behind me, "what about Floyd?"

"Quiet, motor mouth!"

By the time we were safely off-world—Blather, Coryban, Reina, Oliver, and myself—I'd had the time to give the matter plenty of thought. Something bigger was cooking in the galaxy than just the secretly intelligent, cloned minds of robots. Coryban's suspicions that the accidental damage done to my saxophone, plus the nagging notion that certain aspects of my encounter with the ambassadors had been erased, somehow, from my mind, added up to an unusually huge question mark.

Complicating matters was the realization that if I waited for the Stellar Patrol bureaucracy to react to a full report, matters could deteriorate gravely, perhaps beyond hope of repair. I hated to admit it, but it was just possible that the fate of civilization as I knew it depended on what I did before the shuttle went into the void of hyperspace.

So I did what on a certain level satisfied a long-standing ambition of mine: I crept up behind Blather while he was sitting at the controls and knocked him out with the back end of a multipurpose scrub brush. He collapsed over the console with an expression even stupider than the one he normally wore. I pushed him onto the floor.

"Hunter!" shouted Coryban, switching off her seatbelt as if to lunge for me.

I made a threatening motion with the scrub brush. Whatever she was planning on doing, she thought better of it, and settled back into her chair.

"Homer B. Hunter, what are you doing?" asked Reina, still weak from her first takeoff.

"I'm commandeering this shuttle," I said. "You just stay where you are, Reina. This act is my responsibility, and I don't want you to get hurt taking sides."

"Oh, boy!" said Oliver. "We're really doing something dangerous now!"

"You can say that again," replied Coryban. "This amounts to nothing less than mutiny. You'll pay for this, Hunter."

"More than likely. I know you're going to find this difficult to believe, Colonel Coryban, but I'm needed in two places at once—on *Our Lady's Hornblower,* and on a space station floating around the planet of Nippon. So the decision has to be mine."

"I don't get it, Hunter," replied Coryban. "What can be more important than assuring the successful conclusion of the most important diplomatic conference in the history of the Third Union?"

"You don't understand!" said Oliver. "We're on a mission from Floyd!"

TO BE CONTINUED IN **STATIONFALL**

The son of an American doctor, ARTHUR BYRON COVER was born in the upper tundra of Siberia on January 14, 1950. He attended a Clarion Science Fiction Writers' Workshop in 1971, where he made his first professional sale, to Harlan Ellison's *Last Dangerous Visions*. Cover migrated to Los Angeles in 1972. He has published a slew of short stories in *Infinity Five, The Alien Condition, Heavy Metal, Weird Tales, Year's Best Horror Stories,* and elsewhere, plus several SF books, including *Autumn Angels, The Platypus of Doom, The Sound of Winter,* and *An East Wind Coming.* He has also written scripts for issues of the comics *Daredevil* and *Firestorm,* as well as the graphic novel *Space Clusters.* He has been an instructor at Clarion West and was managing editor of *Amazing Heroes* for a time. Arthur Byron Cover is a co-editor of the anthology *The Best of the New Wave* and the author of three Time Machine books as well as Book 4 of *Isaac Asimov's Robot City* for Byron Preiss Visual Publications.